Devil Take the Hindmost

Devil Take the Hindmost

Martin Cathcart Froden

PAPL
DISCARDED

**FREIGHT
BOOKS**

First published 2016

Freight Books
49–53 Virginia Street
Glasgow, G1 1TS
www.freightbooks.co.uk

Copyright © 2016 Martin Cathcart Froden
The moral right of Martin Cathcart Froden to be identified as the author of
this work has been asserted by him in accordance with the Copyright, Designs
and Patents Act, 1988.

All rights reserved. No part of this publication may be reproduced or
transmitted in any form by any means, electronic or mechanical, including
photocopying, recording or any information storage or retrieval system,
without either prior permission in writing from the publisher or by licence,
permitting restricted copying. In the United Kingdom such licences are issued
by the Copyright Licensing Agency, 90 Tottenham Court Road, London,
W1P 0LP.

A CIP catalogue reference for this book is available from the British Library.

ISBN 978-1-910449-91-2
eISBN 978-1-910449-92-9

Typeset by Freight in Plantin
Printed and bound by Bell and Bain, Glasgow

the publisher acknowledges investment from
Creative Scotland toward the publication of this book

Originally from Sweden, Martin Cathcart Froden has lived in Canada, Israel, Argentina, almost Finland and London and worked as a drummer, avocado picker, magazine editor and prison teacher. He won the 2015 Dundee International Book Prize with this novel, and his story 'The Underwater Cathedral' won the 2013 BBC Opening Lines competition. He has just embarked on a doctorate in creative writing/criminology/architecture in Glasgow where he lives with his wife and three young children.

For Lucy. I can't thank you enough.

Prologue

It's Good Friday 1929 and a record crowd has paid to see the cyclists. Down on the oval I watch Paul focus on his hands. Hands that used to handle white-eyed horses, deliver lambs, right fence posts blown over in Campsie gales and put his drunk father to bed.

The Herne Hill grandstand sits dignified along the home strait of the velodrome and today it's full of clueless celebrities (Barbara Hepworth, Vita Sackville-West, Lord Pritchards, Riccardo Bertazzolo, the boxer) and people in the know (A. A. Weir, F. T. Bidlake, G. Hillier – and me). The arena heaves under the pressure of people fighting, betting, spilling gin and smoking.

The cyclists line up, then *Crack!* With a jostle of elbows and straining thighs they're off. We're all cheering, all drinking, all hoping the weather will hold up so that we can see the boys swirl round the concrete bowl like so many eggs whisked for an omelette.

Paul gives himself over to the centrifugal force and to the animal he usually keeps caged in his lungs. Today he can't settle for anything less than a miracle. He lives by his lungs and by the grace of Mr Morton. I dry my hands on my trousers, something I've not had to do for many years.

About a third into the race Paul drops down in the field. His grimace says he's hurting. My hands are now sweating so much the cummerbund of my cigar has become attached to my ring finger. I claw at the piece of paper like a married man given a once-in-a-lifetime chance to spend the night with Vilma Bánky.

Halfway through the race I know he won't win. My heart sinks for Paul, and for myself, as I have to start planning for his disappearance. I stand up, spilling ashes all down my front.

I walk outside to one of the stands selling Venetian Ice Cream. As soon as I'm finished with my ice cream, I vomit in the gutter. People laugh and ask if the beer's too strong this side of the river. Standing up, wiping my mouth with the back of my hand I hear the shouts from the arena, but can't bear to witness the defeat. I walk away.

One of the little grimy boys I have working the crowds for me runs up. Pulling my sleeve, something I never allow, he says 'Silas, Mr Silas, your man, Paul. Come, come quickly!'

Chapter 1

It's Easter 1928, and a lot of people are travelling. Seeing family. I'm not. I'm just standing here enjoying the spectacle of humanity. For the last half hour I have been watching one man in particular. King's Cross, with its tangle of tracks and rabid porters shouting and shoving, can be overwhelming, but it's absurd for such a robust man to pace the same spot. His hat tucked into his armpit. His hands – big, strong hands – come up to his eyes every so often. Wiping tears?

I don't usually have time to stand and sip coffee in draughty train stations, looking at men, but I've got another few hours before I have to see Mr Morton. I don't especially appreciate being summoned by the Elephant Emperor, as I now secretly refer to him, but I'm not worried. These days I'm in his good books. Since that little job at Dartmoor, which I pulled off myself, and the one out by the Greenwich docks, which took a few hands, he trusts me. I just hope it's not something too tiresome this time. I'm not one to shy away from slicing a man up like a ham if it's warranted, if he's put himself in trouble, but some of the other boys *enjoy* it. I wish he could leave that aspect of the work to them. Blood spots are beastly to get rid of.

After I've seen Mr Morton, I plan to quietly celebrate my birthday. No party, no band or cake, no dancing girls or coach trips to the seaside to ride on deathly tired ponies. Just a drink or two with the son of a very wealthy shipping merchant. The boy, young, with dark intense eyes, and a sharp sense of dress and entitlement, is in need of a shoulder to lean on, someone to talk with in the dark hours of the night. I have no interest in becoming his go-to, but I am happy to be a rung on the ladder, and I've never regarded being paid for one's troubles in champagne much of a chore.

I finish my drink. It has warmed my hands if nothing else. The big man, incredibly, is still pacing. I walk over. It'll pass the time if nothing else.

'Can I help you?' I ask. Possibly the least used phrase in London. Sometimes I'm more than half-foreign. More Greek than I like to admit to myself, may my father rest in peace. The man, who is younger than I thought, looks at me like I've said something indecent.

'No thanks,' he says and continues rifling through his pockets. By now he's probably even run out of lint. Then he looks up, eyes shining, and says, 'Actually, yes. Yes please, you can.'

'That's fine. What's your name son?'

'Paul MacAllister.'

'Pleasure,' I squeeze his hand and my knuckles roll like marbles in a bag. I put my other hand on his shoulder to steady myself, and also for professional, appreciative reasons. 'Silas Halkias.'

'That's an unusual name,' he says, looking at me and the melee of the station.

'There are a few funny sounding names around here,' I say. 'I take it you've never been to London?'

'I've never been anywhere bigger than Glasgow,' he says and shuffles his feet.

'Now, tell me what's made you this flustered,' I ask. He doesn't say anything at first and I nod my head to coax him on a little.

He smiles a row of pearly whites, looks both proud and ashamed at the same time and says, 'Well, it began with a fight with my father.'

'On the train?'

'Oh no, a couple of days ago. Before I ran into trouble here.'

We start walking, and immediately I sense that he has no idea where we are going. He talks and I smile and nod, 'I have a bike, or rather, I had a bike. A beautiful thing, my uncle gave it to me,' he says. When I was getting off the train this boy came up to me and asked me if he could help me with my luggage. I thought that was very friendly, but I told him I didn't have much. Then he noticed my stub, and said he'd fetch the item for me. Before I could do anything about it I saw him cycle off on my bike.'

'That's terrible,' I say, but I'm not really listening. I've heard this story before. 'My uncle brought it back from the Meteor Works in Coventry. It was a Rover, the Imperial model. Do you know it?'

'No, I don't know much about bicycles.'

'Well, it's the most expensive thing I've ever owned, probably the most expensive thing I'll ever own.' Here I have to guide him past a flock of a certain kind of women trying to get his attention.

'Don't be so sure,' I say.

'I ran after the boy but he was too fast. When I came back I saw two other little boys run off with my bag which had my wallet in it.'

'I'm sorry to hear it.'

He nods and continues, 'Now I've got nothing for food or lodging or anything, not even the trip back, if I was so inclined.'

Judging by Paul's size, by his ruddy face and straight teeth, he could be useful. I could put him to use in the yard out at Sandown if he knows his way around horses. Or make him a wrestler, smeared in petroleum jelly. His strong arms locked around another man's waist, in tight black breeches, no top. As we cross the road I make up my mind and say, 'Right, let's get something warm into you. My treat.'

'I don't know how to thank you.'

'We'll think of something,' I say smiling.

I guide him out of the station, now with half a plan. I find myself sheltering from the wind behind him. It's supposed to be spring but the weather hasn't turned yet.

There's a place on Bidborough Street that serves jellied eel with plenty of nutmeg. Not my cup of tea, but cheap. The woman who runs it wasn't always as respectable as she looks now, and she owes me a favour or two. I'll stuff him full of as much mash as he can stomach and by then I should know what to do with him. I can tell he's not used to people being this close to him. The way he bumps into street vendors, the way he looks at fashionable women, the way he smiles at children, the way he says sorry too often, but not to the right people.

I guide him inside the café. It looks like a miniature chapel, but with two shop windows letting in light. There's a middle aisle with booths – marble tables and dark wood, touched by many greasy hands, all the way down the rectangular room. The walls are tiled white up to about chest-height, and above painted a light green. Seaside scenes are pinned at regular intervals. It's nice to come inside. I feel my hands thaw a little. I nod to one of the girls and she moves a dirty man from a good table, wipes it and curtsies.

Once we're sitting down, Paul says, 'Maybe it was a mistake coming to London. I just didn't know what else to do.'

I nod, and raise a finger to order for him. Belinda nods from behind her counter.

As he eats, his high cheekbones become flushed, from being inside. From the smoke and the beer I put in front of him. He seems thirsty but not a very seasoned drinker. Good for me.

'Sounds like you were quite desperate,' I say while looking around the room for familiar faces. My eyes get stuck on a picture of the Eastbourne pier. It looks awful.

Paul finishes his beer, and starts on the next one I've thoughtfully provided. Wiping foam from his upper lip he continues, 'My father's a...' He doesn't finish the sentence. 'I don't want to sound like I'm the disrespecting kind,' he says instead, 'but he's done a thing, and though I have forgiven him in the past, this time it was too much.'

'You want more mash?' I ask. He nods while separating another piece of eel from the block of jelly. I shout for Belinda and one of her little girls scurries over with another plate of the stuff. Makes my stomach turn, but for Paul it seems to do the trick.

I sit and look at him. He's huge. Effortlessly so, just by birth and accentuated by regular, manual work. Ruddy and with eyes set wide in a freckled face, cheeks with slight stubble, shifting between ginger and gold depending on the light from the window. One hand around his beer glass, the other steadily forking food into his mouth. He looks so pure.

I'm tired of being me. This thought creeps up on me like a vicious cat, and it scratches at my heart. I've been caught off guard by myself, and I quickly look around to see if anyone's seen me falter.

Then, luckily, he interrupts my thoughts.

'Mr Halky, this is delicious. Especially after such a long journey,' he says.

'It's Halkias.'

'Sorry.'

'Don't apologise.'

I remind myself I'm a lender and a promoter, not a lovesick spinster, and that if I play my cards right, he could be profitable. Paul pushes his empty plate away. Leans back and after a short flicker of contentment he starts to look worried again.

'I'm a long way from home,' he says and wipes his mouth on his sleeve. When he realises I noticed he looks embarrassed.

'Then we need to find you somewhere to stay,' I say. 'What are you good at?'

'My father has a dairy farm. I've been running it for a long time but he doesn't own it any more. A man he gambled with owns it now.'

'Well, there are no forests or farms in the city, so I'm not quite sure what you expected.'

'I just presumed with so many people living in the one place there would be plenty of jobs needing done.'

It strikes me he might not be so good with horses. Maybe farm horses, but not race horses. He is perhaps like a horse himself. A machine you put grain into and get power out from. I sigh and change tack.

'How comfortable are you with violence?' I ask.

'If an animal is hurt and can't be fixed we kill it. With some practice I could probably work as a butcher.'

'I've no interest in animal butchers. How about humans?'

'I'm not a murderer.' The poor boy pales, and looks over my shoulder to see if anyone's heard us. I smile and continue, 'I know you're not. I meant human violence. Boxing, wrestling, that kind of thing. You're a big man, ever tried fighting in a ring?'

'Never liked it much. I've been in a few fights, like everyone. Nothing organised, mind you, bar fights. People get excited when they've been paid, or angry when they haven't been, and the whisky's pretty strong where I'm from.'

'Which is?'

'Lennoxtown.'

'Never heard of it.'

'Very pretty, apart from the chemical works.'

'Like I said, never heard of it. But, how about boxing? You're a big man, you must have broken a nose or two in your day?'

'Can't say I have. I've been close to it with my old man, but no. I'm strong, but not much of a fighter to be honest. My hands are not very fast, like you see on some. Or maybe people don't want to pick fights with me because I'm this tall.'

'That's another thing that won't be the same here in London. Here people will pick fights for the flimsiest of reasons. Just to have something to do. The distraction of a good fight has led many men into unforeseen circumstances. Regardless, I might have some work for you, then again I might not.'

'I'll do anything.'

'Well, judging from how you've answered my questions you wouldn't.'

'Ask me again.'

'I won't.'

'Ask,' he says, so earnest.

'Fine. If a widow with fourteen children owed you money, and couldn't pay because all her money went to pay the doctor who couldn't help her now dead husband, would you kill her youngest daughter? With your bare hands, in front of her mother? Would you set fire to a hospital, starting in the ward with people in wheelchairs? Would you deliberately blow up a boat full of returning soldiers, all heroes? Would you take a shot at King George? Burn down a church?'

'No! No. Is that what you do?' he says.

'No, I'm just proving that you wouldn't do anything.'

'I'm an honest man.'

'I have no need for honest men. No one does.'

'Well if that's the case, it was nice meeting you, and I am very much in your debt, thanks for helping me. If you give me your address I will reimburse you for the meal.' Paul stands up. He holds onto the table trying hard to look at some kind of nominal horizon. The beer has gotten the better of him. I'm a tiny bit afraid I'll lose him, but I know that he needs me more than I need him.

'Sit down, Paul. As I was saying before you turned into Saint Andrew. I think I can find other uses for you. In the meantime you need somewhere to stay until you find a job. I have somewhere you can stay. I'm lending you a month's rent, plus some money for food and such. Don't ask me why. If you decide to disappear, I will find you, wherever you go. Lennoxtown, Macedonia, or Antarctica. Just trust me, I will. That's my job.'

'I don't understand.'

'I don't expect you to.'

'I'll pay you back as quickly as I can.'

'I know you will. If you're a bad apple, I will know within the hour.

'I'm a good apple.'

'You would say that.'

'Why are you so kind?'

'I'll be honest with you. I own a house and I've got tenants who are about to move out, that's my business. 'But I'm a nice man, and since you're in serious trouble I will give you a favourable rate, don't worry.'

He still looks suspicious, I can see that he's weighing for and against in his head. I go over and pay for the food and when I come back he's still there, which certainly means he's not going anywhere.

'Paul, don't worry, you've not borrowed anything yet, and you're just coming with me to have a look at a room, no obligations.' He nods so I tell him, 'Say bye-bye to Belinda, the one in the apron. This is a good, cheap place to come and eat, and you might want to return. When you do, speak nicely to her, she's a bad apple turned good, and once you can afford it, pay a little extra and she will give you the best bits and a table.'

Paul walks over to her and even makes her smile. A rare thing with strangers, but it proves me right. He is handsome, and he has a way, an innocent, childlike way. And as he rolls his r's and undulates his vowels more than one person looks up and smiles. He shakes hands with Belinda, the first person to do that in at least ten years. Maybe he genuinely liked the eel? When he turns Belinda touches her nose with her index finger. I'll be damned if I can't get this boy to eat out of my hand, and make me some money in the meantime.

I take him the long way to the house on Copenhagen Street. It's not far from the station, but I want to confuse him a little, see what he's made of. The crowds seem to get to him, but he does well considering. The shouting and pushing masses don't bother me. It's second nature. Some people lift their hats when they see me, one or two come up to me to shake my hand. These are the ones I've let pay back a day or two later than they should have. To some poor souls, a little rebate on their debts seems to be manna from heaven. If I can afford it I don't mind these crumbs of perceived compassion.

We pause so I can light a cigar. Paul cranes his neck and looks down Pentonville Road where it meets Euston Road and Caledonian Road. Says something about the mass of people, and how busy everyone looks. I nod and muse as my Pyramide glows. He turned down my offer of a cigar. Not a smoker, who would have thought? I don't think I have ever met a man who doesn't smoke.

'Mr Halkias, look at that, what a beauty,' he says, pointing across the street, at two women holding bikes.

'Which one? The tall one? I suppose, if you like them gangly, horses for courses. But a word of advice, I'd steer clear of some women, ones dressed up that nicely, loitering on street corners. They're either married to someone richer than you, or not the marrying kind, if you know what I mean.'

'No, no. The red bike. The BSA. That's their Path Racer, look at the sloping head tube, that's lovely. Good quality steel. My bike was good, but no match for that. Look it's even got aluminium rims. Amazing. People in London must be very wealthy.'

'It looks like a bike to me. Nothing more, nothing less. What's the idea? Surely a car is better in every way?'

'I'll never be able to afford a car.'

'There is that. But you could aspire to something more than two triangles with a bit of rubber attached.'

'Horses for courses, eh?'

'That's the spirit. So you're a racer then?'

'I've cycled on tracks a little. I've been to the velodrome at Celtic Park in Glasgow a few times. I cycle a lot on roads around where I'm from.'

Velodrome cyclists are everywhere down here. They're celebrities and some of them make more per race than I do in a month.

'Is there a track near here?' he asks.

I feel a plan niggling me, and smile at him, 'Of course. I'll even take you to Preston Park one of these days. That's by the sea, in Brighton you know. We'll make a holiday out of it. Get you a straw hat and a bit of rock to lick. Have you ever competed?'

'No, but my uncle was a racer. Never at national level, just below. He once took me to the track in Glasgow. After, as I was so keen on cycling, kept sending me magazines and clippings about it.'

'Sounds like a nice man,' I say absentmindedly while looking at a shopkeeper who owes me money.

Paul continues, 'He worked at the Park velodrome for the 1897 World Championships, before I was born and I think he once even met Cyril Alden and Horace Johnson.'

'I see,' I decide to let the shopkeeper be for another day. I take Paul's arm as we cross the busy road. His arm is completely solid, like a plank.

He's still rambling, 'I trained with my uncle for a while, even in a velodrome a couple of times, but after mother passed away we saw less of him. With the farm and everything, there was never time, or money to travel for leisure. My father threw away the magazines one day when I was at church.'

'The question is – are you any good at it?'

'I cycle as much as I can. There's a great big hill just where I grew up and I was always the fastest one up it.'

'So if you were able to make a little money on top of what you're paying me back would you buy a bike?'

'Without hesitation.'

'And if you were able to race, would you win?'

I don't know cycling, I'm happy to admit, but I do know people. I've made their motivations, their honesty and varying ability to lie, my life's work. His conviction is an unexpected bonus.

'I would do my best,' he says, earnest.

'Would you win?'

'At least now and again.'

'Let's try you out.' I smile, thinking that I know horses, and dogs, and boxers and rowers and strong men, and maybe soon cyclists. They're popular, it's big business, I know that much, but humans are different from animals. I'm happy to whip a horse, I'm just not sure how to whip a human into winning. 'Now and again is no good to me. How would I get a racer to win all the time?'

'One way would be to pay his rent,' he says.

'I'll pretend I didn't hear that. But you're saying you're pretty good?'

'As there is a distinct lack of farms and useful animals here, I would say yes. Yes I am.'

I want him to be dependent on me. So I tell him a white lie, and a solid truth. It's a mixture I tend to use.

'I'm going away for a little while after I've shown you your accommodation. Only a couple of days, but once I'm back I'll look into the velodrome circuit.'

'Fantastic.' He extends his hand which I ignore.

'Well, don't get too excited. You're going to need a job, but I'm telling you to train while I'm away.'

'How can I? I don't have a bike.'

'I'm beginning to think you're either a bit slow in the head, or maybe you're a curse that my mother has put on me.'

'I wasn't asking for one.'

'But you were, and credit to you, there must be a brain on top of those legs of yours. I'm going to get you one. Take your landlord with you to a shop and he'll make sure my money is spent well.'

'I don't know what to say.'

'Say your prayers, that's what. You'd better be good.'

'Thank you. I won't let you down.'

'It's a business transaction, nothing else. Remember that. I don't care about you.'

We get to my building on Denmark Street. It's dreadful, with plaster coming off in big chunks. The weedy front garden, a step or so long, the three crooked steps, the door swinging open on bent hinges, all mine. All very good for my wallet. No costs, no tax, all below board. We get inside and I point him towards a door where someone has scribbled *Ofiss*. I'm surrounded by cretins.

I don't knock and catch Rupert, the landlord and my small-time fixer, sleeping, cradling a bottle, his feet up on the desk. I cough loudly, and he wakes up. I won't shout at him today, but I remind myself to drop in every now and then.

The room is dim and full of smoke. Rupert's desk is small and cluttered, apart from where he rested his feet. Over by the window, I have a bigger desk and a better chair. Both are the cleanest items in the whole house. On the desk sits a metal box with a huge padlock. Inside I keep a giant, starved rat. A nice surprise for anyone foolish enough to steal from me.

I introduce Paul to the embarrassed Rupert, who, once he sees my wink, tells Paul there are no rooms available. We've done this before. 'But,' Rupert says, 'we have got a small place in the attic.' He then mentions a sum that scares the wits out of Paul. Counting on his fingers he looks like a child in a sweetie shop, one that's lost his money. Shaking his head he asks to be shown the attic. After we've been over the terms, he decides to go for it. I shake his hand and give him a little pocket money to sweeten the deal.

Truth be told I'm not taking much of a financial risk. I employ the boys who took his bike, and I know how much they've sold it for already. I know how much was in his wallet, a cheap imitation one, as Belinda slipped me the money when we were at the eel house. The boys will have left the money untouched. They all remember what happened to their friend who didn't.

With him settled in, and Rupert holding his hand as it were, I am off to see what bee is in Mr Morton's bonnet this time. Then I'll go to the Strand for something much more agreeable. *Happy Birthday Mr Silas* I hum to myself hailing a taxi, thinking of the gift horse sleeping under the eaves.

Chapter 2

Rupert gives him a mattress of sorts. Two sacks sewn together stuffed with rags and newsprint. Paul realises that a blanket is another thing he will have to buy, then tries to stop himself from thinking about all the things he will have to find in the future.

'Come and find me in the morning,' Rupert says, 'we'll sort you out.' Then he climbs out of the attic.

Lying down on the bed Paul realises he's made the worst mistake of his life. He should never have come here, should never have left Scotland. Horrendous father or not, there must have been a better solution. But he's here now. A horse in a mire. No ropes, no rider, no rescue.

He thinks about the money he kept in a battered Hovis all those years. Money his mother left him in secret. Occasional gifts from his uncle Stephen. His earnings from farm work. That tin was his future, his escape from his father. But somehow the old man found out. He must have been spying on Paul through the curtainless windows. Maybe when returning from the pub? Relieving himself in the garden before being sick on the front step, as was his habit. Maybe he spied through the keyhole? Watched Paul counting, and counting again, planning and hoping.

A week before Paul's eighteenth birthday – when he was set to become his own man, make a down payment on a small farm – the tin disappeared. Then his father came back from Glasgow, drunk and proud as a cock. He told Paul the farm was now mostly theirs again.

'Where did you get the money from?' Paul asked. 'And isn't it strange that my savings have just gone missing?'

'How dare you?' His father spat. 'You wee upstart! Think

you're a big man, do you? I run this farm and I won't be told otherwise, especially not by you!'

'That's not fair! It wasn't your money to take,' Paul said, raising his voice.

Pushing Paul in the chest, his father drew himself up tall. Seething with anger, he hissed, 'This is the land of my father, and his father before him. Generations of men who have known better than their sons. I've kept you. Fed you. Housed you. You think you deserve that money?'

'You haven't properly worked for years. Not since Mum—'

Paul's father gasped, cheeks purple. Then he lunged at Paul.

'You and your brother killed her. You wouldn't let her have a minute's sleep when she was pregnant. He wouldn't let her give birth to him. Then he went and died too. Silly sod.'

Then his father, panting like he'd been carrying logs, took a step back and said in a calmer voice, 'Anyway, this is what your mother would have wanted.'

Paul lashed out, quick as the kick of a mule.

Silent for the first time in years, his father gurgled blood and finally spat out a shard of a tooth. Cradling his right fist in his left palm Paul walked to his room. He threw some things in a knapsack and retrieved his bike from one of the outbuildings. He cycled for almost an hour before he realised he was shaking and crying. Luckily it was raining so no one could see his tears.

He had just been paid for some work on a neighbour's field, the envelope still in his pocket. It wasn't much, but enough to give him some options. He hadn't been thinking about where to go, so for want of a better idea he cycled to Glasgow and then got on the morning train to London. He had read somewhere that there were plenty of work opportunities down south. Wanted to be as far away from his father's land as possible.

And now he is here, in this room, lying on sacks filled with rotting newspaper for the mice to gorge on. Outside, Copenhagen Street is noisy. Paul turns over from his back and onto his side in an attempt to sleep. With his nose pressed against the wall he can hear the mice scuttling up and down in their passageways. He hears a scream, half laughter, half fear from the street below him. There are pigeons on the roof, endlessly settling and re-settling and a pack of cats ramble back and forward, scratching and whining.

Paul says his prayers, thanks God for Silas finding him, for the eel supper, the room. He decides the beer he had with his supper was the last alcohol he'll ever drink and that he will take every measure not to end up like his father. He will never gamble. Never. Then, turning onto his back and clasping his hands he asks forgiveness for what he did to his father. He falls asleep while mumbling and will never know where his confession ended.

★★★

In the morning he goes downstairs to find Rupert, but no one seems to be in the office. Paul walks up and down the stairs a couple of times, hoping to bump into him. After a while he decides to speak to his neighbours, to see if they know where Rupert might be.

There are three storeys, with three doors on each landing. Seeing that all the doors on the third floor are boarded up he decides to ask Rupert why he can't have one of the rooms on the third floor instead of the little space he's been assigned.

Walking downstairs he knocks on 2A.

'I'm ill,' a coarse voice shouts. Paul knocks again. When he receives no answer he shouts, 'Can I help?' through the door.

'Go away,' the same person shouts.

Paul tries the doorknob of 2C and to his surprise it comes loose in his hand. He tries to put it back but the screws must have landed on the inside of the door. He pockets it, thinking he might be able to sell it or swap it for an onion or an apple. He pushes the door open with his foot. A black lump hangs from the doorframe. It's as big as his head, shrouded in what looks like dusty cobweb. At first he thinks it's a hat and reaches for it, then he notices a snout and wings. The mass of bats screeches and flaps past him, and he jumps backwards, trying to make himself small. The black horde disappears upwards in the building. There must be an exit somewhere up there he thinks, hoping it's not his attic space they're after.

He crawls up to the door on all fours. Looking into the room he realises there is no floor. The room is just a shell with a deep shaft going down into the basement. Finding one of the screws from the doorknob on the floor in the corridor, he throws it into the abyss but can't hear the sound of it landing. Whether that's because of the drop, the dirt floor, or whatever other organic matter might lie at the bottom, he doesn't know.

Getting up on shaky legs he pulls the door shut, shuddering.

On the first floor he knows there's no need to try 1C, as he's seen the shaft extend far beneath the first floor. 1A is Rupert's office. In 1B, as the door swings open from his soft knock, he finds a very drunk man.

'Have you checked the yeast?' the man asks, fumes of alcohol rolling out of him like storm clouds.

'No, my name is Paul, I'm your new neighbour.' This seems to upset the man greatly.

'Go and check the yeast. It can't, I mean, it *cannot* get wet,' the man grunts.

'I don't know what you mean,' Paul says opening his arms in a half pacifying, half questioning gesture.

'Oh, don't play games with me!'

'I'm not, I'm your neighbour.'

'Have you checked the yeast?'

Paul gives up, and tells the man that yes, he has checked the yeast.

'You stay away from that yeast!'

The man attempts to stand up, waving his arms wildly, trying to reach for Paul. 'If I find that you've been stealing yeast again, you bastard!'

Paul backs out of the room, only to bump into a man covered in flour.

'Don't mind my brother,' the man says.

'I'm sorry. I was just passing by. I live upstairs,' Paul says trying to negotiate past the man.

'Nice to meet you. I'm Henry, and the drunk is David. And unless we help him, he's going to be late for work. Would you mind fetching a bucket of water?'

'There's water?' Paul asks.

'In the tap in the cupboard on this floor only,' says Henry.

Paul goes off for the water, and when he returns, Henry, now in shorts and a vest, chucks the whole pail over his brother. David comes up screaming and clawing the air. Henry calmly punches him in the nose.

'I don't like doing it, but it's the only way to wake him up. Cold water and adrenaline. Then off to work for him.'

'Speaking of work, you wouldn't know of any going? Anything?'

'We're bakers. Not much trade at the moment, so I'm afraid not. But with your size surely you could get something. Lots of cargo ships I hear at St Katherine's.'

'I haven't tried yet. I'm very new to London.'

'Well, we're all beginners in the beginning.'

Paul nods and says goodbye. He's not eaten anything since the eel supper and he's famished. He goes out to buy something to eat, but quickly realises the money Silas left him won't buy him much. London prices are very different from those at home. He buys a bag of apples and thinks about the bike he's been promised. About how weak he feels.

On the way back to the building he sees ice cream with sticks of candied sugar and fancy pastries. Carcasses of heifers so big they look like skiffs hanging on hooks.

Once he's back at the building, he sits down on the steps. He's hoping to catch Rupert, or, even better, Silas. But for the next four hours he has no luck.

He stumbles upstairs and on the lumpy mattress he thinks about getting on the train back to his father's farm. To trudge all the way back, this time without a bike, and grovel. To apologise and to be hitched to the yoke again. He can't do it, even if he had the money for the train fare. He tries to listen out for Silas or Rupert entering the building, but despite trying his hardest he drifts off. When he wakes up in the morning he's so thirsty and hungry that he can't think straight.

He tries to speak to the neighbours again. He knocks on the door to Rupert's office, and sits on the doorstep. Drinks from the tap David showed him. But essentially the day is spent waiting in vain. Wasting more money on apples.

Chapter 3

We're standing in the sun on Copenhagen Street. I can tell Paul has lost weight in the two weeks since I saw him last. I enjoy assessing size, leg length, inseam, chest width, girth, that sort of thing. I could have become a master tailor, had I been inclined.

From what I understand, from speaking to other cyclists and coaches, weight loss is not a bad thing. The trick seems to be to find a racer who can pedal for hours. Not a showman or circus act, but one who won't give up. The more weight this racer carts around, the more energy he has to spend doing it. Elementary physics, really. With the amount of training and racing these boys are required to do there isn't much time to eat, and whatever they eat, dissipates into energy. Runs off as steam from the engines they have turned themselves into.

Paul has told me he's so happy I'm back a hundred times already, and though I should really tell him to stop, it's nice to hear. This puppylike devotion, however much it is based on the treats I get him, might prove useful in the future.

'Well, let's have a look at this bike then,' I say.

'It's great isn't it?' He smiles.

'It's not a toy, you realise. It's an investment.'

He turns to me, earnest, 'Hopefully I can make us some money.'

'You better make some money quickly.'

'Well, with this machine I think we have a chance.' He runs a finger along the frame.

'What's so special about it?' I ask, not that I'm all that interested, but he's nice to talk to and if this is my new investment, at least I should know something about it. Same as chatting with a jockey I suppose. Or patting a greyhound.

'It's a 1921 Iver Johnson Special, The man in the shop told me it was once owned by Dusty Chalmers.'

'Who?'

'Eric "Dusty" Chalmers, an American racer. I'm surprised you haven't heard of him. The man in the shop told me Eric came over here for the 1920 Olympics in Antwerp. There's a sticker on the seat tube: "*Vélodrome d'Anvers Zuremborg*". He didn't do too well in the games, and afterward, he came to London. He brought a team of people and two bikes, can you imagine? Two bikes! Both this bright yellow. This is one he left behind.'

'Well it's a nice colour.'

'Eric sold it to someone to pay for his hotel. It's light too. Feel it, lift it.'

I lift it, and raise my eyebrows for effect. 'Well I don't know what to compare it to but I suppose that's quite light, but you won't be carrying it will you? You'll be cycling on it mostly, won't you?'

'Yes. It'd be a shame not to. Look it came with laminated wooden rims, adjustable stem. Look here, the bars are made-to-measure by Mr Lauterwasser himself.'

'Mr Lauter... who is that?'

'The man who runs the shop of course.'

'That's fine. Where is it?' I say, looking at him; a boy by the Christmas tree, the biggest gift ripped open.

'On Holloway Road.'

'I'll make a point of popping in to see them.' I want to know Paul got a good price.

'Speak to Jack if you do. He's the guy who owns the shop. It was nice of Rupert to go with me. He took Jack off to the pub, to do a bit of haggling. When they came back, Jack's face was quite flushed, and the price had dropped considerably,' he says, the manchild.

'That's good. Makes it easier for you to pay back.' I shuffle my feet a little. I'm not that interested in bikes, but his enthusiasm is quite contagious. I light a cigarette and allow him to indulge a little more.

'You know Iver Johnson Company sponsored Marshall "Major" Taylor?' he continues.

'Who?'

'You're kidding?' he says.

'Almost never.' I blow smoke out of the side of my mouth.

'Only one of the greatest cyclists ever,' Paul's even taken his eyes off the bike in astonishment at my ignorance.

'Was he in the army?' I ask, looking at the sun. It feels like it has been a century since I saw it last.

'No, he was black.' he says.

'Dressed in black?' I say, closing my eyes and feeling the warmth of the weather.

'No, black skin.'

'In the army?'

'No. When Iver first started sponsoring him he was mostly doing tricks outside the bicycle shop to attract customers, and for some reason, maybe he was lent one, or maybe it was the closest to a suit he could find, he wore a uniform.' Paul taps his finger along the top tube of the bike, listening intently for something. Then he goes on, 'Anyway, he went on to be a legendary racer, but people found it very hard to see him win, because of the colour of his skin, and he retired early.'

'Well lucky you're ginger. People mind that less, I believe.'

'I think I'll wear a cap just in case,' he nods seriously and wheels the bike back and forward a couple of inches.

'I can never tell if you're actually quite funny, or just a child.' I say.

'I think maybe neither.'

'I think maybe both.' Chapter 4

I have decided to treat the whole episode like an outing to the Zoo. The best way to run this new branch of my enterprise is to see the cyclists as horses, dogs, cocks – animals, plain and simple. Speaking animals.

I've set Paul up for a trial, with the three famous brothers: Harry, Leonard, and Percy Wyld. *The Wyld Bunch*, as they're advertised. They grumble a bit but when it transpires that their manager owes a considerable amount of money to Mr Morton, they stop. They gather around Paul's bike, and nod approvingly, feel the handlebars, lift it once or twice, hold it by the saddle and spin the back wheel. These men are like dogs; I'm expecting them to sniff each other's crotches, and pee in the banked corners.

It turns out Harry has had a fall. He'll be coaching from the side of the track instead, something he seems quite happy with.

As Paul, Leonard and Percy warm up. I go and stand to one side. I am the only person on the stands apart from a caretaker, who is picking up litter from the night before. Judging by the size of his sack it was a successful evening. When I ask him about it he shrugs his shoulders, says it was quite average. About eight, eight-and-a-half-thousand people. The financial cogs in my head turn a little faster. The man's words, and my experience of drunk people betting and getting it wrong, make me smile. I know Saturdays and sometimes Sundays at Herne Hill are big, but a Tuesday night right after Easter? At Moorgate? At a small oval with rundown stalls? At a place with no glamour? Astonishing.

The cyclists warm up at a blistering pace. It's beautiful the way they fly. It makes my lungs hurt just watching them. I light a cigar while they do sprints and formations, pedalling too fast for me to see whose legs are whose. Afterwards they slow down, come high up on the banks, and swoop down – ballerinas on bikes.

Harry shouts something about fifty laps and they come off the track. They stand in front of me; a crescent of men with slicked-back hair. The experts and the apprentice.

'He goes too high up, comes too close, isn't too sure of himself or how to handle the bike, can't properly judge distances or speed,' says Leonard. Paul hangs his head. He's strong but has nowhere near the level of stamina the Wyld boys possess. Even I can see that.

There is silence for a moment.

'But for a first-timer, he's not too bad,' Leonard continues, and the surge of relief on Paul's face is so obvious and childlike I can't help but smile.

'He's obviously a quick learner,' Leonard says 'but, as he'll tell you himself, he needs a lot of training to keep up with the big boys.'

Paul nods.

'He would be good in a team time trial. He's so broad, he blocks a lot of the wind. And if he was fast enough and Percy could hide behind him, he could prove to be useful.'

I send Paul out on the track for another few laps. Nothing too strenuous, just to get some exercise, more experience. In the meantime I speak with Harry, and arrange for him to meet me at the Rising Sun on Chalton Street later in the evening. I think he and I could strike up something quite interesting.

★★★

After the trial I take Paul to the eel and pie house. He looks happy and exhausted at the same time.

'I was hoping you'd be faster than them,' I say winking to Belinda as she takes our order.

'I'm sorry,' he says. 'But I will be. Just need to get to know the tricks and the pace.'

'And how will you do that?'

'By going to the races, by speaking to Mr Lauterwasser, by training and trying to get into the races myself.'

'This offer of money has a time limit, you realise?'

'Yes, I do.'

'And you need to start performing soon, or my patience will run out.'

'I understand,' he nods seriously.

'I'm not sure if you do.'

To do my job properly, to get the most out of him, I'm pretending to be angry with him. As it is I don't mind what he does. It's good if he stays in my house, it's great if he starts winning races, and the combination would be fabulous. He looks at me, all earnest youth, and says, 'I promise to do my best.'

I wave his sincerity away like a bee. Then we order. Or at least he orders. I don't like eel much.

'Oh, I meant to tell you,' he says once we get the food, 'I've got a job.'

'You have?'

'Well, the fruitmonger on the corner came and saw me in the house. He'd heard I was looking for a job. Luckily his horse went lame on the same day, so I said I would deliver all his vegetables for the same price as the oats and straw he would have spent on the horse, till he sorted it out. I would even provide my own bike.'

'That's a terrible deal for you.'

'I know. But that horse is not going to get any better soon. If it's lame it's headed for the knacker's yard.'

'So you hope that once he realises you're cheaper than buying a new horse, feeding it, keeping it and so on, he'll hire you properly?'

'Something like that.'

'You're an errand boy?'

'The way I see it I'm being paid to train, and I like getting to know the streets anyway.

'So you're a professional? The fruit and veg man just happens to be your main sponsor?'

'That's a good way to describe it.'

'You are peculiar.'

'Thank you,' he says, smiling.

'It's not a compliment. Not necessarily.'

I watch him load mashed potato into his mouth. Don't tell

him the fruitmonger was so scared his teeth were chattering when I spoke to him. He would have offered Paul a job even if Paul was lame. But I won't mention it. A man's pride is more important than his hunger or money, in fact more important than anything. Besides I made sure the fruit man got a decent price for his old horse.

'I worked all day today in fact. Deliveries from five to five,' Paul says. 'Went straight to the velodrome.'

He moves his shoulders, as though there's something sitting between his shoulder blades, and I think of the hundreds of kilos of potatoes and apples he must have carted around in the morning before the Wyld trial. He should have said something.

I order more food for him and lean back in my seat. I like to sit and watch him regain his strength.

'Have you been in to see Belinda?' I ask, but he just shakes his head, mouth full.

Once we're done I tell him to go and rest or something. He lumbers off with the air of a dismissed employee. That's not to be underestimated, but in fact I was pleasantly surprised by his form and his ability on the bike. I'm no expert, but I could tell there is potential in the boy.

I walk over to the Rising Sun and sit so that I can see the people coming in. Turns out Harry is quite the drinker, but before he gets too incomprehensible, we agree to some kind of terms whereby he advises Paul on racing, but only gets paid once Paul starts winning. We also agree to enter Paul into a race sooner rather than later.

'There's only so much training you can do,' Harry tells me. 'Besides, you can't really prepare for races. So we might as well push him in with both feet.'

I nod and order more drinks.

Harry continues, 'There's an easy one at Peckham in a couple of weeks. If you make sure he gets there, I'll see him right.'

Eventually I get up, but Harry stays on. I leave him a little bit of money and he looks up at me with the grateful eyes of a Spaniel. I like the man, he's competent and knows a great deal about cycling and cyclists. He can bridge the gap in my knowledge until I've learned enough for this new venture. Once I know a little I can transfer my skills from horses and boxing and so on. Till then, I'll use Harry as a teacher for Paul.

I put on my hat and walk outside looking for a taxi. Not finding one I decide to walk for a while instead. Swinging my cane and whistling. I smile to myself, I'm either drunk, or excited about the future. Maybe both. It's been a long time.

Chapter 5

Since coming to London almost a month ago and making that vow about alcohol, Paul has developed a taste for sarsaparilla. His favourite is Baldwin's, which they serve at the eel house. Once or twice he has offered to pickup the vats of the stuff from the supplier on Walworth Road as a favour to Belinda. The sugary drink helps when he's tired after cycling. Most people drink beer for lunch, but it just makes him sleepy.

Dropping off the vats, Belinda often tells him there's a man, in Fremantle, Australia, who writes to her about once a month. Long letters on thick paper, asking her to send him a case or two of the bottles. The man's done well for himself, he's a landowner, with his own herd of camels for rent. People use them when crossing the scorched plains. She tells Paul the man has enough money for dresses and meat on the table every day, but that he misses the eel and the drinks of England. Belinda has a way of leaning into him when he's sitting down, her hip resting against him. She usually brings over more drinks than he has to pay for, always smiling. Most days he's too tired to think properly about women, and anyway they're too complicated.

In the past few weeks he's lost weight and gained speed. Silas has had Harry look him over and offer him tips a few times, but with all the work Paul's not had a chance to practise in a velodrome. But that's about to change today, he's been told. Silas has arranged for him to race in Peckham.

Paul has gone past the small arena a few times doing deliveries, so it's easy enough for him to find the way there today. By the looks of it, the little arena is about to be demolished, but there are still races. Posters scream of *Daredevils* and *Prize Money*. The faded colours of the flags on top of the stadium don't inspire much confidence but it's a welcome change from the deliveries.

He looks at the signs and streamers, at the crowds and the stalls selling oysters and clams, at the colourful tricycles selling drinks. He walks past the service entrance to the velodrome when someone runs out, shouting about how late he is. After a few stammered excuses, Paul realises Silas has given him the time the race starts, and not the time, about an hour earlier, he was supposed to turn up to register and warm up.

Paul apologises and asks about prize money. The answer is pleasantly surprising. The sum is more generous than the velodrome suggests. He's still not used to the inflated economy of the nation's capital.

He's been told Harry will meet him and make sure everything runs smoothly, but since Silas got the time wrong Paul's not counting on Harry being there.

He rolls into the velodrome and warms up for a couple of laps, to get a feel for the gradient and the concrete surface. The oval is 1,175 feet. Just a distance to be broken down into laps, pedal strokes and breaths.

At the sound of the starter gun Paul takes a chance on his legs and lungs. After just a few laps his thoughts are dreamy yet clear. The race seems to pass in front of him like a play at the theatre.

It's very different from practising with the Wyld boys. There was order, there. Commands shouted out by the team captain. A well-drilled line of men surging around him. This is dangerous. This is chaos. After a few laps, where he has been out front, smirking with the ease of cycling on a track as opposed to the streets, he is caught. Left behind. He looks up at the sign board by the finish line. His heart stops when he realises how many laps are left.

He pushes hard. His breath rasps through his lungs as he catches up with the main group of riders. Spurred on by the jolt of happiness he feels when he passes another racer, he climbs up in the line of men, until he's third. Then second. He stays there. Focusses on not losing an inch. Keeps his eyes on the man's calves. Up, down, up, down.

After what seems like an eternity, he hears a bell. He has just entered the last lap. He decides he will wait forty pedal strokes before launching an attack. *Thirty-thirty-one-two-three-four...* a violent tide of pain. Sawing on his handlebars, swinging his bike as if it was an axe, the man in front of him stands up and sets off. Paul assembles everything he's got left, which isn't much. With half a lap left he hasn't caught up. With a quarter of a lap left – even in the last bend – he hasn't caught up. Out on the home straight at last, he leaves the air stream behind the man and pulls out next to him.With twenty feet left they're neck and neck, with ten no different. With five feet the man's front wheel is in front of Paul's. With three feet Paul pushes the bike out in front of him, as if he wanted to get rid of it, which is true at that moment, and that seals it. Paul wins by a tyre.

He can't breathe for two more laps. He feels the man he just beat pat him on the back, a friendly gesture of defeat, before they both slow down and get off their bikes. Walk, on unsteady legs, back to their bags and woollen suit jackets.

Sitting down after the race, looking at the winner's envelope, Paul starts to plan which flat on which street with which colour front door and what food in the cupboards he'll buy now that he can make so much money in an afternoon just by sweating a little. Or actually quite a lot, as it has been a few hours of cycling. It has been hard work but at times almost enjoyable.

Harry comes over and pats him on the back, says, 'You did well today, really well. I missed the start as Silas told me the wrong time, what a dumbbell.'

Paul nods. Harry continues, 'Just now I'm late for something but I'll see you at the next race, if not before.'

Paul's head is spinning. Not from tiredness or hunger, but from the prospect of making money as a cyclist.

An oily little man comes over and demands a thirty percent

cut for the booking and handling fee. Paul tries to argue, but the man shrugs his shoulders and says, 'It's part and parcel.'

Paul pays and the man, who promises him more races, then walks off.

In the middle of his elation Paul realises that there are much faster and fitter cyclists than the Saturday crowd in Peckham. But with that comes the insight that there are races that will pay a lot more to win. Today was good, but he knows he can do better. He will have to train well, eat well, sleep well. Devote himself in a way he didn't think was necessary. Or imaginable. The prospect of it makes him smile as he gets back on the bike again for the cycle back across the river to his waiting bed, his buttocks only smarting a bit.

Chapter 6

I follow him to Peckham. At a distance of course. Just want to see what he is up to. I have no desire to be his trainer or too close to the actual racing. I thought it'd be nice to see his first race, since that would be my first too, fitting that. I get a good seat and wait for things to get going.

Inside the velodrome is a busy mixture of people. Women from all social strata. Mechanics with oily rags hanging out of their back pockets, competitors eating gruel, smoking or drawing deep nasal breaths of ammonia or one of the new powders you can get in a paper cone if you know a chemist. The ones that make you extra alert, but sad in two days' time.

Paul stands still next to his bike, his skin like marble. An Apollo in tight woollen shorts. He looks tense and lost, like a farmhand recently made knight.

I signal for a drink, down it and ask for another. 'Less crème de menthe, more gin, and the real stuff. Not your back room poison this time,' I shout. I'm on edge.

I close my eyes for a minute while Paul completes a wobbly exhibition lap, like they do at Kempton Park.

The starter gun sounds, and I'm pulled back to the racing and the reality of the monetary risk I'm taking on this boy. At the moment it's not much, but if things go well I'm going to have to introduce him to Mr Morton, the vulture always perching above me.

At the moment I'm in Mr Morton's good books, and by extension so is Paul. This veneer of understanding is easily cracked. Debts and insubordination are just two ways to rile Mr Morton. As the current leader of the Elephant and Castle Gang, recently reinstated after that debacle out in Bradford, Mr Morton owes me a huge favour. If he chooses to honour it. A terrible temper on that man, but rich pickings if you can play him right.

I light my Punch Petit Pyramide and toast Paul, who's sweating profusely now.

Against my hopes and wishes, I am now part of Mr Morton's awful family, but I have made a good living from the scraps he has thrown me. There's no denying that.

The men down on the oval are surging. I can't see the numbers from here, but there's an attractive girl turning a flap over every lap, once the leading man has passed. I'm disappointed to see it's not Paul. If I'm going to make a go of this cycling thing maybe I should be on the lookout not only for handsome cyclists, but ones that actually win races. To my delight though I notice that Paul is second. Didn't recognize him at first, bent double and as red as a tomato.

I concentrate on the race. Seems it's soon coming to an end. I watch the men straining, bustling, shouldering each other, jostling for position, and realise just how dangerous a fall would be. In a stampede on wheels like this I would hate to be on the ground. Eight laps, seven, six. I like the speed. Four, three. What is Paul doing? Why isn't he trying to win? Two. Am I backing the wrong man? One. Now there's a bell. Still, Paul just sits on the wheel of the man in front of him. Half a lap. Now I see movement. I find myself standing up. I'm clenching my fists, I'm on my toes, neck straining to see every inch of the race. There's a wild shout, a deranged howl of happiness as Paul crosses the line first. Only when I close my mouth do I realise I've been shouting. First I'm ashamed, then I realise the men next to me have been shouting too. Not knowing what to do, but feeling that we've been through something significant together I turn to my left, then to my right, and shake hands with my fellow spectators. They don't bat an eyelid. It's done solemnly, respectfully.

I leave the arena convinced I'm backing the right man. But I won't let on.

Chapter 7

After training one day, Harry pulls Paul aside. Sits him down on the side of the track and plonks a cup of tea down in front of him.

'Paul, I need to ask you what you take.'

'How do you mean, take?'

'Any medication?'

'I'm not ill,' Paul says, hands around the mug.

'I mean, you now, none of the other boys are cycling dry. They all have a little something every now and then to help them along.'

'Like what?'

'Capsules, powders and vials from the sports apothecary. Whatever suits them.'

Paul nods and Harry continues, 'Benzedrine for quicker legs, Laudanum for the pain after a race. There's plenty to choose from. Codeine, cocaine, diamorphine, chlorodyne. It's a list with no end really. We'll do some experiments, work out what suits you best.'

'Are you sure it's safe?'

'A cyclist's private pill box is as important as a good set of tyres and cranks. Sometimes more so.'

'I'm not sure. I feel fine, I feel fast.'

'But that won't last, you see. I wouldn't ask you to take anything I haven't used myself,' Harry says, 'Silas will sort you out. I know he has contacts in the medical trade. I'll help you with doses and timing. We'll do some training on that as well.' Harry slaps Paul on the back before leaving him with a parting thought, 'The next time we'll talk about endurance races. The ones where you cycle for twelve, twenty-four hours, or six days in a row. Then you'll understand why you need your drugs. Wouldn't want you to fall asleep in the saddle. Or be in so much pain that you can't complete by day five.'

★★★

Paul returns to Peckham a week later, registered as Paul MacAllister, of Copenhagen Street. The next week he squeezes in two midweek races as well as the Peckham one, where they now recognize and rightly fear him. More and more of his time is devoted to the track.

He continues to work for the fruit and veg shop. It's hard going, and he is indeed treated like the horse he replaced, only no one slips him apples or pats him. No one puts a warm blanket over his shoulders when it's raining. But it's good training and it teaches him more about the city of London. It's a city he fears and warms to in equal measures. With the weekday work and the weekend races, he makes more money in a month than his father ever made in a year of hard, hard work on the family farm. Again all his money goes into a tin. This time a Warburton's one. At the end of the month he finds Silas in Rupert's office and presents the box to him.

'I'm not hungry. And I wouldn't want to steal your bread, you're poor enough as it is,' Silas says smiling.

'It's the inside that counts,' Paul says proudly, straightening his back.

'So you've managed to pay rent this month?' Silas says once he's prised off the lid of the tin. He sounds surprised, but there's a knowing smile playing over his lips. Implying he knows more than he's letting on. 'And the bike?'

'I've put a little something in the box towards it. Ten percent agreeable?' Paul says, with a sense of pride that can't be hidden.

'It is indeed. And is this all fruit and veg money?'

'It's mostly from smaller races. I've not been able to enter as many races as I would like to. Some of them are further away and I would have to go on a train, maybe stay overnight, and there's no way I can be back for the deliveries on those days.'

'So what does that tell you?' Silas says twirling a pen.

'I don't know.'

'Do you want me to tell you?' He taps the pen twice on the green writing pad on his desk.

'If you think it's important.'

'It's your life.'

'Some of it belongs to you,' Paul says, looking at his fingernails.

'Well, it tells me that you have to speak to your boss and tell him you will need a day off every now and then.'

'Which would be fine if I won the race. If not I'd be losing money.'

'You would have to be pretty successful, that's true.'

'He only cares about his deliveries.'

'I don't blame him. But the other thing you can do is to find another job.'

'I tried, and still do whenever I can, but it seems pretty impossible.'

'You should perhaps look elsewhere. You need something which pays more so that you can work less, so that you can compete more, so that you can rake in more winnings with that bike of yours. Or should I say my bike?'

'As of today one tenth is mine,' he says, proudly.

'Which tenth would you like?' Silas asks, now drawing a row of interlinked eights on a legal pad.

'The wheels please,' Paul says after thinking about it for a second or two.

'You can have one.'

'Deal. I can be a circus bear on a unicycle,' Paul says smiling.

'Tell me more about your... our... finances.'

'It's hard to make much when I'm forced to pay someone at the various tracks thirty percent of my winnings,' Paul says, quietly.

Silas shakes his head and gets up from his chair. Starts

pacing the small room, brushing past Paul, who is leaning against a wall.

Silas stops and says, 'I worry about you. This is elementary maths. You need to improve your income and lower your costs. From now on I want you to inform me of any races you plan to enter, these other jokers are robbing you of your money. You should leave that up to me.'

'That's fine.'

'Good, so, I want to make you a proposition. Any races you win I take twenty percent, any you lose, you pay me ten percent of what the winner made.'

'And if I come second, or third?'

'Then we'll do ten and five percent.'

Paul counts on his fingers for a second or two, then says, 'Deal.'

'Smart move my boy,' Silas says and extends his hand and they shake on it.

'Let's see how we get on.'

'Let's see indeed.'

'So what about the starting fees?' Paul asks.

'You just tell me in advance where you're going to be racing, and I'll make sure you won't have to pay any starter fee, or anything beyond our deal.

'How will you do that?'

'Not that it's your business, but I have connections myself, and I work for a man with more fingers in more pies than you could possibly imagine. Sports and gambling is just one branch. It keeps expanding, so you'd do well to be under his protection anyway. Whether it's financially sound for you or not.'

Silas opens the door and gestures for Paul to come outside with him. They walk half a block before Silas speaks again. 'So, if we are going to be a team – you the cyclist, me the financier, you the legs, me the brain – you need to meet Mr Morton. I've told him about you and he was quite interested.

Not too interested though, don't flatter yourself. But for various reasons you wouldn't understand he needs to meet you. So, tomorrow.'

They've come to a stop in front of a newsagent.

'Tomorrow suits me fine,' Paul says.

'I wasn't asking,' Silas replies, and opens the door, setting off the bell. 'Mr Morton has a place out in Elephant and Castle,' he continues. 'What time are you done with deliveries tomorrow? Around ten?'

'I should be done by then.'

'I'll meet you there. Just go to Walworth Road and ask for the Carousel, that's his place out there. Everyone knows where it is. Give my name to the orangutans at the door, and they'll show you upstairs,' Silas says before going inside to purchase his American weeklies.

Chapter 8

May arrives but the weather is still crisp. The irregular cobblestones of Paul's usual routes glisten in the fleeting sun. He's had a puncture but the day is sunny and Silas wasn't all too precise about when to arrive, so instead of looking for a taxi, he looks at the water, eats an apple. He slowly rolls the bike, turning the front wheel this way and that, painting oblong eights in the mud. He walks towards Southwark Bridge asking people if they know a bicycle shop nearby, but no one does.

The bridge itself is painted bright green and yellow; fresh peas with butter. The lampposts are darker and look like sentries with their arms outstretched, each crowned by a princess' crown in brass. Children stick their hands out through the gaps in the railings like prisoners, fenced in by gravity and parents. Paul leans the bike against a lamppost and squints at the river full of barges. Double-decker trams are flying both ways. The tracks are screaming in protest as the behemoths, filled to the brink with people, accelerate and stop in a never-ending waltz.

Paul hears a car revving hard, then an explosion. He turns to look and there's a blue Talbot crumpled up against a lamppost, smoke coming out of its bonnet. Behind him a horse whinnies, and before Paul has a chance to step out of the way the huge Clydesdale pulling a beer cart is on top of him. Paul's belt snags on the cart. The man holding the reins is screaming to the horse, and can't see Paul being pulled along like a rag doll tied to a steam train.

As the horse picks up speed Paul trips and falls. Now he's scraping along the ground, hanging from his belt. The massive wheels of the cart are only inches away from his face.

He can see the pattern of the spokes, blurry. It's curious and compelling. He hears the crunch of the ironclad wheels as they destroy everything in their way.

Time slows down almost to a standstill. Now the horse changes tack. From the middle of the road it's now veering over towards the right pavement, crossing tram tracks, the man on top cursing. A bow wave of traffic and people in front of it. Paul is squeezed up against the high kerb. He hears glass bottles being crushed, popping like deadly fireworks, under the wheels of the cart. People are screaming and jumping out of the way of the now frothing horse. The paving stones, with their grouting of human and animal sludge, are a blurry mess coming closer and closer to his face.

His belt snaps and he hits the ground, ending up underneath the cart, between the wheels. He feels the wind from the spokes ruffle his hair and brush up against the soles of his feet, as the cart passes overhead.

He stands up and looks down the street at the horse, still galloping with the broken cart careening behind it, and almost passes out from the relief. Then he feels the sting of gravel and bits of glass.

He looks over in panic to see where his bike is. It's still where he left it and the relief surging through his body almost cancels the pain. He starts to hobble towards the bike then the pain takes over.

Paul sits down on the pavement, feet in the gutter, his shoes near a pile of cabbage and manure. Stars dance in front of his eyes and he can't make his hands stop shaking however hard he tries. He turns his palms this way and that, looks at them like two lobsters he's never seen before, ones that are alive and will snip off his fingers if he's not careful. Finally he sits on them, to keep them still. He can't see anything to either side of him. He's in a tunnel of relief, but it's hard to breathe, his chest not big enough for all the air he feels he needs to calm down. He takes off his jacket. Lays it across his legs, building a little tent for his wounded knee.

A woman runs up to him, asks if he's ok. She tells him she saw the whole thing. All he can do is nod. When she doesn't walk on, he straightens up and looks at her. She's slender but not thin. Wears her clothes well but not ostentatiously. She has a long neck and her face is cute as a button, he thinks, but not without experienced lines. Her eyes are light green, the colour of a William's pear, and her hair is coppery and chestnut. She's lost her hat running after him, and a little boy comes over with it. She holds it in her hands, turning it slowly by the brim. It's one of the modern ones that hide women's faces. Paul tries to give the boy a coin, but the woman waves Paul's hand away and gives the boy a little nod. He disappears into the forest of people on the bridge.

Getting up, groaning a little, Paul tells her he is fine. Smiles as much as he can. Thanks her for her concern, while hiding the wound on his leg from her with his jacket. The shakes won't subside, but after gulping down air for a while he's less disorientated. He tells her he needs to be somewhere, which was the he last rational thought he had before the horse almost killed him.

'I was going to cycle,' he says. 'Now I can't cycle, and I would rather not walk. All I want to do is to sit down.'

'I don't think you should be walking anywhere,' she says.

'I don't want to but I have to,' he replies, trying to bend his knees.

'We'll see about that,' she says, and puts her hat back on. Before she was just beautiful. Now she is more than beautiful. Then she smiles at him and says, 'My name is Miriam. What's yours?'

'Paul MacAllister. Nice to meet you.' His hands are still trembling, but he lifts one up for her to shake.

She takes his hand in his. Her skin is warm and dry. The opposite of his. She holds on a split second longer than she needs to he thinks. Maybe.

'Thanks for taking pity on me,' he says, and folds his hands in his lap. Interlaced as though he was in church. Can't stop thinking about the sparkles of mica in her eyes. Crushed gravel on moss.

'Nonsense. It's what any normal person would do,' she says.

'Well in that case, you're the only normal person on this bridge,' he laughs.

'Where are you going? Or where were you going?' she says.

'I was just trying to calm the horse,' he says, panting.

Miriam looks up and down the bridge.

'I'm from a farm, I know my way around horses,' Paul says.

'I can tell you're from out of town. Not sure about your way with horses,' she says smiling. She looks out over the water. Over the morass of streets and lanes. She turns back to him.

'Maybe you're right,' hanging his head a little.

'Anyway, I meant where were you going, before the accident?'

'Oh, I see,' Paul says. 'I was going to Elephant and Castle.'

'You're in luck. So am I.'

'There's a place called the Carousel there. Know it?'

She shakes her head. 'If you're going to the Elephant, we can easily catch a tram, it's the least I can do. One should come along any minute.'

'But my bike, I can't leave it here,' he says, looking across the road.

'You shouldn't be on it,' she says. 'If you start walking over to the stop I'll see to it.'

He limps over to the queue of people. Stands with his forehead against the cool bridge railing. The world is spinning, his leg is dripping with blood, and he has to concentrate very hard on not being sick.

He turns around, leaning against the railing. The woman, Miriam, flags down a man on a delivery cart. She points to the bike about a hundred yards away. Tells him to load the bike onto the cart, and to take it to the pub called the Ram's

Head on Heygate Street. Paul hears her instruct the man to leave the bike with Isaac Holben, the landlord, the man with three fingers on his left-hand. He's not to give it to anyone else. Paul stares in wonder. Miriam seems used to getting her way. Through his pain and nausea he smiles. He's glad she seems to be on his side.

The man on the cart starts to protest, but she hushes him and pulls out a purse, giving him what looks like two days' wages. Then she leans close and mentions a name Paul can't quite catch.

On hearing this, the man promptly hands back the money, jumps down from the cart and sprints over to the bike. He loads it and sets off. Lifts his hat and smiles a drawn smile. Miriam has been standing stock-still, arms akimbo, her brow knitted. Now she bows a little, flashes her teeth, possibly the tip of her tongue, and walks over to Paul. He smiles and tries to raise a hand to thank her, but he's still focusing on not vomiting.

'Paul, Paul,' she shouts for him. To bring him back from where his brain, rung like a church bell, has taken him. 'That's our tram coming now.' In the distance, emerging from the crowds of the north, he sees a double-decker tram, painted bright red and blue, advertising Yorkston Pies. 'Come on.' He hobbles over to the end of the queue, mouth set in a grimace. The wound is not too painful, but it's raw, and his jacket brushing up against the exposed flesh is a very unpleasant feeling.

The conductor, taking Paul's fare, says, 'So, one for The Elephant – the Piccadilly of South London? Return?'

'Yes. No. Does it matter?' says Paul.

'I'd take the return if I was you. If you have somewhere nicer to return to. You're looking pretty beat up, but it's even rougher out there.'

The woman now sitting across from him smiles and tells Paul the conductor is just joking. Then she notices his leg and gasps, puts a hand up to cover her mouth, 'Paul! You should have said.'

'I'm fine,' he replies, smiling as much as he can.

'You need that looked at!'

'I'm late for something.'

'Something or someone?'

'Someone,' he says, shrugging his shoulders.

'A woman?' She arches both eyebrows. Leans forward.

'No. A man, two men. Business, you know.'

'Well if it was a woman I would have let you go. She could have taken care of you. And one should never be late for a woman.'

'I wouldn't know,' he smiles.

'That's good. I like that in a man. One who admits he doesn't know.'

He smiles, finds it hard not to. It's like there are fishing lines attached to the sides of his lips, and someone above is pulling at them. She quickly looks up and down the tram, doesn't nod to anyone. Then her eyes return to him, and hold his until he has to blink.

'Thank you,' he says. Then the lurching tram makes him feel queasy again.

Holding a hand to his mouth he whispers, 'I'm sorry. I'm not feeling too well.'

'I can see that. You're almost green.'

'Thanks.'

'Paul, you can't go to your meeting looking like that. Your leg looks like raw mince. We're getting off one stop earlier. I'll patch you up. Then you can go.'

'I'm not sure...'

'I'll tell you what. Pretend I'm an army nurse or something, and that this is an order.'

'Fine. I surrender,' he says.

She sits back in her seat, looks out through the window behind him. Then she starts rummaging in her bag.

'Here, have this Walnut Whip,' she says. 'It's good for your colour, they say.'

Through his pain he looks at her as much as he thinks is polite.

After a short while she pulls the cord and helps him off the tram. Takes him upstairs to a small, but not tiny, apartment. She apologises for the mess. He can't see a mess. She sits him down on a high stool in the kitchen and goes to the bathroom, returning with several strongly smelling liquids which she pours over his leg. He winces and wriggles a little, and she calls him a brave boy. He can't tell if she's joking or not. She stands in front of him, looking him over, appraising her work. Then she walks off into another room, returning with a pair of men's trousers she insists he puts on. He tries to protest but it's useless. She's half spun sugar, half pickaxe.

'Do you want a glass of water?' she asks once he tells her the coast is clear.

'No. Do you?' he answers.

'Do you want anything else?' she says.

'A cup of tea?'

'Gin?' she offers, with one eyebrow raised, leaning against the sink.

'No thanks. Anyway, I thought you were in the army?'

'Be quiet. Can you walk?'

He stands up and limps a little, then over the course of three or four steps he softens and then walks almost normally. 'Yes,' he smiles.

'Good. Well, let's get the blood circulating. Please could you get me a glass from the cupboard in the hall? One of the nice, crystal ones. I'll put the kettle on in the meantime.'

Once he comes limping back she pours a deep measure into the glass, then quickly drinks most of it in one go. He whistles softly and she smiles. When he turns back from dealing with the kettle she has refilled her glass.

'I don't usually do this kind of thing, taking stray dogs like yourself home with me,' she says.

'Me neither. I never have accidents,' he smiles, shamedfaced.

'It's just…'

'I'm quite good with traffic. It's sort of my job. If I had been on a bike it wouldn't have happened I'm sure. Well, I wouldn't have stopped to deal with the horse anyway.'

'It's just, my brother…' she says, and suddenly she turns pale and he thinks she's about to fall.

He says, 'How are you feeling? Sit down. Is it the blood?' he asks, now half standing up.

'I'm fine with blood. It's just before I came to London… never mind. You have a peculiar way of speaking. Are you Glaswegian?' she says gingerly turning her glass in her hands.

'Not too far from it,' he says, suddenly aware of his accent.

She put her glass down on the table, and says, 'I've known a few. I might sound like a Londoner but I'm not from here. It's a long time ago.' She looks down at her hands gripping the edge of the table, then she sits down, smoothing her skirt. As if on cue, he sits too, grunting as the knee bends.

She continues, 'Up there, in Birmingham where we were living, the horses are huge. He was only five, I was seven. It was just the two of us, out doing something, stealing food probably, and he was knocked over by a cart.'

Her hands are fidgeting from the glass to the tablecloth and back. Again and again. Then she gulps down the full glass of gin. 'Unlike you, he didn't make it,' she says, holding her empty glass high. 'He died. Right there in the street. And no one noticed,' she says, her voice flat.

The room is silent. To him it feels like the whole town is all of a sudden deserted. It's a very strange feeling in London. Then one by one little sounds come back. The tram, a horse, a woman shouting about the evening news, a child crying.

'I'm sorry,' he says. It's the only thing he can think of.

'It's a long time ago. My brother was a child. I was a child.' Paul is quiet. Looks into her green eyes.

'No one knows. I don't know why I'm telling you,' she says. He looks around the room, then his eyes settle on a small pile of napkins, folded on a sideboard. 'Here, take this, you're crying,' he says, handing her one.

She starts to dab her eyes, and then unfolds the napkin and buries her face in it. Her shoulders shake. The sobs tear at her body. He feels utterly useless. Then she looks up, smiles a sad smile and says, 'It's been a long time since that too.'

'Can I help you? In any way?' he says.

'No.'

'I owe you that.'

'Don't be silly, it's just a bit of bandage,' she says. Then they both lapse into silence. Her eyes are still wet, still very green. He's not sure where to look. The kitchen feels too small and too big at the same time. Eventually he says, 'I should go.'

'You should,' she answers quickly.

'Do you want a drink?' he says, looking at the glass she's still holding high.

'It's my house isn't it?' she says with glassy eyes.

He watches her cry a little while. She doesn't seem to mind. He watches her drink, watches the green specks of colour in her eyes. Then she tells him it's time to go. And he does. Leaves his cup of tea steaming on the sideboard.

Once he's out in the street again he looks up and down the tram tracks to see where the next stop is. After walking two blocks, still in pain, but not as bad as before, he asks a man about the Carousel. The man, with raised eyebrows and a very obvious up-down-up look, says, 'Turn left up there, then left again. Got that?'

Chapter 9

'Where in God's name have you been Paul?' I say, shaking with anger.

'I was held up,' he says, shrugging his shoulders.

'It's almost twelve. Are you crazy? We said ten.'

'I'm sorry. I had a puncture. And then I had an accident.'

'I don't care,' I say and try to spit but can't, as my mouth is as dry as sand. 'You can be late for Mr Morton, once. Only once.'

'I didn't realise…'

'You must be the luckiest Scot in England. He's been in a meeting with one of his lawyers all morning, and he's still expecting us. Let's go and when we get there be so quiet he doesn't even hear you breathe. Pretend you're a ghost. A dead ghost.'

'That doesn't even make sense.'

'Shut your mouth. Just let me do the talking.'

Two men, both taller than Paul's not insignificant six feet and three inches, come outside and look us over. There's a stage with baby blue velvet drapes, a bar the length of a rugby pitch, and chandeliers wider than buses. Bartenders loiter in white shirts, silver arm garters and matching baby blue double breasted waistcoats with dull silver buttons. Polish glasses with the proud, dismissive smiles of their profession. As there are no tables or chairs the space feels empty. I tell Paul that Mr Morton reasons he can fit in more drinkers if they stand rather than sit.

We follow the impatient security man in front of us through a door and come to an equally large room. This one is carpeted apart from a large hexagon in the middle of the room which is sprinkled with fresh sawdust. There are ten or twelve clusters of comfortable seats with emblazoned antimacassars, all with views of the hexagon. Next to the seats are small tables with kerosene lamps and pedestal ashtrays. There's a smell of naphthalene balls and spilled whisky. Old cigar and pomade. We walk single file along an aisle of floorboards painted white and red, like a bleeding zebra.

Our guardians march us in single file. I had hoped to prepare Paul. To give him stern pointers. I'm not usually summoned like this. Whenever I've seen Mr Morton I've been to his other office. This one, this crow's nest, I've never been to. Only heard talk of.

After coming up a carpeted staircase, we stop at an unadorned door. It looks like so many of the doors we have passed. One of the giants knocks once, then opens the door an inch, then they both leave, walking quickly. I motion for Paul to enter.

Swallowing hard, wiping his hands, patting his hair once, twice, three times, he walks in, and I follow. Once into the room he stops. The room is completely white. The first thing I see is a crucifix. A simple cross, one bit of wood slightly longer than the other, tied with a bit of coarse twine, hung on the wall by a crooked nail. Not ostentatious like the rest of the Elephant's life.

'I'm a devout catholic,' Mr Morton says from behind the open door. He waddles over to the middle of the room where he sits down in an armchair, puffing. He wears a white morning coat, white tie, waistcoat with ivory buttons and white trousers, baby blue socks with an Argyle pattern of white and grey, which look to be made from silk. His shoes are grey on white wingtips, polished to an impossible sheen and laced tight. He stretches his hand out for the tumbler on the little table next to him and stares at us. Looking uncomfortable, Paul scans the room, but there's nothing else on the walls. I know better, I just stand. There's nothing for the mind to rest on. Nothing but the incredibly fat man in a white Chesterfield.

'I'm drinking Cointreau,' he says, but doesn't offer us

anything. 'Sit,' he says, and before we have had time to react, 'SIT.'

We bend our legs and sit on the floor just inside the door. Like schoolchildren.

Mr Morton looks at me and says, 'Silas, will you undo my shoelaces? I've been on my feet all day.' I stand up stiffly and walk over to Mr Morton where I have to kneel. Cradling the man's feet in my lap I untie the shoes, first one then the other. Place them next to the chair, not on the same side as the table. Mr Morton then cups a hand under my chin and tenderly tilts my head upwards. He looks at me for twenty seconds.

'Thank you. That's better,' he says and then his eyes turn to Paul.

'So is this your newest investment, Silas?

'Hello. My name is...' Paul says, and I turn to look at him sharply.

'I don't really mind what your name is,' Mr Morton says. 'But if you're ever late again your man here will do unspeakable things to you.'

'I'm sorry.'

'You should be. I've half a mind to make an example of you.'

I don't like where this is going, so I gently raise my hand and say, 'May we talk business, Mr Morton?'

Mr Morton takes a sip and sets the glass down hard on the table.

'I'm not in the mood. Something about this boy annoys me,' he says. 'It's a shame because as you said Silas, he's big, he could have been turned into a winner. I know you know better Silas, and I know you're sorry about your lateness. This boy on the other hand will receive punishment.'

My heart stops. I think I might have grown to like the boy. Mr Morton slowly takes off all six signet rings, inspects them, and then threads them back on. Taking his time. Then he says, 'Silas will you go downstairs and ask for my man Drago?'

Paul starts to speak but Mr Morton's hand waves him silent, before he continues, 'Silas, now be a good man and ask Drago to come up, and tell him to bring ropes and piano wire. We'll see what this boy is made of. Can't have latecomers in my organisation.'

I try to catch Paul's eye, but he looks petrified. Maybe it's dawned on him just how badly this meeting has started to slide.

Before I have time to go downstairs, the door opens and a woman saunters in. I've seen her before but we have never spoken. The fact that she doesn't knock or seem to need an excuse to walk in on us in the middle of a meeting sends a shiver of respect down my back. She walks up to Mr Morton and whispers something in his ear, not even glancing at us. Again we're like wheelbarrows – just tools.

Mr Morton smiles benevolently and says, 'Miriam, will you excuse us. I was about to make an example of this boy. He's insubordinate and he was late. You know I don't like time-wasters.'

She looks at us, swallows once, then turns to Mr Morton and says, 'He was helping me. I'll take the blame.'

'You must be joking. This half-wit, this ginger dog, helping you?'

'He did. Punched a man in the face. Knocked his teeth out, kicked him in the head.'

'I don't believe you,' Mr Morton says.

'Have a look at his leg. See the blood? That's not his. It's the other fellow's.'

'Really? I find that hard to believe. No one bothers you. Unless they don't know who you are.'

'I was tired. Forgot to think. Left my purse on the shop counter, next thing I knew someone was running for the door, and this man, what's his name?'

Demonstratively Mr Morton turns to me and asks, 'What's his name?'

'Paul,' I say.

'This man, Paul? Paul, runs after the thief and, well, gets my purse back,' she says.

'You're losing your touch Miriam,' says Mr Morton.

'Maybe,' she says.

Mr Morton continues, 'So, there's more to you than meets the eye, Paul,' says Mr Morton. Paul looks hard at the woman. I'm keeping completely still. I honestly don't know what to think. She's got lovely eyes, great sense of clothes and a nice cloche hat. She's pretty. Too pretty for him.

'So it seems Miriam can vouch for your arms, and Silas here has been talking about your legs,' Mr Morton says. 'Fine. You're forgiven. All I want to do is ask a few questions, regarding your head, and depending on your answers I might have a job for you.'

Paul looks at me, I nod, and look down at his hands. They are shaking. I don't like it. Mr Morton's voice jolts me out of it, 'Silas, run downstairs will you and fetch my abacus. It's behind the bar. I want to speak to Paul here. Miriam, you can show Silas out. You can also bring the abacus up, and bring another bottle of Cointreau for me and a drink for Paul.'

'I'd be happy to stay,' I say.

'And I'd be happier if you didn't,' Mr Morton says, looking at Miriam's legs.

I stand up as Mr Morton leans forward. 'What's your poison Paul?' he asks looking down at his empty glass.

Paul says 'Sarsaparilla,' and in the deathly silence which follows Mr Morton looks at him, weighs him on a scale no one can understand.

'Are you a woman under those trousers?' Mr Morton asks, then waves away the notion of an answer. 'Miriam, bring up two bottles of sarsaparilla, one AJ Stephans, and one Bickford's – so we can have a little taste test, Paul and I – and two frosted glasses. Seems Paul needs to feed himself sugar lumps dissolved in water. As for me I would still like another bottle of this French orange liqueur, I feel it's very good for my joints.'

'Yes Mr Morton,' says Miriam, while I say nothing but I look at Paul as though we are now on either side of a ship snapped in half by a torpedo, one side sinking, the other floating.

'I've got a proposition for you Paul,' Mr Morton says. 'I understand you run deliveries for a fruit and veg man? Well that ends today. You work for me and no one else. I will ask you to deliver messages. An envelope here. A small package there. Silas tells me you're fast and I know you're harbouring dreams of becoming a velodrome racer, which is fine. Just remember I own all your time from now on. You understand?'

'Yes.'

'Have you ever seen a cheese wire?'

'Yes I have.'

'Your thighs are of more or less the same consistency as a large Italian hard cheese. Keep that in mind.'

Mr Morton suddenly turns to me and shouts, 'Why are you still here? Off you go. Both of you.'

While I stand up and Miriam walks over to open the door, Mr Morton leans back in the chair and asks Paul, 'So how long before you're an Olympic champion?' Paul looks at us standing in the doorway. In my nose the smell of lemon, geranium, pine tar, Miriam. As Miriam and I leave, again accompanied and kept quiet by the two big men, Paul turns to face the full moon of Mr Morton's face.

Chapter 10

The next morning Paul receives two messages, delivered by little boys, not ten minutes apart. The first one is a note saying 'Be careful. Get out if you can!' There's no signature, but the handwriting is round, and slanted. The other is a boy telling him to come to the Carousel for lunch. It sounds like an invitation but he knows it isn't.

Paul goes to tell the fruitmonger he needs to leave. Mr Morton has told Paul he won't have the time to cart around apples between races and delivering messages. Also, the vegetable shop doesn't have a Drago waiting in the wings, so Paul's decision is easy, even if it means disappointing the fruitmonger.

Mr Morton is not there to receive Paul for lunch. Neither is there any food. Just a set of short, snappy instructions issued by one of the many well-dressed men at the club.

***

The next day, his messenger services begin. At set times Paul picks up envelopes with a slip of paper inside. Sometimes from Mr Morton's place in Elephant and Castle, sometimes from William Knapp, a bookmaker working from a back booth at the Southampton Arms on Nine Elms Lane.

The envelopes are always glued shut, apart from one time, about two weeks after the meeting in the white room, when the envelope was open. Paul resisted the urge to look inside. After the message was delivered Mr Morton seemed especially pleased, and told Paul he had passed a test. Mr Morton told Paul he had hidden a blonde hair inside the envelope, and showed Paul that it was still in place. Other than that the contents of the envelope were nothing but a small bit of paper with a series of typed numbers on it. First eight, then a space, then four. On the other side a picture of a woman in nothing but her bloomers, her long hair covering her upper body.

Mr Morton had told him he could keep the card once the receiving man had been given the numbers. On the way out of the building Paul eased the photo out of the envelope to doublecheck. It was dark inside, the electric lights kept off in anticipation for the evening's revellers, so he stood by the windows in the room with the giant bar.

One of the bartenders came up behind him, and once he realised what Paul was looking at he shouted *'Pervert!'*

He pointed at Paul, backing away while the rest of the bartenders laughed at him. Paul tried to explain, tried to show them the back of the card, only to realise the numbers were probably secret, and though they might not mean much to him, they might mean things to other people. And he was in a hurry. Should have been in a hurry. Not looking for nipples in a pub.

Once outside Paul ripped the picture into as many bits as he could manage before feeding them down a drain. Though the light was poor inside he was able to ascertain the girl in the picture was Miriam. The same wideset eyes, the same nose, and while he can't know about her chest, her hair looked similar.

★★★

Today he delivers an envelope to a bald, uniformed man sitting in the foyer of the Cumberland Hotel by Marble Arch. Same as for the last week. The man jots down the sequence on a page of yesterday's Evening News. He tells Paul next week he'll be sitting in the Kensington Hotel on Bayswater Road, and that Paul can never come to the Cumberland again.

Despite the passing of time the picture of Miriam is still

firmly stuck in his mind as he cycles off to the Peckham velodrome. He's trying hard to make the image, and any implications, go away. Once at the velodrome it fades a bit. Here he's Paul MacAllister of Copenhagen Street, cyclist. He changes in a daze, folds his clothes, and walks out onto the track. He nods to some, tries to sum up others. Judging by bikes and thighs today might be harder than he had anticipated.

He hears someone shout his name from the side. It's Harry Wyld. Paul rolls over and asks how things are.

'Same, but different,' is Harry's answer. His breath is heavy with beer. 'Paul, look around you. They're all good enough cyclists, but the difference is not so much in the legs, we're all born with pretty much the same legs. It's in the mind. And I sense that you have a pretty one-track mind. That's tricky in life, and great in sport.'

'That's one of the most backhand compliments I've ever had,' Paul smiles, glad to be distracted from the impending race.

'I'll tell you something else Paul,' Harry continues, 'I've been looking at these boys warm up, and to be honest there are some pretty good ones, but, and this is a big but, they are mostly road racers. They think velodrome cycling is the same as road racing. It's not. You know this. You're better constructed for the velodrome.'

'Maybe,' is all Paul can say.

'Road racers dream of the tour finish in Paris, sprinting around Parc des Princes, wearing a wreath the size of a lifebelt. Your goal in the velodrome is the handlebar: the bent bit of metal half an arm's length in front of you. Knees pumping, legs disappearing down and coming back up. The momentum created by the pistons your cranks become. Just forward movement, just pain.'

'I suppose,' Paul says, one eye on the starting line where racers and organisers are starting to congregate.

Harry takes a deep drink from a brown bottle, and looks

Paul in the eye. Then he says, 'You're going to do well today. I can sense your hunger. That's another thing that separates you from a lot of the boys here. They enjoy it. You need it. Make sure you translate that into a win.'

'I'll try my best.'

'Be aggressive. And be careful.'

'Thanks Harry.'

'I believe in you son.' Harry sits down. Beaming like a favourite uncle at a christening.

Lining up, Paul takes ten deep breaths, knowing that it will be the last time in a couple of hours that his heart will be beating at a normal pace. A commissaire in an outmoded stovepipe hat nods and it's time to straddle the bike and strive again for more, better, faster.

Two minutes to go, and he looks at his hands. They are shaking. They are the same hands that would like to touch Miriam more than by accident. The man in the hat comes out of the men's lavatory and Paul forces himself to put his thoughts away. The commissaire raises his arm, in his hand a gleaming starter gun. Paul pushes down hard with his right leg, the pedal almost bending under his weight. He's off just as the echo of the gun starts bouncing between the walls of the stadium.

Chapter 11

Paul has been given a day off. No races, no deliveries. It's about as likely as winning the lottery. It's a lovely bright day in June, and after being paid upon completion of his first month with Mr Morton, Paul cycles to Jack Lauterwasser's shop. Feeling like royalty Paul can spend money on things not absolutely necessary for his survival. The sensation is unfamiliar to him, and he grins like a maniac coming through the door of the shop. The jingle-jangle of the bell and the smell of grease, leather and oil come to meet him in a familiar embrace. Jack laughs at him and asks Paul who the lucky lady is, to which Paul replies, 'No one. There's one lucky man, and it's me.' Jack looks doubtful but Paul continues, 'I've been paid.'

'I see.' Jack smiles.

'So, what's new? What are the professionals using?' Paul says sauntering around the shop.

Bowing, Jack directs him to a display by the counter.

'I've got something here,' Jack says, wiping his hands on a rag from his back pocket. Gleaming dully on a pillow of wood shavings are a set of pedals. They're like nothing Paul's ever seen, far from the simple platforms he uses.

'You clip your shoes into them,' Jack tells him. 'This way you can pull your leg up as well as push down. In a sense this doubles your output.'

'Can I hold them?' Paul asks, and at Jack's nod he picks them up. They're light but feel solid. There's a spring holding a plate in place. He tries it a few times with his thumb.

Jack gently takes the pedals back from Paul. He's not a stupid salesman, he knows the power of holding something, the ebb and flow of ownership. He takes a pen from behind his ear and starts to point to the pieces of the mechanism.

To Paul the pedals are as intricate as the inner workings of a pocket watch, and possibly as expensive. And that's before considering the specialist shoes that no doubt will have to be purchased to go with the pedals.

Jack reads out loud from a catalogue, sounding like a school teacher. The words coming out of his mouth are like a different language to Paul. He soon stops listening and lets the torrent of words wash over him. It's a foreign tune of technical terms, a hymn heard in passing.

'It's a Belgian make. *Dinant.* The Dutch Olympic team used them for the games in Amsterdam this year,' Jack says, and points to a series of pictures at the back of the catalogue, adding *Gerard Bosch van Drakenstein, Johannes Maas, Piet van der Horst,* to the melody of mechanisms and merchandise.

With the shoes, an extra set of springs and a small bottle of clear oil, the pedals end up costing Paul more than a month's rent. Paul smiles and walks a full lap of the shop. Then he returns to the counter.

You need to spend to earn, Silas has told him more than once. While Jack puts them on his bike Paul walks around the shop, fingering objects of desire, then abruptly stops himself. He forces himself to stand by the window. To not touch anything, to stop thinking that he can afford anything. The only thing he allows himself to do is to look at the people passing by. This is the last free activity in London; the experience of lives flicking past like snowflakes.

In a gap between two cars, he sees a woman who looks like Miriam. He runs out of the door, the bell doing a double jingle-jangle behind him. Leaping this way and that, running in the gutter, being sworn at by coachmen, drivers and cyclists, he eventually catches up with the woman. The fox fur on her shoulders gleams in the afternoon sun. Her step is forceful but not hurried. He overtakes her, a silly grin on his face, his mind blank as to what to say, but his body telling him it is very important he speaks to her.

It's not Miriam.

After apologising to the surprised woman, Paul returns to the shop, and has to explain to Jack why he dashed out. Jack laughs, and finishes putting the pedals on the bike before following Paul out of the shop. He smokes a cigarette, wiping his hands on his apron.

'It must be a woman that's made you this happy,' Jack says.

Paul is on the bike struggling with the action of the pedals, tip of his tongue pointing out, and can only nod.

Jack, turns his cigarette to inspect the tip, says, 'By the way Paul, a Mr Halkias was here a couple of weeks ago. He said he was your friend.'

'What else did he say?' Paul says, a hand on the shop window, now strapped in.

Jack exhales and says, 'Nothing much. Didn't seem to be very interested in bikes.'

'He's not,' Paul says.

Jack grinds out the cigarette with his heel, and asks, 'Is he your financier? A sponsor?'

'He paid my rent when I first got here. And bought me the bike. You remember I was here with another man, Rupert?'

Jack nods, and asks, 'And what do you have to do in return?'

'Nothing. Pay him back.'

'Look, it's not my business, but I've heard rumours about this Mr Halkias. Be careful.'

'I am.'

'I'm just speaking as cyclist to cyclist. I've seen some bad deals and more than my share of scary managers in the past. I was winning a lot of races for a while but wasn't getting any money out of it, until I realised what my backer was doing.'

'I appreciate your concern, but I'm fine.'

'Well, from now on I want to sponsor you too. To even the odds. I've got a couple of racing tops I had made for a guy I was racing a tandem with ages ago. He was huge. As big as you. The perfect stoker. But he's retired from cycling now.

You might as well have them.'

'Thanks Jack,'

'I'll give the tops to you if you promise to wear them when you race. And if you send people this way for their purchases, I'll give you a good price on whatever you need for the bike in the future. What do you say to that?'

'I'd be delighted to race for you.'

Jack nods and ducks into the store room to fetch a box. The tops are on the big side, but Jack tells him they've never been washed and will come down a bit in size, if he knows someone who can do his laundry extra hot. Paul says he does, but he doesn't. He'll be doing it himself. The top he prefers is a black one with two yellow lines across the chest, and the same lines with the name of the shop in an arch over his shoulder blades, and space for a number, on this one 34, underneath, on the back.

'There's a white and a yellow one too. One long-sleeved, one sleeveless, one for every condition,' Jack says, smiling proudly.

Out in the street Paul clips into the pedals and immediately falls off. Laughing to himself and ignoring the whistles and jibes from coal porters and newspaper boys, he gets back up. He takes it slow. Cycles round and round De Beauvoir Square for a while. Soon he's mastered it and gets out on a real road for some speed. He quickly realises his *power transfer*, as Jack called it, has increased significantly. As he eases out into Holloway Road into heavy traffic, it feels like there's more space in his head now to think about other things. Breathing, traffic, the wind, horses, women, children, the road, potholes and the highway oysters dropped by horses. How to find the way to where he is going. Then realises for the first time in a long while that he doesn't know where he is. He doesn't need to. He's still got change in his pocket and would like this to be a day of celebration. So he cycles to Elephant and Castle. But not to the Carousel, not to the Ram's Head, not to the apartment up three creaky stairs. To a coffeehouse across the road from it.

Chapter 12

Paul sits in the coffeehouse for hours. Once the man behind the bar realises Paul doesn't even like coffee he sells him milkshakes instead. The cold drink is something fashionable the proprietor is very proud over. Paul gets a sore neck from his head darting back and forward, as if he was watching a fast badminton game, but his efforts yield no sightings of Miriam. Disappointed and with a solemn promise to himself never to drink milkshake again he cycles home when the place closes.

The morning after he rushes around the city in a seemingly endless chain of deliveries, made slightly easier by his new pedals. There are envelopes going back and forward between the Carousel and various drops. Some are new but most of his deliveries are to well-known addresses. Paul cycles to a man above a Russian restaurant, to a little old lady in Barnet who runs a pet shop. She never looks at the envelope, just puts it in a bag of birdfeed and sets it behind the counter. Always offers Paul a glass of lemonade, if he's got time, which today he hasn't. To a tall, completely hairless man who dresses in rags, but usually slips Paul a big note out of a golden money clip, if he's been quick getting there.

He ends up eating apples all day and drinking out of water fountains when he can. The evening continues much the same. Except that Mr Morton stands outside the Carousel when he comes back for what is usually the last pick up at around nine. The Elephant Emperor tells him to be careful when he picks up the next envelope from the Russian. 'And be fast, very fast,' Mr Morton continues. 'Or very dead. It's a big weekend. A lot of cups and races and scores and prize fights.'

Paul nods and tries to ask one of the men working in the bar for a glass of water.

Mr Morton puts his thumbs through his suspenders, then says, 'Why am I telling you? You're just an ape on a bike.' Then he slaps Paul on the cheek with his bunched up gloves, and sends him out without a drink.

'What do you think this is, some sort of sanatorium?' Mr Morton shouts after him.

Paul looks out for policemen and their whistles. He speeds up whenever he can. Acts recklessly whenever he has to. He is sworn and shouted at twice a mile, but he feels himself getting faster too. Developing both his eyes and his legs.

Once Paul has been dismissed for the day he has milkshake after milkshake to restore his mind and body. Still hopeful he'll spot her.

The manager has already made a note of him. Due to Paul's size, his lack of proper spending and the sheer amount of time he has been sitting over his milkshakes. Most people drink them standing up, or at least less than one an hour.

Paul brings out a newspaper he bought. To look less conspicuous, not to read. Despite his best efforts an article on the possible creation of the Vatican city state catches his eye.

'Hello Paul, how are you?' Miriam suddenly says at his elbow, bringing over a shake for him.

'I'm... me? I'm fine. You?'

'Stanley,' she says, looking over her shoulder at the manager who salutes like an old soldier, 'tells me you've started coming here. Are you looking for me?'

'No.' He picks up the paper. 'Yes.' He folds it three times, an uncomfortable number. It keeps flipping up under his hand and he tries to subdue it to no effect. 'Yes.'

She stands, hand on hip, and smiles a half-smile. 'Well, here I am. I might get one of these milkshakes for myself. You seem to enjoy them so much. Mind if I join you?'

She walks over to the bar and laughs with Stanley, leaving Paul to blush. Stanley and Miriam chat behind his back. She orders a giant Knickerbocker Glory. She tries to pay but

Stanley won't hear of it.

'How's the leg?' she asks, once she's back with Paul.

'Fine.'

'And your eyes?'

'Why do you ask?'

'You've been spying all day, on the wrong girl.'

'I've not been spying,' Paul says, his face going beetroot red.

'I've seen you. You have.' Miriam smirks and winks at him.

'I just wanted to see you I suppose,' Paul says, feeling his embarrassed pulse settle a little. 'It was a bit of a shock to see you at the Carousel,' he says. He looks out the window, then turns to Miriam. She's looking out the window, so he turns to the window and feels her turn away from the street scene to him. When he turns to face her, her eyes are back on the trams and carts outside.

'Which one are you today?' he asks.

'How do you mean?'

'Army nurse or Mata Hari?'

'Paul,' she turns in her seat to look right at him. Her eyes big, serious, lovely, 'I'm always the same. I might have to wear different dresses sometimes, but I'm always the same.'

'I'm sorry. It's none of my business.'

'You're right,' she says, smiling.

He tries not to think about the picture he has seen. He tries not to think about rushing out of Jack's shop, chasing her mirage. He tries not to think about anything.

'You want another?' she asks after they have spent a while watching the ebb and flow of traffic.

'No thanks. I don't even like milkshake all that much.'

'That's dedication. Well then, I've got a couple of errands to run. You can come with me if you want, or you can sit here and read about the Vatican and drink milk.'

Paul leaves his bike with Stanley, who's now much less suspicious, and they stroll down the street. An almost familiar distance between them, interrupted only by other pedestrians, by lamp posts, by horses and cars. Sometimes they bounce into each other, sometimes they are separated for a second or two.

'How's the cycling?' she asks after a few blocks.

'Which one do you mean? In my mind I do two kinds.'

'I don't know. Cycling and not falling over? That cycling.'

'The velodrome racing is going quite well.'

'In those round things?' she says, drawing an 'O' in the air with her index finger.

'Oval, but yes, I go round and round.'

'And you race for a living?'

'I race, but not yet for a living.'

They turn a corner and have to stop talking. They can't hear over a team of raucous newspaper boys shouting about something *Extra! Extra!*

Paul doesn't want to find out just yet what the disaster is; he'd rather continue talking. As more and more people come running to see what the papers say, he takes Miriam's arm. Doesn't think first, just takes it and leads her out of the growing crowd. She doesn't thank him, but neither does she take her arm away. They turn another corner into a dormant street with no shops.

'Can I watch you compete sometime?'

Paul's heart surges. Pride, and nerves all congregating into a blush.

'Of course. Have you been before?'

'No.' He realises inexperience doesn't deter her.

'Then it's important to choose the right race. Somewhere you can see, be out of the rain, get a drink, that sort of thing,' he says stretching. Proud of his knowledge.

'Is there more than one velodrome?'

'There are maybe six or eight in London, and then more in the neighbouring counties, you know, Essex. Then a few up north, Nottingham, Mansfield, Manchester so on. I've not been to any of those. A couple in Wales, a couple in Scotland,' he says, a schoolboy's confidence in his knowledge. He could have been talking about diplodocuses or the moons of Jupiter.

'Well, then you'll have to tell me which one I should come to,' she smiles.

'This weekend I'm in Preston Park, Brighton. It's a cinder track, a real bastard,' he says putting a hand to his mouth. 'Sorry, I didn't mean to...'

'You think I'm offended by a little coarse language?' she says, laughing and punching him playfully in the arm.

'To be honest I don't know what to think.'

'Don't think too much pretty boy. Back to the racing, and me seeing you,' she says.

'If you come off the bike at the Brighton track you end up with splinters everywhere and someone has to brush them out with hot soapy water.'

'So make sure you stay on your bike this time.'

'I certainly will. Wouldn't want anyone but my personal nurse to care for me.'

'Steady on,' she warns him, index finger wagging, dimples showing.

'So next week then, here in London is probably better. Or the week after? There's always a good crowd at Kensal Rise, especially if the weather is nice. It's on a Tuesday, at six.'

'I'll try to be there.' She smiles and starts to say something, when she is interrupted by a boy with a flat cap pulled low delivering a note to her. She unfolds the note, nods, and gives the boy something from her purse. Paul can't see if it's another envelope or a coin.

'I'm really sorry Paul, I have to go.'

'That's a shame,' Paul says.

She nods and pushes a lock of hair behind her ear. Looks up the street, asks him, 'Do you want to meet tomorrow?'

He can't help but let out a giggle. She looks at him, confused.

'Sorry, that was just a bit of happiness that slipped out,' he says, feeling his ears burn. He continues, saying, 'It'd be nice to see you again. In daylight. Milkshake?'

'No thank you. No, it's a little bit of work I have to carry out. I could say that I could use a burly man like yourself, but I don't. We manage quite well by ourselves, but it'd be nice to see you.'

'Burly, is that the term these days?' he says.

'Athletic. Big. Whatever makes you happy.'

'What do you want me to do?'

'Nothing, just stand there.'

'Where?'

'I'll show you tomorrow. Meet me here?' she says and points to the coffeehouse.

'Sure,' he nods.

'Six in the morning too early for you?'

'No problem, I was born on a farm. I'm not as lazy as you townsfolk.'

The boy tugs at Miriam's coat and she nods down to him.

'It was nice to bump into you Paul. Thanks for spying on me.'

'I wasn't…' he says.

'See you tomorrow,' she says and sails away. She picks the hat off the boy's head and tousles his hair as they cross the road together.

Paul stands rooted until he can't see her any more. Then he walks over to his bike and rides home. His legs are weightless and his lungs bottomless.

★★★

After a night of very little sleep, due to the kaleidoscope of butterflies in his stomach and an early rise to get across town in time, he gets to the coffeehouse. Miriam is standing chatting to Stanley when Paul arrives. She says hello and smiles, Stanley nods.

'We're late,' she says.

'I'm sorry, did we not say six?' Paul says.

'You're not late, you're bang on time. Other things have changed. I had hoped that we could go and have breakfast somewhere, but that's now out of the question.'

'Shame,' Paul says.

'Give Stanley here your bike,' is all she says, and steps out into the street to hail a taxi. Then she says, 'You never told me yesterday what the other kind of cycling you do is? The circus?'

Paul shrugs and says, 'Well, in a way…' He's interrupted by a car horn. A High Lot Austin with a red-eyed driver stops by the kerb. Paul opens the door for Miriam.

'Are you still happy to come with me?' she asks.

He pretends to think long and hard, putting a finger on his lips and humming, then he cracks up in a smile. 'Move over,' he says, stepping into the taxi. 'Will we be back by eight?'

'I hope so.'

The streets are already full of horses and cars. It takes the driver a while to find a clear bit of road. Not that Paul minds. Miriam sits, hands in her lap, content, composed. Chiselled out of soft marble. Smelling like a pine forest and lemon peel all at once. Then suddenly she turns to him. Puts one gloved hand on his hand. She leaves it there for a heartbeat or two. Then pats his warm hand once, twice, three times. Looks at him and then to the window, the sun peeking through a gap in the buildings.

Once the city is streaming past he asks her where they are going.

'To a pawnbroker in Angel,' she says. 'The man, a Mr Gullard, has a couple of things belonging to a friend of mine. My friend says she's paid, but he's not giving her the things, so I thought I'd go up there and have a chat. And you're a big man, you'll look good next to me.' She puts a hand on his arm as they bounce over the cobblestones and tram tracks of

Southwark Bridge. She lets it stay there.

'What was that about the circus? Do you handle lions and tigers too?' she asks once they're underway.

'In a way,' he says.

'Be honest with me,' she says in a low voice.

He turns away from the Ferris wheel of the streets and says, 'If you're honest with me.'

'I will,' she says, quite seriously.

'Don't worry,' he says once he notices her expression. 'I can handle it,' he smiles.

'I believe you. Well, I believe you believe that. But that's not true.' She shakes her head a little.

As they come to a stop at a junction Paul looks out of the taxi into the window of a dressmaker. Tries to imagine Miriam in the place of one of the slim mannequins. One is wearing a green tunic past its knees and the other a golden dress and a feather boa. He knows Miriam would look great in anything. Then the image Mr Morton gave him in the envelope strikes like lightning and he has to look at his feet.

The taxi lurches forward and Paul takes a deep breath, to clear his head from the outfits, and of Miriam changing between them. He says, 'I deliver messages for Mr Morton. That's my circus act.'

'I was afraid of that,' she says.

'It's a new thing. Silas set it up for me.'

'How do you know Silas?'

'He's my landlord. And he's been helping me with the cycling, the racing, I mean.'

'Good lord,' she gasps.

'Landlord,' he says, with a straight face.

'I heard you,' she smiles. 'At least you're not in bed with him.'

'No, I've got my own little place. It's not much. Just a room really, I'm hoping to move soon. As soon as the velodrome racing starts to go a bit better.'

'I thought you said you were good.'

'I am. But sometimes others are faster. And sometimes I'm too tired from running Mr Morton's messages. Or he wants me to do runs that clash with starting times at the velodrome.'

'That seems a shame.'

'I don't know what it seems, but it pays my rent. Keeps me alive.'

'And that's a London rent,' she offers. The weather and rent, safe ground of conversation.

'I could have bought Lennoxtown several times over with the money I pay for rent here,' he says.

She smiles at him. Her hand still on his arm. He's not moved an inch since he got into the taxi. He fears putting her off, breaking the spell. Also because being in a taxi, in a car, is a pretty novel experience for him. The speed doesn't impress him, he knows he could've covered the same distance much faster. But it makes the trip longer, and sitting ensconced in the big leather seat in the relative privacy of the taxi is very pleasant. Outside: people, trees, buildings, landmarks, smells, shouts, fights – the patchwork quilt of London.

'What do you know about Silas?' he asks once they gather speed again after a traffic jam on Grays Inn Road.

'He's Greek.'

'And?'

'He's a sharp dresser, with a lot of friends. And though he's polite enough he can be a dangerous man to cross,' she says.

'And Mr Morton is his boss?' Paul asks.

'In a way. But in a way Mr Morton is a lot of people's boss,' Miriam says sharply.

'Yours?'

'He'd like to think so,' she says.

'How do you mean?'

'Don't tell him I said that,' she whispers.

'I won't. I make sure I speak to him as little as possible.'

'Keep it that way.'

'What do you do?' he asks, still as immobile as a statue.

Miriam turns to him, smiles. 'I help people in trouble. Like my friend who can't seem to get her things back from the pawnbroker.'

'That's very charitable of you.'

'You could say that. But it wouldn't be right.'

'I don't understand.'

'Here we are. Get out you big oaf. Watch out Mr Gullard, I've brought my own strongman.'

She pays the taxi and they get out. They walk down Goswell Street. She's in no hurry, letting prams, horses, cars, bales of wares pass them by. Every so often Miriam asks him what time it is. When they get close to Clerkenwell Road and Old Street, she motions him into a narrow lane, Gee Street, and asks him to carry her jacket. She just stands there, eventually glancing down at her shoulders, at him, then nodding.

He starts to help her out of it. She turns slowly in his hands. The jacket peels off, and she does a little twirl with one arm, her wrist bent, above her head. Then she reaches over to him and takes a long black feather with a golden top out of her inner pocket. This she puts in the brim of her hat. She looks him in the eye for a few seconds while he forgets how to breathe. A half-smile on her lips. Standing on her tiptoes she plants a kiss on his cheek. He spends the next few seconds trying to triangulate whether it was closer to his ear, or to his mouth, whether it was a friendly continental kiss like he's seen in the movies, or a Judas kiss like he's heard about elsewhere.

Waving him toward the exit of the lane she says, 'Now be careful. These old boys hoarding other people's stuff are usually pretty keen to keep as much money as they can, and they're reluctant to deal with honest folk like me and you, so things sometimes get a little rough.'

'I'm sure I'll be fine.'

'Just stick close to me.'

When they come out of the lane they turn right, and Paul

gasps. The pawnbroker's shop is huge. Half a block long, with wide windows properly lit up. There must be thousands of things on display, under a big sign reading Gullard & Mathews. But what catches Paul's breath is the sight of a crowd of women in front of the shops, all with the same black and gold feather. Like Miriam they are all well dressed and lethal. The bells in St John's toll for two and the women all nod in unison. Then, in one fluid motion, about half of them bring out cricket bats and set about smashing the windows, while the other half walks straight into the shop. They start carrying things out into the street. After a minute some of the cricketers discard their bats and start putting the contents of the smashed windows, trinkets, jewellery and gold, in jute sacks. One woman comes around the corner, apologising for being late, pushing an empty wheelbarrow which soon fills up with sacks. The whole thing is so unexpected that Paul stands stock still until Miriam gently closes his jaw with a gloved hand.

'There must be a hundred of them,' Paul says.

'They act like it, but it's only thirty-nine. Actually thirty-eight, Alice Barrett has gone into labour. If we're lucky, and if she's lucky, we might go and see her after this is over. It's her fourth so she should know what to do. I might take her a diamond cluster ring or something. It's always nice to bring a little something to a baby.'

'Come on, time for you to do some work too,' she says to him. 'Follow me.'

Once inside the shop, a warehouse full of thousands of objects, everything from trinkets to four-poster beds. The debris of broke citizens.

'The owner has a safe, and one of the girls is working on getting the combination for it. It's just a small Charts & Bedell, but it's full. Worst case I might ask you to carry it upstairs and throw it out of the window.' They come to the office, and then someone shouts for her, she points to the floor and looks at Paul, then runs off.

He stands there looking at the spectacle for what feels like a long time. Little ants, scurrying off with golden grains of rice. He peeks into the office, realises it's almost eight o'clock. Time seems to fly when you rob people. He wonders where Miriam is, and if he should be doing things, carrying things, or if it'd be best to disappear before the police turn up. If they do? He realises he has no idea on which side of the law he is.

Suddenly he hears a loud whistle and jumps, only to realise it's Miriam, standing not far from him, conducting the show to an end.

'What's happening?' he asks her.

Disregarding him, she whistles again 'Time to go girls!' she shouts. 'Can you not hear the whistle? Think you'd enjoy a little holiday behind bars?'

She winks at Paul. Once they are outside in the street she tells him they got the combination. 'It was shamefully easy. A pity to miss out on you carting the box upstairs.' As the women file by, Miriam grabs a tall woman by the arm and asks, 'Brenda, did you get the paperwork, the books?'

'Yes I did. Right here in my bag, Mimi.'

The raid has a festival feel to it. Like a May Day parade. Then Miriam shoots a glance over her shoulder and her face goes sharp and dark.

'Paul,' she hisses, 'come with me. He's one jealous bat face.'

'Who? I can disappear in the crowd. I'll give one of the girls a hand if you want me to,' he says.

'If you value your life, do as I say. If he realises I've been seeing you, or even using your services we're both in deep trouble. Now,' she hisses. She looks over his shoulder again and takes his hand. They half-run up towards the quieter, narrower Gee Street. When they are just a few yards away they both hear Mr Morton's voice shouting, 'Miriam, Miriam is that you?'

She looks around her, at Paul, her eyes big and wet. She mouths 'Sorry', and 'the Coffeehouse', and pushes him down the backstairs to the Garter and Sceptre. He tumbles into the basement room and judging by the startled looks on the faces of the men drinking, he decides to play drunk rather than explain himself. Reeling and singing, he heads for the stairs. Once outside, he walks in the opposite direction to the pawnbroker. His bike is at the coffeehouse and he has no choice but to spend money on a taxi, something he doesn't like. The return leg of his journey is nowhere near as pleasant.

He's both scared by how serious Miriam turned, and excited to have seen her in her element. To have seen her lithe and dangerous; a smiling crocodile, snapping.

Once he gets to the coffeehouse, he finds it's shut. No explanation, just a turned over sign, telling him it's 'Closed – Please come back tomorrow.'

If he can't get his bike, and Mr Morton asks him to make a delivery, he's sure to be killed. The realisation sends a wave of fever down his back. Then someone moving inside the café catches his eye, and he bangs on the door. First nothing happens, then he sees the movement again. He bangs harder. Hears 'We're closed,' from the bowels of the place.

'It's me,' Paul says through the gap between door and doorpost. Stanley comes to the door but doesn't open it.

'What do you want?' asks Stanley.

'My bike?'

'What about it?'

'Is it still here?'

Stanley just nods.

'I'm sorry. Why are you closed?' Paul asks.

Stanley offers no explanation, but unlocks the door and ushers Paul in. 'Don't worry about it. I'm only pulling your leg. I'm a friend of Miriam's and any friend of hers is a friend of mine. What's your name son?'

'Paul MacAllister.'

'Pleasure.'

'Will you be open later? She told me to come here tonight,'

Paul says.

'Why on earth would she do that?' Stanley straightens up, pushes his cap further up his forehead.

'I'm not sure.'

'Well, I usually tell her friends who come calling for her to find her at the Bamboo Lounge if she's not here or has left instructions with me.'

'What's that?'

'A bar. You're quite new to London aren't you?'

'Or I could go to her flat,' Paul says.

'You know where she lives?'

'Yes. Just across the road.'

'And you've been inside?'

'She asked me to come inside.'

Stanley looks incredulous. Then he says, 'That changes things. To me, you're now category B.'

'What do you mean?' Paul asks, sitting down on one of the high bar stools.

'I like everything classified. From milk to people. My wife calls me bovine, I think of myself as structured and big-hearted,' Jack replies.

'I see.'

'Well, the lady invited you home.'

'It wasn't quite like that.'

'Whichever way it was, this morning you were F, just some fellow. Then she spoke to you. That made you E. After that you left together and she seemed to know your name. That made you D. Now you come here expecting a message, that makes you C, and since you know her lodgings that makes you B.'

'Are there a lot of friends, a lot of men, who come calling for her?'

'Hundreds.'

'Hundreds?'

'Relax, Mr B. Not many. A baker's dozen.'

'Still…'

'But the category B ones I can count on one hand.'

'So thirteen down to five, that's still not too encouraging.'

'Well, I can count it on a pirate's hand, one with a hook, how's that?'

'Better. Much better. Who is he, if I may ask?'

'He is a she, and I believe she's dead. Or at least not to be found in Europe as far as I've been told.'

'Are you joking?'

'No.'

'So you think she might be at this bamboo place?'

'To be honest she could be anywhere. The Carousel, Norwich, Tower Bridge, anywhere really. Your best bet is probably at the Turkish Baths by Hampstead Heath, but not till after midnight. Do you know your way there?'

'I think so. Well, to the Heath anyway.'

'Ask anyone once you're there, then find Ralph or Suzanne in the reception and they can send word upstairs for her. If she's there.'

'Thanks I'll go there tonight then.'

'Make sure to stay Mr B. If I hear you're slipping down you're probably on the way to getting yourself killed.'

Paul wheels the bike out into the dusk. Waves to Stanley and sets off. Pushes hard on the pedals. ## Chapter 13

After running errands most of the day and then eating dinner on his own at a working man's place in Bethnal Green – cheap stodge and as much tea as he wants – Paul's ready.

He cycles to the Heath, where he finds a big sandstone building with a sign saying: *Hot & cold baths & water therapy & nourishment,* next to a crescent moon and a star. Neither of the two people he's to ask for are there. He stands in the vestibule of the baths, feeling stupid. He's ridden across town faster than he has ever managed, on top of a tiring day.

He hears her voice and turns, 'Paul? What are you doing here?' Miriam, with a towel wrapped around her hair, says.

'Stanley told me I could come.'

'I'm usually not here until after midnight.' Lucky you caught me.'

Miriam tucks a strand of hair back into the towel and says, 'I'm sorry I had to push you into that pub. I had to spend the day with Mr Morton. He was looking for a stuffed bear's head. Apparently grizzlies are hard to come by. I didn't know he was going to show up, but he had me go through a lot of the back store with him.'

'Sounds rough.'

'It was fine actually. I don't like that he *happened* to come by though. Of course he didn't mind what I was doing, I mean it was sanctioned by him, it's just, he usually lets me get on with it. I always put my profits in his books.

'So do I. Or at least, Silas does.'

'Mr Morton likes storming in, you know, making a big entrance of it in his white car. At least I provided him with a nice crowd.'

'You did.'

'I wouldn't want him to see us together. I can't be associated with any other man. That's partly why my crew is all women.'

'Won't they tell him about me?'

'They're more loyal to me than to him.' Miriam nods to herself then says, 'I'm glad you found this place. Are you hungry? I'm starving.'

'Come to think of it I had four milkshakes this morning, but I've not really had anything since.'

'They have a private room upstairs. I'll ask Ralph to send up some lamb stew and a loaf of bread.'

Upstairs, Paul walks over to the window. The inner courtyard is fenced in by the building on all four sides. There are two pools, 'One steaming hot, one cold,' Miriam says behind him. A peacock struts around pecking, a troupe of sparrows endlessly settle and take off. No people disturb the calm as the bathers have all gone home. Paul closes the curtain, feels good to not be in danger of being seen even from neighbouring rooftops.

The room is painted dark red, the windows framed by dark green tasselled curtains. On the walls hang hammered copper plates, a watercolour of a cathedral labelled *Hagia Sophia* and a grainy photo of a wide bay labelled *the Bosphorus*. Over the door hangs a long curved sable with a long sash in white and red tied to the scabbard. There's a low table to kneel at, and two round leather cushions filled with horsehair.

Miriam takes both his hands in hers and says, 'You can never tell anyone about this place. It's my haven. Even Mr Morton doesn't know about it.' He nods. Then there's a knock on the door.

She drinks most of a bottle of wine with the meal. He's still loyal to his promise of prohibition, but the mood of the evening has gone to his head. They pile the dishes outside the door and push the table to one side. Sit with their backs against the wall. His face is warm and her hair is coming loose from its pins. She looks at him. Holds his gaze for several heartbeats. Nodding to herself she gets up and walks over to her bag. Brings out a book.

'I got this when I was at home, thought I'd keep it here instead.'

'What is it?'

'Towards the end of her life my mother told me some things about my family, and she gave me a drawing of our family tree. I sometimes write things about the people in my family. About my past.'

'Sounds interesting,' he says, extending his arm. Both to bring her back to his side, and to have a look at the notebook.

'I try to write in it, or read it, whenever life gets a bit much for me.'

'Like a diary.'

'Yes, and no,' she says and comes over to him.

He nods and watches her sit. She folds herself gracefully

into a small bundle of legs and arms. Sits on one of the round cushions. Then moves an inch closer to him, and asks, 'Will you read to me?'

'If you want.'

'I do.' She giggles a little, and then sways over to the window where she throws the curtains open and unlatches the window.

'Have you ever had Turkish coffee?' she asks.

'No, can't say I have,' he says, one hand on the empty cushion.

'It's a good remedy for red wine. As is fresh air.'

She comes back and they sit in content silence, until a woman Miriam introduces as Suzanne, comes up and pours thick, black coffee into small cups. She leaves the pot on a little burner, places copper bowls of cardamom seed and Barbados sugar on the table, and retreats without a word. But with a wide smile directed to Miriam.

Miriam sips the coffee, looks at Paul, moves closer to him, leans back and closes her eyes, says, 'Please read.'

He clears his throat, opens the book, angles it to catch the light from the candles, and then begins:

No. 14
Three brothers, all decent men
The fourth a misfit, and then,
The Great War made heroes of all but one
The youngest with scars and a gun
Discharged early and alone
Broke her like a dog a bone

He looks down at her and she opens her eyes.

'Thank you,' she says quietly. 'It's about my mum. And her uncle.' Miriam takes his hand. 'It's a shame that I write like a child,' she says.

'I don't know anything about poetry but I think it was nice.'

'I wouldn't call it poetry, and maybe I will always be that

child when I try to put pen to paper.'

'What about your mother? What happened?'

'I've never told anyone, but since we are here, since I've had this rather nice wine, since you read to me, and for reasons you can't, and I can't explain, I will tell you.'

'You don't have to.'

'I know. But I will.' She dips a finger in an almost empty water glass and dabs her eyelids. 'When the family came over to England from Norway, the three older brothers did well for themselves. The oldest one married and had a daughter, my mother. The three oldest brothers went into the navy and the fourth went into the army. Then came the war. When it ended, the navy men had moved up in the ranks, while the youngest had stayed where he began. He had been injured, and not honourable. When he returned from the front he was wrong in the head.'

'I hear battle can do that to a man,' Paul says.

Miriam looks at him. Hesitates. Then she grips his hand, swallows and opens her mouth. Nothing comes out. Paul stretches for a glass of water. She gratefully gulps some down, then manages to continue, 'When he returned home from the frontlines he found my mother home alone, she was very young.'

'That's... I don't know what to say,' Paul sits still. Like he was made out of glass.

'My mother was never the same. Not that I knew her before. Sometimes I felt like she had not always been the person she was with us.' Miriam reaches up and intercepts a tear that escapes her right eye. One from her left lands on his hand, the one still holding her. 'She could never forgive him. She could never forgive me,' she says.

'I'm sorry.' It sounds empty, but it's better than nothing, he thinks.

'Later, I had a brother.' Miriam empties her wine glass. The second bottle now almost empty. Then she continues, 'I was to protect him but you already know what happened to him. I don't know who his father was, and I don't think my mother did either.'

'You don't have to tell me this if it's hard work.'

'It's fine, really.'

'What happened to the other brothers?'

She doesn't answer. He doesn't know what to say. Or do. She doesn't cry again, but he can see it's not far off. Drops of salty water slowly, slowly gathering, increasing in size, caught by her lower eyelashes. He wishes he could help. Wishes he was more experienced, then he would know what to do. A hug? A kiss? Something more? Or leave her alone? In the end he just sits there. Asks if she wants a cup of tea, to which she just shakes her head.

After a while she looks up at him from under her fringe and says, 'Paul, I think you're a lovely man.' She stands up and shakes a little, waking up her limbs. 'I've been drinking, and now I'm very sleepy. But before you get any ideas, I am going to send you home. I think it's best that way.'

'Maybe,' he says, eyes like a puppy. Half on purpose.

'We wouldn't want Silas to wonder where you are.'

'He doesn't own me.'

'Relax, I'm not making fun of you.'

'Can I see you again?' he asks.

She smiles. Pushes an escaped lock of hair behind her left ear, and says, 'If you want to. If you dare.'

'I do.'

Chapter 14

Since Paul struck the deal about percentages, no officials or collectors around the various tracks ever ask him for money or fees, but neither do they present him his prize when he wins, or does well enough to be paid. Instead he receives a kind of salary from Silas.

The only thing Silas has said on the matter is that Paul must always, always wear the same black and yellow top, the one with the same number 34. If someone else has the same number and won't change, even after Silas' name has been mentioned, Paul is to pull out of the race.

Paul soon realises Silas must have eyes and ears at every race because Silas is never present, but seems to know how he has placed, who has won, fallen over, tried to cheat, pulled out. And he has never tried to race in any other sweater, or number, but that's more to do with wanting to do Jack proud and a tiny flicker of superstition, than Silas' warnings.

Once a month Rupert hands Paul a box with money and a wide baby blue ledger with six columns. *In*, *Out*, *Places*, *Percentage*, *Silas' total*, and, in red, *Paul's total*. Rupert tells Paul he has to sign the ledger. There's a handwritten slip telling him how much he owes for rent and how much he still owes for the bike. The suggestion is that he gives as much as he can afford. Paul always follows the advice in regards to rent and usually for the bike. In the back of the ledger Rupert notes the sum, and under it pens, tip of his tongue jotting out, wriggling like a fish on land, a long squiggly signature as impossible to forge as it is to read.

A week after his dinner with Miriam – a busy week of deliveries and races – he is scheduled to compete.

He puts petroleum jelly on the insides of his thighs. When

he races, sometimes sweat pours off him, sometimes it's so cold that only the crystals of salt are left. He wants to avoid the constant chafing, avoid slowly turning his thighs into sandpaper.

It's very early as he crawls down the ladder, bum sticking out into the air because of the angle. His life as a farmer proves helpful when he needs to get up before dawn. He walks down the creaking stairs, carrying his bike over his shoulder and a small bag packed with his vials and three apples.

On Copenhagen Street, a little boy, noticing the bike and the race gear, waves at him and shouts 'Good luck'. Paul smiles and waves back, taking the lack of rain and the boy's wide smile as a good sign.

Paul hopes he'll return with a medal and enough money for rent and food, as well as lighter tyres or something from Jack. The streets are quiet, but it's London so people are on their way home, or on their way to work. Drunks are getting drunker, sober preachers are preaching to the deaf, taxis are trying to kill him and women are waving after him. When he first came to London he thought they were cycling fans, maybe they recognized him. Then he realised they are the sort of women who wave to any kind of man at this time in the morning. In the hope that the man is on his way home from something dismal, rather than on his way to something exciting.

His main concern is to stay clear of the huge, still steaming mounds of manure. Of the veritable lakes of horse piss and human piss and the streaks of vomit that line both streets and pavement. As if the people being sick were in a great hurry, vomiting as they ran along. There's broken glass, nails, wood splinters, sharp shards of metal, stolen cobblestones, inexplicable holes and sharp edges in the road surface that he has to look out for too. He learned this on his first trip across Southwark Bridge, and, this time, he doesn't want to be late. Over his shoulders, under the bag, he carries two spare inner tyres. They form a black X over his jumper.

Now onto London Road, wider, faster. Full of potentially deadly trams. And he wants to ride as fast as he can past the areas that he knows Mr Morton controls. He doesn't want to be seen. He knows he's not doing anything wrong, but still being seen is being dragged into more of the business than he already is. And he's had enough of the man in white for a long time.

Elephant and Castle flies by, and luckily he doesn't spot anyone from Mr Morton's establishments. He picks up speed again along Hollingbourne Road, his legs and chest now warm, nothing more. This kind of cycling is not tiring, it's like walking, but not boring. Then, his destination: the velodrome. He feels the flutters, the expectant orb in the centre of him. The prospective speed, and a fair amount of fear, puts him in the right mind for two days of cycling. He rolls up to the racer's entrance and after signing in and small-talking with one of the janitors he finds his allotted space.

Harry's not here today. Paul knew that was going to be the case. But the conversation they had about enhancing his races is still vivid in his mind.

'Paul, you've been learning a lot these last couple of months,' Harry had said. 'You have learned to dose out the extra push depending on the length of the races. One pill per hour the first two hours. Then one every half hour. And you make sure to keep an extra back. In case something unexpected happens in the last twenty laps. I know the sweats, the suppression of hunger, the extra wind in your lungs, the way the light comes in more clearly, like you've opened the blinds of your head. The effect is absolutely fantastic. You wouldn't dare take the pill if you weren't cycling, or in mortal pain. Be careful son.'

Paul nodded. He wasn't sure how he felt about the extra power coursing through him, but soon realised it was both useful and necessary.

Harry continued, 'As the first pill, always the strongest,

kicks in, you want to sing and shout but there's not enough air in your lungs for that. It's best to be quiet, it's best to save your breath for later. But remember, it's too early to celebrate, even though you feel so happy that winning seems secondary. You know you are paying a price. A high one. You know that tomorrow you will be starving but not feel the hunger. You will shake. Both from not taking the pills, and from your body being tired almost beyond repair. You will be annoyed with everything, you will feel sad for no real reason. Make sure you explain this to the ones you love. They might be more forgiving that way.'

Paul smiled and thought about the smell of pine and how much trouble he would be in if he was rude to Miriam.

'As the race wears on you will be broken. You know you're riding the chemical imbalance. It's a serrated knife's edge. You know you'll one day end up crushed by the rush, by the vials and paper cones. You know you can't stop. Everyone else is riding the wave, so you continue. It's a fragile balance. The stakes, and dosages, always going up.'

After Harry packed away the things he said, in a voice thick with seriousness, 'You make sure to keep on the right side of all this Paul. As soon as you stop cycling you stop taking pills. I've seen too many good men disappear into the shadows once their careers were over. I'll be watching over you like a hawk.'

Today, thinking about Harry's pep talk, Paul prepares as best he can, tries to find the tunnel vision that seems to work best for him. He nods to some of the others. It's now six o'clock. A man. A gun. Then it starts. He feels the pills in his back pocket. He knows he will have to use them. Everybody else does.

Paul has spent the weekend coming second to a Welsh cyclist, Emrys Rees. He decides to chat to Rees and see what equipment he has been using.

Emrys sits smoking and drinking a tall glass of frothy beer on a fold-out chair in a corner of the infield, by the easement curve. There's a tub of steaming water on a chair across from him, across his shoulders is a towel ready to be pulled up over his head.

When Paul comes over, Emrys nods and extends his hand for a shake, but is enjoying the cigarette too much to speak just yet. He doesn't seem too offended by the possibility of a chat.

'Congratulations,' Paul says. The man nods again, downs half his beer and raising it, mimes the question if Paul wants one. Paul replies he only drinks sarsaparilla and laughing the man says that's one he's not heard before.

'What's in the tub? Smells nice,' Paul says.

'Hot water, a sprig of rosemary, a little St John's wort oil and a thimbleful of eucalyptus oil from Madeira. And ethanol. It's this month's concoction.'

'I don't understand.'

'My dad is a pharmacist, sends me the stuff.'

'And you inhale this after every race?'

'And before. Have a sniff. Sure you don't want a beer?'

Paul shakes his head and takes a long deep breath, inhaling the steam that rises from the basin. It makes his nose and eyes run, it makes his lungs sting, it makes his head ring, all very unpleasant. Seconds later he feels cleaned out, hollowed out like an egg ready for display.

'That's very strong,' he says wiping his eyes with the back of his hands.

'Great for colds too.'

'I won't disturb you any longer. Just thought I would congratulate you. Today was hard. You did well. Your wheel did well.'

'Stay around, you're Scottish aren't you? I've seen you around. A real workhorse.'

Paul grunts.

'It was meant as a compliment, not to offend you.'

'None taken, I've heard worse,' Paul says.

'Sure you don't want a beer?' Paul shakes his head, and

Emrys continues, 'Well, I'm not like the other ones, the ones who refuse to talk. I don't mind a little discussion after a race, or indeed before. I like a laugh you know. And anyway I usually sit with my face in a bucket for an hour before I can make myself leave the velodrome.

'Great.'

'You're going to catch me any week soon you know. I can sense it. And I don't like it. But that's life.'

Paul assures him he's nowhere close to beating him and Emrys shouts for one of the boys who always seem to be hanging around to run out and buy another couple of beers and some sarsaparilla. He drapes the towel over his head, like a bride about to enter the church and moving his chair closer to the basin, he bends over, a human penknife in shorts, resting his elbows on the chair and lowering his nose to just above the surface.

'Would you mind if I asked you some things? About your bike?'

'Yes and no,' Emrys says, his voice muffled, 'but go ahead. Some secrets I will take with me to my grave, other knowledge you'll find out sooner or later so I might as well share some of mine. Just let me breathe this in for a moment will you?'

Emrys inhales and exhales, slowly, a coarse wheeze escaping him. Paul relaxes, lets his legs shiver and go soft. The boy soon returns and stands awkwardly with the bottles and the change.

'Keep it,' Emrys says from under the towel. Then a long sniffle.

Paul thinks the concoction smells very sharp and wonders if that is maybe one of the secrets to Emrys' speed – the fact that he has nothing left of his nose, his throat. His lungs must be burnt out like a forest fire has ravaged them. Looking at the white pallor of the man's legs, a shade whiter even than his own, Paul thinks something must be wrong.

Paul downs his drink, feels the light sweat it always brings on. He looks at the track around him, where a group of riders are training on tandems now that the crowd has left. The front riders, the captains, shouting for the riders behind them on the bike, the stokers. The teams are going faster and faster, higher and higher up while a team on a five-man tandem, a Quint, warm up on the inner field. They will need to gather a lot of speed to be able to stay up, he thinks. As they enter the velodrome Paul tries not to look at them, fears for them. Despite himself his eyes are drawn to the bike. It's as long as a shopfront, more a spectacle than for serious competitors, he thinks. But then again, five times the manpower for not much more weight might be fun. Then Emrys emerges from the towel, small sweat beads on his nose and forehead.

'Do you have a cold?' Paul asks.

'Oh, you mean all this?'

'Seems like a lot of trouble.'

'I grew up not far from the track at Carmarthen Park, that's how I got interested in the first place. Watching my older brother and his friends tear around. I was never allowed on the track, my mother would have killed me if she found out that I did any kind of exercise, let alone sprint round a concrete track in freezing conditions. That was pretty hard for me, for any boy growing up I suppose. I never got to play football or climb trees. I wasn't allowed to do any of the things my body told me to do.'

'Why?'

'I had very bad asthma. Still do, but I'm not thinking about it now, and it has gotten a bit better. People seem to think it's something I have made up, or that it's something that I've brought on myself, some kind of queerness in the head, but I assure you I would trade everything I have to be able to breathe properly. As it is I treat it like a bad cold. It's really not the same, but I can't be a victim. And clearly I'm doing something right.'

'Well, you're beating me over and over again.'

'I mean I'm still alive. And these days my mother is my biggest fan.'

'Have you always done this with the basin then?'

'I used to rub myself with chloroform liniment before getting on the bike, but I got a terrible rash, like eczema. I was prescribed sulphur by my dad to fix it but the powder made it worse. Then borage oil, which made no difference, then evening primrose oil, which made me smell like compost, plus it made very little difference.'

'That sounds pretty complicated. I drink water, try to eat an egg with my breakfast porridge. That's about it.'

'I think I'm a bit of a guinea pig for my dad. I don't mind, and I do it to myself these days. I think about it as a scientific experiment. Whatever it takes, whatever helps. I tried smoking Grimault's Indian Cigarettes, a pack a day prescribed by a doctor, to see if that would clear up the airways. It didn't work.'

'I had no idea. You seem perfectly healthy out on the track.'

'And you? Any allergies or sensitivities, or defects, or injuries?'

'Not really I'm afraid. No excuses.'

'Wishful thinking really. Just joking. Good for you.' Emrys returns to his vigil under the shroud. Paul asks him about his bike, his training, his thinking, and many other things. Receives muted answers from under the towel.

'At least you're not too ill to talk,' Paul laughs after a story particularly loose with the truth.

'That'll be the day I die,' says Emrys. He sits back up and shouts for the boy to get more beer. The boy is watching the tandem too, perched on a fence. Once he had delivered the drinks he didn't go far. In the hope of more chores and change. After looking at Paul's bike for a moment or two, Emrys turns to Paul.

'One of the differences between you and me is the handlebar you're using. You have opted for a more traditional one, while I have a lower, narrower one. That keeps me down. Keeps the wind from getting to me, and I'm not pushing too much air in front of me. I'm giving less help to the people just behind me, people like yourself.'

'I see.'

'Have you thought about your position?'

'I've just gotten used to it I suppose. It came with the bike and it's not anything I've thought about. I've been focusing on my legs and my lungs. And besides I'm riding for a shop. A man called Jack Lauterwasser, and he's the man who crafted these bars.'

'Have a go on my bike if you fancy it. Just don't break it, you're a heavy ox. Just a lap or two to get a feel for the handlebars. You need to focus on everything. Not just your legs and lungs. Every part of the bike and your body. Get smart, you're not a horse pulling a canal boat. You're an artist. A professional.'

Paul walks over to Emrys' bike. It's a dark red Rudge-Whitworth. Emrys tells him it was tailored for him alone.

'Are you sure you don't mind?'

'Well, I've been wanting to try the pedals you're using for a while and as soon as I've finished this beer I intend to take your bike for a spin. Hand me your shoes, will you? I'll stuff a bit of newspaper in the toe. Exchange of experience, you might want to call it.'

They circle the unused inner field. Then the tandem teams come back in from their session and the velodrome closes for the night. Paul and Emrys swap back, shake hands and go their separate ways.

On the Monday after his delivery Paul meets Emrys outside Jack's shop and they go in together. Paul rambles for a while, trying not to ask what he wants to ask. Emrys eventually asks Jack if he would be offended if Paul decided to use another set of handlebars than the ones Jack made. Jack laughs out loud, and says he is surprised to see Paul still using the old handlebars.

'They're antiques now Paul,' Jack says, and continues, 'You need to move with the times if you want to win. Even if that means stepping on people's toes, something you're unlikely to manage doing with me.'

Then choosing a handsome handlebar, deep, narrow, with new brown tape for Paul, he fits it to the Iver Johnson Special and sends the boys out of his shop. Emrys is clutching a box with a set of pedals similar to Paul's.

Chapter 15

The weather has been good to me lately. July sometimes means sun, sometimes just means disappointment, but this year it has been fine. I think my complexion and my heritage come into their own whenever the sun is out, and temperatures rise. Paul's doing well – he's not dead and he's sometimes winning. No major troubles in any of the properties. Tenants come and go, but as long as rents and deposits are collected I'm a happy man. I've even had the opportunity to purchase a couple of new summer hats. Some really exciting developments on that front. The shows in Paris and New York must have been good this year. Maybe one day I'll get the time to travel a little.

When Mr Morton and the weather allow it, I go and see Paul race. Which isn't that often but more often than one might think. Maybe because he races a lot, or because I have started to understand a little of the racing.

At first I tried to treat it like horses. The closest thing I could think of. The oval, the muscles, the staring eyes, the occasional death from exhaustion. Then I realised cycling was, if not better, then at least very different. I still can't shake the image of horses, but I have come to develop a special place in my heart for the velodrome. It is rather exciting, and some of the men are real specimens, real power houses.

As with any sport, it's difficult to be interested if you don't understand it. It's the same with most things. Unless you know, it's hard to judge a pretty painting from a dog's dinner. Same with a fantastic effort on the track. But there are racers who seem to be one with the bike, who can sense where there will be a gap, where a back wheel will be in a split second's time. Racers who shine even to the untrained eye.

Paul is one of these. He floats as if friction and fitness are concepts he needn't concern himself with. He never sees me, I make sure of it. I don't want to disrupt him. He's doing well enough without some man in a cravat shouting from the stands. Someone who, despite my recently acquired knowledge and my budding passion, has no idea about racing. And I think I'd probably add pressure he doesn't need. My presence signals he owes me money and that I wish to collect soon. I have no intention of spoiling his winning streak. It is, if not making me rich, certainly bringing in money I never thought would come. And I enjoy watching him. It's become an essential part of my weekend routine. So I'm happy to let things be the way they are. A bonus, a gift horse, and all that.

Mr Morton checks my book. The blue ledger where I note my ins and outs is always kept in his second office. It's a kind of casual library where everyone's account ledgers are kept. It's casual until he needs access to your book and it's not there when it should have been. That happened once to a man, and the result wasn't pretty: Closed casket.

Besides, compared to some, I'm a man of modest means and pleasures. I own the Copenhagen Street property, and two smaller houses, as well as a few debts that I collect interest on and a couple of gambling schemes. In essence, just enough to tide me over.

I'm good at always returning, or having Rupert return, the ledger. Mr Morton has never showed my smaller side-businesses much interest, other than to ask for a small cut every now and then. I never lie, and he always snorts at the insignificance of the money I make. My gambling and the collateral income must be shoelace money for him. I am glad about that. The less we are in contact the better.

This changed after one of his random inspections. Just after Paul, sporting his new handlebars – these days I notice things like that – won twice in one weekend against Emrys, Mr Morton called me in and shouted at me for not calling his attention to the money I had made from the bikes.

Mr Morton told me all my business was done *'Under my protection you'll be wise to remember.'*

I told him it was meagre profits. I'm not managing or sponsoring any other racers. By now I probably could, as I know a bit more who's who. But I won't tell Mr Morton that. I was issued the decree that from now on I was to keep a closer eye on Paul. To influence him for the better, to make sure he slept well, stayed in, trained. That he was kept busy racing, making money, apart from when delivering, and kept away from trouble and women. Especially women. The deliveries would also increase. I was to tell Paul he had been tried and he had passed, but his holiday was now over.

'And for you too Silas.'

I nodded and thought about nothing. Then I forced myself to think of a hot bath and a cold drink and everything felt better. For a second or so.

'I'm the first to admit Paul's been good for business. In a small way. The boy is fast, the police clueless, and he is very cheap compared to some of the other methods I've tried,' Mr Morton said. 'But for the money I'm paying him to run my errands, you need to make him more profitable. You understand this. And you will see to it. In fact you should have solved it before I was forced to bring it up. '

For the first Saturday in August I arrange for Paul to be at the Carousel. Race ready for nine o'clock at night. It's not his usual time to start, but it happens to be when my working day starts to pick up speed. I tell him I'll give him some money, and that I'll double the amount if he can find a partner.

I make it sound like an exhibition, a room full of fans, a little something they can do for cash in their spare time. They can prance around like horses at the circus, and easily pay rent that month. It isn't going to be quite like that but I don't have to tell him he doesn't have a choice. That I didn't have a choice. I'm going to make him more profitable, and that always requires a show. I can't be concerned about his comfort or dignity.

The day comes and I dress to impress. Saunter over to the Carousel. I am early. Seeing the arrangements Mr Morton has made causes me to feel sorry for Paul and his friend. I'm paying them both handsomely, but as Mr Morton, who was quite enthusiastic about my idea when I first told him, shows me around the inner room, and talks me through the evening, and the people he has invited, I'm starting to feel a bit funny. It's not a race or exhibition that's for sure.

'Tonight Silas, this is called the paddock.' Mr Morton's hand is on my shoulder, half fatherly, half a leash. He's talking about the hexagon in the middle of the inner room.

'And tonight we'll hopefully see the birth of a new sport, or the death of two men. Either or: it's publicity,' he continues.

'It's great, really great,' I say.

'Come here,' he says, with his hand like a vice on me, and he shows me four blocks where the axles of the two cyclists' rear wheel will go. He's had a scared-looking joiner working for him all day. The man is now busy nailing the blocks to the floor, the two sets of blocks facing each other.

The hexagon is usually sprinkled with sawdust and sucks up blood, sweat, vomit and the tears of the defeated most nights a week. Today, though, it's scrubbed clean, and the lines have been repainted. Not that it matters on this occasion. Boxers and wrestlers might stray outside the boundary lines, and be penalised for it, but where will the two cyclists go?

Once Mr Morton lets go of me, I go and hide in the Ram's Head across the road. Under the pretext of wanting to change and think up odds. I'm feeling too queer to drink gin and ask Isaac, the man in charge, for a good hangover cure.

'I've got just the thing here. Very popular with the revellers.'

He pours me something called Bib-Label Lithiated Lemon-Lime Soda, or a Bibi, for short. He explains something about

Lithium that I can't hear or understand. After a few glasses of Bibi, I feel a bit calmer and more clear-headed. I've not changed or thought about odds, but I doubt Mr Morton will notice. Besides he'll have the betting under control tonight.'

I walk back to the Carousel. I see that Mr Morton has changed into his evening wear. His customary white, with baby blue dashes, with his abacus, his business rosary, tucked into one armpit. A lot of the seats, especially the ones closest to the ring, are occupied by men smoking cigars and clasping his hand as he makes his rounds.

'Silas, where's your man?' he shouts as soon as he sees me.

'I told him to be here at nine sir. In about an hour,' I say after consulting my watch.

'That's too late,' Mr Morton shouts. 'Make him come faster.' He laughs and turns to his next guest, but not without wagging a finger at me. I stand in a corner sincerely hoping Paul hasn't had an accident on the way over. It's a nervous thirty minutes, the Bibi can't help with that, until he walks in, his sportsman's strut impossible to hide.

To my disappointment Paul has brought with him an asthmatic Welshman. A man called Emrys, who despite wheezing, and plunging his head in formaldehyde or something before we get going with the warm-up challenge seems fit enough. As he's getting on the bike, Paul, who has noticed my initial disproval, tells me Emrys wins a lot of races, quite often beating Paul. There's no telling with cyclists I find. Boxers, fighters, horses and dogs I can gauge. Cyclists are still an unknown quantity.

Mr Morton has arranged the evening like a gladiatorial tournament. Only there are no animals and no Coliseum. This doesn't deter a man like the Elephant Emperor. Instead he hushes the crowd. Walks around with his arms up in the air, officiating a séance by the looks of it. He proceeds to introduce the two cyclists with fanciful Latin names: Paulus Maximus and Caesar Emrys. Gets them to strip to their waists, and parades them around the room for the patrons to pinch and admire.

He has each cyclist take off their rear tyres and remove the inner tube, all with a great sense of drama. Then he sets them up on their bikes, or chariots as he calls them, and has the rear axles of their bikes inserted into the slots in the wooden blocks. Then, with the rear wheels, now naked, spinning in the air, he has the same unlucky joiner attach a belt to the wheel. This belt is attached to a cog on a stand. One each for Paul and Emrys. The joiner, now flushed and with shaking hands, fits the instrument of the first battle to the wheel. It's a whisk. And the game that people are now betting on and laughing at too for that matter – which is great; happy people are more loose with their money – is to see which of the two cyclists can first turn milk into butter. The person whose legs first manage to whisk a bowl of milk to a consistency where it can be turned upside down without anything landing on the floor, will win. Mr Morton has even found a retired dairy manager, all dressed in white, as a co-judge. The man, a Mr Stanley, stands in one corner cutting up bread in preparation for the butter. The whole thing is truly awful.

Soon the two boys are sweating, milk splattering in every direction, and Mr Morton goes over to slap Paul's back.

'Give the man a beer,' he shouts to no one in particular, 'No. Ginger ale. No, wait. This one has a hard-on for sarsaparilla. Mr Morton turns around to receive the laughs. 'A pint! No, a pitcher! Can't you see he's a thirsty man? And bring a couple of straws.' He points to a bartender who scurries out of the room. Then he continues, 'This one's hungry for a win. Come on Paulus! You get to eat the butter you make.' Then he laughs, and resumes his tour of the room. Once the bartender returns Mr Morton shakes his head and Paul never gets a drink.

As the people in the wingchairs become increasingly drunk, the games turn more ridiculous. Also harder on the boys. I can see from the way Mr Morton is working the room, the way his upper lip is shining, that he's content. The way his eye whites are showing and the way he gestures for one of his orangutans to come over and take bundles of cash to be put in a strongbox upstairs lets me know things are going well. In a way this makes me happy. Or at least relieved. After the butter, which Paul wins, Emrys is the first to saw through a log, then he's also the quickest to reel in an anchor, and I get a bit worried in case, despite the lucrative nature of the evening, Mr Morton thinks I am, and by extension, he is, backing the wrong racer. Luckily Emrys has a massive coughing attack. Then, he collapses and falls off the bike. A harsh seallike sound escapes him and he can't get back on the bike. Emrys is spluttering and trying to say something about the smoke and the sawdust, then he goes all white and has to be carried outside into the alley for some fresh air. Wagers from the chairs collected, wealth redistributed, drinks and smokes continuing, and there's talk of a whole series of these events. The Emperor is happy.

The Carousel doesn't close for another couple of hours, but the Roman feast is over. I can't look Paul in the eye, but I give him twice the amount I had promised him and the same for his friend. As soon as he's allowed he runs out into the alley to check on Emrys, while Mr Morton walks around the room with a toga and a laurel wreath made from bay leaves for the winner he can't find. He hands it to Miriam, who's standing in the shadows. I hadn't noticed her.

I go across the road for another Bibi. Sitting by the window in the Ram's Head I see Paul come limping out with Emrys draped over his shoulder. Miriam comes out and tries to hand him the wreath, but he shakes his head. Instead she hangs it around the neck of a drunk sleeping against a lamp post. Then she goes inside. Paul hails a taxi which he piles Emrys into, pays and then goes back in for the bikes. I pay for my drink. All I want to do is to go home and have a bath. Clean myself.

Chapter 16

After passing a few barber's shops around Victoria station on Tuesday morning after the Roman Feast, Paul goes inside one and asks for a fashionable haircut. Once he's done he is sold a bottle of Stephenson's Hair Pomade – *For the Discerning Gentleman*, which he's not sure he is. He comes out feeling silly, and vain, but after a few hours of rubbing his unusually naked neck and trying to look at his reflection in shop windows without being caught, he starts feeling good about it. And he thinks, but can't swear, that a pretty girl at a flower stall smiles a little extra to him. But then again that's how flowers are sold after all, and he retraces his steps and buys a bouquet of red, white and yellow tulips from her. He lugs around the flowers all day, and that earns him more smiles from passing women than any haircut could. Then he makes his last delivery and cycles to Kensal Rise, eating apples all the way there.

It's a midweek meet. The racing calendar calls it *The Tuesday Tumble* as the track is quite tight and not all that smooth in places. People like Paul, who have raced on the track a few times know where the worst parts in the decking are, but it's always enjoyable to see the more inexperienced riders come off, usually flying forwards over their handlebars. The accidents happen either high up on the banking in curve two, or close down by the black line in curve four. The race is a part of a monthly series, *the Cadbury's Cup*. There are also biweekly races, the main spectacle on Sundays as well as a smaller race every Thursday. Usually out of town. This concentration was Silas' suggestion, but Paul knows who's behind it. Paul knows and Silas knows who is wielding the whip.

Paul knows, or knows of, most of the other racers. As it's a Tuesday the crowd will be small but dedicated. Possibly even near to sober. Enthusiasts. Not just happy to be out in the sun, not at work, watching other people almost kill themselves, but knowledgeable. It won't be the gin-fuelled Saturday night revellers you sometimes get at the bigger velodromes, or the Sunday crowd who have decided to make a day of it; the ones who save up, steal, borrow, pawn, to come and enjoy themselves, almost disregarding the racers. For the weekend crowd, the entertainment could be anything from tigers killing ocelots, to boxing, rowdy soapbox preachers, or bearded ladies on stilts. It just happens that this year they have decided to flock to cycling. Next year it might be something else. But today at Kensal Rise, it'll be a crowd with stubs, with notebooks and pens behind their ears, mumbling odds and race pedigrees. Offering litanies to the gods who reign in the Kingdom of Money. Praying to the numbers they have chosen, or feel have chosen them.

Almost two months ago, in the back of a taxi on their way to Mr Gullard, the pawn broker, Paul asked Miriam if she'd like to come and see him race at Kensal Rise sometime. He's not sure what she usually does on a Tuesday night, but hopes she's above routine.

Warming up, circling the track slowly, avoiding high up in turn two, and low down in curve four, he looks out for her. He knows where she'll be sitting if she turns up. She said she would, but her business, whatever it is, is probably as fickle as his. He knows he would have to drop everything and leave the track if a message came through from Mr Morton that something was to be picked up and delivered. Even if it was just a piece of paper.

By the time the commissarie calls the racers in for a quick speech about the rules, the number of laps, the standings in the cup and the points they are able to earn today by placing in certain ways, Miriam is nowhere to be seen. With a sigh the commissarie explains about the two extra sprints where sponsors and a certain unnamed film star are offering cash prizes. Gives no word about the bad track. He's an old hand who knows that despite the apparent sophistication of the crowd, they too like blood and screams as much as anyone else.

Recognizing Paul, Emrys and Percy Wyld as regular racers, he winks and walks off. Paul shakes Percy's hand, feeling like it was a hundred years ago that he was being tested for his abilities. Pleased now to think he's surpassed his old heroes, he rolls out onto the track. Still she's not in her seat.

Harry walks up to him after a brief chat with his brother Percy.

'Paul, come here,' he says. 'You know this track don't you. The pitfalls and all that?'

'I've been on it before.'

'Well, you might think it's the actual track that's your biggest enemy today, but that'd be wrong. Today, as any day, the track is full of new men as desperate as you.

'Some are angry, others are by nature more easy-going. Light-hearted racers for whom exhaustion is a laugh, something they do to pass the time. The angry ones run out of anger, especially if they occasionally win. But the happy ones – the ones undeterred, and simple-minded in their beaglelike contentment to just run and row and race and then eat and then sleep – these boys you ought to fear like the plague. If you are not like them you will have a harder time of it. You will think too much, laugh too little and generally lose to them.'

'I'll make sure to read less, and race more.'

'Joke all you like young man. I know the competition. You have to think yourself invincible. Rely on your strength in finding the calm while your lungs are rasping. You have to train your ability to shut out the daily problems, the distractions of life. Just seeing the front wheel, the person in front, and making sure that that person ends up being behind you. That money, rent, love, racing politics, managers, sponsors, hurts and any intelligent thoughts all stay outside the bubble. It's an absolute calm in the eye of the chaos of spokes and legs.'

'I hear you Harry.'

'I'm only telling you this to scare you a little. I'm just trying to make you faster, which will make me richer, and Silas too, so – best of luck.'

'Thanks,' Paul says and rubs a little more liniment into his left thigh, always his weakest leg. Harry walks up to his spot by the starting line, grinning to Paul over his shoulder.

The official in the black tails starts brandishing the starter gun, a sure sign that things are about to kick off. Paul lines up, holding onto the barrier on the top side of the straight. It's such a long race today that he hasn't bothered asking for someone to hold him upright as he starts off. The jostling and positioning will come later, when people have been racing for close to three hours. When they are tired and thirsty and irritated and angry at themselves and their bodies for not responding to the messages they are trying to send. Annoyed that the commands sent from brain to legs are not being followed. This will go on until the brain gives in too, when any motivation dies under a blanket of exhaustion. That what he's saving himself for, the last fifteen laps or so. Until then he'll make sure to be in the first ten riders, maybe go for one of the cash sprints. Staying in the race is the key. Still she's not there.

She would have been sitting very close to where he's balancing now. She would have smiled, maybe even noticed his haircut, she would have bent her head and buried her nose in the flowers he's had left on the railing where he thought she would stand, but still she's not there.

Then he spots a face he knows well. A face he's dependent on: Silas. Paul raises a hand in greeting. Takes his eyes off the bike. The gun cracks and he tears himself off the balustrade, almost falling over. It's a terrible start. He's last by almost half a lap before the pace has even picked up, and still she's not there. He didn't think it'd mean so much to him, but pedalling off to try to catch them, he realises he's thought about and planned every move up until now. And after the race too. Little comments, excuses, compliments and jokes. Without her watching him, Paul feels like a different man. He's the same as before he ever had the thought of involving her in his life. It's an independence and innocence he feels he can't go back to. On lap twenty, when he's caught up properly, avoided three crashes, and found himself in a secure enough position in the depleted field he raises his head. Looks again, but nothing. Silas looks up from his papers and waves to him. A lazy hand brushing off a fly mid-air. Not great, but at least someone has come to see him, to keep him company from the stands.

He regains control of his breathing and overtakes a red-faced Yorkshireman. Paul now tries to control the pace from one or two places behind the first man. He would let one man go off into the distance, maybe even two, but if there were three sprinting away, he would like to be one of the three. He tries to keep the pace high enough to tire the less seasoned riders, and possibly put a dent in the lungs of the fitter ones, but low enough that he still has some energy, or *dynamite* as Harry calls it, for the last ten percent of the race. This is experienced racing, not exciting racing. This is him maturing, not necessarily gaining any new fans on the stands. But then again, a Tuesday race is less about being flamboyant, or a daredevil, and more about being consistent. About guarding his position and controlling the situation.

Then all hell breaks loose.

Chapter 17

After the race I walk down to catch Paul in the middle of the circle. It's almost midnight, and I'm starving. I've been sitting on the emptying grandstand, just looking at him for a while. As I enter the circle he is talking to a man in one of those ridiculous Caradine Airway hats. The kind that looks as though mice have been at the front of it.

Paul introduces him as Morgan Lindsey from the Sunday Times. The man goes on to explain that Paul's the youngest ever leader of the cup, and that he's been predicted to win the thing. I nod, making sure he doesn't catch my name. I have other interests than being known in the papers. Paul is speaking and the man is scribbling away furiously in a little notebook. After a few minutes I send Mr Lindsey away. Hacks like being treated with disrespect. Makes them think they're speaking to someone busy. And either way my appetite is acting as a great motivator to get going.

'Come on Paul, I'll take you out for some food,' I say. 'To celebrate.'

'You sure? Haven't you got somewhere more important to be?'

'Where else should I be you think?'

'I don't know.'

'It's just something to eat.'

'Fine, just not to Belinda's.'

'Why not? You don't like seafood any more?'

'Eels are not from the sea.'

'They're from the Sargasso.'

'But they're caught in the Thames,' he says slowly, like he's speaking to a child.

'Let's not get bogged down in details. Are you hungry or

not?'

'I am, but not Belinda's food. I always feel a bit funny after a race.'

'You used to be very keen on it. This recent success has gotten to your head.'

'It's not that.'

By now we've locked the bike up in an overnight storage unit, and walked out into the night.

'I'm sorry. Is it that obvious?'

'What?'

'Is she reading you the letters from the camel herder?'

He stops abruptly, 'You know them?' he asks.

'Do they sound a little like fairy tales to you?'

'Is he not real?' he says, eyes wide open.

'Did it make you jealous?'

'Not really.'

'Shame.'

'More confused as to why she wouldn't, I don't know, emigrate if he was that perfect.'

'*Only mirages are perfect*, my mother used to say.'

'So he's a fake?'

'She's just lonely I think. Besides why do you dislike her so much?'

'I don't. I think she's nice,' Paul says, throwing his hands out either side of him.

'But she's not for you?' I offer.

'Something like that.' Relief on his face.

We have now crossed the canal, walking down Ladbroke Grove. We're in Portobello which is not the nicest part of town to be honest, but I know a place, a small place, unassuming, where the food is marvellous.

'Because you take your pleasures from other things?' I ask.

'I'm not sure what you mean.' His brow knitted.

'You prefer men?'

'No, no I wouldn't say that,' he says looking shocked.

'But you've never tried?'

'Never had the urge.'

'Do you want to try?'

'No. NO!' He looks at me like I've got rabies. I smile and tell him it was just a joke. That his post-race nerves are playing havoc with him. I continue, 'So, go and see Belinda. God knows my mother and father didn't choose each other.'

'You really want me to?'

'Either you'll begin to like her, or start to hate her. Then at least you'll have strong feelings. That'd be better than this bland indifference you British people seem to wallow in, thrive on, even.'

'Why are you so keen for me and Belinda to be together?'

'I'm just curious as to why you don't have a lady friend. And besides I like you both and think you could be happy.'

I don't tell him it'd be easier to keep track of them together than as now, separate.

'Well, I think she's not for me,' he says.

We cross the road. The boy who can judge where a bicycle wheel will be in five seconds' time almost walks into a taxi. I take hold of his lapel, save him from death, although he doesn't seem to notice. He shrugs me off. But doesn't thank me. It's not the first time he's seemed uncomfortable with me touching him. Once we've reached the relative safety of the pavement, he blurts out, 'I've got a girl.'

'Who hasn't? What makes you think Belinda doesn't have a man?'

'Nothing. I've not thought about her situation at all.'

'Well, there are five or six other men that come and listen to her letters. Men better than you.'

'Good for her. Do you send them?'

'Yes.'

We walk down the street. Me noticing everything. Him like a lumbering ox, oblivious to the world. He seems distracted. Then it hits me. He's in love. This can cause mild heartache, nausea, confusion and an increased aversion to risk in young people.

'Watch out,' I tell him. He's almost stepped on a sleeping dog. Then I resume my thinking. For me his new development can work two ways. I just need to make sure it's going to work my way.

'So you've got a girl?' I ask.

He looks at me, a child who's found a sugar lump, and says, 'Yes.'

'And has she got you?'

'How do you mean?'

'Is this a mutual affection?'

'I think so.'

I put an arm around his shoulders, and say, 'You're sure?'

'I've not asked her.'

'Do. A lot of broken hearts could have stayed whole if people had been reading from the same page.'

'Is that your mother's wisdom again?'

'Be quiet.' I smile. I'm not sure he has any concept of how much he should fear me, but his cockiness is quite refreshing.

'Yes sir.' He spins around, big grin on his face, and salutes like a soldier. My arm comes flying off him.

I say, 'So not eel? That's fine. Despite it being my treat I'll let you be fussy. I've already made up my mind though, and Kalamaki it is.'

'Don't tell Belinda.'

'Of course not. And don't feel bad about it. These other five fellows who come in and don't accept their change are well-bred, single. With normal hair colours and interests. Lots of money.'

'I'm sure.'

'Belinda's a nice woman. She's come a long way,' I say.

We've now circled the same block three times, passing the restaurant twice. He's not noticed. He's clearly affected by the woman. I hope he soon parts with her. Can't see how she'd be good for him. But then again, women have always struck me as a bit peculiar.

'What is Kalakaki?'

'I don't know? A sailor's disease?'

'But…' he says, looking confused.

'*Kalamaki* on the other hand is a dish you won't find properly done in many places in London. Nor Athens for that matter, but I know where.'

'Is it eel? Greek eel?'

'What an ignoramus you are. Stick to bikes and let me do the rest of life.'

'Fine by me.'

'By the way, it was a great race. I was surprised. You told me Tuesdays were usually dull, but tonight wasn't. You're tonight's champion so we should celebrate properly.'

We're now right outside the restaurant. I stop him, one hand resting on his arm, my other hand on his chest. I turn him around and point him in through the door of the place. He's so incredibly taut. I can't but admire him, and it pains me to think of the woman. Then he puts his hand on mine. It looks like a pancake compared to my dainty, money-counting ones, and gently, gently removes my other hand from his chest. He holds on for a second too long. Does he hold on for a second too long? I shake the feeling and the old, sunny, couldn't-care-less Silas returns. I throw a mock punch and ask, 'Now, this woman. Who is she?'

He grins widely. 'Let's eat,' is all he says before ducking into the smells of my childhood.

That's all I manage to get out of him for the rest of the evening. I must confess I'm impressed. This reluctance means it's not just some floozy, some barmaid he's toppled by chance. This is not some exotic dancer who's taken his brain and turned it into mashed potato for her to enjoy. It must be serious. And it must be someone I know. Otherwise he would just say a name. His secrecy whets my mind.

After the meal he leaves to get his bike from the velodrome. I stay in the restaurant. Footing the bill, chatting with the owner. I enjoy a second coffee, some ouzo, a little music.

I think about the economic climate. In general terms we all have what we need. Much more than we need. The war really sparked something in people, myself included. We are more inclined to spend than ever, and our industries are churning out material goods we're more than happy to gobble up. When people spend more money they are more likely to end up in debt, which is great news. But I have a niggling suspicion that we're riding high on a somewhat inflated market. I can't be the only person thinking this. I must make sure to read the financial sections of my American papers closer. If anything's going to happen it'll come from over there. Pushing these less than happy thoughts out of my mind I rise to leave the restaurant.

I have just started rolling a Pyramide between my fingers when I realise who it may be. My heart stops. Please don't let it be her. I have to get out into the fresh air. I leave the cigar on a windowsill and walk off into the night. In the back of the taxi, going home alone, I'm suddenly terrified for him. My stomach is full of food that tastes of summers in Athens and beyond. My heart is cold.

Chapter 18

Paul picks up envelopes late Monday nights, and then again on Wednesday morning all through August. Occasionally on a random day, the information passed on either by Rupert, Silas or one of the runners. There seems to be a whole horde of boys, and as he's usually on his way to a race, at a race, or recuperating after a race, he's quite easy to find. Silas has the race calendar after all.

The only time he's scared to miss a pickup is when he's spending time with Miriam. Especially when he's with her at Hampstead Heath. But he reckons he should be allowed to be out of touch every now and then. Mr Morton would disagree, but Paul can always blame his absence on being out training, or mechanical mishaps. So far it's not been a problem. Also, whenever he's with Miriam he relaxes a little, as she seems to know when he's due to come in and check with the people at the Carousel.

The danger makes her irresistible. He fears being caught with her, but if he didn't see her, sleep next to her, or spend time beyond the grasp of Mr Morton, he wouldn't be human. He loves racing and the rush of the crowd, the feeling of winning, but more and more Miriam is on his mind. And in a way these emotions excite him more than the racing, which is why most of his rivals are bachelors. His feelings for her scare him more than Mr Morton.

Making the deliveries he's learned to take the shortest of shortcuts, and equally the long ways around certain points where he knows the police usually stand. He sometimes wishes he had a box or two of vegetables, to make him seem less like a private post service. In a way he just looks like a man in a hurry, but he realises that he must be seen quite a lot by the people who work or live on the streets where he goes. It's hard to blend in when you're big. When you're in a mortal hurry, zooming by on a bike, seemingly out of control.

Mr Morton has not said Paul's work is illegal. Not in an outright fashion. But then Mr Morton might not ever do anything legal, so for him perhaps the norm is so murky he doesn't reflect on it.

Lately he's not had to visit the Carousel, which is a relief. Instead he's been in to see William Knapp, the bookmaker at the Southampton Arms a lot. It's as though the command centre has moved. William's a barking German Shepherd of a man, with long mutton chops, black from birth, whitened from age, yellowed from tobacco.

The most recent deliveries have been to the same three addresses. Little glued-shut envelopes, containing first eight then a space then four numbers. The numbers are incomprehensible to Paul. A few times he's seen them, while in the presence of the people he delivers them to as they open them. Sometimes they make a point of showing him the slip of paper, as if that is a tip in itself. And maybe it would be to some people.

One cloudy Monday Mr Knapp says that he's run out of envelopes. Paul's just going to have to take the slip of paper in his pocket and make sure a man called Ilya on Gresse Street, in Fitzrovia, sees it properly. 'Off you go.'

On the way there Paul tries a new path through the warren of streets. How else will Paul ever find better, faster ways? He knows it's not a great idea, but Mr Knapp didn't say there was any extra hurry.

Paul winds in and out of traffic. He's twice as fast as some horses, a third faster than most cyclists he sees. Admittedly they usually cart much heavier things than a slip of paper. He sometimes feels like he's able to see into the future. In a way he's doing Mr Morton, and Mr Knapp, and Silas and all those other men who are too busy, too lazy, too old, to do the dirty work, the hard physical labour, a favour. By enduring the extra pain in his legs he's likely to save time in the long run. By spending the extra breath on finding a better, faster, more efficient way from one point to another, he's bound to make his boss, and his boss, happier.

Slowly, he realises he is lost in Marylebone. He's following hunches, craning his neck for landmarks. The sky is getting darker and darker, but the streets are still dry. Eventually he has to admit to himself he has no idea where he is. Mr Knapp usually writes the address on the front of the envelope – but not today. Paul remembers having been there before, but there have been many deliveries, many addresses and details to remember since. He knows the building, a three-storey one with a Russian restaurant on the bottom floor, and Ilya's apartment above.

Paul knows the building – the whole block – well, if he comes at it from the right way. He knows the turns, the things to look out for on the way there, on his usual way from Mr Knapp. Now though he's lost and he can't ask for anything more than Fitzrovia, which is broad enough.

Then the hailstorm starts. He's still on the bike trying to retrace his steps, and the little white shavings from the sky have a sharp bite. It feels like pinpricks if he tries to go any faster than walking pace. The hail is followed by torrential rain. This makes for slower going as the gutters and streets become rivers and lakes. Pedestrians under umbrellas crowd corners Paul usually cuts, and they also have a tendency to just walk out into the street. Paul's harder to spot than a horse or a taxi, and this slows him down. In a matter of minutes he's soaked through. He contemplates standing under an awning by a café but there's already quite a crowd and the owner is walking around taking orders, and pushing the ones who don't want anything out into the rain.

Paul gives up on being dry. He stands and looks at the traffic for a minute. Tries to get his bearings. Annoyed with himself for being an idiot. Now a wet idiot. He puts his hand in his pocket, only to find a small ball of grey pulp. This has never happened before. He's never been lost. He's never not delivered a number. He's been wet before, but the envelopes, and the relatively short time he's been on the way to the receiver, seem to have been enough for the slips of paper to survive.

Standing with his head in his hands, water streaming down as though he is under a waterfall, Paul decides he has two options. He can either return to Mr Knapp, tell him about the deluge, ask for a new slip of paper, and hope that Mr Knapp doesn't report him. But if Mr Morton even heard a whisper about Paul not being able to deliver, things would turn unpleasant very quickly. Also, and he admits to himself this is guesswork, he was hired because he's fast. So there must be a time limit, something that makes the numbers expire, or else Mr Morton could just put a stamp on the envelopes and let someone else carry them across the city.

The only thing left to do, besides suicide or boarding a ship for Japan is to make up a number. He knows it's crazy, but hopes Mr Morton's system doesn't involve receipts. As it's a number that expires, it must have something to do with bets. Paul guesses horses, or boxing, the lottery, something along those lines. Tries to think about what sports would use the combination of numbers. First eight then a space then four. For results or odds. Instructions perhaps.

In the end he can't work it out, but walking into a first floor office he tells the girls behind one of the desks a long and convoluted story about a girlfriend. How they have been seeing each other for almost a year, and he wants to surprise her. She's a keen cartographer, and he has buried a secret treasure for her. Paul hints at a hidden engagement ring. He was on his way to give her the coordinates, but now, with the weather, the note has been destroyed, and would she mind helping him? He shows her the ball of pulp.

'It'll only take a minute, tops,' he says. 'I'd be happy to pay you for your time,' he continues and pulls out a big crinkly note. One that's to last him a month. The girl smiles and calls him a silly romantic. She puts a fresh sheet of paper in her machine.

'What numbers do you want?' she asks, fingers poised.

He thinks hard, tries to remember if he ever saw the number he put in his pocket this time, but realises the note was folded over. He tries to remember any of the other numbers he's seen, but draws a blank. They're just numbers, and not ones that make any sense to him.

First eight then a space then four, he thinks. How hard can that be? Surprisingly hard he realises, trying to make them up from thin air. In the end he looks at the clock, tells the girl, 'three', then outside at the row of parked taxis, says 'nine', looks at the girl's hands. First the left. On it an engagement ring, the only kind of jewellery she has that he can see. The ring has a couple of white stones set in a ring of five red ones. So he says 'One, two, five,' then after a pause, he looks at her right hand. It hovers over the top row of keys, and so he says 'Nine, seven, eight'.

Drawing a deep breath, he asks the girl to make a space between the first set of numbers, and what's to follow.

He can't remember how he came up with the remaining four numbers, but once he's out in the street his legs are shaking like after the worst of his races. The rain has stopped and he asks a paperboy for directions to Fitzrovia.

When he finally gets to Ilya's place he's told he's late by a snooty maître d' on the bottom floor. Paul's told he's not to worry. Ilya is coming back. Just had to see someone about a delivery of fish. In the meantime the maître d' has been instructed to hold onto the envelope Ilya is waiting for.

Paul tells the man there is no envelope, not this time, and this part is true. A simple clerical error by Mr Knapp. After putting his index finger to his pursed lips the man folds a newspaper he has in front of him, and asks Paul to deposit the slip inside, and properly witness how he, the maître d', has not, and will not, look at the slip. The numbers are Ilya's business.

Paul's pulse threatens to kill him, but he nods and walks out of the building, to his locked bike. Through the window he sees the man unfold the newspaper and have a good long look at the number. Then laboriously copying down the combination in the margin of another paper, anxiously looking up to see if anyone sees him.

Paul briefly considers going back in to catch the man, but decides he's had enough for one day.

Chapter 19

September comes to London with no wind but plenty thunder. It's muggy and damp to begin with, then the haze clears and for weeks it seems like the world is a warm, kind place, where you can trust that one day will be like the next. One where there's no need for wool sweaters or galoshes. Mother Nature is deceitful. She lulls us into a comfortable dream where one layer is enough. It will end, everybody knows, but for the time being, for three glorious weeks it's marvellous.

Paul's glad to be outside with the wind in his face. He keeps on going all day till the afternoon turns to evening and the cooler air rolls off the river and the parks to greet him. He heads for the heath and finds Miriam crouched over her book of poems. As she doesn't greet him, just holds one finger up in the air to stop him interrupting, he sits in a chair, quiet as a mouse, waiting until she is done. Then she looks up and smiles and his world starts turning again.

'Come on Paul. Let's see if we can catch the sun coming up.'

They sit on the roof of the baths looking out over the Heath. Miriam has her hair wrapped in a towel and is smoking a cigarette stuck in an oxblood Bakelite holder, looking far away onto the horizon.

'Paul, I'm trying to not think about how high up we are,' she says. 'I know it was my idea to come up here. I've never been, wouldn't have wanted to come up alone, but this is nice.'

The night is about to turn into day. Paul's hands are a little shaky. Not because he's tired or thirsty. Because he's got a present for Miriam in his pocket. It was her birthday a few days ago, but at the time she never told him. He only found out by accident. She was wearing a new scarf, bright pink, and he commented on it, and it slipped out that Miriam's friend Alice Barrett gave it to Miriam for her birthday.

Putting a hand in front of her mouth when the story came out she made him promise not to buy her anything. She told him she doesn't like birthdays. So he's not bought Miriam anything, he's had something made for her. It's in a box, in a little velvet-lined box, in his pocket. The jeweller advised him, with a wry smile, to get one much too big to hold a ring. A flat one, with no hints of hearts or doves, so there's no mistaking. No use either sending the wrong message or having the girl be disappointed.

He's just looking for the right moment to sing 'Happy Birthday'. And in the meantime he's happy just to look at Miriam.

'You know I came to that race,' she says. 'The one at Kensal Rise.'

'You did? I looked everywhere for you,' he says.

'I thought you were great by the way,' Miriam says and looks up at him.

'Thanks, it turned out to be a pretty exciting race in the end. Where were you sitting?'

'Well, I spotted Silas in the queue, and thought that maybe you had put us together, for some stupid suicidal reason.'

'I wouldn't do that,' Paul says. 'Besides there are no seat numbers apart from the very posh ones. You just stand where you find a place. Or sit if people are polite enough. I had left a ticket for you in the office, but it was general admission one with a note to say where would be good to stand.'

'I don't know what I was thinking. He and I are like your family down here. Maybe you wanted us to meet?'

'No.'

'Well, at least I thought my seat would be a good one, and people are usually easy to spot in good seats, like you know boxes in theatres. Instead I got myself a cheap ticket, a standing one up on the hill. It was mostly men, but they were surprisingly polite.'

'Tuesday crowd. Did you get the flowers in the end?'

'No. Were they nice?'

'Quite nice. Sorry, no, they were probably the nicest, biggest, most elaborate bunch of flowers ever seen. Since the last coronation or royal wedding at least. You would have had to hire an extra horse and carriage to transport them home, would have had to rent an extra flat for them.'

'Well, if that was the case, I'm sorry,' she says and blows him a kiss.

He shuffles his feet. Fingers the box in his pocket.

'So are we a secret?' he asks, decidedly not looking at her.

'I don't see the need for Silas to know everything. Sometimes untold things hold a power in themselves.'

He nods. He knows the score.

'If my mother could see me now,' she says, 'all perfumed, expensive slippers, Christy's terry cloth robe, a strong man, an imported cigarette.'

'And if mine could see me. Socialising with a ringleader,' he smiles.

'Is that how you think of me?'

'No. But she would have.'

'Tell me something about her.'

'I don't really remember my mother,' he says, then stops. Looks at Miriam and smiles. She is somewhere between her two guises. She has had a bath, but the night still lingers in the air and so does some of her make-up and manner. He looks at her, then continues, 'Growing up there were one or two pictures but my father hid them when I got older. It's possible he destroyed them. He couldn't bear to look at them any more, he said. They were photographs, must have been taken before they were married, as she was very young in them. I used to stand looking at them on the mantelpiece. They were behind glass, in little oval, black frames. The glass reflected and I would try to line up my face with hers to see how much we

119

looked like each other. It didn't help that whenever we met my uncle, her brother, he'd say that I was an exact replica of her, apart from the hair.'

'Was she not ginger?'

'Her hair was as black as coal at night. My father's hair was red when I was a child but now it's all white. Well it was the last time I saw him.'

She looks at the brightening horizon, then she says, 'Keep talking Paul. I'm still not sure about the height.'

'She died in childbirth,' he says, 'when I was six.' He looks where she looks, then continues. 'I would have had a brother but they both died. My father and I never talked about it. I remember him coming home only to change into black and leaving again, instead of coming home with Mum. I was left with a neighbour, then later, a cousin of mine came to stay. She managed to stay on for a year or two, then she left. My father was either out in the fields or drinking. I was sent to school, my uncle paying the fees, but that soon stopped. I was needed on the farm, my father decided. I was strong even at ten, free labour. My uncle's money continued going to the schoolmaster, who took a big cut, then sent the money to my father, who spent it on drink and bad odds.'

'I'm so sorry,' Miriam says and moves closer. Takes one of his hands in both of hers.

'I don't know,' he says and shakes his head. 'I became quite good friends with some of the farmhands. It suited me to be outside all day, to do things, look after animals. I know that's some people's idea of hell but I was good at it and I enjoyed it. I made sure I didn't see my father too much, and in limited doses he was always fine. Could even be nice to me every now and then.'

'At least you had a home.'

'I've never thought about it like that.'

'I've lived in more places than I can remember,' she says looking out over the park.

'I've lived in two.'

'Maybe we're too different to be together?'

'Are we?'

'I'm joking. It doesn't matter how many places you've lived in,' she smiles.

'I meant,' he says quite seriously, 'are we a couple? Secret or not.'

'Do you want to?'

'Do you?' he says looking up at her, one hand on the box in his pocket.

'I asked first.'

'I asked second,' he shoots right back.

'Well, you keep avoiding the question, which to me speaks volumes,' she says quite seriously.

'I do want to stay Mr B, I mean category B,' he says.

'What are you talking about?'

Paul explains the conversation he had with Stanley in the coffeehouse. This makes Miriam laugh so much she starts to cough. She has to stand up to clear her airway. She staggers over to the edge of the roof, and holds onto the little barrier. She's laughing and crying and eventually drops the towel. Her hair comes cascading out. Wet, fragrant, long, curly, unpinned. Two stories down, a pack of dogs start fighting over the towel and it's soon ripped to pieces. Her vertigo has been distracted by the laughter, by the towel, by the canine brawl, but as the dogs limp off to lick their wounds it comes surging back.

'Paul!' she shouts, frozen.

He quickly gets up from his chair, runs over and takes her in his arms. 'Don't worry. I've got you,' he says.

'That's good,' she says, quietly. She buries her head against his chest. 'I'm just going to stay right here for a minute,' she says. Paul nods. His chin resting on her head. His nose full of her scent. She wriggles closer to him and says, 'I can't decide whether to go to bed or take a vial, you know just get on with it.'

He stays quiet. Puts his arms tighter around her.

'I can feel your heart beating,' she says.

'My pulse is usually a lot slower.'

'Not when you race.'

'Even then it's not this fast.'

'I'll take that as a compliment.'

'You should.'

Now they are hip against hip. She holds him harder, feels the man underneath the clothes. His head comes away from her head. She looks up at him. In case something is wrong. In case he's seen something, heard someone coming. He hasn't. Almost imperceptibly his face moves closer to hers. She mirrors his movement. When they kiss she has to crane her neck. He puts a hand on her cheek. She puts more pressure on the small of his back. A sound escapes him, like a small animal. She winces. In the best way.

After a while she takes his hands and puts one over her eyes, for the descent of the stairs.

'To help with the vertigo,' she says. She leads him to a room she's never shown anyone. One behind the dining room with all the copper things and pictures of the Bosphorus.

She tells him to sit down on the bed, but remains standing herself.

'Before you can come too close, there are things you need to know,' she says.

'Whatever it is, it can wait. Miriam, let's not talk any more.'

'This is important, and it's not easy. If I stop now I might never try again. And I've been waiting many years.'

He sits on her bed, a pillow in his lap. Disappointed. Attentive. Confused. He nods, and she starts, doesn't look at him, 'Years ago, before I came to London, a friend of mine told me about a man she sometimes serviced. My friend, who knew me, knew my family, said he was the kind who would cry and talk about his memories after. And this one told her things she didn't want to hear. Things about a niece. He was an old soldier. Always wore a uniform, tattered and foul, with more medals than she had ever seen on any man's chest. Even on real heroes in parades. One evening I walked with her, by her usual territory down by the docks, and I recognized him. My mother's enemy: my father. I hid quickly, while she lured him in. As my friend worked him I put my scarf around his neck and pulled and pulled. It looked like a snake winding up and down his back as he struggled. I pretended it was just an animal with its own will to make the thing easier. When he stopped breathing we pushed him into the water and a guillemot picked up my scarf in its beak and flew off.'

Paul looks at her. She asks if he can still like her despite knowing what she's capable of. He smiles, nods, swallows, and walks over to kiss her again. Her hands shake as she starts to unbutton his shirt. Then she stops. Pushes him away from her and steps out of her dressing gown. Then she comes close again and helps him with the buttons.

***

Afterwards, they listen to each other's breathing. The morning now well on its way. A bullfinch comes to rest on the windowsill, then it sets off, a blurred ball of red and black and grey. In the trees, crows. In Paul's stomach, butterflies.

Miriam says, 'You spoke about your parents, now I'll tell you some about my mother, or about me rather.'

'Mmm,' he says. He's very sleepy.

'My mum named me Kråke. I never use it. Never tell anyone.'

'What does it mean?' he says.

'It means crow in Norwegian.'

He says, 'Little crow.'

She smiles and puts a warm hand to a stubbly cheek. He says, 'Why not use it? It's nice.'

'Thanks.' She looks out the window. Continues, 'My mum was never happy. I think I looked a lot like *him*, and I think some of his madness got into her. She liked reading and she liked books, and one of the last memories I have of her is telling me about my names. *Miriam*, that's from the Bible. *Kråke* is different,' she says. 'She told me I was born with very dark hair, lots of it too.' She looks away from him. Behind him, out of the window again. 'Will you please get me the book from the shelf? Read to me, from where the bookmark is. I like your voice.'

He gets up, and she tells him cycling has been good to his bottom. 'Especially in this light,' she laughs. He pretends to be outraged. Picks up a cushion on the way back to bed.

Once under the covers he puts a couple of pillows behind his head and she settles on his chest. He feels his heart slow again. His breathing returned to normal. A few minutes ago he was breathing quickly, not sure how to continue, until he couldn't stop. Now he's calm, and warm and hers.

No. 26
Kråke she called me – her Little Crow
Black against the whitest snow
Just before passing she told me a story
A Viking princess, shrewd plans and late glory
Protected by snakes and killed by the same
And that's how she found my name

When he puts the book down she is asleep. A snail's trail of saliva on his chest. He puts the book on the floor. A mid-morning sun is blazing outside the window, and he looks at Miriam. Her eyes move behind her eyelids, like planets moving back and forward across the heavens. In his jacket pocket a flat box. On the floor, next to the book a black feather with a gold top. He moves down under the covers and knows it won't be long until he is asleep too.

Chapter 20

Today's race is important. It's a qualifier for a whole series of big races later in the year, some even on the continent, and unfortunately a troupe of incredibly fit Dutchmen have turned up. Paul does a long warm-up to disassociate himself from life outside the velodrome. Just before he lines up for the start he glimpses Silas on the grandstand. That puts fear into him. Not necessarily a bad thing. As he rests, Harry ambles up to him.

'Hello Paul, how are you?'

'Fine. A little out of breath, but not more than I should be.'

'You look fine. It's a tricky track. And that's if your bike and your health are both up to scratch.'

'I feel I'm quite fit, have been doing a lot of training lately, and the bike is in as good a nick as it'll ever be.'

'Sometimes, it's got nothing to do with that. Sometimes cycling goes beyond reality. On a good day your chain purrs like a fat cat being stroked in the sunshine. Your spokes whisper sweet nothings, your tyres remain hard and your saddle is part of you rather than a separate piece of leather.'

'That's true. Let's just hope today is a good day,' Paul says, glancing towards the starting line.

'On bad days, the opposite,' Harry continues. 'You can't get into any rhythm. Your wheels seem softer, heavier than your opponent's. Your bike is an admiralty anchor, your legs are made from slag, and it feels like you're swimming wearing a chainmail suit. Yet still you push. You silence the voice inside telling you to give up, to let your heart rest from the torture.'

Paul gets off his bike. Weary of what Harry is saying and of the cramps that come and go, unexplainable like weather systems, he's stretching. Holding onto the top tube and bending at the waist. Keeping his legs, back, and arms straight. His mind too.

Harry smiles and says, 'The ability to disregard, to pretend to yourself that today you're having a great time and glory will be yours, is the main difference between you and the other cyclists.'

Paul nods and gets back on the bike. Clicks his feet into place. Pulls up his shorts, pulls down his top. Flexes his arms.

'I know you'll do well out there. You always do,' Harry says.

Paul leaves the side of the track and rolls toward his designated place on the starting line.

He takes three deep breaths. Then comes the crack of the gun and the immediate pain of hoped-for glory. He gets a good start. Manages to squeeze in to be third in a big field, close to the bottom line, where the distance he'll be riding is a lot shorter than if he was higher up. The sun is out and he affords himself a little smile now that he's underway. Now that he doesn't have to think about anything besides racing. After the long warm-up his legs are used to the motion, and he relaxes a little. Nothing's going to happen in the first five laps. Then, after that, anything can.

The first time he ever rode the velodrome at Kensal Rise he didn't know about high turn two and low turn four and buckled his front wheel. Paul had an important race on the Monday, at Fallowfield Stadium in Manchester. An awful shale track, long and steep, cold and unforgiving, the site of the controversial 1919 Championship. Jack fixed the bike overnight and cycled it to Copenhagen Street in time for Paul to catch the train.

That was many months ago now, and Paul feels like he knows the track well. Like an old dog, a well-worn jacket. The first fifteen laps pass before anyone really does anything other than positioning. They are all trying to sense the pace, the wind, the mood, the willingness of the others.

He hears shouts and what he presumes are jokes in Dutch.

A strange guttural sound. Two of the Dutchmen, gangly greyhounds, possibly brothers, weave in and out of the field with expertise they can only have gained from years of racing. They are freckled and fair like Paul. Their shared complexion doesn't mean that the brothers won't do their best to kill him.

On lap forty-two the shouts and jokes stop and the professionals, he now realises that's what they are, knuckle down to do some real racing. It's beyond human. He tells himself it's impossible. His body now turns into pig iron as he tells himself nothing should hurt this much.

The pace picks up.

The Dutchmen are pushing for a fast pace. Paul runs out of water long before he should. He feels like he's got nothing to stoke his fire with. Some days his body just won't listen to his commands. It has turned into an unruly army, a mass of deserters. His limbs threaten to give up. He can't have that. It doesn't work like that, he tells himself. The gulf between mind and body grows wider and wider for every lap, for every push on the pedals. Then a group of three riders try to break free. Or is it four? He can't see properly though eyes running with sweat, frustrated tears, and the sharp prickles of dust from the riders in front of him. It feels like he's swallowed sandpaper, but he won't give up. The group, three riders, he can see now, are still pushing hard. The fourth rider, an Englishman with a great moustache and what looks like the kind of swimming caps cross-Channel swimmers use, has pulled back, screaming in pain and frustration. His ears standing out like wing nuts, now that he's pulled off his hat.

Paul decides to make a point of asking the man about his headgear after the race, but soon forgets in the sheet lightning of pain coursing through his body.

'Bloody Dutchmen,' he groans under his breath, over and over until he's caught up with the group of three. The last man looks over his shoulder, and notices Paul. He shouts something in that gruff tongue of theirs and the first and second man, nodding as if this was all going to plan, simultaneously stand up. *Push, push, push.* Half a lap. Paul is still on the back wheel of the last one.

The Dutchmen have devised a strategy whereby the last person, the one just in front of Paul, eases off. The gap between Paul and the two riders out front widens. The third man looks over his shoulder and smiles, still easing off, pulling to the right, up on the track. Making it hard for Paul to pass, even if he had the lungs and legs to do so. The Dutchman now looks over his shoulder and changes the position of his hands on the handlebars, from a grip up on the top to the vertical bend. Still monitoring Paul; an owl eyeing a mouse. The Dutchman turns his attention back to the track, to the gap up to his countrymen.

Just as the man's eyes leave him, Paul swerves down from the line he's been holding slightly above. For a split second Paul eases off, lets the momentum and gravity propel him forwards to the inside of the Dutchman. To a place the man never thought Paul could fit in. This is his one chance to leave some of the competition behind, to catch the two out-runners. He feels his mind go blank and his vision go black. His muscles pull him back into his body. Only the acute pain keeps him conscious.

When he can see again he's closer to the leading pack than he is to the Dutchman groaning behind him. Another couple of pushes and he changes that balance more and more. Now he reaches behind him to the pocket of his sweater and fishes out two pills. One he shouldn't be taking for another thirty laps. The other is an emergency one he always carries in case he was to drop a pill. He greedily swallows them both. Soon he can't feel anything. Soon he's all speed.

Chapter 21

An hour after the race I find Paul sitting in an alley behind the racetrack. I've been looking everywhere for him. He's shivering uncontrollably, distraught and disorientated. His lucky jersey torn all down the back. It looks like he's fallen because his shoulder blades are bleeding, then I realise it's from sliding down the rough wall.

I've been asking janitors and competitors for him. I've been annoyed, then worried for him. When I find him relief washes over me. Then anger. Not at him. At the situation. I say his name but he doesn't react. I walk up to him, but he doesn't seem to recognize me. Even when I stand right in front of him. Even when our noses touch.

I can tell he's had too much of the powders Mr Morton has prescribed. I've never been against them, realise they're useful, crucial in fact. But some of the pills Mr Morton procures for the boy are clearly too strong. They make him very active, then very down. It's awful to see, but it means Paul can enter twice as many races in a week than before.

'Silas?' he says, momentarily coming to.

'Shh,' I say, putting both my hands on his cheeks. 'Don't speak. I'll fix you Paul.'

'Did I win?' he asks.

'Don't worry about that. Worry about yourself,' I say.

'Did I?'

'Bronze. A very good bronze,' I say, one hand now supporting his neck, the other still on his clammy cheek. 'You qualified. Now rest.'

He's in terrible shape. A boy champion, passed out in a seedy alley, all hopped up.

I don't know what comes over me but I kiss him. He doesn't

even react. He tastes of salt. Butter and toast on his breath. Immediately after I regret it. I berate myself for letting my emotions get the better of me. What if we had been spotted? What if Paul will remember?

He seems oblivious to the world as I lead him out of the alley. I walk home on light feet. Paul lumbers by my side quite unaware. A dull, copper-coloured medal dangling from his neck. I can tell it was hard to come by tonight. It was the last position to qualify, and Paul did so by less than half a wheel.

I decide against a taxi. He needs to walk off whatever Mr Morton crams into the pills I've been told to supply Paul with. Luckily it's not far to my place. The air will do us both good.

I take his hand. Tell him it's fine, that men do that all the time in Greece. He tells me the pain in his left lung and leg is too much for him. His eyes water like he's been chopping onions, just from walking.

After many breaks, and him drinking pint after pint of water from a flask I refill in every pub we pass, we're on my street. I take him upstairs to my big rooms, newly appointed with saffron velvet and the latest *Atelier d'Or* wallpaper. White and yellow digitalis on an oxblood background. Cost me a fortune, but worth every sou.

Paul stands in the middle of the hall while I busy myself getting the bath ready. In the past he's told me he needs one cold then one hot. I oblige. He gets in the first, the ice cold one, and I stand to the side and look. He doesn't seem to mind, or notice me.

He's explained that the pain from the shock of the cold water takes his mind from his body. Makes his muscles seize up, in a good way. Then down the drain the cold water goes and I bring a huge vat of water just about to boil. Paul, wet and cold to the touch, stands up and cups his privates with one hand. I leave him and fetch the next big pan. He still doesn't seem to know quite where he is. The hot water goes in, and it steams up the room, I turn on the cold tap, blend the water with my hand, my face at his hip.

'Sit down,' I tell him. 'I'll make it right just for you.'

Now the swirl of the hand, the hand that can brush his thighs, the hand that can brush his chest. It's just mixing, a tool for the best bath. It's a hand that puts in bath salts, and pats Paul's back. Squeezes his neck and shoulders. I'm just helping him recuperate.

'Take it easy. You won a place on the next tier, the next qualifier. It's as good as gold,' I say. I look down on Paul. His eyes are now closed. 'That's it my boy.' Paul's now breathing slowly, slowly. 'You can come here whenever you want,' I say. I'm pretty sure I'm talking to deaf ears.

When it looks like Paul is sleeping I kneel by the bath. Slowly add more hot water. I watch my hand move from the neck, down Paul's chest. His heart slow now. I'm fascinated. My hand is a five-legged crab crawling over freckled sand. It stops by his navel.

I stop myself. I take my hand out of the water and sit on the floor by the bath and listen to his breathing. It's warm and steamy in the bathroom, and some condensation must have gotten into my eyes. I feel myself crying a little. Surely just a cold.

After the bath he looks better. We sit dressed in thick bathrobes. I'm drinking copiously. He's both high and coming down at the same time. We talk absolute rubbish, giggle like girls and decide to cut Mr Morton out of our lives. We don't talk about the crab crawling around on his thighs. I've decided it was just a dream.

The last bus thunders by, and I make a bed for Paul on the sofa. I say goodnight to him. I can't sleep, so I check on him every now and then through the night. His breathing isn't all that regular which worries me a little. Wouldn't want him swallowing his tongue, or choking on his own vomit. I turn him over a couple of times. Tuck him in. Finally I must have fallen asleep.

***

When Paul wakes up in the afternoon he tells me his whole body aches.

'It's not the exercise,' he says. 'I'm used to that. I don't mind the drugs so much. They make me faster. But after a race I feel horrible.'

'You don't look too good,' I say. It's both true and a bit of a lie. 'You must stay here. I'll keep an eye on you.'

'I'm fine, I can go home, wouldn't want to be any trouble.'

'No trouble. Can't afford to have you in hospital.'

'Thanks,' he says.

'It's just business. I don't care either way,' I say, then go and make him a cup of tea. Throughout the day I provide Paul with freshly ironed, emblazoned handkerchiefs to spit blood into. My mother would have been proud.

As the evening becomes night outside we listen to the radio in silence. He falls asleep in the middle of a symphony. I sit by the window, his slow breaths behind me. I drink another two inches of whisky, then pull his covers over him and go to bed. I toss and turn but can't go to sleep. It's because he's right there. It's because of what would happen to me if anyone realised. This makes me so angry that I don't know what to do. I leap out of bed, snatch my robe and stride out to the sleeping shape on the sofa. While the anger and the bile about the whole situation is still up I shake him. I prod him and push him till he wakes up. I say sternly to his face, 'Paul. This has been a holiday that will never be repeated. I will be sleeping late in the morning but you can show yourself out before six. This is not a private hospital, you realise.' I hate myself for it, but that's how it's got to be. He just nods once and goes back to sleep.

I can't sleep. I hear him leave in the morning.

***

The next time I see Mr Morton he tells me he wants Paul to race more. For less. He tells me again I need to make the boy more profitable, mentions he knows a doctor who's come up with some miraculous new mixtures. I nod and say yes, but I'm not listening. I think about the strongbox in his office. Mr Morton doesn't know that I know the combination, as I was there when it was installed. I know also that it's not been emptied between last week and now and that it's been a bank holiday, which always means more drinkers. Mr Morton talks about injections and slowly upping the dosage. I nod. I say yes. I can't possibly continue this. It has to stop. For Paul's sake. Still I nod and agree to all sorts of things.

When I finally get away from the Carousel I sit in a pub where I'm unlikely to bump into anyone I know. I think about things, I think about the future. I try to make a plan and think about the odds of me succeeding. It doesn't look too good. My lapse in judgement is unforgivable. The flaw in my defences, taking him home and letting him stay like that, has really shaken me up. I might need some violence to level me. I drink and drink. Then I go looking for Rupert.

Chapter 22

Rupert stands just inside the front door, looking dazed, when Paul comes down the stairs. 'Morning Rupert. How are you?' Paul says, but gets no reply. He's come home to pay rent. This is usually done by slipping an envelope under the door of 1A at Copenhagen Street, the *Ofiss*. But today he's racing early, so he's up and about even though it's only half past five. He's been spending less and less time under the eaves and more and more time with Miriam in the room at Hampstead. Between that, racing and running things across the city for Mr Morton he's barely been in the house for weeks. September has become October and Paul feels like he is married to one of his woollen jumpers.

Rupert looks surprised to see him, 'Fine, just fine. I'm a little busy right now, could you come back in a while?'

'I'm off to Wood Green, big race weekend coming up. I'm just here to pick up some things, and pay rent. I was wondering, have you seen Silas lately? I've got some money for him. Would like to pay off this bike before it breaks you know.'

Rupert is standing in the corridor, hasn't opened the office door yet. There are two big sacks leaning against the banister. Rupert moves as to pick them up, then seems to change his mind.

'Need a hand with those?' Paul asks.

'No, no.'

'Should I just put the rent under the door then?'

'Give it here.' Without looking inside the envelope, something that surprises Paul, Rupert folds it over in a hurry and stuffs it into his inner pocket. But he doesn't move either to unlock the office or for the sacks. The front door opens and the two bakers walk in. David happy, Henry with black rings around his eyes. Each carrying another sack like the ones at Rupert's feet on their shoulders, aprons flapping around their legs like hungry lapdogs. Henry shoots Rupert a questioning look, and Rupert drags a hand across his face. He looks up the stairs, at the bags. At Paul, then at Henry, and nods. David stands, sack still on his shoulder, with his forehead leaning against the wall, arms hanging by his sides, eyes closed.

'Come on then Paul. You've got time before you go I'm sure,' Rupert says to Paul. 'See if you can lift those two,' he continues with a smirk. Straining, Paul manages and the four of them walk up the stairs to the door of 2C. Rupert gets a key out and Paul notices a new clasp and a padlock.

'Someone has been fiddling with the door. Stolen the knob. Some people.'

'Who would do that?' asks Henry.

'Probably that man Sorensen upstairs,' says Rupert getting the lock open.

'So Paul, this is something you don't see every day.' He pushes the door open and invites Paul to come and have a look. Paul acts surprised to see the black void. Even plays along when Rupert jokingly pushes him a little in the back.

'When they redug some of the sewage system they came too close to the surface or something under this house. The floor under one of the flats collapsed into the underground. Luckily no one was in. With Silas and Mr Morton's connections in the insurance world we were able to get a decent amount of money to compensate for the damage.'

Paul can see there are still pictures hanging up on the wall on the opposite side of the door, and the curtains are still drawn.

'And what are we doing with the bags? Is it flour?' asks Paul.

David closes his eyes, Henry looks at his feet. Rupert looks at Paul as if he's expecting him to say something more, but then he nods and smiles.

'Yes. Yes, that's what it is. It's flour. Isn't that right Henry?' Henry nods but doesn't open his eyes.

'We've got a deal with their boss. We pour the leftovers, or the flour that's gone off, down this shaft and it disappears. Either into the ground or into the sewage system. Also helps with the smell.'

'Paul, let the boys rest, they've had a hard night,' Rupert says. 'You wouldn't mind pouring this stuff down there would you? I've got some things to discuss with them in the office. Might even pour them a drink, talk a little about the baking they did last night,' the last comment directed straight at David.

'I'm in a hurry Rupert,' Paul says.

'Consider it an order from Mr Morton.'

'Sure, fine.' Paul says. 'Then I'm off. Tell Silas I'm looking for him, or he can come out to Wood Green if he wants to.'

'Not a problem Paul,' Rupert says, letting go of the doorframe. 'I've left the key in the padlock. Just lock and slide the key under my door when you're done. Good man.'

The three men leave. Rupert shaking his head, Henry stumbling down the stairs, David whistling. Paul hears clinking glasses and someone opening a bottle of beer even before the office door is closed. Then someone kicks it shut and Henry's voice starts rumbling, indecipherable.

Paul carries the first sack over, rips it open with the skeleton key he gets out of the lock and pours the flour into the darkness. He doesn't know much about flour but this stings his eyes and smells sharp. He reasons that's because it's gone off, or maybe it's infested with mealworm? Once he's done with the fourth round he wonders where to put the empty sacks but if the shaft is big enough to swallow pounds and pounds of flour surely the hessian bags can go down too. He bunches the first three sacks up and drops them over the threshold. Then, picking up the fourth, he notices writing on the side of it. It says '*NaOH – Sodium Hydroxide – Not for domestic use – Handle with care.*'

Is that really for baking? he wonders. Or is it baking powder, rising agent, that kind of thing? As his nose prickles and his eyes sting he decides to throw the last bag into the gap and close the door. Coughing his way down the stairs he slips the key under the door.

'That's you done then?' Rupert shouts from inside, not opening.

'Yes. I put the bags down the shaft too. Hope that was the right thing to do?'

'That's fine. Run along now.'

Paul can hear David and it sounds like he's laughing, but he could also be crying. It's something right between: a hacking hysterical noise.

Paul runs upstairs and stuffs his meagre possessions into a haversack. A couple of medals, a shirt, the spare cycling top he can never use as it has the wrong number on the back of it, two books, both presents from Miriam that he's not read but pretends he has at least started. Some clothes for life, some for cycling. A hat and a coat. A few bits and bobs for the bike, a picture of Glen Coe he found in a magazine, a meerschaum pipe Emrys gave him once after winning a race, the wager from Paul was his old handlebars, now sold back to Jack for sentimental value. It's not much, but it's all his. On his way down he passes the office again. A voice shrieks from behind the door. Not a word, not a command – a wounded seagull's death wish.

Paul leaves for the track, hoping to see Silas there as he sometimes does. The house is getting to be too much for him. Maybe Silas owns other houses where Paul can rent a room. Or maybe it's time they went their separate ways. That's what Paul wants to discuss. He's been saving and there might just be enough, providing that he wins the remaining races of the month, to pay off the bike and the rent he still owes along with whatever other costs Silas will surely tell him have been incurred. Coughing up phlegm he cycles over to Wood Green.

Chapter 23

Today I'm at Wood Green. Though I'm usually a bit secretive about telling Paul I'm here, I've decided to make my presence known. Since I saw him last, only one thought has been on my mind. I'm going to ask him to meet me in ultra-secret, maybe even leave town for a day or two. I want to talk to him about any plans we might hatch for severing our ties to Mr Morton. The boy has given me hope. Foolish definitely, but an addictive line of thought.

I find him in the racer's area twenty minutes before the race is about to start. It's extremely early. I've not been home yet. I've been to an absolutely splendid champagne reception down on the strand all evening. Just caught a taxi to the velodrome.

'What's happened to your face?' It looks sunburnt or as if he's painted it. He says something about sweat, and fleas in the room he's renting. With everyone else I would have heard a veiled accusation, with him just a fact: there are fleas.

He talks about bags of flour poured down the shaft in the house. I realise I have to talk to Rupert, and tell Paul he's not making any sense. I make sure he gets to the starting line on time, tell him I want to speak to him after the race. My ears are still burning from the bubbly drink and previous night's adventure. I wish him luck and retire to the stands for some reading. On the way over I had the presence of mind to buy a few of the national broadsheets. These races go on for absolute hours. Throughout I'll cast the occasional look. Unless he crashes he doesn't need me. Or if he's in a bad way after he might need me too. Sometimes. Once.

I've got the stack of newspapers next to me. A steaming cup of coffee, a breakfast roll in a brown paper bag balanced on top. The sun is out. My boy's looking good, has been doing well lately. This means I've been getting richer, and almost more importantly, more and more in favour with the old Elephant Emperor. I hear the crack of the starter's gun. I watch the first few laps, nothing too strange, nothing too exciting happens. Paul stays second or third, like he usually does. He looks relaxed enough. I ask one of the girls behind the bar to bring me a coffee and some breakfast if they have any.

I undo my scarf, a lovely mohair number I've imported at great cost, and turn my attention to the world beyond the oval. In the Spectator I read an article on the upcoming election in America. A chap named Hoover is the favourite for the next president, and the paper has tried to get a statement from the current president, Mr Coolidge, but has been quite unable even to get a decent quote. Not because they haven't been able to reach him, but because he's such a quiet man. This Coolidge is probably as good or as bad, as genuine or addicted to sex and money as any other old man in politics. A former lawyer, which tells me everything I need to know about the man. He fell into the post as president quite by accident when Harding, the real president, suddenly expired from a heart attack. Rumours say he was poisoned, by his jealous wife, but nothing was proved.

I laugh to myself. This high drama so unlike our own House of Commons. I've always been fascinated by America. Have always tried to keep on top of the news and rumours from over there. It seems quite often their trends and ideas trickle over to us, and it's good to keep abreast of these things. I suppose it used to be the other way around. Europe was all the rage, our ways of thinking, and the languages. That tide is changing now.

Under the article is an advertisement for paint. My eyes are reading along before I can stop them, I'm not interested in paint. I will always hire people to do the work for me. I will have nice tastes. Not too showy, not too classy either. I'm measured and cultured and stuck. I wish I wasn't tied to Mr Morton. He owns me and that feels like a pair of seamstress scissors hacking at my insides. He knows that. He knows I hate him, and he loves that I do. Like a kicked dog I return to him again and again.

I lift my eyes from the paper I have long since stopped reading. I look at Paul, he's in the lead, sweating and panting, a big pack of cyclists chasing him round and round.

I think of my mother and, not for the first time, I wish she was here, tucked away in a cosy flat in Palmers Green. She would have liked Paul. She would have pinched his cheeks and made him promise to come over for lunch every Sunday. I have let him starve, which is good for the cycling. I am now more a Londoner than Greek. A slick, wise-cracking, corner-cutting bastard. When I think of myself in the light of my mother I am ashamed.

I've added cognac to the coffee. It helps. Keeps me drunk. I concentrate on the paper. Eat a roll and drink my coffee. Force myself back to the life I've created.

After the race Paul can hardly hold the pen someone gives him, asking for an autograph. I take him by the elbow and steer him away, out, home. I can't take him to mine. That can't ever happen again. I'm happy to take advantage of people in general and sculptural boys in particular but despite having decided not to think of the episode I do. That's something I'm not used to. *Harvest, then move on,* is a motto I've lived by a long time.

A man walks up and asks Paul to sign a bit of card, for his child. Paul wants to but can't. Hand, eye, shake, eye, shrug, shaking worse and worse now. He can't. He needs to go, to sit in a bath, to lie in a bed, to close his eyes.

'Sorry my friend. It won't work,' he says. 'Can you come next week? I'll be fine by then,' Paul says to the boy, disregarding the father. 'Silas, please give the boy two tickets for next week,' Paul says, and I do.

I put an arm around Paul's waist as I can't reach around his shoulders, and address the man, 'He'll race again on the third and then on the fourth. Thank you.'

I should have left as soon as the race was over. Or employed someone to carry Paul's stuff, wheel his bike, find him a taxi, open beers and provide jam sandwiches. Instead I'm getting involved. What happened to the business agreement? The cold using of this specimen, this horse of a man? Instead I'm tenderly ensuring his way out of the crowded stadium.

He soon looks a little better, but not by much. I can tell the throng wasn't helping. Once again I remember he's from a place where there probably lived fewer people than would fit in the arena. I was always an Athens boy, then a London man. Crowds of people don't bother me. Unless they owe me money. It's the silence and the empty spaces I fear.

I take him to a classy place to have a quiet drink on the way home. He needs to sit, he says. He needs to drink something strong I say. He says he can't. I tell him he needs to. But all he does is to order his old, silly drink. So there we sit in a club not far from my home. He has sarsaparilla, his eyelids heavy. I drink quite a lot of beer. I'm all souped up from drinking all night, staying up all day, boosting myself with pills whenever I need to. I talk and talk. Not sure about what, but it's not the ultra-secret plans, not the precise extraction I had planned to discuss.

He looks at me but I'm not sure whether he's grateful, or if he blames me for his pain. Eventually I tire of my own voice. I know I have to remove him from my neighbourhood. I lead him to a taxi. Getting in he looks so helpless. I curse myself and jump in beside him. We don't talk much. Once we get to Copenhagen Street I have to help him up the ladder. Once he's in bed he says he's cold. I put an extra blanket over him, hold onto the edge of the cover for just a minute as he drops off.

***

Two hours later I wake up and he's on his back, almost comatose in his exhaustion. I've been sleeping in a foetal position, my back to his. We have been sharing the pillow and my saliva has formed a big round mark on it. The effect of the beer has left me, all I need to do now is to pee.

I begin to sneak down the ladder and the stairs, then I remember that this is my building. I can do whatever I want. Whenever I want. With my back straight I walk down the stairs.

I make it home without falling asleep in the taxi, but it's not far from it.

In the morning I wake up with a terrible hangover which is a rare thing. I'm feeling a touch bad for letting Paul get involved with Mr Morton. And with me. With London and the whole thing. To cure my headache and possibly my conscience I walk over to Copenhagen Street.

'Come on, I'll take you out for breakfast,' I say once he's come down the ladder from his crawl space. He's not wearing a shirt, and sleep still lingers in the corners of his eyes. His hair is tousled and he looks absolutely pure.

There's a hint of red on his high cheekbones. Maybe he remembers me sleeping next to him. Maybe he's just tired. Either way he needs to be built back up. Quickly. He's got a race on in the afternoon. This time in Catford. He races so much I'm starting to lose track of all the places. West Ham, Putney, Paddington, Herne Hill, God Knows Where and then the same again, week in week out. And that's just in London. He's a machine, but he's also a man, and I'm taking him out for a proper feed. To make my mother proud, if nothing else.

★★★

After the race I buy Harry Wylde a drink. I tell him I need to make Paul make more money. At this Harry sighs. He tells me Paul is doing remarkably well in the series he's in, that he needs time to grow and mature, to master the tactical side of cycling as well as the physical.

Here I tell him to stop. 'Whose side are you on?' He starts

to speak but I cut him off, 'Just remember who puts bread on your table. And beer for that matter.' He cocks his head, he's a clever clod after all. After drinking half a pint in one go he sits back and tells me about bets and odds. As if I wasn't the master of those things already. But one thing I wasn't aware of is something he calls *Endurance Racing*.

Harry says, 'They're almost closer to a circus act than real racing, but the money is good.'

'He's used to that from the gladiator games Mr Morton puts on,' I tell him.

'Well then. There are a couple, and if you think you've got the manpower you could organize one yourself I suppose.'

'Go on.' Half of me is attracted to this idea of more money for the same effort from me. The other half realises that more money means more effort on Paul's part.

'There are twelve-hour, and twenty-four hour races, and even much longer ones. The aim is to rack up as many miles as possible. You can ride however you want. Either go quickly and then rest, eat, sleep if you need it. Or just go at a steady pace for the duration of the race. It depends on your style of racing and on the quality of drugs you can get.'

'And the money.'

'The longer the race, the better. Especially as there are intermediate sprints and prices for the first person to complete ten, twenty, a hundred miles and so on.'

'And what's the longest?'

'The six-day race.'

'You mean cycling for six days straight?'

'The Lord rested on the seventh. If it wasn't for that...'

My mind is reeling. I couldn't do anything continuously for twelve hours, let alone a week. Harry continues, 'Sometimes you race in teams of two, making sure one of you is always on the track. Sometimes you're on your own. There are little shacks, like the ones at allotments set up in the middle of the velodrome, where racers eat, sleep, see to their needs, be they medical or more basic.'

'How have I not heard of this?'

'You're not a cyclist. No offence. And besides these races are bigger in France and Germany than here, but there are still enough of them to enter Paul into if you feel that would be the right thing to do. There's a man out at Olympia trying to set one up at the moment. You should go and see him.'

'Thank you Harry, this has been most informative,' I say after he's talked a bit more about the finer points, most of which I don't understand. 'I wouldn't usually ask an employee for advice, but seeing that this is a new venture I'll ask you: Do you think I should enter Paul into one of these six-day races?'

'To be honest. No, not yet. He's too explosive, too young. You need to know yourself, your limits and strengths better before setting out on something like that. It's absolute agony you must understand. I can't think of anything harder.'

'But…?'

'But, I think that maybe next year, or the year after that, once he's lost a bit more weight, and knows himself, and the bike, a bit better, he could be a contender for some of the bigger races. Also if you're going to send him to places like Berlin or Toulouse where these races are big and where the real money is made, you need to either be prepared to travel with him, or trust him on his own. Or send me I suppose.' He smiles.

'I see your point.' I think about this, about Paul's age and legs for a minute. Then I just want to go home. I stand up and signal for another drink for Harry. I leave, thinking about what I'm doing in six days' time, and how horrible it would be to know I would be cycling almost the whole time till then.

Chapter 24

A month of racing and hard graft has passed. The occasional warmth of October is about to topple over into the hoarfrosts of November. Wet cobblestones, slippery from the night's cold, greet Paul in the mornings. Mr Morton's commands stand above seasons and the passing of time, disregarding Paul's every possible discomfort.

It's Monday evening and Paul's just parked his bike outside the Southampton Arms on Nine Elms Lane. There's usually a big, burly ox of a man on the door. Paul has never been able to get his name.

The man stands by the door, waiting for an excuse to explode. The first time Paul saw him he thought to himself that the pub must be doing well, or be especially important in some other way, as the size of the man on the door usually tells punters what they can expect. Later when Paul knew the place as one of Morton's main pickup points he realised there must either be a lot of secrets or a lot of cash on the unassuming premises.

As Paul is a regular, not in the drinking sense, but in frequency and punctuality, the man nods. That's the most polite he's ever going to be. When Paul asks if he can leave the bike outside unlocked, this again the same question every time, the man nods again. Only this time the man raises an eyebrow and points with one thumb over his shoulder into the pub, as if he's trying to convey some sort of message. This is different from the usual, but the meaning is lost on Paul. He presumes the ox is asking if he's going in which he is, or having a drink, which he isn't. But Paul thinks not having a drink might offend the man, so he just nods.

Once in the pub he heads for the back corner where he

usually finds Mr Knapp. The booth is empty so he walks over to the bar to ask if anyone's seen the boss. There's only a young girl on duty and she doesn't seem to know anything, let alone how to pull a pint. Paul asks her for a drink, either milk or sarsaparilla. After struggling with the bottle opener she reaches over to him and places a bottle of Sioux City on a small folded napkin in front of him. This is something he's never seen anyone do in a pub.

He smiles and turns around, puts his elbows on the bar top, one foot behind him on the footrest. Drinks a few gulps. Looks at the front door, where the giant man has stuck his head in, as if to check. Paul finishes the bottle and puts it down hard on the bar top. He's in a hurry, he thinks, he needs to leave as soon as he has seen Mr Knapp. Turning back to the pub he catches a man's eye and feels the blood drain from his face.

'Paul, would you come over here?'

Paul manages to croak, 'Mr Morton. Pleasure.'

'Come closer, sit,' the big man implores. He moves his fingers over a silver rosary, eyes half-closed. He sits in a booth opposite where Mr Knapp usually does his business. In a blind corner of the pub.

'Thank you. I was just looking for Mr Knapp. I'm due to pick up a number.'

'I know. But we have other worries now.'

'Where is Mr Knapp?' Paul says once he's sitting down.

'He's here somewhere. Don't worry.'

'I should go. Do you have the number? I wouldn't want to be late for Ilya.'

'Which brings us exactly to where I wanted this conversation to be going,' Mr Morton says. 'Good. That saves us time.'

Now Mr Knapp comes out of the bathroom, tugging at his trousers. Paul sees that he too is very surprised by the presence of Mr Morton. Quickly recovering, Mr Knapp smiles and comes rushing over.

'Mr Knapp, would you join us please?' Mr Morton says pleasantly. As if they were just three mates meeting up for a pint.

'Sure,' Mr Knapp says, his voice faltering slightly. 'What are you fellows drinking?'

'Well as you might know I'm partial to Cointreau, and this man here I believe likes his drinks soft and sugary. And American by the looks of the label. I'm sure he'll have another. I find this influence from the States tedious myself.'

Mr Knapp walks over to the bar and starts berating the girl who is soon in tears, but manages to pour a large glass of the orange drink, open a bottle and find a clean glass for Mr Knapp's beer. Her tears drop on the little napkins she has been busy folding.

Not being used to bartending Mr Knapp has to go twice for the three drinks. Once he's seated next to Paul, Mr Morton beams at them both. He smooths his tie and takes a long slow sip of his drink. He smacks his lips, nods, exhales. All while the two men opposite him – one giant, one small – hold their breath.

'I don't usually come to this part of town. I don't mind it, it's nice enough with the water and all, but I prefer being home. I prefer my own turf. That's maybe what happens when you get a bit older. When you get a bit wiser.'

'We could have come to you,' Mr Knapp offers, while Paul stays as still and quiet as he possibly can.

'Be quiet when I'm talking,' Mr Morton says, then takes another sip. 'Now, I came here to inform you of something. There are to be no more deliveries to Captain Sergei Ilyashenko Petrovich, or Ilya as you know him. Knew him. He died this morning, in tragic circumstances. The first train to Manchester this morning had to be cancelled. They told me they found his head almost fifty yards from the body. It must have gotten stuck on something I suppose. Other than that he was spread out over the tracks for about a hundred yards.

There were bits of him stuck to the engine that they had to get specialist cleaners to remove. I believe they used high-pressure hoses, a bit like the fire department. Fascinating really.'

Mr Morton takes off his hat and inspects it. Not finding any faults he slowly returns it to his head. He touches it ever so gently three times to make sure it's sitting right. 'If it hadn't been for the uniform he was wearing no one would have been able to identify him. As it was, he was in full regalia, all his medals and the ceremonial sable present and correct. The sable was clean. If I know, knew, him right, it had mostly been used to guillotine bottles of champagne. The police had to get both his wives out to look at him. What was left of him. The women must have had quite a surprise. First seeing him. Then meeting each other for the first time. Turns out they were not aware of each other. I mean, the scene must have been hilarious.' Mr Morton laughs for a while, then gets a handkerchief out of his top pocket and wipes his eyes and the corners of his mouth. Then he continues, 'Mr Knapp, could you stand me another drink, I seem to have forgotten my wallet today.

Mr Knapp shouts for the girl behind the bar, then swears at her under his breath. Both Paul and Mr Knapp keep as quiet as they can, while Mr Morton continues, 'Apparently Ilya was a decorated war hero. The medals he sported must have weighed almost a pound.'

Their drinks arrive, but something is wrong with Mr Morton's glass he says and he pours the drink out on the floor asking the girl to get him a new one. Then he says, 'Now you might be asking yourselves why I'm here. I'll tell you, it's partly a social visit. This is a family company in a way, just that we're not related. I want to see who does what and make sure that the standards are kept up, but also that people are happy. So Paul are you happy?'

'Yes.'

'Yes, what?'

'Yes sir.'

'Mr Knapp? You?'

'Yes sir, I'm happy.

'Mr Knapp, I think we have known each other long enough. Drop the 'sir', it doesn't become you. You were once a proud man. You once had dreams for this place. Now it's a bit downtrodden. You've even got children working the bar for you. Which I don't object to per se. It's just when they're incompetent it's a bit embarrassing.' Mr Morton looks up on the walls, inspects a corner, then says, 'Maybe a lick of paint would do the place good. I like white. I will send a team of painters over sometime next week. They won't be too expensive.' He nods to himself, then says, 'And I'll find someone to replace that girl.'

'Don't feel you have to Mr Morton,' Mr Knapp says.

'I don't feel like I have to do anything, but I want to do you a favour. I want this place to be more profitable as much as you do.'

'Thank you, yes.'

'Now, one person we know who's not happy is Ilya. He was unhappy for a while before he died. That's what neighbours and wives are telling the police now. Partly because it is true, partly because I've asked them to. Suicide is never easy on the family. Especially not for men with a past in the army. They have such a strong sense of pride you know.'

The girl is back, although it doesn't seem like Mr Morton notices her. He appears content with his drink.

'I also happen to know that Ilya was very unhappy right before he so sadly passed away,' he continues. 'The moments before, he was delirious. When asked he kept saying the numbers were wrong. That this had never happened to him before. He wasn't to blame. He had done nothing wrong. He deserved a second chance. These kinds of things are hard to hear. Especially when they are coming from a man who used to look death straight in the eye on the battlefield.'

Mr Morton gulps down the rest of his drink in one go, then

reaches for Mr Knapp's beer without breaking his stride, 'Now, I have decided to conduct my own investigation. The police in this city can be painfully slow sometime. And between you and me: Thank heaven for that.'

Mr Morton turns to look both men straight in the eye. Then he smiles and makes a man with his two fingers. Walks it to the edge of the table, jumps off. Pretends to cry. Then lets out a loud cackle. He falls suddenly silent and turns to Paul, 'How did he seem to you when you delivered the numbers last week Paul? It seems you were one of the last people from my organisation, apart from me and Drago, to see him.'

'I didn't see him.'

'How do you mean?'

'He wasn't in when I got to his place.'

'That's highly irregular. Why?'

'I don't know.'

'Were you late? Pray to God you weren't late, Paul.'

'No I wasn't. In fact I was early. That must be it. I was early, I found a new shortcut. I don't know the name of the street, but it was quite neat really, I could show you sometime Mr Morton, I must have shaved a couple of minutes of the time from here to there.'

'I'm not interested in cycling, you know that.'

Paul goes on, 'Maybe he had a prior engagement, you said yourself he had two wives. That must take some seeing to. He could have been in a meeting or something, maybe he was in the bathroom just like Mr Knapp here when I came in. Maybe I just missed him.'

'So who did you give the envelope to?'

'Well, I don't know if Mr Knapp has told you, but there were no envelopes.'

'No envelopes? That's not how I want to run my business. Lucky I came here to check. It seems standards are slipping. We will talk more about this later Mr Knapp, yes we will.'

Mr Knapp looks pale and shoots Paul a look of disgust,

but Paul, happy to have diverted the questions for a moment, pretends he doesn't see.

'So who did you give the number, the number not in an envelope, to?'

'Well, whenever I have been there in the past there has always been the same man, this maître d'. I asked where Ilya was, and the man said he wasn't in, but that he would happily give the slip to him whenever he did come in.'

'That seems correct, from what we've been able to put together. My problem now is that we can't find this employee of Ilya. This is unusual. That, to me, suggests the two of them had an agreement of some sort. It also suggests that this other individual might know more than he should about our line of work.'

Paul hesitates a second. Then, wanting to push the subject as far from himself as possible, ventures 'I'm not sure if I saw this correctly, but as I was leaving I'm pretty sure the maître d' copied down the numbers.' Mr Morton's face goes purple. Paul still doesn't know what the numbers are for, but decides not to ask. Mr Knapp might or might not know. Paul can't tell, but he looks petrified, wringing his hands. He hasn't even got his beer to hold onto. Mr Morton is sipping on it.

'You realise this would never have happened if you had put the slip in a sealed envelope? This is serious Mr Knapp. Very serious business,' Mr Morton says, then clears his throat and puts his hands square on the table top, 'So, in short, you Mr Knapp, gave Paul the right number?'

'Yes.'

'Not in an envelope?'

'Not as such.'

'Yes or no?'

'No.'

'I see. And you said goodbye to Paul who cycled across town, extra fast due to some new shortcut, to Ilya's place, with this piece of paper. And he gave it to the now disappeared man?'

Both men nod.

'So the fact that Ilya ended up owing me a considerable sum of money, a debt which has now been transferred to his remaining family, and in effect been cut in half, as the dirty old boy had two wives, is down to either the secretary or Ilya himself tampering?' Again both men nod.

'Good. Well, I'm glad we cleared that up. It's just as I suspected. Apart from some minor details. I'm also glad there won't be any more delays to the Manchester train, because I know the two of them wouldn't dare lie to me.'

Mr Morton drains the beer and stands up. He's huffing and pulling his suit jacket down over his stomach. The buttons are all strained, but luckily they remain in place.

'Thank you Mr Knapp. I owe you a drink,' he says, squeezing out of the booth. 'I'll be in touch in regards to future numbers Mr Knapp,' he says, 'and of course subsequent pickups.' Mr Morton starts to waddle out of the pub, then half turns to the men, 'Paul come here. Walk with me.'

Paul jogs up to him and Mr Morton says, 'Actually I've been wanting to see you about something entirely different, but I've got a prior engagement I have to honour.' Paul nods and Mr Morton continues past the doorman, 'Can you come by my office? The one over the pub, not the other. Just ask any bartender. I can't be bothered with the stairs today in all honesty. Eleven o'clock tonight suit you?'

Without waiting for an answer Mr Morton turns around and starts berating his driver for not having the engine running, or the door open. He settles in the back seat sofa of his white and chrome Packard Big Eight. Mr Morton nods for Paul to close the car door. Then he nods to the driver and the car sets off. A fat Caesar on his way to quash barbarians in all known corners of his empire.

Without a word to either Mr Knapp or the ox man, Paul walks to his bike and sets off. Later, in the coffeehouse, he can't remember anything of the journey there. Sitting down with a pint of milk he feels unsteady, like an hour-old foal.

Luckily Stanley is there, and he tells Paul that Miriam is in her flat just across the road. Stanley must have thought Paul had come to meet her. He tells Paul that Miriam was just over for a quick chat, a half-pint of milk, full cream. Paul buys a cheese and onion sandwich as well as some other things, and stands outside in the sun feeling the shivers slowly leave him. As much as they will for now, which is far from very much. Then he sees Miriam in one of the windows, walking back and forwards, slowly taking off her earrings. One seems to have become tangled in her hair, and it looks like she's singing.

Chapter 25

Miriam opens the door and immediately looks over her shoulder. Not the kiss and cuddle he was expecting. Or needs.

'Paul? What are you doing here? Come in quickly.'

'I'm sorry. Are you busy? Should I go?'

'Yes you should go. But now that you're here come inside. Hurry.'

He bends his head and scuttles in, and she quickly closes the door behind him.

'Did anyone see you?' she asks.

'I don't think so.'

'Thinking is not the same as knowing Paul. Sometimes you drive me crazy.'

'I'm sorry.'

She stalks into the kitchen and starts banging pots and pans. All she achieves is spilling a bottle of milk and then, after he's mopped it up, she puts on the kettle. He sits on a kitchen chair, looking at his hands. The little bag of presents he bought underneath the table. She leans back against the wall, her hands behind her, her face turned to him, inquisitive. Waiting for the water to boil.

'I'm sorry. OK. You look pale, have you eaten properly?' she says.

Paul clears his throat unnecessarily and says, 'I just had a funny morning. A little run-in with a Mr Knapp.'

'Never heard of him.'

'He's a bookie over on Nine Elms Lane. I pick up messages from him a couple of times a week, nothing more. But today Mr Morton was there and he wasn't pleased.'

Miriam pales, lifts the boiling kettle off the hob with a shaky hand. Then she speaks in a hushed voice, 'Why? Tell me you haven't done something wrong. Or something stupid?'

'No, no. It wasn't that. It was about one of the people I deliver to. A Russian man who killed himself over a debt to Mr Morton. Nothing to do with me really, only I was the last of Mr Morton's employees to see him. Only I never saw him.'

'And did you tell all this to Mr Morton?' she asks.

'I told him what had happened, yes.'

'And he seemed fine with that?'

'I don't know him well enough to know how he seemed, but he was happy enough when he left.'

She thinks for a second, then nods and comes over to him. Puts a hand on his shoulder. Her foot brushing the bag under the table.

'What's in this?' she asks.

'Just some scones, some chocolates. These little white hearts with sprinkles.'

'From across the road?'

'Yes, Stanley told me they were very nice. That a lot of girls come in for them. Or at least that a lot of men come in to buy them for women.'

'So someone saw you come in here?'

'He told me you were home. But I mean he's harmless.'

'Doesn't matter. You have to be more careful. I'm not in any safer a position than Ilya.'

'You know about him?'

'Of course I do. I saw how upset Mr Morton was when he found out how much money he had lost. It wasn't pretty. I just didn't know that you were involved.'

'I'm not involved.'

'You are. We all are. Everyone is.'

'I don't want to be.'

'It doesn't matter.'

The kettle whistles and she makes them a pot of tea so strong he thinks she's trying to punish him. The only smile he seems to be able to get out of her is when she tastes one of the little chocolates. But then again, that's maybe more Stanley's smile than his. 'Mr Morton asked me to come back later in the evening,' Paul says as she refills his teacup. He really doesn't want any more tea, but feels it would be rude to decline.

'That's not good.'

'It might just be about the cycling. You know I've been doing these competitions for him. Special evenings.'

'But usually he wouldn't ask you. He would deal with Silas wouldn't he?'

'So far yes. But I don't think Silas likes these things, the competitions.'

'And do you?'

'No, but I don't have the luxury of a choice. Some things I'm just told to do.'

He reaches for the milk. Miriam sits back. Looking content for the first time since he showed up at the door. She reaches for him, puts her hands on his forearms, and looks him in the eye.

'I'm so sorry you've been drawn into this whole mess.'

'But I've been drawn in with you.'

There's silence for a moment. 'Come here you big oaf.'

He forces himself to return her smile. 'No, you come here.'

She stands up, brushes some scone crumbs off her skirt and walks around the table to him. Sits on his lap and puts one hand in his hair.

'You need to look out for yourself Paul. Look over your shoulder. Try to be a bit more streetsmart.'

'I will. I promise.'

'I know you won't be able to. It's not in your nature. And that's why I like you. Don't worry, I'll look out for the both of us.'

'And I'll get more white chocolate hearts for us next time. Did they all just disappear? Were they nice?'

'I'm afraid so. A curse on Stanley and his witchcraft.'

She tousles his hair and strokes his cheeks, first going with the grain of his shave and then against it. Seeming satisfied, she kisses him. Perfunctory at first, then deeper. He puts his arms on her shoulder blades and pulls her in. This is what he needs to counter the fear which welled up when speaking to Mr Morton. Then he pulls away and asks, 'What are you doing today?'

'I have a rare morning off,' she says. 'I was going to maybe bake a cake, feed the ducks, buy a dress I can't afford, go to church.'

'Really?'

'No, not at all. But don't you sometimes feel like doing normal, mundane things?'

'Like all the people you see?'

'Not the people I see,' she smiles.

He shrugs and says, 'I mean the people in the street. Going to work, coming home from work. Playing with children, putting them to bed. Reading, singing in a choir, that sort of thing?'

'Yes, that sort of thing. I couldn't bear it in all honesty, but sometimes, even just for an hour I would like to feel drab, and slow, and run-of-the-mill.'

'You'll never be drab,' he says and kisses her.

'Thank you. I wasn't fishing for a compliment, but thank you all the same.'

'So for an hour or so let's have a cup of tea, like normal people, then we can go to the park if you want. Have you got any old breadcrumbs you want rid of?'

'You're too sweet. I'm going to sleep. I'm only just back. Last night got a little out of hand. Another collection. A big one.'

'How are you feeling?'

'I'm a peach.'

'So you are.'

'When was it you had to be in for tonight?'

'Eleven.'

'Then I'll go in with you. Or not with you, just before, or just after.'

'You don't have to.'

'I just want to be in the building in case Mr Morton wants to discuss anything other than cycling.'

'What would you do?'

'I don't know.'

'He's surrounded by apes, and that man, Drago, seems to always be floating by his side.'

'I got a new pistol from the raid yesterday.'

'You have a gun?'

'Don't sound so shocked. It's not like it's my first one.'

'Not the first one?'

'Nor the last. I think there would be more cause for concern if I told you I had just gotten myself an embroidery frame.'

'Can I see it?'

She pulls out a purple velvet pouch with a golden drawstring from her handbag, hands it to him, and nods for him to open it. He fishes out a tiny gun, so small that it disappears in his hand.

'Does it fire properly?' he asks.

'I tried it last night.'

'On someone?'

'No. In the air. To shut someone up.'

'And?'

'To be honest, it's more a showpiece. A decoration for someone's wife. A deterrent rather than a killer I would say.'

'But it fires real bullets.'

'Of course, I just mean it wouldn't rip off an arm or stop a speeding train.'

He looks at it. Turns it this way and that. She takes it from him and says, 'It's mother of pearl, this bit on the handle. The man we were collecting from had a big collection of accordions and concertinas, some of them quite valuable we found out, some of them covered in this pearly stuff. Silly man had this gun to protect himself. It kind of goes well with some of the instruments.'

'It's very small.'

'He had small hands. As do I,' Miriam says and smiles.

'And apart from firing into the air, does it work?'

'I reckon if I put it close enough to someone's temple they wouldn't be able to dodge the bullet. Especially if they were big and fat,' she says.

'You scare me sometimes.'

'Do you mind?' she smiles.

'Not really, as you're so pretty. I find it pretty exciting to be honest.'

'Paul, you're in a funny mood today.'

'I'm sorry. I'm a bit shaken up from meeting him in the pub.' He reaches out and touches her collarbone, just where it meets her throat, just where it's visible.

'Don't worry about it,' she smiles.

'I forget that you're a lady.'

'I am a lady. I'm also not a lady. I like it when you speak your mind.' She turns to face him, looks straight into his eyes, and says, 'Always be honest with me Paul, promise that.'

'I will. On one condition.'

'What?'

'That I don't have to finish this cup of tea.'

She stands up, laughing, and takes his hand. In the front room on a little table are the earrings she managed to wrangle out of her earlobes before she received him. She sits him down on the sofa and closes the curtains. Sits still next to him and asks him to read.

No. 33
Eating, washing, playing, sleeping
A thousand secrets not worth keeping
I was one blood, he another
I still miss him, my little brother

She lies down, putting her head in his lap. In less time than it takes for him to survey the room, the bookshelf, the curtains, she is asleep. Soon he is too, hand in her hair.

***

In the afternoon, when Paul comes back to Copenhagen Street, it's as though he is seeing his attic space for the first time. The scene is atrocious. A long time ago when he moved in he made a conscious decision not to see the room for what it was. A hovel. He couldn't afford to think about it, and the last few months he's been home so little. Sleeping every now and then, but nothing more, and only when he's not away for races, or at Hampstead Heath. Miriam made him promise to never come knocking on the door to her city apartment again. She said she understood he was in some kind of shock, after he explained about seeing Mr Morton in the pub, but he couldn't come by unannounced. Or at all. It was too dangerous. He didn't tell her about the real reason he was so afraid. About the rain, the delay, the forgery. About his luck with the vanished maître d' and the apparent suicide.

Seeing Miriam in her home, rather than at the Turkish baths was different. He lies on his lumpy mattress and wishes he could set up a real home with her. A little house somewhere. Maybe a dog or two. A plot of land. No cows whatsoever. Then he blushes, telling himself to stop being such a girl. She will never leave the city, and neither will he probably. He can't make enough money for a house, and even if he did own a house in the countryside and had ten bread tins of money, he's not sure if she would come with him.

He makes a quick headcount of the money he's made so far. Deducts rent and other costs, mostly inner tubes, apples, eel, and the down payments on the bike. He considers which races are coming up, then he climbs down the ladder and walks down the creaky stairs to Rupert's office. He knocks and to his surprise Silas shouts from the other side of the door.

'You're late. Come in.'

'I'm sorry. I didn't realise we had...'

'Oh, it's you Paul, I didn't know you were in. I was hoping Madame Dubois was coming in today with this month's rent. She's gone over her time you see.'

'Madame Dubois?'

'She's in 2B'

'I see. The one with the friendly women. Always socialising.'

'That's the ones.'

Silas stands up and walks over to the little window. Peers out for a second. Then turns back into the room.

'Now how can I help you Paul?' Silas asks. He looks uncomfortable. Paul thinks it's maybe the heat of the room. Then Paul thinks back on some of the blurry evenings in the summer. And their plans. Their stupid, stupid, drunk and dangerous plans in regards to Mr Morton.

Paul looks down. Suddenly he feels ashamed and he's not sure why, but then he pushes that thought aside, a brusque sweeping of the mind. He looks up and says, 'I want to move out. I wanted to ask Rupert, or yourself, if you know somewhere else. You know a bit bigger. Better.'

'You still owe me a lot of money.'

'I know. And I'm sorry. But I'm doing quite well and I think I should live somewhere where I can sleep properly. Stand up. Have a thing or two of my own. A proper window.'

'I don't want you to move,' Silas blurts out.

'I can't stay.'

'I like to know where you are,' Silas says uncrossing his legs.

'You're afraid I'm not going to pay back the money?'

'Not really. I told you I would find you wherever you went if you chose to disregard our arrangement.'

'So why can't I move?'

'I like to know where you are, that's all. After all, you're my star.'

'I see.'

'And some nights you're not here, is that right?'

'Rupert does a headcount? Does he tuck us all in?'

'It's for your safety, nothing else. Mr Morton has a very short fuse, no one knows quite what will ignite it. I just care about you, that's all,' Silas says leaning back.

'I'd be more than happy to give you the address of where I'm going, if I can find somewhere,' Paul says, now eager to push the sore point.

'Leave it with me,' Silas says and returns to the papers on his desk.

'What do you mean?'

'Just leave it with me and I'll see what I can do.'

'Sure. Thanks.'

'You're not in a rush are you? No one's coming after you? You don't owe money to other people as well?'

'No, no. It's just you.'

'Good. Fine. You know it's just with you running Mr Morton's numbers, I have to be able to get hold of you at short notice.'

'Sure,' Paul says, then continues, 'Speaking of Mr Morton, I'm meeting him tonight.'

'Tonight? Why?'

'I don't know. Because he asked me to come see him at the Carousel.'

'And did he tell you to ask me too?'

'No, not really.'

'Yes or no?'

'He didn't tell me to ask you, but he didn't forbid me to tell you.'

'This isn't good,' Silas says and puts down his pen, 'What made him ask you?'

'I met him at one of the pickup points. I think he's upset about some Russian.'

'Ilya. Bloody bad business that. You know they found his

head two hundred yards further up the line. It had become lodged in one of the headlights of the train engine.'

Paul tries to ignore the icy sheaf in his belly. It's not proving too easy. Changing the subject from what he has done, to what he can do, he asks, 'Anyway I can get out of it you think? You know any late night races I could be going to?'

'I don't think that's a good idea,' Silas answers with a wry smile. A lemon stuck in his throat, kind of smile.

'I'm sure it's harmless,' Paul says. 'He didn't seem too upset. Maybe it's something about the Roman races. Maybe he didn't want to bother you about the details?'

'Maybe. Maybe not. Either way I'm coming with you. He'll have to throw me out if he doesn't want me there. When are you meeting?'

'Eleven. Will I just meet you there?'

'Meet me at the Ram's Head at ten, sharp. Speak to Isaac Holben as soon as you get there. If I can't make it or have any instructions for you I'll leave a message with him.'

Silas crosses his legs again, pulling slightly on the upper trouser leg. Puts an index finger on his lips. Still as a picture. Then he turns to Paul and says, 'You short of money my friend?'

'I won't be late with my rent.'

'I know you won't. That's not what I meant.'

'Well, then yes and no.'

'Here take this.' Silas puts his hand in his jacket pocket and hands Paul a roll of bills held by a rubber band. 'It's not much, but I had some luck with a horse called Tipperary Tim last night. Hundred to One,' Silas says, shaking his head. 'I know the jockey, Little Willie D, and his horse was looking terrible just before the race, so I called out and promised I would be betting on him, just to cheer him up a little, but the only way he would win would be if all the other horses died or fell over. And lo and behold, they did, forty-one horses down, can you imagine?'

'That's mad.'

'I know. It's good to remember the long odds too sometimes. My pocket change made me quite happy so see it as an early Christmas bonus.'

'But it's only November.'

'Very early then.'

There is a shuffle by the door and a giant, heavily made-up woman – a walking empire biscuit – comes in wringing her hands.

'Madame Dubois, so nice to see you,' says Silas.

The woman, in a very deep voice, says 'I'm sorry Silas. There was a mix-up last night, a whole company of sailors, you know how it goes, rum and the girls busy looking at tattoos and talking about foreign places, all wanting to get married to these men, follow them to hot islands, drinking out of coconuts.'

'I'm not sure if I follow you.'

'I'm surrounded by fools, these girls sometimes forget that they work for me.'

'As you forget sometimes that you work for me Madame.'

'No, never. I never forget.'

'Rent. Let's talk about rent. And why it's not here on my desk today.'

'Well, I can explain. You see...'

Silas turns to Paul with an apologetic smile, 'This might take a while. I'll see you later.'

Then he turns back to the woman who wears a dress too small for her and says, 'Let's get this over with, shall we?'

Chapter 26

I knew it. I knew it. I knew it. The boy is going to end up getting himself killed. Not because he'd ever do anything bad, but because he's a giant, trusting boy in a man's exquisite body.

After Madame Dubois leaves, promising rent plus ten percent in the next three days, I sit and look out the grimy window. I pour a drink from a bottle I keep in the desk. The rat is scurrying around in its box and I feed it some dry bacon from a tin I keep next to my bottle. My head is still empty after the second drink, so I put on my suit jacket and my coat, unfurl my umbrella, and leave the house. Copenhagen Street and its inhabitants, the human rats I keep in the brick box, soon behind me. It's easier to think when walking. It's raining, but I don't mind. Less people to bump into.

People don't think I am very compassionate. Some would say all I am is an opportunist; a lowly moneylender and fixer of boxing matches, cock fights, greyhound races. But people don't know me. I care for Paul. For Rupert and the Baker brothers in a way. I care for Madame Dubois and her girls. I even gave her an extra week to come up with the funds.

And now I have to go over to the Elephant Emperor's palace. Not what I had in mind for my evening. I've never liked the place. It's massive for one, you never know who's there and who's not. Who's coming or going. You can never get to know the people, never maintain any useful contacts. And maybe that's exactly what Mr Morton wants. He ensures such a high turnover of staff that none of them ever get to know anything. No routines, no secret paths, no schemes. No congeniality, no friendships, no plans, will ever take root there. There's too little time for the luckless few who are forced by circumstances to work for him to get acquainted, and it's always so busy. Mr

Morton is also very good at sneaking up on people, sniffing out any kinds of intrigue, that I don't think it ever enters people's heads to revolt.

Over the years I must have met hundreds of his employees, but I can't say I remember many of them. Apart from Miriam, his pretty orphan, Drago the despicable Austro-Hungarian or whatever he is, and the two monkey men on the front door, whom I don't credit with speaking English, or any other language, there seems to be an ever-changing sea of faces.

I leave Copenhagen Street and walk for about twenty minutes with no particular destination in my mind. The rain, which at first was charming, has now gotten heavier. It's bouncing an inch off the pavement so I hail a taxi. I was going to nurse my hangover, read the Washington Post, and as my luck was quite remarkable last night, have dinner at the Savoy. Later on I'm booked on the last train to Cheltenham with Rupert. It's a postal train leaving half past twelve. They usually hitch a first-class carriage onto the back, a service they put on for the Cheltenham events. Speeding west, they will sort the mail while we gossip about jockeys.

I have lost my appetite and instead of enjoying the day I have to worry. I will miss the train, my outing and reward. There's also a real possibility that Mr Morton has plans which will result in the death of Paul. I would miss the boy terribly if that was the case. The taxi stops outside my house and I hurry inside to have a bath and to think.

***

To my relief Paul is waiting for me at the Ram's Head, chatting away to Isaac. Paul's wearing what almost could pass as a new shirt, with a kind of Chinese collar to it, not sure if I like it. He's got an elbow propped up on the bar, foot on the brass rail, looking more relaxed than he should be. Than I am. I buy Isaac a drink, and a whisky for myself, but I don't have much to say. Too many things going through my mind. I half listen to Paul describing something to do with motor-paced racing, where the cyclists are pulled along the circuit by a man on a motorbike.

'Speeds of up to twenty miles an hour,' Paul says. Isaac laughs a drunk's laugh and shakes his head. He holds onto the cashier so as to not fall over. Someone could walk off with Isaac's trousers and he wouldn't notice. He catches me looking at him, and without asking hands me a Bibi and a small glass of ice, as though I was the one who was drunk. After listening some more to Paul, Isaac's called upstairs by a rough-looking man in a Fur Felt Broadway. A terrible hat for a strongarm, if you ask me. Isaac leans heavily on the man who doesn't seem to notice, must be used to it. As they go upstairs the shouts and insults of patrons and punters increase. Seconds later I hear the crashes of another drinking session gone sour. It is clear that Isaac's man was straining at the leash. He just needed his master to come upstairs and release him.

I glance at the clock above the bar mirror. Then, not trusting it I get out my own watch. It's a buckled, rubbed old thing on a chain. It's only a *Chemin de Fer*, nothing special, used for sentimental reasons more than anything. My doublechecking pays off, the bar clock is slow by twenty minutes, that way they extend the licensing hour a little. I put a hand on Paul's shoulder, indicating it's time to go across the road. A table crashes against the balustrade upstairs and then two chairs come toppling down the broad stairs. Cartwheeling disasters made from oak.

'Come on Paul, time for us to go. Unless you want to join in upstairs?'

'No, thank you. Besides you told me to never be late for Mr Morton again.'

I can't tell if he's serious or pulling my leg. Never can.

The Elephant Emperor receives us in his hidden office with his usual flourishes. Inquires about our health. Parents.

Prospects. As if we had a communal life Paul and I. Asks about our day, as if we spent every waking minute together, grooming each other like a pair of monkeys. As if we were on honeymoon and not summoned.

'Silas, I'm surprised to see you here,' he says. He's standing behind his desk, the two of us are sitting on uncomfortable kitchen chairs in front of it.

'Well, I was in the area. Just bumped into Paul at the Ram's Head. Thought I'd drop by.'

'You were in the area?'

'Yes. But you know, if this is something you want to discuss with just Paul that's fine, I'm happy to go back. I had a good run on the cards with some clueless chaps from Somerset.'

'No, stay. It's good that you're here actually. Saves me explaining the same thing twice.'

I can see he's annoyed. In my mind I resign myself to leading a simple life on a small island somewhere. A goat, a chicken or two. A small, tattered library. Half a bottle of ouzo. Maybe getting by with one arm less, or if I'm lucky, just a hand. I don't know what we have done, but judging by the gaiety in Mr Morton's voice, the way he trips around like a portly frog in raw white silk, he must have a bloodbath on his mind.

So when he says, 'You two have become my favourite little thing to think about,' I am at first scared witless. Then I realise he's serious, and I'm so relieved I almost pee in my pants. I have to wiggle a little in my seat to stop a drop from escaping.

'I think you've found yourself a good project Silas. You're fattening him up, whetting him, all that. In short, making him a champ.'

'Thank you,' I stammer like a girl at her first communion. Out of turn.

'Now, I've been looking at the books. Apart from a week here and there I feel Paul could maybe have done a little better. Pushed himself a little harder. But I'm not complaining. You'd know if I was.'

He puts a finger in his ear, holds it there for a second, looking into the middle distance, then shakes it in a series of spasms. Then he takes out his finger, and looks at it. There's a wistful, disappointed look about him. More human than I have ever seen him, and this over the lack of wax. Then he looks up, 'The venture is not a great earner,' he continues, 'but luckily I have other areas which bring in money for food on the table. This messing about on bikes is a nice little sideline, something that amuses me. Like pigeons, or darts or something. It's inconsequential, but fun. Well done Paul.'

'You're welcome,' the boy says, as if he's made a cake for the local society.

'You see young man,' Mr Morton continues, for the first time tonight addressing Paul, 'Silas here had been on the ropes for a while, a few years in fact, and I was debating not when, but where, to put him out to pasture. But that was before you came along. And look at him now, the coat, the lustre in his little Greek eyes when he looks at you. If you didn't know better you'd think he was a man in love.'

He walks around the desk and gives me a playful punch in the arm, and I die many deaths inside. Mr Morton always thought of himself as some sort of natural boxer, waylaid by his godlike ability to make money. I smile, a strained smile. It's one that I know looks natural, from years of practice with a mirror.

'Now gents,' Mr Morton says bringing over his abacus from a shelf, 'I've got a suggestion.'

He sits down behind his desk and fiddles with the beads. Moves all the ones in the top row to the right, the ones on the second tier all the way to the left and so on. Then he continues, 'I think that with a little more discipline and training, sufficient physical exercise and a more restrained diet, Paul you could really make something of yourself. I speak to a lot of people, and when I mention your name, they quite often whisper 'Olympics, next time around,' back to me. Wouldn't that be exciting? What an honour. Imagine how proud your family would be to see their son in the paper? A golden medal around his neck. I wouldn't expect anything less. Representing his country. Representing me.'

'Yes, yes that would be great,' Paul says shooting a glance at me. This is all news to me and I shrug my shoulders as imperceptibly as I can.

Should Paul play along, telling Mr Morton that 'Yes, I would like to become an Olympian'? Should he deny his wish to cycle and swear his allegiance to Mr Morton's business empire? It could go either way. I don't know. Speaking to Mr Morton is like being forced out on thin spring ice. You know it's going to crack, you know you'll end up wet, probably with hypothermia and pneumonia, but you have to walk on, not knowing where the crack is going to appear.

'To achieve this goal,' Mr Morton continues, 'I have decided to bring in an auxiliary trainer. A friend of mine. He has recently left the army. Something unsavoury that you'll probably hear about anyway, but I'm convinced it's a stitch-up. You know those Sandhurst types, they'd sell their own grandma for another bar on the chest.'

'I think we are doing fine, with all due respect, Mr Morton,' I say, forgetting to think before I open my mouth.

'Yes, you might think you are, but your thoughts don't account for much. I hold the money, I hold the reins. Try to remember this Silas.'

He continues, 'Nathaniel Jones, his name is. Served in the Kent Cyclist Battalion. As soon as he's had a drink he talks about cycling through the ruined villages of the Somme, in that high-pitched theatrical voice of failed war poets. Just make sure you water down his beer, and he needs help remembering his quinine tablets.'

'Sounds great,' I pitch in, in a neutral voice, beyond reproach.

'He's a hero, did more than you to win the war Silas. He

saw some action in that Anglo-Afghan affair too, I'm not sure what that did to him. Last time I saw him he affected a limp, something he claimed had to do with being shot, but I'm not so sure. I think it's gout rather than shrapnel.'

'Quite the man,' Paul says in a similar neutral voice to mine. He's learned something, which, despite the situation, makes me proud.

Mr Morton nods and goes on, 'Nathaniel's a real hard man. He swears by strict routines and a healthy lifestyle. I think he could really whip you into shape Paul. And also keep an eye on your comings and goings, young man. This isn't a holiday in the sun you realise.'

'I don't know what to say Mr Morton.'

'Thank you?'

'Thank you,' Paul says, then looks at me and I say the same.

'When is he joining us?' I ask.

'I've had considerable trouble finding him. He's been holed up somewhere in India for months, waiting for his marching orders, as he puts it, but I know better. It has 'dishonourable' all over it, not that I mind. Do you Silas?'

'About what? The man, the Afghan war, the end to his career? All of the above? No, no.'

'Good man. I think Nathaniel could be good for you too. He doesn't miss a thing, and he could get rid of that flabby stomach of yours too. Make sure you're in bed early.'

'Good,' I say, 'I could use a man like that. A nanny.' No irony in my voice whatsoever.

'I've arranged for a passage for him and he should be here to crack his whip before the end of the month.'

Mr Morton puts the abacus, which he has been cradling like a lapdog on its last legs, on the desk and stands up. Groans a little. 'So gentlemen, we're in agreement that this is a good idea? That this will lift Paul's cycling to the next level? To an Olympian level? That he'll bring me at least a silver medal, yes?'

The two of us nod. There's nothing else to do.

'Good. I'm glad. Now, if you'll excuse me, I've got a couple of things on my desk today. Things that bring in money, real money.'

He roots about in a drawer and brings up a box of cigars. He pats his pockets in constrained frenzy. Like a Red Indian dance to make matches appear, or at least like the Red Indian I once saw on Margate Pier. Then he waves his hand, five flying Cumberland sausages, in our direction. To end the misery I light a match from my box for him. He nods and says, 'Goodbye gentlemen. Please show yourselves out.'

Just as we reach the door, Mr Morton turns from the secret window overlooking the pub and plucks the cigar out of his mouth, 'Paul, before you go.'

'Yes?'

'There is one thing relating to Captain Sergei Ilyashenko Petrovich that I wanted to ask you.'

'Anything. I only met the man a handful of times.'

'Still.'

'I don't think I can shed any light. Look, I don't even know what the trouble is. Was. What he did. Is it money?'

'Of course it's about money, but this is different.'

Mr Morton turns to us, a certain glint in his eye.

'I was wondering if you wanted to do me a favour,' he asks.

'Of course.'

'I wasn't asking. When will you learn?'

'Sorry.'

'Ilya's apartment in Fitzrovia is a mess. You know where it is don't you? You've been there?'

'I have, but not inside. Mostly downstairs at the restaurant. Up the servant's backstairs a couple of times.'

'But you wouldn't get lost trying to get there?'

'No I wouldn't,' Paul says, his voice flat.

Mr Morton looks at him for a few long seconds, then continues, 'I'm renting out the apartment to a rich Belgian. He's a diplomat or something, and he's bringing his own furniture. I've sold most of Ilya's possessions. In the middle of the dining room is a pile of carpets, all rolled up, you can't miss them. I want you to hire a cart. You're used to horses aren't you? You're from some sort of farm I believe. Take these carpets to Copenhagen Street, which is handy, because Silas tells me that's where you live.'

'Where do you want me to store the carpets? In the office?'

'No, no that wouldn't be very suitable. Not very suitable at all. No, here's what I want you to do, throw them down the shaft. Has Rupert shown you?'

Paul nods.

'Good. Well these carpets, though initially quite expensive, Persian I believe, are now ruined. Wine, gravy, that kind of thing. They're an insurance write-off. It's better for everyone if they are never found.'

'That's fine. Consider it done sir.'

'I do.'

'When do you want me to do it?'

'Are you joking?'

'No. Sorry.'

'I just asked you. I want it done now.'

'Of course, immediately.'

'Now get out of my sight you two. I have some real business to deal with before I leave tonight. If I'm late for confession I'm blaming you.'

Mr Morton then unbuttons his jacket, and says to Paul, 'You're a big strong man, I would usually ask two people to do this but the ones I tend to use are busy somewhere else. You've met David and Henry, the baker brothers, haven't you?'

'Only in passing.'

'Here's a key for Ilya's house, and the flat. Just leave it in Rupert's office once you're done.'

Paul and I stand up, then Mr Morton turns to me, 'Are you not going to thank me?'

'Sorry sir, I don't quite follow,' I say.

'Well, I thought I'd be nice to you. Finish early.'

'I don't understand, but I appreciate it all the same.'

'Well don't you have a train to catch at half past? For Cheltenham I believe.'

'I do, with your permission.' Mr Morton chuckles and waves his hand in mid-air.

'Goodbye you old fruitcake and take your giant with you. Make sure he doesn't screw up.'

We leave and step outside in the dark. Behind us, in front of us, the shouts of revellers. I glance at my pocket watch, then wave to one of the many taxis Mr Morton forces to idle outside. 'To make it easier for people to come and go,' he says.

'I'm away for a night or two Paul, and so is Rupert. I mean it doesn't matter, we've been away in the past, but would you mind just keeping an extra eye on the house for us?'

'Doing what?'

'Alert the fire services if there's a fire. Throw out Madame Dubois' men if they are found sleeping in the corridors. That sort of thing.'

'Alright. I'll probably be up all night carting carpets anyway.'

'Yes, now, go and do that as soon as you can. At any cost. Buy a cart if you have to. He's sure to check tomorrow morning.'

'I will. I will,' Paul says, looking tired. Rolling his shoulders.

'I'm off. Wish me luck on the horses,' I say before retreating into a taxi.

And with that I tap the driver on the shoulder and tell him to go to Paddington. He looks relieved to be on his way somewhere else. And so am I. I always enjoy seeing the Carousel getting smaller and smaller in the rear-view mirror of a taxi.

Chapter 27

Paul watches the taxi disappear into the darkness. Then he hears Miriam saying 'Coffeehouse' in an urgent whisper, but he can't see her. It sounds like the voice is coming from above him, but it's hard to tell. He looks around the corner and up at the façade of the Carousel, but can't see anything.

He walks towards the coffeehouse, which is closed, as it's now past midnight. The windows are dark and the shutters are pulled down. Coming closer he sees a black and gold feather in the lock and tries the door. It's open. He walks in and at first he can't see anything. Then he sees the red pinprick of a cigarette move slowly, like Mars in the night sky.

As his eyes get used to the dark he can see her outlines. She's sitting on a high stool, one high-heeled shoe dangling off her right foot. Her hat is on the counter and she's holding the oxblood Bakelite holder in her right hand. Next to her an almost empty glass of milk.

'How was it Paul?' she asks.

'Fine.'

'Really?'

'Really. All he wanted to tell us was that he's bringing in some sort of physical trainer for me.'

'You don't need that. All you do is exercise.'

'I know, but Mr Morton wants this Major to come and work for him, work on me, so that's that.'

'Who is he?'

'I don't know. A Nathaniel something. You know him?'

'Never heard of him.'

He walks over to her and she puts out the cigarette in the last centimetre of milk. Wafts away the smoke before offering her cheek for a kiss.

'Not on the lips, this red stuff takes ages to apply. I have to go back to work in five minutes, told them I was only stepping outside for some fresh air.'

'Shame.'

'I know.'

'Did you bring that gun?'

'Of course, why? Do you want it?'

'No, just wondering.'

'What's on your mind?'

'Well, if it's not safe for me in there, then it can't be all that safe for you either.'

'Don't worry about me,' she says, putting her head to one side. 'You don't worry about me do you?'

'Of course I do.'

'That's sweet, come and kiss me on the other cheek.' He obeys, happily. Then she continues, 'You don't have to. I can manage.'

'I know. But I still worry.'

'Come here, I can put on more lipstick later. Give me a kiss. Then I have to be off.'

Their clothes rustle in the dark of the coffeehouse as they kiss. He bites her earlobes, kisses her on the neck as far down as her blouse will let him. Her hands are strong, gripping him around the head, like a heavy urn she is afraid of dropping. Then finally she pushes him away from her.

'My time is up,' she says and pulls her dress into shape again.

'When will I see you again?' he asks.

'Whenever you want to. Just not now.'

'Fine,' he smiles.

'Why don't you invite me to see your place? I know it's dangerous, but I want to see where you live. We can be careful.'

'You mean my room at Copenhagen Street?'

'Is that Silas' house?'

'Yes. I'll tell you why I've not asked you over.'

'Don't tell me – you're married, and have eleven children.'

'Twelve, these last ones were twins.'

'Be quiet. Tell me why.'

'Because it's awful, and small.'

'We don't have to do ballroom dancing. Just a quick drink and then we can go somewhere else. Come on.'

'Well, I suspect you knew this before you asked, but both Silas and Rupert are away for two nights, Cheltenham I think, you know, the horses.'

'And?'

'So I would like to invite you for dinner. Tomorrow, at seven? Even though it's just in an attic space.'

'And I will gracefully accept, but come on now, get out of here so that I can lock up.'

She puts her hat on, asks him to help her with the feather. 'You going home now?'

'No, I've got a small errand to run first, something Mr Morton asked me to do. Then the baker, the butcher, the cleaner, the washing lady, the candlestick maker, the florist, and whoever else I need to make you happy.'

She just smiles at him. Out in the street, she says, 'I'm fine with porridge.'

'Salty?'

'No thanks,' she says slipping the key out of the lock, 'just a little cream and a lot of honey,' she laughs. She slips off into the night, back towards the club.

Paul walks off, his eyes trained on carts and horses. He walks for almost half an hour, asking people if they will lend him a horse and cart. Some people laugh. Most spit. Even when he offers them money.

He starts to worry and think of cheese wire and walks faster, tries to cover as much ground as possible, still heading towards Fitzrovia. On a corner outside a pub called the White Anchor stands a huge, blinkered Shire tethered to an empty cart. Paul leans against a lamppost until he is sure no one is walking in and out of the pub, using the cart for deliveries.

As Paul is used to these hay-munching machines – different beasts altogether from the nervous ballerinas Silas talks about – he makes a big show of not being in a hurry. Despite being about to steal a living animal Paul smiles to himself. Sneaking about in the dark was something he could never do before. Before coming to London, before meeting Silas, before starting to move in the kind of social pond the Greek swims in like a graceful carp.

Paul straightens one of the horse's blinkers, pats its flank. He decides to name the horse Terry Grant, after the current, motor-paced champion. He thinks this is very funny as the horse couldn't be any more unlike the cyclist, who's a whippet; a lightning-fast starter and famous for not eating vegetables. Unlike the horse, who could happily be munching through bale after bale by the looks of it.

'Meat and bread, cream and milk, boiled sweets,' the real Terry told Paul one afternoon after a race, 'that's my diet, my winning formula.' Paul had just won the race and Terry had come over to congratulate him. He himself was due to try for a one-hour record behind the motorbike in the afternoon. Paul wished him luck and watched him wheel his curious-looking bike over to the weights and measures table manned by stern judges. It had a smaller front wheel than back wheel, forks turned backwards to make the front wheel come closer to the down tube, and a long low handlebar. All this to enable him to get closer to the back wheel of the motorbike and to reduce the amount of wind he has to push in front of him.

Paul unites the reins from the railing and slowly, slowly, walks over to the cart and gets up. He slowly rolls away from the kerb, hoping the owner has decided to treat himself to one more pint. To Paul, the clip-clop of Terry's hooves sound like gunshots in the night, but no one comes running out of the pub.

Paul heads over to Fitzrovia, sliding around on the well-worn bench as the wheels jump on cobbles. He pats his pocket every now and then to make sure the keys for the apartment haven't fallen out.

Finding the right building, he steps down from the cart. He surveys the closed Russian restaurant on the ground floor. No sound, no light, no movement.

'Mind waiting here for a moment Mr Grant?' he says and ties the reins to a lamppost.

As there's no one to receive him at the front he goes to the back staircase, the servant's entrance. Once in the flat he moves around in the dawn light, going through bare rooms, like a museum robbed of all its riches, counting his steps. It's as big as a rugby pitch, he thinks. The parquet floors creak a little. The walls still show marks of habitation. The empty spaces of paintings removed. Where cigar smoke hasn't been able to penetrate as readily, where sunlight has been unable to bleach. All the furniture has been taken away apart from in an office the size of a train carriage. There's a big desk covered in a white sheet. Six brass lion paws peeking out from under the shroud.

In the centre of the apartment, nearer the main entrance, is the circular grand hall. An inlaid compass rose, faux marine marquetry, takes up most of the floor. The big double doors open up to the main marble staircase, Paul finds out when he tries one of his keys.

Just beyond the hall, in what looks like it was the library, he finds the six rolls of carpet on a bottle-green tarp. All tied together with coarse bits of string, all plugged either side with bits of fabric.

He carries them down, straining a bit as they're heavier than they look. After six trips, up and down the slippery, worn marble stairs, he's happy to lean against the cart. Terry hasn't moved at all. A statue of a horse without a general on top stealing the limelight.

Paul takes the reins and, only stopping for a cup of tea and a roll – a well-deserved breakfast he feels – takes the cart to

Copenhagen Street. He dumps the carpet rolls by the door to 2C. Once they're all up he opens the door, now ready to duck for bats. Only this time none come out. He pushes five of the rolls over the edge and is just about to push the last one over the threshold when one of the fabric plugs comes out. Trying to put it back, and accidentally reaching inside the roll he feels something odd. Something soft. And wet.

He takes out his hand and it's covered in red. He can't understand what it is at first. Then it hits him. His hand is drenched in red blood, and strands of dark hair cling to his fingers like seaweed. His stomach lurches as he realises what he's seeing. He prods the carpet with his foot, now suddenly afraid of it. It stays still. He kicks it again. It's the same weight and girth as the other ones. With shaking hands he unties the rope and slowly unfolds the carpet. One quick look shows him a small, dark man. Dead. Hair matted and plastered with blood. Skull caved in, a dark hole where his forehead used to be. Eyes wide open.

Paul carefully closes the carpet. Then he's violently sick. Holding onto the door frame he hacks up phlegm, bile, and what feels like all the food he's ever eaten. He hangs there, face cold with sweat, arms seizing up from holding on, head spinning from the disgusting reality and the terrifying implications.

Then a door downstairs opens and he hears slow steps come up towards him. He doesn't think to move the carpet. David comes around the corner of the stairs out onto the landing and walks slowly towards Paul.

'How you getting on?' David asks looking at the carpet.

'I'm fine,' Paul says dragging the back of his hand across his mouth. It becomes wet with saliva and vomit.

'You look terrible.'

'Sorry.'

'Nothing to apologise for. I take it you're doing Mr Morton a favour?'

'How did you know?'

'Well, I shouldn't really tell you this, but you would have found out sooner or later anyway, and being as close to Silas as you are, you must come across some pretty interesting scenarios.'

'I'm not sure what you mean. I mostly just cycle.'

'Sure you do. I mean, did you really think we were bakers?'

'Are you not?'

'And did you really think we were pouring flour down the shaft?'

'What were you pouring?'

'Is that carpet roll full of what I think it is?'

'What do you think it is?'

'A body.'

'The last of six.'

'We call that a *medium-sized batch of bread*.'

'I see,' is all Paul can say.

'Come on, let's go and get a couple of bags of flour,' David says gently pulling Paul back from the precipice.

'Flour?' Paul asks.

'Lye,' David smiles sadly. 'It eats up the flesh and dissolves the bones in a couple of days.'

'You do this all the time?'

'Every now and then. It pays the rent.'

'It's not right.'

'I know. I used to get angry too. I used to be sick as well,' David says looking at Paul's splattered shoes. 'But over time I've become immune to it. My brother, on the other hand, can't handle it. It drives him to drink.'

'I'm going to be sick again I'm afraid.'

'Go outside, get some fresh air. I'll tip this last unfortunate bastard in. Meet me by my door for the flour?'

Paul runs down the stairs, and outside to a drain. However much he heaves there's nothing more to come out of his stomach. After a while of sitting on the ground thinking of nothing, absolutely nothing, he hears Terry snort. He's still standing where Paul left him. He walks over to the horse and puts his head against its flanks. Paul's cheeks are wet and he thinks of the ticket he made up, and how his silly mistake, and the weather, has now killed at least seven people. If not more.

Eventually David shouts at him from the front door, and Paul unties Terry. Kisses him on the twitching ears, then slaps him on the flank, sending him into a slow trot. The name and address of a brewer is printed in large letters on the side of the cart so Paul hopes someone will take the horse home. Or that Terry like a giant homing pigeon will find his way to the White Anchor.

Paul returns to the house to help David carry the massive bags, marked *Flour*, up to 2C. Holding their breath they pour lye down into the black hole, onto the bodies of men he's carried but never known.

Then David says, 'I've got a surprise for you.'

'What is it?'

'Something Rupert asked me to do, something nice. On a decree from Silas I think. Nothing to do with this,' he says and nods towards the open door. Then he reaches in and closes it. 'You'll see in the morning. It'll make you feel better I think.'

David walks off whistling a Christmas carol. Paul trundles upstairs and up the ladder. It's not easy going to sleep, but he takes some of his after-race pills. *Neutralisers*, Silas calls them. Paul's heart rate drops and soon his thoughts are treacle slow. He can't remember falling asleep, but he wakes up thirsty and dazed.

Downstairs there is the sound of someone screaming and cursing. Paul comes down his ladder and finds David standing with folded arms in front of the Sorensen's door. Mr Sorensen is shouting. First at his wife, telling her to take the children downstairs. Then he turns to David. 'You can't do this. We have always paid on time. We are only late by a day. Come on.'

David just shakes his head and points to the stairs. Mr

Sorensen starts walking away, then he suddenly turns and lunges for David. Quicker than a bird in flight David punches Mr Sorensen in the nose, then follows in with a left hook to the eye. After that he steps to one side, and Mr Sorensen, still carried by his own momentum, goes down. He falls into the wall and comes up shaking his head, bleeding from a cut eyebrow.

'Goodbye Mr Sorensen. Now please leave before I ask Henry to come and help me escort you out.'

Then Mr Sorensen notices Paul standing on the other side of the landing. He points and shouts, 'Your pimp did this. This is all your fault.'

David gives Mr Sorensen a shove in the back and the man stumbles down the stairs, spattering the stairs with blood. David starts down the stairs after him and says to Paul, 'Rupert asked me to do this. You can move in your things this afternoon if you fancy. We'll just have the cleaner make it a bit nicer.'

'What about rent?'

'It stays the same.'

'Did Silas do this?' Paul asks, incredulous.

David just nods, before shouting to Mr Sorensen to get out of the house.

In one trip Paul transfers his belongings from the attic to the vacated room. He carries the bike down the ladder, like always. He's relieved he doesn't have to show Miriam his attic space. The house is bad enough as it is, but at least he now has a room where he can stand straight.

He places his belongings on the little table by the window. The room is bare, nothing on the walls or in the two cupboards mounted to the wall above the single ring cooker. There is a wide mattress though which makes him smile. It's old and well used, probably twice his age, but it's sprung – and it's not too lumpy, he decides after a quick test. He wheels his bike in from the corridor. He leans it against the wall by the sleeping alcove. He still can't believe his luck at getting his hands on such a fine bike. It's been his most trusted friend since coming to London.

He decides to buy an offcut of carpet that can house the bike, have a special place for it, like a favourite dog. He wants to treat it better in the future, now that he has the space to fiddle with it standing up. He makes a shopping list in his mind. First the carpet, then oil, the best Mr Lauterwasser has, maybe even a bit of polish for the chrome and new bar tape.

Laughing softly at his own silliness for treating the bike like a pet he strokes the saddle. The leather is scuffed but not beyond repair. The shape perfectly formed, a mould of his hardworking buttocks. On the list in his mind goes leather saddle soap. Maybe even a new chain. On top of all this – a giant bag of dried apricots. Very expensive, but a treat to have when he's out and about.

Then he stands by the window for a moment or two, watching Copenhagen Street. It's a river of people, buses, bikes, carts, horses and stalls. Then the magic happens. Feathers of snow, slowly at first, but quickly increasing in size and weight, start to whirl in the air. It's icing sugar on a grey world. Soon people are pulling scarves tighter, putting up umbrellas and looking for taxis.

Getting a pen and a paper out of his knapsack Paul walks around the room, like a potential buyer. First he writes down all the bike-related things. It'll be nice to see Jack at the bike shop again, he thinks. Realises it's been ages. Then he writes: curtains, a pillow, a warm duvet; the thickest he can afford, now that winter is here. He writes a list of essentials.

A knock on the door surprises him. As he puts his hand on the handle, he realises it feels like a great luxury to have a door again. No more ladder, no more always banging his head, no more of the lumpy mattress. The cleaning lady stands outside, and though he tries to tell her the room is fine, she tells him Silas would kill her if she didn't do her job. He lets her in, takes the list, but leaves the bike, that's a novel feeling too, and heads out into the gentle snow.

First thing he does outside is to buy two lengths of fabric. Then he runs straight back up and asks the cleaning lady to help him put them up. She smiles at him, tells him they don't just go up, he needs a rail and a bit of sewing. Then, seeing his shock, she tells him to fetch a hammer and a dozen nails from her cupboard downstairs, and he puts them up that way. Temporarily, but more cosy than just the bare window. Once they're done he asks her if she can bake him a cake, and she says she will.

Later in the evening, after he's bought wine, and suffered the jokes from Madame Dubois after he realised he didn't have a corkscrew and went down to borrow one, he boils potatoes, cuts up mint, makes gravy and checks on a joint of meat. While he waits for the greengrocer's boy to deliver the rest of the things he's bought he puts on a fresh shirt and polishes his new secondhand boots till he can see his own grinning face in them. There's a knock on the door and since he's expecting the cleaning lady with a cake, he shouts for her to enter. Turning around, after rearranging the two candles and the vase of flowers on the table for the fourth time in as many minutes, he sees her: Miriam. She's early. She's perfect. His heart skips a beat. She looks different in his house. She's too beautiful, too clear. Too much for him surely. It must be a trick. For her to like him, to want to spend her time with him, can't be normal.

'Come in, let me take your coat,' he says, abandoning the candles and the flowers. She smiles but doesn't say anything. On his way over he pushes a pile of greaseproof wrapping papers and his wet jacket under the bed. She circles the room, runs a finger along some of the surfaces. She stands by the window for a minute, still with her coat and hat on.

'It's not much, but it's mine. Well not mine, but you know what I mean,' he stammers, suddenly nervous.

'Sorry I'm early,' she says, smiling.

'That's fine. It's nice to have you here. But how did you know this was my flat? I only just moved in.'

'Your bike is outside.'

He swears and runs out to get it, bumping into the cleaning woman. She apologises for putting the bike outside, but the floor is nice and clean now, he must have noticed. Paul brings the cake and the bicycle inside, causing Miriam to laugh. Then the little boy turns up with a mountain of bags and boxes, and the little congregation stand on the small landing. Paul is beaming and starts doling out money to the woman and the boy, who both laugh at his happiness. It's a friendly sound rarely heard in the house.

'Good thing I was inside already,' she says once the boy and the woman leave. 'It's probably better if I'm seen as little as possible.'

He nods, serious all of a sudden. Puts down the cake on the table.

'It's nice,' she says once he's back to take her coat.

He shrugs. 'It's bare and it's cold, but it's the beginnings of something like a home I think.'

She gives him her coat and stands by the stove rubbing her hands. He pours wine into two glasses and they clink them together. She's quiet, and he's fidgety. She's cold and he's hot from the running around.

He pulls out a chair and she sits, unfolding a napkin in her lap. She watches him put clam broth from a tin, in two tea-cups.

'It's maybe not Quaglino's,' he says, 'but I really like this stuff. Sorry, I only have two dinner plates.'

They eat in silence. As if they have known each other for longer than a few months. He likes it. He knows he could ask her things, make her smile, laugh even, but at the moment it's nice to just chew, and watch, and sip and live.

After the main course he clears the table. He serves her

cognac and himself hot ginger beer in the same teacups they had the clam broth in.

'It's good to put something strong and warming on top of the meat and potato,' he says. And onto the crystallized lemon cake the woman made for him. He stretches his legs and she smiles a tired smile, looks at the bed. Without a word they walk over to it. He folds away a thick tartan blanket and the new duvet and pillow as she undresses. Then he walks over to the table and blows out the candles. Not because it's not romantic, but because he knows he wants to fall asleep quickly. Today he's made sure to be really busy, to never stop to think. With the events of the previous night he wants to either be distracted by Miriam or go to sleep as soon as possible. They distract each other for a while, until they are nice and warm, then they fall asleep.

Chapter 28

In the morning Paul can tell she's worried. Or at least not as comfortable as she could be. He realises the risk they are taking, whether Silas and Rupert are away or not. She asks him to come to the Heath later in the evening as she has to go to work. Miriam's coat and general look is more unremarkable than usual and she slips away from the house unnoticed.

Paul spends the morning slowly clearing up. Enjoying the space and the heavy feeling in his bones from the night before. After lunch he cycles over to Jack's to celebrate. The snow didn't lie. The only evidence it was ever there are tiny banks of sleet gathered in places the sun hasn't reached.

He chats a little to Jack, who is apologetic, but the shop is busy. Christmas isn't too far off. Paul is glad to have gone out and glad to come back home. Glad to put his bike up and clean it properly, put new grease in the headset, put the new chain on. Glad to fill his mind with safe, tangible, predictable machinery.

He potters around for ages in his shirtsleeves, with cups of tea on the go, with tools and bits spread around him like water lilies on a pond. Then one of Mr Morton's runner boys comes to the door and tells him he's needed for a delivery.

Paul fears it's going to be something connected with Ilya, but it turns out to be the birthday of one of Mr Morton's mistresses and Paul has to go to various florists and boutiques to pick up parcels going to an address off Regent Street. It takes Paul most of the afternoon to sort out Mr Morton's love life, but he doesn't mind. Anything is better than carpets or even the same runs of numbers to the same places week after week.

After the last delivery Paul goes out to the Carousel to

report, and to check if there's anything else he needs to do. He's relieved to speak only to Drago and not to Mr Morton himself. Paul's let off the hook for the rest of evening, and goes out to Hampstead Heath, Miriam waits for him in the lobby, and, when he arrives home, sweeps him upstairs and straight into bed. A polite knock on the door a while later tells them that dinner is standing on a tray outside the door. Paul puts on a bathrobe and gets the food, and they eat in silence. Then he gets back into bed. He puts another pillow behind his head. He's warm, sleepy and waiting for her to come back from the bathroom. They could have stayed at his, the evening before was near perfect, he thinks, although she had fallen asleep in his bed before he had even cleared the table. But they couldn't risk it. Just in case the horses weren't working out for Silas, or in case they really had come up trumps, and he came back early to celebrate.

When she comes back, her hair unpinned, she picks up her Family Tree book. She opens it for him, folds back the covers and comes wriggling up to him. Really close, with one leg over his. Her feet blocks of ice. Then she looks up at him. Her eyes are big and childlike, but her commanding nod would scare a furious Angus bull.

So he starts:

> No. 36
> *As a python coils around its prey*
> *As a starling sings at the break of day*
> *Two sides compete in me for space*
> *Violence and deceit, beauty and grace*

He reads it twice, then looks down at her. Fully expecting she will be asleep, her breathing slow since he started reading. But she's not, and she mouths 'Thank you', and kisses him on the hand.

'These verses aren't very good,' she says.

'I think they're lovely.'

'It's alright Paul. They're mine and that matters more.'

He bends down to kiss her. She kisses him back, slowly, slowly. Her feet are soon warm and her legs too.

They sleep close.

In the morning she is up well before him. He lies in bed, eyes half-closed. Then she comes back to bed and properly wakes him up with kisses.

Putting an arm behind her head, he asks, 'Have you ever been to Coventry?'

'No, but I've been in that part of the country more than I care to remember,' she says with a frown.

'I see. Would you like to go? Maybe this time it will be better?'

'Why Coventry? Oh let me guess, some bloody velodrome?'

'It's my job. It's not that bad surely?'

'Oh, and here's me thinking you had planned something romantic. Whisking me off to a seaside hotel or a Scottish castle, and all you've got to offer is Coventry. You think I'm going to ride through the city naked with you on the bike. Like Godiva and you the peeping Tom?'

'What are you talking about?'

'Never mind,' she smiles.

'If you let me finish, I would really like your company, both on the trip and after the race. I've told Silas it's a three-day affair, but in reality it's only two. The third day is a race for this cup I've already qualified for.'

'You are becoming quite sneaky.'

'Maybe. Even if I wanted to race on the Sunday I wouldn't be allowed.'

'Get to the romantic bit. I'm not too interested in the inner workings of the league tables of cyclists,' she says and gets out of bed wrapped in the covers.

'My, you're in some mood today. Have you had your coffee?' he smiles, left bare on the bed.

'Yes.'

'Have you had your tobacco?'

'Yes.'

'Have you had your breakfast?'

'I have, thank you very much. But I could do with a proper kiss. Not a peck or friendly, *Hello, I'm your second cousin* kind of kiss. A real kiss from a real man. A crusher, I haven't had that today. I think that might help.'

He jumps out of bed and kisses her until, giggling, she asks him to stop. 'In essence I've earned myself a day off', he says, 'and I don't know what you had planned for Sunday, but I doubt it was church, so I was wondering if you would want to go on a little trip with me. I'll find us somewhere to stay. Maybe even a castle?'

'Yes my prince.'

'Do you want to come just for the Sunday?'

'When are you going up?'

'Quite early on the Friday. The race starts just after lunch. It's one of these long ones that will run into the night. It will get busier and busier as first offices, then factories, then pubs clear out. And by the end of it, I think about ten at night, we should be ready for the final. I mean if you're able to come you could come in the afternoon, or to be honest, the last train of the day is probably fine, you'd still get there in time. Then it's the same on the Saturday.'

'Or, I could come up with you and then stroll around looking in shops, sipping tea in the botanic garden, if there is one. Is there?'

'I don't know. I've never been.'

'And then I'll come over to the race, with hundreds of bags and hat boxes.'

'I'll see about getting you a good seat. A row of seats,' he smiles.

'Sounds nice. I'll speak to the girls and see if any of them can cover, while I'm off, deadly ill,' she says.

'Seems like the kisses worked, you're in a better mood already.'

'Don't try your luck. But yes, kissing usually works. Remember that.'

'You're funny. We can either leave at the same time, but go on different trains, meeting up somewhere outside London. Or we can go on the same line at different times. Which would you prefer?'

'I don't fancy sitting in a carriage on my own all the way to Coventry. So if you can find two trains that leave London one after the other, meaning you'll wait for me at some platform somewhere in Godforsaken-Hole-On-Sea, and then jump on to find me.'

'Sounds grand.'

'Don't book us into the Station Hotel, try a little harder. I don't mind taking a taxi to the better bits. If there are better bits of Coventry?'

'I'll see what I can do. I'm not quite sure where the stadium is. It's called Butts, but I don't know if that's a man's name or an area. Should be a good fast race, the track is made from asphalt, which is great. I don't fancy racing on shale ever again. Once you get used to the speed of wooden boards, cement, asphalt, even some of the quicker gravel tracks, it's hard to go back.'

Miriam mimics a yawn, then smiles. 'What should I pack?' she says. 'Will there be a ball in your honour? Are you expecting to win? Will they hand you the keys to the city?'

'I'm hoping to do quite well in the race, at least a medal, but other than free water, I'd be surprised if they even gave me a fish supper. But don't you worry, I'll look out for a nice restaurant for us to go to on the Saturday evening. On the Friday night I think I'll have to take it easy, maybe just stay in.'

'That's fine. I'll bring a book and my knitting. You can read for me and I'll make you a scarf. Like we were an old couple.'

'Easy does it.' Now it's his turn to smile.

'Only kidding, don't count your chickens. I might not come along after all. In fact I might not even like you,' she says.

'But you will, and you do,' he replies.

'What chance do I have in this world if I'm that bad a liar?' She lies back on the bed. Her back on a pile of pillows, her arm draped dramatically over her forehead.

'Against me? None,' he smiles smugly.

***

He's told whoever wants to know that he's going to Coventry for a big race. A three-day affair, pulling the absolute elite of cyclists from the North and Scotland, and even some of the bigger names from the South and London itself. In addition, the Belgians have started sending very young, very talented riders to a lot of smaller races. Something for them to cut their teeth on. They're usually well behaved, tall, but not powerful in the same way that he is. Though they are gifted and used to pain, used to riding the flat marshlands in what they have told him is always a headwind, their enthusiasm and youthful panache can't match his experience.

Paul makes sure to speak to Harry before he leaves. He finds him at the grandstand on Herne Hill watching his brothers practise.

First they talk about the weather and Harry's leg, which isn't healing quick enough to be of any use to Harry this season, then they talk about women, in particular and in general, but Paul doesn't mention Miriam, never does.

Harry's raced at the quick Coventry track before. Now he sits down with a groan and says, 'Paul, when you wake up in the morning after a race like that you will ache. You will be on fire, and it's a fire no baths, liniments, cold towels, creams or potions can put out. You've torn your muscles to shreds and now they will speak up. Your body, the more reasonable of the two entities you are – body and mind – is trying to come back to life. It's trying to reconstruct itself.'

'I'm getting used to it,' Paul says.

Harry continues, 'Your kneecaps will crack like kindling. Your thighs will be numb. Lying, sitting, standing, walking: it doesn't matter, it's all agony. Cramps will come and go in spasms. Every now and then, if there's a lull in the contracting of muscles, your shoulder blades will come alive with pain. This can be slightly subdued, by drink, some drugs, some massage, but you can't escape it. It's part of the bargain.'

'Makes you wonder why we do this to ourselves, doesn't it Harry?'

'You know this about the pain, but you can't stop racing. In some sense it's about money and fame. But it is bigger than that. If you're just in it for the cash you won't last long. It's too much for you, for anyone. For any payment.'

'I know,' Paul nods.

'You're here because you can't stop yourself racing. And this pain is the portal you pass through, the ritual you live with. This is the rent you're paying to your body, for letting you use it to win.'

Paul looks at Harry's profile. It's dominated by a bulbous nose that Paul thinks wasn't always that way. Paul reaches out and shakes Harry's hand. Tells him to take care of himself. Almost tells him to switch to water, but doesn't.

'Good luck, son,' Harry says. 'Don't let this old man put you off. You and I know it's the most beautiful sport in the world. We're artists, dealing in pain and glory.' Paul nods and smiles. 'You're young, you're going to go far,' Harry says. 'Now off you go, I've got things to do. Can't sit here all day, chatting like an old fishwife.'

Paul nods and waves down to the brothers standing in the midfield, probably discussing tactics. Paul says goodbye to Harry who grunts and fishes a hipflask from the inner pocket of his jacket. Paul gets on his bike and rolls home, to get ready for the trip.

Once he's packed he descends the stairs with the bike over one shoulder and a haversack over the other. It's packed with his shoes and his special race shirt, the number 34 shining on its back, as well as shorts for racing and long johns for the warm-up. His pillbox – the private apothecary he can't race without. A book, not for him, for her, and a pair of pants and the bottle of Stephenson's Hair Pomade, in case they go out for a meal or dance, or if there's a photographer after the race.

He makes his way over to Euston. Not quickly, not slowly, just meandering on the bike. He's got plenty of time and although it's cold it's not unbearable. A lot of shops on the streets have put up their Christmas displays, and though he knows he won't be getting anything today, he likes to whittle away his time this way rather than go and sit in the station. The smell of roasting chestnuts propels him forward. As does the excitement of the secret holiday.

By separate means of transport, by separate paths Paul and Miriam will travel towards each other. They have agreed that she will come to the station after him, looking out for a seat on the 1.11 train. By then he will already be underway on the 12.11 train for Coventry. He will disembark and wait for her in Berkswell. Bike and everything no doubt causing annoyance. But today nothing can wipe the smile from his face.

The image of the man inside the carpet hasn't faded, but he makes sure to keep it locked up in a dark place in his mind. He couldn't stand the thought of going on holiday with one of Mr Morton's employees, otherwise.

Chapter 29

I'm sitting in one of my favourite cafés on Moscow Road, on the corner across from Pembridge Square Garden, not far from my house. It's a known haunt of mine, and I'm well received, but not fussed over. I'm a bit worse for wear. Cheltenham was good to me this year, and the way I marked the success was to drink lots of champagne. *Blanc de noirs, blanc de blancs,* ending on a couple of bottles of *doux.* All roads lead to Rome. All drinks to a hangover.

I'm glad to be back, and my head is thanking me for the coffee and the simple poached egg. In the paper in front of me, the Washington Post – imported at great cost by a friendly newsagent – I read about the big land to the west. In general and particular. Despite the absurd amount of money and the fact that the actual news is about ten or more days old by the time I get the paper, I make sure to read most of it.

Apart from the articles and letters I see several British firms advertise. Radios, trips, bloody paint again, but mostly fashion. Clothes for men and women. Some cuts, some brands, some houses I know. Some I don't, but I could learn quickly. I've got a good eye for what looks good, I've got an eye for lines and fabric. Maybe I should leave all this and move to America, become a tailor? Start with a men's shop, then move into women's. Women are harder to please, but happier to pay, purchase things more often. Many small rivers of Crêpe de Chine could pay my bills. And if I settled on the East Coast I could import Harris Tweed and woollen jumpers from here.

I read on: *Flapper Step-in underwear, Combination underwear, Slip-on bloused dress, Slip-on evening dress, Kimono, Square Yoke, House dress, Bungalow apron, Empire dress, Porch & Morning dress, Frock, Bolero jacket, Beach Negligée.* It's wonderful. This could be my homework. I sit and think that I can re-invent myself somewhere new. I would stay within the – quite frankly – reasonable limits of the law. Pay tax, vote, get a little dog maybe. A friend. Someone people would think of as my lodger, and I as my lover.

Paul would like America. I know from the press that velodrome cycling is as big in America as it is here. And knowing the Yanks they probably pay better, and race harder. That could suit him. He would like it. Maybe I could go one day? Leave?

Then one of the little grimy boys comes up to me and tells me I'm to go to Mr Morton's damned club at my earliest convenience. 'My earliest convenience,' that's some nerve from the fat Elephant. He knows I'll be scurrying there as fast as a rat smelling peanut butter.

Suddenly my thoughts seem like insubstantial dreams; the candy floss of a young girl's head. I slap my own cheeks, to bring out the man, the killer in me. Putting away what could have been.

Walking out of the café I put the Washington Post in a bin. Who am I kidding? I can't leave. I am trapped here. I make a living here. I am part of London, a worker bee locked to its hive, to its Queen, as much as I am a part of Mr Morton's family. However awful I think that is, that's still the conclusion life has drawn for me. The sum of my actions and choices. At the beck and call of a psychopath in white.

I slip the boy a coin, and he runs off to find me a taxi. As soon as I am in the car I regret throwing the paper away. With the traffic it will be a tedious journey across town. The driver, though I'm sure he's competent at what he does, doesn't look like the kind of man to take any interest in the political field across the great big pond.

I put my hands in my pockets. Get my folding razor out and try the edge on my thumb. It's still sharp. I like that. I try to take it in to be sharpened by this old man in China Town every Wednesday, but this week has been too busy to allow that. Despite this I'm pleased to see a small bead of blood bubbling up from the line I easily drew on my thumb.

I put the blade back into my pocket and try to look out for something beautiful or interesting in the city I'm travelling through. I fail to find anything. And in this mood I enter the juggernaut that is the Carousel.

'Silas, come have a seat', I hear his voice from up above. He's leaning against the door frame of his little office above the bar. Trudging up the stairs it strikes me I have no idea what the meeting is about. It could be my execution, my promotion, the way I wear my hat, the price of sand in Arabia. I never know what to expect, and that counts for more than half of my fear, a fear that increases with every footstep. It culminates in a little spray of stomach acid coming up into my gullet as my foot hits the last step. I disguise it as a cough and quickly swallow the drink he offers me. An unusual, and frankly worrying, gesture.

He thinks it old and venerated whisky. Casked and kept at great cost. I know how his bar works, possibly better than him, and how his distributors work. They know as well as I that he can't tell the difference between a good and a bad drink, or even a terrible mix of leftovers. Between rainwater and the Virgin's tears. He keeps a little vial of her tears in a shrine on one of the walls in the office, imported from the Holy Land for a small fortune.

He pours me another drink and smiles – looking just like the stuffed head of the Grizzly he has put up over his head, only the bear, even dead, has something regal about him.

'I'm going to cut straight to the point Silas. I'm looking for someone to send to prison. Not now, not for another six or seven months. I need this someone to be a known associate of *our band of brothers*.'

If it was me he wouldn't have told me. If this was some sort of blackmail he wouldn't have chosen me, he knows my finances as well as I do. Probably better. It's not hard to work out who he means, but it galls me that he thinks Paul is a crippled race horse. Something easily sent to slaughter.

'I'm not sure I can help,' I say, hoping to evade the inevitable. He turns to me with a look like he has just found a molar in his morning porridge. One that isn't his.

'I'm convinced you can. I need someone to find things out. Someone who's not going to die on me. A tough nut,' he says.

'As in someone quite big? And ginger?' I answer unprompted, a *faux pas* usually punished.

'You'll go far Silas, that's what I've always said,' he muses, rolling a cigar between his fingers.

'How long?' I ask, trying to get myself to sit straight.

'Just a couple of years. Seven to ten should do the trick. I'll even pay him a sort of nominal wage while he's in. Providing he supplies me with a steady flow of information.'

'And if he doesn't?'

'No one is strong enough to survive a knife through a kidney. Inside or outside prison.'

He plies me with drink and talks to me about boxing, something else he's ignorant about. An hour and forty minutes later I stagger down the stairs, back into the world I know. It seems both brighter and a lot more sinister than I remember it. I am very drunk, but can't recall having more than three or four drinks. There's a hairy sensation on my tongue, and my hands are itching. I wonder what I've agreed to, what I've been punished for, what we've been celebrating.

I conclude that Mr Morton has spiced up my drink with one of the many cones of powder he keeps in his office cabinet. I should be fine, I just need to remember to drink lots of water and to do what I set out to do. Stick to my plan. Maybe get a Bibi or two down me. I should manage, the drugging is not insurmountable, though it will soon start to feel like it.

I'm outside, trying to walk off the seasick feeling. The street lights are floating around in clouds of nausea. I try not to look at them. I walk, slowly and in as straight a line as I can to an all-night pharmacy I know: Peat and Pepper on Lafone Street. The man behind the counter mixes me a drink with caffeine, digitalis and turmeric, as well as sugar and acetylsalicylic acid. Then, commenting on my pallor, he adds a little something new. He says it's something that will perk me up.

'Very popular with sportsmen these days,' he tells me, adding quinine into the mix for good measure, without asking me if I've been to the tropics lately, or have malaria. Then the doctor, who I'm pretty sure is a quack, tells me his drink has become a real hit with some of the wealthier people returning from foreign countries. So popular in fact that he's been thinking of patenting it as 'Dr Pepper's All-Curing Tonic'.

'Between you and me, these East India men are happy to buy this for twice the price. The mark-up potential is substantial. I'm looking for investors actually. Would you be interested?'

I nod and down the drink he's prepared while talking. It tastes vile, like licking a wet wolfhound, but I know it will help clear my head in a matter of minutes. Like it has many times in the past. I ask him to make me another and to make it extra potent. Fighting fire with fire in a way. At first he refuses, but when I pull out my billfold he relents.

I walk for hours, quite detached from myself. I'm gesturing, speaking, probably crying. Caught in the embrace of Mr Morton's dark fairies. My feet ache but the view of Hyde Park first thing in the morning is a great way to be compensated for a night's walking. The sunlit frost. A dark coppice of trees. Trying to ignore my broken mind, I revel in the things that are beautiful about the day. The lack of people, the three Royal Guards in shiny uniforms, galloping towards me, horses steaming like transatlantic ships going against the tide. I force myself to stop mumbling and gesticulating. Solemnly nod to the men who ignore me. I take a quick note of the horses they're on – adequate but no more.

The result of the two concoctions is that I can't sleep. I'm more alert and it feels like my eyesight has improved to the point where I can spot gravy stains on people's neck ties from miles away and wood lice in the crowns of the trees lining the streets.

What Mr Morton has planned is obviously out of the question. I didn't suggest that. When he ran out of boxing anecdotes I made sure we talked about my first love: horses. I told him the mile would one day take over from the furlong, and pretended to be outraged about that. I told him a funny story about a vet castrating the wrong horse because the stable boy couldn't read properly and had mixed up the horses.

I was hoping to get him mired in the subject. I've seen this happen before. He has an idea, and he talks about nothing else for a month. Then something else comes along and drowns that idea out. He's not stupid, but in many ways he's a simple man. He can't keep to many ideas in his head, which is great for me. I'll just have to be drowning him in ideas and updates. The unfortunate side effect of this is that it'll bring me closer to him. It will make me see him more often, something I'm trying to avoid. This is the tightrope I'm walking.

I head towards the coppice in the middle of Hyde Park. I'm deadly tired. Once within the evergreen bosom I lie and watch the clouds. I speak to my dead mother for what turns out to be four hours.

★★★

Getting up, aching terribly and shaking from the cold and from the substances leaving my body I resolutely walk out to Marble Arch where I get into a taxi. I ask the driver to stop by the nearest coffeehouse. Tell him there's a hot drink in it for him if he's quick about it.

Mr Morton's words still haunt me: 'Paul will have to take a dive. That's not unreasonable. I'm the one who put him where he is now. I can retract that offer any time I want. And I will.

In the summer.'

'I see.'

'I know you don't.'

'Maybe not.'

'Just don't tell him. This stays between you and me. We wouldn't want our little ginger bird flying the coop would we?'

With a shudder I get out of the taxi and buy the man sitting in the idling car a cup of tea. Then I look for answers in my deep mug of black, tarry brew. I can't find any.

Chapter 30

Paul does well in Coventry. He's not on the podium on the Friday, but he's in with an overall chance if he places within the first five on the Saturday. He is used to riding every day, not just once or twice a week for a race like some of the others, so he's quietly confident about his overall chances. That's about the only advantage his job has.

In the evening of the Friday he wants to stay in the room. Rest, drink water, sleep. He knows full well the pain he will have to endure in the morning. The initial one before his creaking joints have gotten used to moving again, then the other kind of pain once he starts racing, and then the same, but worse, the morning after that. That's part of his life. The cyclist who can endure the most pain over the longest period of time, is a sure winner.

But one look at her, in a new dress, with her hair piled high, appraising him as he gets out of the quick bath he's earned after the race, tells him otherwise. She comes close to him. Kisses him and tells him the salty taste on his lips is gone. They kiss some more, just to make sure the salt has been washed off completely.

Once he's dressed they stand on the little French balcony together. Their room overlooks nothing more spectacular than the rail yard, something she has almost forgiven him for.

In the dark, with the lights of the city reflecting on the tracks, the long silvery strands leading into the eternity of the English countryside, even the most trivial of industrial scenes has become a pretty postcard.

He has apologised profusely for getting a room at the station hotel despite her explicit wishes. It was a matter of money, there's still some left of the Christmas bonus from Silas, but it wouldn't stretch very far, and he thought that a place with a lot of people passing through would be better for them – an unmarried couple, a pair that shouldn't be seen together, an athlete and a night moth.

They are both unused to moments of stillness and the quiet acceptance that only a town smaller than London, and a hotel room, their kingdom while in Coventry, can bring.

Downstairs they find a porter in the vestibule and he tells them that if he had a fiancée or wife, he would take her to the Alma. It's not far. Especially not on an evening like this. Paul winces as he walks down the stairs in front of the hotel, but smiles and she smiles with him.

They stroll down Broadgate, her arm linked through his. Occasionally stepping out of the way when trams pass by. Most of them are returning to the terminus. Slow, elephantine in the night. Legions of men are pulling in awnings displaying shop names. Ones that have protected wares from the sun all day. Women leaning on brooms or carrying pails of water talk about the day which has passed and the night to come. What they have sold, what they will eat. Who they served, what they will drink, and with whom.

Once at the restaurant Paul orders one, and then another, pint of oatmeal stout. A dark mass of alcohol. They are both for her, but she wouldn't be sold them. The Alma is both traditional and foreign to them. He has steak, unusual for him as he seldom eats much after a race. Either because he's not hungry, because he's had so much to drink that he doesn't think he's hungry, or because he's nervous about the following day's race. And because of the foreign substances slowly leaving his bloodstream.

She has plaice. Unremarkable. And, after, they both have jelly.

The meal passes almost in silence. A comfortable suspension of dialogue, punctuated by 'Pass me the salt please', by 'How's the fish?' Not deep, not soaring, not dangerous, not words that have to be guarded or pored over. Not things you have to worry about being overheard. Just the things you say. He drinks two jugs of iced water and she finishes the beer. They both have coffee, but it's so weak it doesn't do them any good. He holds her hand, not under the table, but in plain sight.

Leaving the restaurant they leave a huge tip, not because the patron was very nice to them, but because their waitress looked the other way when it was clear that it was Miriam who was drinking the beer. Also the meal was so cheap compared to the London prices they've gotten used to. Happily they meander back the way they came. One of her hands dwarfed in his, fingers laced like the congregation in *This is the church, and this is the steeple*. Her other hand twirling a parasol. Both full. Him on beef, her on hop and malt.

When Paul checked into the hotel he paid a little extra to bring the bike up to the room, and gave an additional two banknotes to the man behind the counter. This made the man ask, 'Mr and Mrs MacAllister then I presume?' to which Paul nodded.

Paul and Miriam ride the elevator in silence, inspecting each other's contorted faces in the polished brass work. Paul's holding the key to the room, and she's already unpinning her hair with one hand, her other hand looking for his.

They kiss all the way from the lift to the door. He struggles with the lock and then they struggle with each other's clothes while tripping to the bed.

Afterwards he asks her, 'Who is Mr Morton?' He's been up to get a drink, the race still in his legs and torso. She's putting on a nightgown and lighting two candles.

'Please don't bring that man into the room,' she says, suddenly subdued.

She walks over to the window and pulls the curtains shut, as if to hide, as if to shut out the world. 'Look Miriam, I know he's not a nice man. I'm just saying that maybe once I start winning a few more of these races like the one today, it can lead to who knows, races on the continent, maybe even America. You can come with me, not always be in London.'

'It's a nice dream to have,' she says shaking her head.

'But what's stopping us? What's stopping you?'

She turns to him, eyes wet. 'I'm stuck. You might not be, but he owns me,' she says.

'What are you talking about? You work for him, but that's not the same. Surely you can just tell him you're leaving?'

'Paul, you're a darling,' she says smiling. A smile which doesn't reach her eyes.

'Don't treat me like a child,' he says and drinks deeply from a bottle of cordial on the bedside table. His muscles screaming in protest as he moves around the room.

Miriam walks away from the window. Doesn't look at him. Fingers a lampshade, picks up a cushion from the floor and places it back on the bed. Then she walks over to a little table with a mirror. Still not looking at him she sits on a chair and combs her hair, slowly. Counting. Once she's reached a hundred she looks at him in the mirror.

'Oh, Paul.' Her eyes wet. Her eyebrows angry.

'We can do something about this Miriam. But you need to tell me what's going on.'

She starts to say something. Then she waves him to her side, puts an arm around his waist and looks at him in the mirror. He puts a hand on her hair. It's as smooth as water. 'When I came to live in London, Mr Morton took me in,' she begins. 'Trained me, treated me like I was a niece, as one of his little family. I came here with nothing. I don't know why but he gave me a home, an education of sorts, and a job. He has always been eccentric, and I knew that some of what he did was on the wrong side of the law. But to my mind he was a harmless, likeable buffoon, even a good Catholic. Because that's what he let me see. '

'And you didn't mind that he was running a criminal gang?'

he asks.

'At first I liked it. I had money for the first time in my life. And I was known, respected.' She looks down into her lap. Tears falling, staining her nightgown.

'Soon after I was initiated into the family I was making a living out of debt collecting and other bits and pieces. It was a quick rise in ranks people told me. Then one day I saw the sinister side of him emerge. And it was too late to get out.'

'What happened?'

'He told me he'd been checking up on my background. That he knew where I came from. Who my parents were. The whole sordid story. My new beginning started to crumble before my eyes. Mr Morton told me he knew all about my father, and what I had done to him. He told me he had proof and a witness, and he told me the name of my old friend, and that she was willing to denounce me, so I knew it wasn't a hoax. Paul, the information he has at his fingertips is more than enough to see me hang.'

Paul's hand has stopped moving on her head.

'If I ever lie to him, or leave him, that's what awaits me. As he never tires of reminding me. That's why my loyalty to him is so unquestioning.'

Paul feels stuck in an icy chokehold, as Miriam continues, 'Every morning I pray to a God I no longer believe in that someone somewhere hates Mr Morton more than they fear him and decides to kill him.'

'That might take years, decades,' Paul says, shaking his head.

'Worst case there's always the pearl-handled revenge in my handbag. First him. Then myself. I'd be a double murderer, but at least my death would be on my own terms.' Then she stares at her own reflection in the mirror. Dangerously composed. Only a small streak of mascara giving away any emotion.

Paul can't breathe. He tries to get her to stand, so that he can hold her, but she slips out of his grasp. Hides her face in her hands. She collapses in the seat and it's only much later that she allows him to carry her to bed. To tuck her in. He turns off the light and tries to sleep. He can't. Not for hours. Instead he lies and listens to the sound of a clock ticking in the room.

In the early hours of Saturday he reaches out for her. He thinks she is sleeping but when she turns his way he can see she's wide awake.

'Not been able to sleep either?' he asks.

'No.'

'You should have told me.'

'And you?' she says.

'Not really. I've been thinking too much.'

Outside, dawn arrives with its cries of birds and men shouting at horses. The hotel room is warm from the heater he has been keeping half an eye on through the night.

He says, 'You are risking death by being here aren't you? In Coventry? In this room with me?'

She nods, 'Now do you understand how much you mean to me? How special you are?'

'But why? I mean, you hardly even know me. What have I got to offer that's worth risking your life for?'

'Paul, you don't understand. Throughout my life, men have been the enemy. Even from before I was born my father was the enemy. Mr Morton is the enemy. Every man who has ever tried to charm me has done so for their own selfish reasons. I can spot it at a hundred yards. And in the same way, I saw you coming and knew straight away that you were different. You're incapable of lying or hiding anything. You are the first man who's ever been genuinely nice to me, without wanting anything in return. I feel safe with you. I feel free with you. For the first time.'

He moves closer to her. Puts an arm behind her head. Side by side, on their backs they look at the ceiling. 'Miriam,' he says, 'I'm sorry all those things happened to you. It makes me so angry. I just want to protect you.'

'Oh Paul,' Miriam laughs, her eyes lighting up briefly for the first time since the conversation began, 'if only it was that simple. But you're too kind, too gentle to take on Mr Morton.'

'Maybe you can train me up to be more like you,' says Paul with a wry smile, continuing, 'I thought you looked fantastic that day on the tram when I had the accident, and you sort of took me in.'

She props herself up on one elbow and looks down on him. 'And you don't think I look fantastic now?'

'You look even better now.'

'Flattery will get you nowhere.'

'It got me here.'

'True.' She smiles and eases out of the bed to open the curtains slightly. A low light comes in through the window. It's December and the sun won't be up properly for a few more hours. Paul looks at her and smiles. Puts her pillow behind his head and says, 'What I mean is that I never thought that a beautiful London woman would ever lay her eyes on me.'

'There's something I have to tell you about that day,' she says from the other side of the room.

Paul motions for her to come back to bed, but she's looking for a glass to have a drink of water. 'Did you put something in my tea to make me like you more?' he says.

'If I remember correctly you never finished your tea, you ungrateful creature.'

'Sorry.'

She comes over and sits on the bed next to him. Tucks her legs in underneath, smooths her nightgown, erasing non-existent creases, looks straight at him.

'Paul. Look at me.' He smiles and tries to pull her closer. But she frowns and shakes him off. 'Paul, it wasn't a coincidence that I met you.'

'How do you mean?' He sits up in bed.

'Well, Mr Morton knew that Silas was up to something, that he was bringing someone new in.' She looks down, then up at Paul again, his mouth wide open. Then she continues, 'Mr Morton keeps a keen eye on all his employees. And I'm his most trusted set of eyes.'

Paul thinks for a second, then he says, 'So you followed me? For how long?'

'Not every day, but I checked in on you every now and then. And if it wasn't me, it was one of the boys.'

His face darkens and he clenches his fists, then he says, 'And you watched me nearly crippling myself on Southwark Bridge?'

Miriam now moves closer to him, but he's sitting absolutely still. She says, putting both hands on his chest, 'Paul, it wasn't like that. You were a mark. Mr Morton doesn't like new faces. He's terrified of infiltrators, says the whole operation is too sensitive.'

'It sounds like you're defending him,' he says in a monotone.

'And I hate it,' she says vehemently, drying her eyes on a corner of a pillowcase. 'I didn't know you were going to fall. I didn't know you were going to be so nice. I didn't know I would like you. Love you in fact. There, I have said it.'

Paul frowns.

'Remember that in all of this, from when I took you in and bandaged your leg, up until now, right now sitting here in this bed, I am risking my life.'

'So what other marks, what other men did you have, or do you have in your life? Is this how you keep an eye on us all? Up close?'

'Don't be crude,' she says, her voice hard, her eyes soft.

Paul takes a deep breath. Tries to look composed. Then says, 'It's a straightforward question.'

'And I'll give you an adult answer,' Miriam says. 'You are not the first. I have had other men. But believe me when I say this, you're the only one I have chosen entirely for myself. You are the one I want to spend all my time with. It's just that I can't.'

'I don't know what to think,' he says.

'Look at me,' she says, steel in her voice.

'I am,' he says turning to her.

'Not like that. Look properly. What do you see?'

'I see you. I see Miriam. I see someone I thought I knew.'

'You do know me Paul,' she says, 'You do know me.'

'I don't,' he says and shakes his head. Breaks eye contact.

She takes his head in her hands, turns him to her, and says, 'You don't know everything about my past, or some parts of my present. That's because I want to protect you, and because I don't enjoy talking about my past, or my present. I want you before, beside, and after all that.'

He looks past her. Bites his lips. He looks at her and it's too much. He wants to be angry with her. He wants to make her feel wretched. He wants to walk away and find a timid girl from the countryside. But not really. Not at all. He nods and says, 'I slept terribly, if at all. I'm here to work. I have a race in a couple of hours. I think it's best if we continue this some other time.'

'Paul, look at me. It's still me. Remember? Miriam. Your Miriam. Can I still be your Miriam?'

'I think so.'

She kisses him on the cheek, doesn't ask for a kiss in return, and they go back to sleep. Soon she is breathing deeply next to him.

***

Later on, racing, he feels absolutely rotten, and it's only by sheer force of will he manages to come third, which coupled with yesterday's result means he places second overall.

Back at the hotel he has a long bath and she sits on a stool next to the tub, writing in her book. They don't talk about that morning's revelations. Late in the evening they go and see a play, and despite the fact that she has to wake him up three or four times, both due to the exhaustion from the race and the tedious nature of the play itself, he tells her he'd like to go again sometime. They behave like a normal couple. Smile and kiss, walk like they're just anyone.

Chapter 31

Their train from Coventry leaves at eleven in the morning on the Sunday and they spend the morning reading the papers and eating breakfast. He toys with the idea of trying to find a bicycle shop or going to the works where his uncle got his first racing bike from. But looking at Miriam, at her relaxed reading pose, so unlike the tightly wound spring she is in London, he decides against it. He decides against doing anything else than just sitting next to her, walking next to her, for the coming hours. He doesn't ask her if she wants to go and see the cathedral, the Coombe Abbey Park, the canal. All he does is to put a hand on her shoulder and smile at her when she looks up. He nods at their two empty cups, singing, '*You're the cream in my coffee*', off key. She joins in, until they run out of lyrics.

'Another coffee?' She smiles and nods, takes his hand and kisses it, then returns to the crossword puzzle in her Pearson's Magazine.

He feels so normal, so happy that he almost forgets what he's coming home to. At one point she puts down the magazine and leans close to him. Tells him, and this is the only time after the Saturday night that she brings it up, that giving him some of the story has lightened her load. 'Even if you decide to leave me, I'm happier for having at least one person about know some of my past,' she says. He just nods and orders another cup of tea for her.

Once she finishes the crossword she turns to Paul, motions for him to come in closer. He thinks it's for a kiss, but she shakes her head. She just wants to speak to him in a whisper.

'Paul. I've not wanted to say this, but I feel like I'm being watched. Like we're being watched.'

He leans back, looks around and says, 'Don't be silly. We are. You're beautiful. People see you, look at you.'

'I don't mean like that.'

'I did quite well yesterday, have done well all year in fact. People might recognize me.'

'I'm only telling you because I feel it's a different kind of looking.' She still keeps her voice low. 'I know men look at me, unless they're cycling fans, then they look at you. I know women look at you. I don't like it but they do. This is not the same though.'

'Relax, we're far away from home. No one knows where you are. Only Silas knows I'm here racing. You're just being paranoid.'

'Maybe,' she says. 'Maybe it's just a bad habit.' Then she sits back in her seat and pulls her hat lower.

Paul looks around but can't see anything out of the ordinary. Families, men, workers, newspaper boys. Same as in London. Only slower, on a smaller scale. A woman drops a bag of apples. A couple of tables over a man writes something in the margin of his newspaper and gets up. An old lady speaks to no one and everyone about the last days.

Paul moves his seat closer to Miriam's and puts a hand on her shoulder. Closes his eyes for a second and lets his mind drift.

At eleven they board their train, and Miriam tells him she's got plans to slowly nod off. Once underway, she smiles up at him and snuggles in, looking out over the fields.

'Sorry about all the fuss,' she says, 'about the things we talked about.'

He doesn't say anything, but kisses her forehead.

She looks up at him, and says, 'Happy Christmas.'

'Still a couple of days to go is it not?' he asks.

'It is, but I won't be able to see you before then. The club gets very busy this time of year. Mr Morton's away over in Ireland, something with a casino. Otherwise I wouldn't have been able to go, never in a million years. Also, this weekend is usually quiet, the last for a while. People are saving up, preparing for Christmas I suppose. That, and a thousand favours cashed with the girls, is how I managed to sneak away with you.'

'Are you not even able to see me for a minute?'

'Not even a second I'm afraid. Most nights I'll be staying in my flat in Elephant and Castle. Just sleeping for three or four hours between shifts and other jobs. There's a lot of debts and money flying around at Christmas. A lot of collections.'

'That's one way to look at it. Never mind the baby in the manger. Or me.'

'Please don't be cross with me. We spoke about this. It's just a couple of days, don't worry pretty boy.'

'I'm sorry. I'm not cross, you know that.'

'You're a darling,' she says and kisses him on the cheek. Then she falls asleep, like a cat in a sunlit alcove.

Being away frees up space in his head. His body is tired but his head swirls with thoughts other than those of immediate survival. The jostlings of the capital crowds. Mr Morton's all-seeing eye. This trip up north, even by about a third to where he came from, triggers emotions he can't contain.

For a brief second he feels a twinge of guilt, thinking about his father who is probably out with the cows. Paul wonders how his father is managing, but the memory of the bread tin still smarts and dragging a hand across his face he puts the feeling aside. He tries to revisit the few shreds he has of his mother but he can't bring her into focus. He can't say he misses her. He never knew her enough.

Some things he thinks about more often than others. The hills just above Lennoxtown. The weather coming down onto him like it just doesn't in England. The air, which at home felt purer, less used. The things he used to know. The simpler life he could have had. The other farmhands and the banter they shared. The music, the dances, the connection to the land he can't feel here. But then he thinks of the real life he would have had, his father owning him. The cold, the terrible lack of food, the hard work until broken or spent. Being reduced to a pack horse on two legs.

He looks at the refined, but flint-hard girl next to him, thinks of the races he's been in, the money he's won. The kisses and warm mornings in bed with her. All things that would never have happened if he hadn't punched his father in the mouth.

A long time later, just as the train pulls into Berkswell, he wakes her up. This is his stop. He kisses her in public one last time before they get back to London, and she gives him sandwiches to eat while he waits for the next train. After another, longer kiss he carries the bike off the train and goes to look for somewhere to sit. The hissing train heaves and breathes while passengers start to board. With a smattering of flags and whistles the train starts to leave.

Paul stands on the platform watching Miriam through the window. She can't see him, and the sensation of looking at someone so beautiful who has allowed him into her life is enough to make him dizzy.

As the train passes by him Paul sees a face he thinks he recognizes. In the compartment behind them, a man in black is tugging at his goatee. At first Paul thinks it's the man from the café who stood up to leave, then he thinks it's one of Mr Morton's many men. Then he can't be sure. But by then, the train has left the station.

Chapter 32

It's Boxing Day and Paul stands shivering in the entrance tunnel to the Kensal Rise velodrome. It's an early race and it's cold, not that the time of day will do much to improve the temperature of the air.

'Perk up,' Silas says, at his shoulder. 'You know full well cyclists don't have holidays. And that applies to Christmas too.' Silas shrugs into his overcoat, and rubs his hands, ensconced in sheepskin gloves. 'I have a little something like the traditional Christmas Box for you. But the way you're going, our roles could be reversed next year.'

Paul smiles. Shakes some of the nerves out of his legs. Tilts his head to the right, then the left.

'We've had a pretty good season, you and I,' Silas says and hands Paul an expensive-looking box, which Paul opens. Under a layer of tissue paper is Paul's old worn out race sweater, the one with number 34 on the ripped back. Paul left it in Silas' apartment when he stayed over on the evening of his near overdose. Silas has had it washed and darned.

'Thanks. You know this is my lucky garment don't you? I thought I had lost it,' Paul says.

'You've used that other one for ages. I don't like it half as much.'

'Me neither. Thanks. I didn't get you anything.'

'I don't want anything,' Silas says and pats Paul's broad back. Then he continues, 'Well, actually that's not true. I want you to win today.'

And with that Paul takes off his back-up sweater and worms his way into his real one. The tight one. The winning one.

'Happy Christmas Paul,' Silas says and kisses each cheek twice. Paul lets it pass as Greek tradition. Then Silas sends

Paul off into centre field. As a mother sends her son to sea for the first time.

Paul asks around to see if anyone's seen Harry, but the only information he gets is that Harry's been drinking for a couple of days and that no one knows where he is. This is worrying for Paul but he doesn't have time to think about it. As the race starts he doesn't have any space for anything but *breathe, breathe, attack, attack*.

Today, Paul wins. But it's a very close race, and the second man, Cyril Horn, the notable vegetarian, is less than half a bicycle-length behind him. When Paul rolls back into the midfield after the race there's a man standing next to his bags of things. It's a big boxy man in a black overcoat, a man whose hair is plastered across his head like forgotten stucco. Paul thinks he's in trouble, as the man looks official somehow. A police man in mufti, or a bailiff, maybe a lawyer of some kind? Paul slows down to let his tired brain place the man. Then he sighs with recognition.

It's the man from the Sunday Times. Paul walks over and out of the corner of his eye he can see Silas sauntering over towards them. As Paul comes close the journalist extends his hand, 'Paul. Good to see you again, I'm Morgan Lindsey, remember we spoke a while ago?'

'I do.'

'You did well today.'

'It's was a bit hairy in the middle, but luckily some of the other boys seemed to tire off, so yes, I suppose.'

'Look I'm not here to do an interview or anything. In fact I'm not even working.'

'If you're after tickets for next week, I'm sure I can sort something out,' Silas says.

'No, no it's not that. My press pass gets me in almost everywhere. It's this.' Here Morgan takes an envelope out of his pocket. 'It was sent to the paper, you know care of, so to me really. But it's for you Paul, from your uncle.'

'What?' he says.

'I looked you up, you're having a great season. I worked out where you'd be so I could deliver this to you.'

Silas tries to slip Morgan some money, but he shakes his head and says, 'The note for me explained the content of the letter. So for this I won't take any money.'

Paul looks at Morgan and eventually accepts the letter he's holding out to him.

'Good luck with the rest of the season son.'

'Thank you,' Paul says before he opens the envelope.

Dear Paul,

I am sorry to inform you that your father was received into the hands of the Lord on Thursday the 23rd of November...

Despite himself, how he left it and how's he's felt about his father for many years, the death of the old man comes down on him like a bucket of cold water. Or boiling oil, he can't decide which.

The words of his uncle Stephen are too quick to brace or duck for. He sits down, puts the letter on a chair beside him. It flutters a little. Silas sits down on a chair next to the letter. Puts a hand on it to keep it from flying off.

Paul looks over at Silas. Then drags a palm across his face. The hand comes away wet with a mixture of sweat and tears. Then he reaches over for the letter. Gently touching Silas' hand Paul removes the letter from under the paperweight of the Greek's palm.

He reads the rest of it. It's short and to the point. His uncle had noticed an article about Paul in the paper and had meant to send it on to Paul's father, but before he got around to it he received news of a fatal heart attack. Not knowing where Paul was, his uncle sent the letter to the paper, hoping for the best. Looking at the postmark, Paul realises this is more than four weeks ago now. He will have missed the funeral.

He doubles over. Looks at his feet a long time. Silas just sits there, until Paul stirs.

'My father is dead,' Paul says. The truth worse as it's said out loud.

'I'm sorry,' Silas says, bowing his head a little.

'I think I am too,' replies Paul.

Silas moves one chair over, now sits next to Paul, then says, 'My parents died a long time ago. I still miss them though.'

'I suppose I will too. I think I miss my mother. Despite not knowing her.'

'But you left home on difficult terms with your father if I recall correctly?'

'I did. But he had been hard to live with for a long time before that.'

'I see.'

Paul turns the envelope this way and that. Unfolds a well-read, yellowed, greasy newspaper clipping. It's the one that appeared in the Sunday Times, it's not a huge article, not more than two or three fingers wide; the length of a palm. No photo, but a sketch of what is supposedly Paul, but in all honesty could be anyone astride a bike, hair slicked back. You can't tell if it's from Stephenson's Hair Pomade, or the wind. He hands it to Silas, who looks at it and smiles.

'I don't know...' says Paul.

'These things are not easy regardless of the circumstances.'

'I suppose,' Paul mutters.

'Can I offer you a drink?'

'No thank you. But I appreciate the concern.'

'Any time, champ.'

'Can you get me out of tomorrow's race? It's Mansfield, a real bastard, and a long train trip away. I'd rather not to be honest.'

'That can't be helped. I probably can't get you out of it. And despite how you feel now, it might be good for you to have something to concentrate on.'

'Maybe.'

'Either way, let's leave. You sure you don't want a drink?'

'I'm sure.'

'That's fine. I'll go outside while you gather your things. I'll try to find a taxi for you. Can be a nightmare this time of day. Especially around Christmas.'

'Thanks. I'm just going home to eat and sleep, and drink water and sleep some more. I'm going to need all the rest I can get if I'm to get on the first train to Brighton tomorrow.'

'That's the right attitude. See you out front.'

Paul struggles out of his race jersey, the big embroidered number 34 shining on the back, dry on an otherwise sweat-soaked garment. He dips his hands in one of the buckets of water which are provided for the racers. Pulls his hands through his hair, over his face, looking through his fingers at the world. Like he only wants to see half of it. He puts on an undershirt, a woollen sweater, a coat and a flat cap.

He wrestles his swollen feet out of his special cycling shoes, dips a facecloth in the pail and washes the bike. Not because it needs it. Today's velodrome was cleaner than most, and the weather is fine if cold. His mind is empty. A blown egg.

Once he's done he takes a first step, then another. Once his legs are moving, he can't seem to stop. It's as if he's on a railroad track.

He wheels the bike outside, tries to take as much time as he can, but he needs his powders, his drinks, his own bed, and to sit down. Silas, smoking, leans against a lamppost. Paul knows he should go home. He wants to go to Hampstead, but Miriam might not be there, and getting to Elephant and Castle can be an ordeal. And either way he has to let Silas leave first.

Eventually a taxi arrives, and Silas steps on his cigarette and raises his hand in a commanding salute. The driver pulls up and Silas instructs him to take Paul home, paying the fare from a thick bundle of notes. Silas takes the bike from Paul and ushers him into the back seat, handing him an inch-thick wad of money, much more than he would have made from the race.

Paul looks at his hands and sees that he's still holding the letter and that Silas is holding onto his bike. He leans out of the taxi, says, 'My father died,' to himself as much as anyone else.

'He's in a better place Paul,' Silas replies, then nods to the bike, 'I'll get this to the house, get one of the boys to take it over.'

'Tell them to walk it. Don't let them ride it. And make sure they're careful.'

'Don't worry. Get a good night's rest.'

Silas closes the door and the taxi takes off. Paul settles into the leather seat. He really, really needs to see Miriam. As it's Friday, he calculates that she's probably still working.

'Is there enough in the fare to get to Elephant and Castle?' he asks the driver.

'Not really,' the man answers vaguely. 'Is that where you want to go now?'

'Yes, just changed my mind. Sorry. You know the Carousel?'

'Sure.'

'I'm meeting someone. I think.'

'It's up to you. But once we get there I'm not waiting around in case you change your mind.'

'I understand.'

'I'll let you know the difference in fare and I'd like you to pay before the car comes to a complete halt.'

'It's not that bad.'

'Maybe not for you. But for a scrawny taxi driver, with loads of cash about his person, no thank you. Unless you're one of *his* drivers.'

★★★

Paul is now the owner of a farm he doesn't want. One with debts and cattle lowing and repairs needed. It's too much to think about.

He's race-weary and angry at his father. It's a sadness he

can't grapple with so he gives in and looks out the window of the taxi. Looks, but can't see anything. His eyes are blurry, his mind sluggish.

He crosses the river. Flies past Miriam's dark window, past the coffeehouse. The streetlights are on, blinking as if they just woke up, lending a nocturnal feel to the day.

This is the first time he's come to the club without being summoned, and he doesn't know how to act. The men on the door let him through, probably think he's a punter, and soon he's at the bar ordering sarsaparilla, trying every brand. Keeping to himself. Looking at the massive chandeliers and the empty smiles of the drinking masses and the lime-sucking sneers of the bartenders. It's easy to see that they don't get to keep their tips, or they would be nicer.

He knows he should go over to Hampstead and, if Miriam is not at home, go and sleep somewhere else until she is. He thinks he could go and stay in a hotel for a night or two, the wad of money from Silas making a little spontaneity possible, to let his feelings settle. But he doesn't. He tries to convince himself to go home. Despite the house on Copenhagen Street being a draughty coffin of a place, it's his. Instead of leaving he drinks so much of the sugary concoction that his teeth feel soft. Until his stomach is begging him, in a rumbly fashion, to stop. Soon he's been to the loo more times than he can remember, each time his urine smelling more and more like candy floss.

He's been through a monstrous run of races lately and he's having trouble concentrating. He knows he should eat, but can't muster up the will. After a very long time he leaves the club. Both disappointed and relieved he has not spotted Miriam.

It's now quite late, judging by the level of drink some people out on the pavement have put away, but he's still not asked anyone for the time. It seems irrelevant to him, though he knows he should be at home, resting.

He walks for a few blocks. Trying, but unable, to think. He knows he has to be in Mansfield, at the Forest Town Welfare track, in less than ten hours for an early race. Suddenly seeing his father's face in his mind's eye he tries to think of racing and bikes and things that he's good at. Things he knows. Things that are real and won't die in him whether he hates them or loves them. Forest Town is one of those flat tracks, ten degrees compared to the steeper ones more common in London. He finds the steeper ones more exciting. There's more scope for manoeuvring, going high up, gaining power, saving up on power by being higher and higher up on the sides, but still keeping pace with the racers on his left. Unleashing this power, sweeping down like an arrow from the sky. Also, Mansfield is not a real track. It's more a rectangle with four curves, in the middle a football pitch, so it has no real riders area either. But it's part of the race calendar so he has to go.

He steps into a deep puddle, soaking his shoes and trouser legs, and decides to go to a hotel after all. His shoes won't dry in time at home. He'll call by Copenhagen Street for his bike in the morning. The decision makes him feel lighter. He will go away, sleep in silence and comparative luxury. Anonymously. He will think of his father, have a dram in his honour. Write a letter to his uncle, asking his advice regarding solicitors and what should be done with the deeds of the farm. It'll be constructive. A ladder of practicalities to climb until he's purged of guilt. He affords himself a wry smile. Thinks about the time his father fell off a horse into a burn. The surprise made the old man laugh and as soon as Paul had pulled him up with the help of a branch, they stood laughing on the bank, sharing lunch while his father's clothes were drying, hung in a juniper bush. Shivering in Paul's coat his father had talked about the time he met Paul's mother. The first and last time that happened.

Paul walks on, a new spring in his step. 'The Excelsior,' he thinks, 'or maybe that one by Kew Gardens, that little smart one set back from the street.' In his mind he goes through the places he's been cycling past over the last few months. The places he would have liked to have a look inside.

Then he hears someone running behind him, the steps coming closer and closer. It's not unusual for someone to run, but these are urgent steps. Someone escaping something. Paul turns around just as a lanky man skids up to him on the loose gravel in the pavement.

'Are you Paul?' the man asks.

'Yes. Who are you? A cycling fan?'

'No, I like airplanes myself.'

'How do you know my name then?'

'Mr Morton spotted you in the bar earlier. He wants to see you.'

'Now?'

'I think we both know what he's like, so let's hurry. And let me warn you, the Cointreau has been flowing in wide rivers already.'

'What's your name?'

'It's not important. I've only been in London for a month, but after some of the things I've seen, I'm not planning to stick around. It's Canada for me. In fact, you know where his office is don't you?'

'Yes, but…'

'I'm off. Pleasure to meet you.

When Paul gets back to the club, Mr Morton stands outside, smoking a long cigarette, his free hand on the shoulder of a slim man dressed in black.

'Ah, Paul, so nice of you to join us. I hope you're enjoying the evening. I was waving to you from inside there. Didn't you see me?'

'Mr Morton, hello. No sorry I didn't. I've just had some news about my father, I was maybe a little bit distracted.'

'Nothing bad I hope?'

'Quite bad I'm afraid. The worst kind.'

'Well, death comes to us all,' Mr Morton says. 'Quicker to some than to others. It took my father years to die.'

'I'm sorry.'

'Don't be. It was many moons ago. And he was always a bastard.' Mr Morton spits a globule onto the ground, then says, 'But here's another thing. Let me introduce you to my great friend and enforcer: Drago. Shake hands boys, that's it. With the two of you working in unison we will go far boys. My powerhouse and my sharp lance. The two of you should become great friends I think.'

Mr Morton, now with his arms around both men, leads them back into the club, to a room one flight up from the big bar. It's an office hidden behind the mirrors over the main bar. Standing in the room Paul realises they are one-way mirrors and that he can now see the crowd of drinkers. Just as Mr Morton would have been able to see him down bottle after bottle a while ago. It's not a nice feeling realising he's been spied on, no matter how innocent his activities.

'It's rather impressive, don't you think?' Mr Morton says, standing behind Paul.

'Yes, very,' Paul nods.

'Lets me monitor the class of people we allow in. Wouldn't want any undesirable elements. Any suspicious men in uniform, or suspicious men out of uniform for that matter. They're always the worst kind of posers when they drink. It's either not enough to get drunk, I mean who comes here for a quiet drink? Or they drink soft drinks. Much like yourself Paul.'

Paul turns to Mr Morton, speaks up, 'It's not that I don't drink. It's just with the races, I always feel I need the sugar and the water more than beer. I always have to get up early in the morning after a race. You know, catching trains, wouldn't want to miss any early deliveries, or not be as fast as I can be. Beer, for me, tends to muddle the brain a bit.'

'You're very sweet Paul. Did you really think I was asking whether you were an undercover policeman?'

'No, no I didn't.'

'If you were police I'd be spoon-feeding you mercury.'

Mr Morton walks over to his desk, laughing softly, pointing over his shoulder with a crooked thumb, letting Drago in on the joke. Paul smiles and tries to think of the outside world. The last days of December the skies have been clear. Sometimes in the mornings the roads are covered in hoarfrost. Before people and the day have thawed the cobbles he has to take special care. Stay focused and upright. Same as with Mr Morton. There's a little heater in one corner of the room, close to Mr Morton's plush chair. The office itself isn't cold, but Paul has goosebumps. He starts rubbing his arms. Mr Morton flashes his teeth, shakes his head, says 'Scotland Yard' out into the air. Then Paul hears steps coming up to the door, and a double knock.

'Ah, that must be her,' Mr Morton says.

'Who?' Paul says, a second too late.

'The Queen, who else?'

Drago treads over softly, opens the door. Outside, applying lipstick, stands Miriam. She doesn't look up when the door opens, just finishes her make-up. Touches the edges of her lips daintily with a napkin. She flicks her hat with an index finger, which sends the black and golden feather quivering, like the insides of Paul, and steps over the threshold. She hands the napkin to Drago who's too surprised to refuse and continues to where Mr Morton is sitting behind a desk, working on his nails with the nib of an empty fountain pen.

'You're late,' he says without looking at her. His left hand now done, so he shifts the pen to his left hand.

'I'm sorry. But not too sorry. It wasn't as easy as you said it would be. The old man had barricaded himself up in his office. He had his two sons with him and several rifles. Victoria had to climb up to the floor above his, where there was a water cistern. She cracked it open, and we flushed him out.'

'He's gone?'

'He won't be operating from those premises any more.'

'Or any other premises I hope.'

Here Miriam nods, and looks at her shoes. She still hasn't looked at Paul. He hasn't looked at her. He knows she's got the poker face required for the situation. He knows he hasn't. He knows she's in control of the world around her, but if asked right now he would confess anything and everything from making a calf out of solid gold to Jack the Ripper's crimes to pissing on Mr Morton's car. Luckily Mr Morton is too interested in his nails.

'You know, the padres told me I was ambidextrous.'

'Sorry?' says Miriam.

'At school. It was a dreary place and I was often bored. I used to sit in class and take notes with my right hand and draw with my left. I was good at animals. Ponies, cats, even zebras you know. I thought I was quite talented, but the people in charge didn't like it at all. Thought it was a devilish trick.'

'That's a shame,' Miriam offers.

'I think so, too. Eventually they tied my left hand behind my back and told me to never do it again. But here I am, with perfect nails on both hands. Who's a little devil now?'

Paul tries to breathe quietly in the hope that he won't take up more space in Mr Morton's mind than a houseplant. He steals a glance at Miriam but catches Drago looking at him and smiles with a cocked eyebrow, a man-to-man expression. Paul makes sure to not look at anything other than the pattern of the floorboards, but Miriam's naked legs keep coming to him. He tries to will those flashes of colour and skin away. It doesn't work. He silently prays to a God he's not prayed to in a long time, not since one of first nights in the attic.

'Paul,' Mr Morton's voice a commanding rasp, 'you remember Miriam don't you?'

'Yes, yes I do,' Paul says trying to keep his voice from trembling.

'When was it that you two met?'

'In your office, your other office I mean, the white one, with the crucifix, that one, the white one,' Paul babbles, feeling his face go red.

'And not since?'

'Well, maybe here in the Carousel, in passing, I suppose.'

'You see Paul, this is important. To me Miriam is a mixture between a woman, a dog and a good commode. I own her. I need her. You see what I mean?'

Paul answers that he does, but the words leave a sour taste in his mouth. Miriam just stands there. Stock still. If he didn't know better he would think she couldn't hear them. Only the blinking of her eyes, much more often than she needs, gives away the fact that she's not one of Madame Tussaud's creations, found over by Regent's Park. They were all destroyed by fire a few years ago, and now they've rebuilt the place, with a restaurant and cinema, he thinks, wilfully trying to distract himself. Maybe he should take Miriam to the wax cabinet for an outing. She could scare punters with her straight face, suddenly winking or whistling. Despite the situation Paul smiles.

'Is that a smile? Anything you want to share with us Paul?' Mr Morton asks. 'Sorry, no. Just a sore gut from too much drink I think.'

Mr Morton raises himself up from his chair. Straightens his jacket. Pats his hair. Walks halfway around the desk and pulls one trouser leg up. He sits on one corner studying his diamond cufflinks.

'You see Paul, this girl belongs to me. From the feet up. From her little toes, past her delicious ankles, up past her dimpled knees, up along those gorgeous thighs, inner thighs too, white and unspoiled by the sun, past the curve of her buttocks and the gentle curve of her hips. You know, I think the hips of a woman are her most redeeming feature. Ships are launched over hips and their secrets. Not faces.'

Mr Morton stands up, picks up the fountain pen from his desk. Starts to slowly circle Miriam. Occasionally pointing to the parts he's talking about. Like a lecturer performing an autopsy in a hushed operating theatre.

'I own her front, her bust, however small or bolstered it may be, I own her throat, her face, her lips, and today they're nice and red. Almost blood red don't you think? Perfect for a kiss.' Mr Morton pouts, then laughs and continues, 'I own her mouth, her teeth, especially the one golden one in the back on the left hand side, not sure if you've seen that one? Beautiful work. Done by a Gypsy dentist I know. Silly girl ran straight into a crowbar one evening a couple of years ago.' Here he gestures for her to open her mouth and invites Paul to come and have a look at the tooth, pointing to it with the pen, deep into her mouth. Miriam obliges, focuses her eyes on the light fixture in the ceiling.

'I own her hair, piled high on top, or under a hat, or shaved off and weaved into a little doll for juju masters to stick needles into. You realise this?'

'Yes sir.'

'Good. But more to the point, I also own her insides. I own her brain, her mind, her thoughts, her fantasies, her secrets, her hopes, and fears. Her soul and future fate. I own all her unborn children, past and future. I own her family tree.'

Paul shifts his weight from one foot to the other, as Mr Morton continues, 'I could have had her years ago, and I might have, that's none of your business young man, but I chose not to. She was keen to of course, but I'm a married man, a good Catholic and wouldn't do such a thing to a poor young woman.'

Paul nods.

'But she's a lovely ripe tomato don't you think Paul?'

Paul doesn't answer. Just looks at Mr Morton's shoes. They gleam.

'Don't you think Paul?'

Eventually Paul says, 'I wouldn't know sir, I've never really paid attention to her.'

'Good,' laughs Mr Morton. 'Good, and let's keep it that way.'

Paul looks at Drago. The man smiles and fingers his goatee. Mr Morton drops the pen in a waste basket and walks up to Paul. He comes to a standstill about three inches from Paul and gestures for him to stoop down a little.

Face to face Paul can smell the Cointreau on his breath – the orange stink – Mr Morton continues, 'I know you wouldn't flirt with her, try anything, see her outside working hours as it were, or try to contact her in any way. You know, see her behind my back. This I know deep in my heart. You know how?'

'No sir.'

'Because if you did I would have to take a week off work and think up a worse death than I have ever offered anyone. Am I making myself clear?

'Yes.'

Mr Morton makes a fist with his right hand. Then his left. His eyes dark. Then he punches Paul in the face with his right, followed by a smart punch in Paul's solar plexus with his left. They're not real punches, but they're not playful either.

'Relax soldier,' Mr Morton says as Paul tries to get his breath back.

'Mmm,' is all he can say, eyes watering. Drago is giggling.

'Don't worry Paul, I know you haven't got it in you,' Mr Morton continues, flexing his fingers. 'She's too good for you. She's many tiers up.'

'No, no I don't,' Paul croaks.

'See I could have become quite a good boxer. Being ambidextrous means I can lead with either hand. I'm not regular, nor a southpaw. I'm dangerous from either angle.' Mr Morton throws another punch in the air. 'You ok son? I thought you sportsmen had more stamina than this.'

'I'm fine, thank you,' Paul manages to say.

'Good, because now I want you to piss off, and go win some races or whatever it is you do when you're not lounging around, receiving pay from me.'

'Thank you.'

As Paul leaves he makes sure he doesn't look at Miriam, who's still standing in the exact same spot since the examination. Mr Morton is back behind his desk, 'Now young lady, let's talk a bit more about this afternoon, and what we're doing tomorrow. It's a big evening. I want something quite spectacular to happen.'

Drago closes the door and leads Paul through the crowds of drinkers. By the cuff, as though he is a man with unpaid debts. Paul finds himself in the street. The left side of his face hurts and he can't think straight. He forces himself to put one foot in front of the other, over and over again, until he's far enough away from the club that he can't see it. Then he can think of home. Of his bed. He makes sure he doesn't think of Miriam.

His shoes and trouser legs are still wet, and the evening is cold. The days between Christmas and New Year have a sad quality to them. People are working. Broke, but covered in tinsel. With the memory of lard and feasting behind them, but the colourful streamers and flying corks not yet in sight.

It's a long way to walk home. He's gone off the idea of staying in a hotel. The night would be too short to make it worth the money anyway. As it is he won't have time for much more than a nap between coming home for his things and having to leave again for the train station. Still feeling winded and with sore teeth he resigns himself to the steady plodding of his feet. Left, right, left, right all the way to Copenhagen Street.

He's relieved to see the bike outside his room when he gets in. Guarded by a grubby boy about ten years old. Once the boy sees Paul he whips his hat off and rushes down the stairs. It's quarter to four in the morning and Paul's teeth are soft from all the sugar he's had, and his head is like a blown-out egg. In just over three hours he needs to be on a train that will take him to an evening race up north.

Chapter 33

The train journey and the exercise takes his mind off the death of his father and the conversation he had with Mr Morton. But not entirely. While waiting for the train back he sends a letter to his uncle, asking about the farm, the deeds and so on, giving a very brief summary of his life in London, his racing and giving his return address as c/o Halkias, Copenhagen Street. Sitting on the train back to London he can't recall much about the race. He's not even entirely sure how he placed. Decides to ask Silas if he knows.

It's New Year's Eve, which means he has two days off from the racing. Once Paul gets back to his room Silas knocks on his door. It's as if he's been waiting for Paul's return. Silas enters and lays out a not new, but nice enough, suit for Paul to put on.

'I heard you did well up north. In fact you've had a good season. I thought you might want to come out for a drink.'

'I'm fine thank you. I need to eat and sleep.'

'Humbug. You need to live and laugh. Here, I even got you a suit.'

'You didn't have to.'

'I know,' Silas says smiling and spreading his arms. 'Go on, I know it fits. I have your measurements with my eyes, though I must say I think your thighs are getting bigger every time I see you.'

Silas says, 'Put it on young man, there's a taxi waiting downstairs. No time to stand about. And put some of that pomade in your hair. This is an upscale club, you can't come in looking like a vagrant, like you usually do.'

As Paul puts on his trousers Silas takes out a glass bottle with a big atomiser ball on a golden string, tasselled and bejewelled. He walks over to Paul and shrouds him in a musky cloud. Then Silas stands back to watch Paul change his shirt, only coming over when he gets stuck on the cufflinks.

Silas commands the driver to the Peacock Club and seats Paul next to him. Ever since their arrival, Silas has been busy speaking to the hordes of people he seems to know. He doesn't seem to remember Paul, which actually suits Paul fine. Silas laughs and waves to people, his cigar sending ash in little puffs and arcs everywhere.

Silas' companion, a young boy impeccably dressed, in what Silas says is a tuxedo with a *notch lapel,* or rather a *step collar,* this side of the Atlantic, stands up, excuses himself with a little curtsey, and walks, as though he was on a tightrope, to the bathroom. It's only then that Silas turns the other way, to Paul.

'I know you don't drink Paul. Did you ever?'

'I used to.'

'But I was thinking maybe today you could make an exception?'

'I'm not sure.'

'How about I'll never ask you again, if you just this once have a glass of bubbly? I just want to see you a bit perkier.'

'I'm fine.'

'I know, but you could be better. I understand the news about your father must have hit you hard, as well as everything else.'

'You're right, but drinking won't fix that.'

'I know, and I'm not suggesting that either, and I'm not trying to convince you to drink yourself into a coma either, I'm just saying, let down your guard for one night only. It's New Year's Eve for God's sake. Have a drink, have a laugh.'

'Fine, but just the one glass.'

'Just the one. I'll get you the Pol-Roger, it's very good.'

Silas signals for a waiter and soon the cork comes flying out, and the golden foam is poured into high flutes. Then the boy comes back, and they get another glass.

'Sorry Paul, I didn't introduce you properly,' Silas says. 'This is Sebastian. I know his father, he's one of those men who owns ocean liners, you know one of those America Line ones, in this case Cunard.' Paul nods and holds out his hand for a limpid shake. 'So, Mr Cunard Junior let me introduce you to Paul MacAllister. Britain's fastest man.' 'You a jockey?' the boy asks, showing his ignorance. No person Paul's size would be any good on a race horse, 'Or is it cars?'

'Bikes.'

'Bikes?'

'Velodromes mostly.'

'I see. It's not for me, but a lot of the people, you know the people working at my father's company, especially at the docks, you know the thicker types, riveters and joiners, they like these spectacles.'

'But you've never been yourself?' Paul asks.

'No.'

'I could get you some seats if you were interested?'

'That's nice of you Paul. Sure, I'll contact you through Silas here, our mutual friend and rogue, if I ever get the urge.'

'Anytime.'

'Speaking of the urge, can I speak to you in private Silas?'

Silas looks to Paul – whose glass is full again – smiles and stands up. Paul empties the glass, the soft bubbles tickling his nose, and starts walking to the bar, then stops and holds onto a pillar, his head a gyroscope. Despite not drinking much, he's not fit to walk. He plots out a route from where he is to where he needs to be, the bar fifteen feet away, past things he can hold onto. This includes plants, the wall, a sturdy man's shoulders, and the beginning of the bar, a service area busy with staff.

Paul's not convinced the effect of the champagne alone could have done this to him. After a while of drinking water and orange juice Paul feels better and risks letting go of the bar he's been holding onto with knuckles going whiter and whiter. Silas catches his eye and beckons him over. This time Paul chances it and walks straight across the floor to their booth. He sways, narrowly missing a waiter carrying a huge platter covered with a silver dome. He bumps into two women dancing; their feet so fast, they're just a blur. The women laugh, take his hands and swing him around to the music – a fast brass-driven ragtime – which doesn't help his progress. When they let go, to dance with another more malleable, and richer, victim, Paul sets off for the table. When he finally arrives he's out of puff. Not bad for a semi-professional athlete.

Silas' friend is off again, ordering something, inhaling something, smoking something. Kissing someone, fixing something, and in general spending an enormous amount of money. Silas leans close to Paul and says, 'Sebastian is a very, very talented artist you see. He asked me to sit for him. He was a bit bashful about asking, that's why he wanted to do it tête-à-tête.'

'That's nice of him. Is it a portrait? Will you end up looking like a king?'

'I don't think it'll be quite as regal as that, but you never know.'

Just then the boy comes over with four waiters behind him. He starts conducting along to the music that's playing and at the end of a big crescendo he waves his arms about and the three waiters in the front, all with reserved smiles, each pop a cork of champagne, GH Mumm this time, Silas tells Paul. The fourth one carrying a large tray of glasses walks into the middle of the circle they form and soon all the glasses are full. With a flick of the wrist Silas sends them out into the crowd, while the first waiter opens another bottle, in a more restrained way, for the booth.

There's singing and shouting. Then, noticing ripples in the crowd, Paul and Silas stand up, to see better. Silas consults his pocket watch and explains that there will be a troupe of girls, twenty-eight of them for the year, who will perform at eleven.

'It's based on Swan Lake, but not as boring as the ballet,' he says.

'And there's one more to join them for a more special show,' here he elbows Paul in the side, 'after the clock's struck twelve.'

Paul nods.

'It's Danica Petrovious if you must know, but don't go telling any of the other men or we'll have a riot on our hands here.'

The name means nothing to Paul but he nods conspiratorially.

After the show, a mixture of string music and white feathers, of blaring trumpets and skirts thrown up to show bottoms, there's just enough time to go out on the balcony to listen to Big Ben toll. Silas being Silas he has reserved a place on the balcony for himself, the shipping boy and Paul.

A man in what looks like mayoral chains stands up on a chair holding a huge hammer. He shouts 'Oy, Oy!' over and over until people fall silent, turn to him. He gets a pocket watch out and nods happily to himself.

'Ladies and gentlemen,' the man says looking out over the crowd, 'and present company. We are on the brink of another year. I don't have any speeches to deliver, I'm not the kind, but I want to thank you for putting your trust in me this year too, and for continuing to come to this watering hole. I consider each and every one of you my friend.' He raises the hammer over his head, and the chain jangles. He's breathing deeply, and looks like an overweight Valkyrie, a god in oversized woman's jewellery.

'Please raise your glasses and join me in a toast, the last of the year.'

Silas produces three not so small glasses and pours greenish liquid into each of them, handing one to Paul and one to Sebastian.

'To us,' the man shouts, and the crowd answers in drunk unison, 'To us.'

Silas says, 'All in one go my boys, all in one go. Best to swallow quickly.'

Paul obeys, the drink setting fire to his mouth.

'What was that?' he asks once he can breathe again.

'You've never had absinthe before?' Sebastian smirks, but Paul can see that the boy's eyes are watering too. 'Better be careful with this stuff. It's enough to drive you to cutting off your ears. But by God is it good for your vision. You look like an angel Silas.'

'I am an angel,' Silas exclaims.

'That would be very boring,' laughs Sebastian and puts a hand on Silas' cheek.

'Now, everyone,' the man with the hammer intones in a voice used to speaking to the masses, 'if you could help me with the countdown.'

Silas busies himself with refilling the glasses as the man, and everyone around them say, Ten, Nine, Eight, then shout, Seven, Six, Five, Four, then scream at the top of their lungs, Three, Two, One; Happy New Year!

'Happy New Year Paul, you lovely man,' smiles Silas, closing his eyes and leaning in to kiss Paul on the mouth. Paul moves awkwardly to one side and Silas stumbles, off balance.

'Happy New Year Silas,' Paul says, giving Silas a firm handshake, and continuing with a bashful smile, 'Silas, London is very different from Lennoxtown. I understand that you are, well, different. But I'm not like that. Whatever it is that makes you tick, well, I am not, not that kind of clock, if you get my meaning.'

Silas dissolves into tipsy giggles, 'Not that kind of clock! I know, my dear boy, I know. You're a tick and I'm a tock. Quite incompatible. I'm sorry. Put it down to New Year delirium.'

They both laugh, relieved, and turn to watch the scene unfold in the room. The Valkyrie has fallen off his chair and is now scampering around the room, laughing demonically. A huge net of balloons is being released into the crowd by a man in a jester's costume and confetti shoots out of cannons set up in every corner of the room, manned by the feathered dancing girls. Then the girls disappear.

'To get ready, shed some feathers, for the next instalment of their show,' Silas says. Silas pours Sebastian another drink, but excuses Paul this time. People are singing and scraps of paper fall like snow around them. The others finish their drink and then Silas laughs. He throws his glass off the balcony and staggers away, making rounds in the crowd, kissing mouths and cheeks. People flock inside for the show and Paul is pulled along. Accepting a drink from one of the dancing cannon girls.

An hour later, after a breathless Danica, more hugs and kisses, the tap Charleston and the Pyramides smoked, Paul is unsteady again. He stands on the balcony looking out over London. Just letting his eyes roam streets he knows so well, corners he's taken a hundred times. He plots shortcuts he's never thought of. The air is cold, but not too cold.

He tries to explain to a woman next to him about the dangers of tram tracks and bicycle wheels, and the unfortunate coincidence that they are of a very similar width. His speech is too slurry, his thoughts fragmented, and he can tell he's boring her. After a while he excuses himself, draws a line over his lips with an unsteady finger, and resumes his mapping of the streets. Eventually he comes back in and walks over to the booth where Silas sits laughing with Sebastian, now sporting a feather tiara. The men are leaning in close, and Paul decides to leave while he can still walk.

By looking carefully at the ground before he decides where to put his foot, he navigates the stairs and comes out at street level. He moves away from the crowds at Piccadilly Circus. He makes it all the way to St James's Square before he's violently sick. He puts his head against a cool lamppost, revelling in the sensation of something in the world standing still. He even considers putting his tongue to the lamppost, despite the low temperature, to wash the taste of the party off his mouth.

Before he has time to act on his impulse he falls over, narrowly missing the flowers he has just defaced.

The shock and the taste of blood in his mouth help a little. His split lower lip stings as he takes great gulps of cold air. He raises himself up on his elbows and then, using the fence, drags himself up. He walks on foal's legs until his head clears a little. By then he's not far from Hampstead Heath and the baths. He's quite happy with the quick progress of the sobering up. That's until he starts singing '*You're the coffee in my cream*', outside Miriam's window. He's unsure of the tune even when sober, off-key at the best of times. He thought he was sober, but realises he's not. Still he can't stop singing. It seems like the funniest thing he's ever done. Standing outside. A shouting tomcat with red ears from the cold, and a red nose from the spirits.

Nothing happens, Miriam doesn't open her window, so he walks over to the main entrance. There he tries to speak to Suzanne who is sitting on a chair reading behind the door in the reception.

'Good evening,' he says, rapping his knuckles on the glass of the door.

'Hello, good morning. How are you Paul?'

'Why are you here?' he says. He's having to concentrate very hard on every syllable, and still mumbles and mispronounces things, like a foreigner.

Suzanne smiles and says, 'Last year we had some trouble with break-ins around this time of year. I don't mind, they're giving me triple pay, and I've got children. These days I prefer money to a hangover.'

'I'm looking for Miriam.'

'I know. But she's not in.'

'Where is she?'

'How should I know? Working, dancing, celebrating,' she says, shrugging her shoulders.

'Can you let me into her apartment?'

'No, sorry. But I can give you a cup of tea and you can wait here if you like.'

'Thank you, that's very kind, but I think I need to lie down.'

'I bet you do.'

'Why can't you just let me in?'

'I don't have the key, simple as that.'

'You have a ladder? She usually leaves the bedroom window open,' Paul says, measuring a shaky inch between his fingers.

'That's more information than I needed to know, but yes there's a ladder at the back.'

'Can I borrow it?' Paul says, animated.

'You shouldn't be on it.'

'But I will.'

'I know. Let me go get it.'

With Suzanne holding the ladder, giggling like a schoolgirl, Paul climbs up and into Miriam's bedroom. He undresses, tries to fold his clothes neatly but can't, goes to the toilet and ends up shadowboxing the long string for the cistern.

Once in bed he smiles at his ingenuity, and the surprise Miriam will get when she comes home. Humming the tune from outside he sends himself to sleep, the window still fully open. A cold wind, the first storm of the year, blowing in.

***

'Paul!' Miriam shrieks when she comes into the room. At eight in the morning. 'I almost killed you.' She puts down the knife she's gotten out of a hidden pocket in her dress.

'Didn't Suzanne tell you I was here?' he says sleepily from the depths of the bed.

'She wasn't there. It was Benjamin on reception.'

'She must have gone home,' he says sleepily into the pillow.

'It's freezing in here.'

'Can you speak a little quieter?' he says, his voice hoarse.

'Paul, you can't just come here, I'm serious, Mr Morton's

not joking you know. He would have you killed in a heartbeat if he knew what we were up to.'

'I'm sorry. I just wanted to surprise you.' He sits up, only now realising how upset she is.

'Well you achieved that. And don't misunderstand me, I like having you here, but this cannot continue. What if he realises you come here? What if he realises how much you mean to me?'

'I didn't mean to scare you. I was outside singing in the night and everything, hoped you'd be home, but you were somewhere dancing.'

'I was not out dancing. I was working, and I'm very tired now. My feet are in pieces.' Then she starts to cry. Paul comes out from under the covers and walks over to her. Holds her.

'Paul,' she says, 'we have to be more careful. He has eyes everywhere. I can't live with this permanent fear. This is the one place I can come to that Mr Morton doesn't know about. I've taken care to keep it secret. I always cover my tracks when I come here. I need you to do the same. To take this seriously. I know you're fast on the bike, but I need you to be faster. Sneakier. Take long detours, narrow lanes, watch your back. Never mention this place to anyone. Not even, in fact especially not, Silas.'

'What a way to start the New Year. I'm sorry.'

'Me too. It's not the way I want it to be, it's just the way it is.'

'Well if we don't like it I think we should think of a way to change our situation.'

'If only it was that easy.'

'I know it's not, I just mean, I can't not see you.'

'We'll think of something. And till then you be careful, always go the long way, stay out of sight, and so will I.'

'Can you trust Suzanne and Benjamin?'

'As far as they know, I look after the pets of a very wealthy man in Richmond. I usually stay over at his mansion, but sometimes I'm here.'

'Who do they think I am?'

'The gardener.'

They go to bed. It's too cold in the room to stand and cry.

'Where were you?' she asks once they've settled under the covers.

'At the Peacock.'

'With Silas?'

'Yes.'

'You should stay away from it, and from drinking with Silas' friends.'

'I will never drink again I promise.'

'You must still be drunk otherwise you'd be more scared of me.'

'I am.'

'Which?'

'Both.' She snuggles up to him, then he says, 'He's dead.'

'What? Who? Silas?'

'No, my father.'

'Oh Paul, I'm sorry. What happened to him?'

'Heart attack. He drank a lot. That's why I don't. Except last night.'

'Are you alright?'

'Fine. Sad that I'm not sadder. And I've missed the funeral.'

'Can I do anything?'

'No, just do what you do. I'm fine, really.'

She puts a hand in his hair and plants a big, wet kiss on his forehead, then she asks, 'Did you climb up?'

'Ladder. Suzanne.'

'I'm going to have a word with her.'

'Shush, just come here.'

★★★

When they wake up it's the afternoon and Paul has stopped being cheeky. His head is exploding, and his tongue feels like it's made of sandpaper. He's cold, then hot, then sick.

When he comes back from the bathroom looking sheepish, Miriam gets up too. Not to be sick, but to call down for eggs and a huge pot of coffee. Then she dresses in a big fur coat, and helps Paul into his jacket too.

'Come on you big oaf. I'm going to cure you. It will hurt, but it's better than having this linger for days.'

She leads him down the stairs and out to the big frozen ponds. They stroll out on a frosty jetty, and then without a word of warning she pushes him off the edge. He comes up spluttering and swearing. At first he tries to swim, then putting his legs under him he realises the water is only knee-deep. His jacket clings to him.

'Shock, adrenaline, cold water, anger, it all helps,' Miriam says from the safety of the jetty. With a roar he pushes himself out of the water and sets off after her. Soon his teeth are chattering so much he can't even shout the revenge plans he thinks up while running. She sprints back to the Baths and up the stairs. Throwing off her fur coat and her shoes she dives into bed. He stands on the doormat and smiles. Miriam's cheeks are flushed, her hair is wild, the sun shining in on the bed picking out tiny diamonds of frost in her curls. She smiles, she's panting from the run and the excitement. Without coming out from under the covers she sheds layer after layer of clothes. She makes sure Paul, who's standing dripping, smiling wider and wider, can see exactly what it is she takes off.

'Paul, get out of your clothes before you catch pneumonia,' she says.

'Are we even now?' he manages to say between shattering teeth.

'Almost.'

He wrestles out of his clothes, keeping his eyes on her.

'You enjoying this?' he asks her.

'Immensely.'

He's soon down to vest and pants.

'Would you be a darling and bring the coffee and the eggs with you when you come to bed?' she asks.

Benjamin has placed a tray laden with coffee, cream, cups, sugar lumps and six fresh eggs, outside the door and Paul carries it over to the bed, his skin burning.

'None of your wet clothes in here please,' she says, taking the tray. Then she almost averts her gaze. Then they are seated. Arm to arm, hip to hip, thigh to thigh. She puts a foot on his and then shouts, 'You're freezing.'

'Now you know how I feel.'

'My feet are never cold.'

'Your feet would be cold in the Sahara.'

'Quiet and drink your coffee.'

After sipping a cup each in silence, she turns to him and says, 'Feeling better now?'

'I do. Actually I do.'

'Here's the last chapter in my recovery plan,' she says, and gets an egg out of the carton. She cracks one into her empty coffee cup, then another, then mixes in cream. She pours the mixture into his empty cup, then tops it with a little coffee.

'Drink this,' she says thrusting the cup at him.

'Why?'

'It's good for you.'

'How?'

'Well it's good for the hangover and...'

'And?'

'It's good for certain other bits too.'

He feels himself blushing, but dutifully downs the mixture. It's revolting, and he quickly pours more coffee into his cup, followed by two sugar lumps. In the meantime Miriam has slipped out of bed and has closed the curtains enough to only let in a shaft of sunshine. Then she turns to him.

★★★

They are still in bed when the evening comes. Which admittedly is very early in January. He's propped up, sitting with his back to the wall, and she's lying on her side, away from him, nestled into his right leg.

'Will you read me something from my book?'

'Of course. Where is it?'

'Here,' she reaches in under the mattress and pulls out the thin notebook. He reads her one or two poems, but he is finding it hard to concentrate.

'That's enough Paul. Let's leave it for another time,' she says, smiling.

He puts the book by the side of the bed and turns to her. He's warm now. His head feels better. The New Year has treated him well so far. Soon they're very warm and sleepy again.

Chapter 34

His brief holiday ends and the usual summons come from Mr Morton. In rain, sleet and snow Paul delivers and picks up. Avoids and outraces the police. January passes with fewer races, as the crowds are less willing to stand outside, but more deliveries as more people owe Mr Morton money after the holidays.

One lunch time, early February, Paul cycles past Belinda's place. Realising he's hungry he doubles back on himself. It's the thought of a friendly face rather than the food that draws him in. He is directed to a freshly wiped table by one of the girls. Then Belinda comes over, one arm on her hip, the other in her hair.

'How are you Paul? It's been a long time.'

'I'm fine. Busy. I've been out and about on that bike for hours.'

'I can see you keep yourself fit.' She looks him up and down. 'You racing tonight?'

'No, not tonight.'

'What are you doing with your night off?'

'Look, I'm sorry Belinda. You know, you're a delightful woman, really, but I can't. I've got a girlfriend.'

'Oh Paul, you daft boy, I was just making conversation. I've been married for almost six years. He's an older man, with some money, no demands really. A nice man.'

'But Silas...'

'Silas what?' Belinda smiles a wide smile.

'He told me you were quite keen on me. On men.'

'Well, I am. But not that way.'

'What way then?'

'I like people. I like chatting. That's all.

'I don't know what to say.' Paul sits back in his chair, feeling his face go red.

'So what Silas has said about you trying to get me to marry you?' he says.

'It's rubbish,' she smiles.

'And the letters you are always showing me? Were they not to make me jealous?'

'Not at all. He's a friend of my brother's. I've always liked him, but I've not seen him for twenty years. I told you for no reason.'

'I'm sorry.'

'Don't worry. I'm a chatterbox, so I'm sure I've told Silas a lot of stuff he thinks is private. He's the sort of man who likes to feel like he knows everything about everybody.'

'That's true.'

'He's a lovely man, don't get me wrong. He tips well, he's dapper, polite, and many years ago, he really helped me out. Lent me enough money to get me out of trouble with a horrible man. Then let me pay back in instalments, no interest.'

'But you're saying he's a bit of a gossip?' Paul says, now smiling.

'The biggest one you'll ever meet. And that's how he's survived his arrangement with that Mr Morton, and how he manages to do so well on the horses. Jockeys and trainers and bookkeepers and owners, they all talk.'

'Makes sense.'

'I bet he doesn't know everything about you.'

'I don't know?'

'I bet there's a special place where you go for a drink, where you can sit with your back to the door and still feel safe. I bet there's a little lady somewhere, someone who makes you feel at home. Maybe even two or three, judging by the pomade.'

Paul self-consciously pats his hair.

'Only joking love, you look fine,' she says laughing. 'If I was ten years younger and not married, I would have made sure you noticed me. As it is I enjoy my games with Silas and the long string of suitors he keeps bringing here. All trying to save me. It's good for business.'

'I won't tell him.'

Belinda lets out a big chortle and smacks him on the shoulder. She keeps her hand there, and says, 'Right what can I get you? On the house?'

'A big portion. But not eel, something else please.'

She walks off, still laughing and starts telling the younger girls what to do. Paul just sits, looks out through the window, delighted to be inside, away from the weather, and relieved not to be moving. Then the food arrives. Cod and mash.

Just as he's about to tuck into the mound of potato one of the little messenger boys comes up with a note saying he's wanted at the greengrocer's around the corner from Copenhagen Street. Excusing himself, and telling Belinda to give his food to someone who's struggling to pay, he walks out of the café. He's so hungry he's seeing stars, but he can't risk not obeying orders immediately.

Once Paul gets to the fruit and veg man he's asked to deliver a heavy sack of potatoes, a sirloin steak folded into waxed paper, as well as an apple, a slice of cheddar and a handful of beetroots to Bergholt Crescent, Stamford Hill. This is a lot more weight and mass than he's used to.

When Paul asks who the delivery is for the man barely nods, just scuttles back down into the basement.

Paul has to stop every now and then to retie the straps across his back and chest.

The house he gets to is small, but clean. The little white gate stands open, and he walks down a crunchy gravel path, his weight, plus all the things he's carrying, making deep imprints in the path.

There's smoke coming from the chimney, and there's a candleholder with nine arms, four on each side and one taller in the middle, in the window next to the door. Next to the knocker on the door he notices a small gold rectangle set on a slant with strange letters on it.

Paul lifts the knocker, and is about to swing it when the door opens. In front of him stands an ancient woman, wrinkled like a plum. She wears a fringed scarf wrapped around her face and a dizzying amount of layers, ending in fur boots. She says something in a language he doesn't understand and smiles a smile so void of teeth it looks like a newborn's. She waves him inside.

He bows low, the doorway no higher than his shoulders, enters and puts the sack food on the floor.

A younger woman in her late forties, in a bright, but old-fashioned and foreign dress, comes out from behind a screen and starts wringing her hands. Just inside the door a pair of riding boots, polished to a sheen like a still loch.

Paul tells her she doesn't owe him any money, but the woman doesn't react. When he asks if everything is alright, if the delivery is what she expected, the younger woman just replies in the same sibilant language as the older, still beyond Paul's understanding.

Paul nods and starts to leave, but the young woman screams, and quickly puts herself between him and the door. The old woman walks over to the door and locks it with a big iron key. She says 'Mr Morton,' and points to a chair in the corner. The woman opens the window and throws the key far out into the garden. Then she blows out all nine candles with a single blow. Paul struggles to suppress the urge to vomit.

The younger woman now motions for Paul to sit by the fire. Gives him a chunk of dark bread and a small glass of hot, sweet tea from a massive urn standing on the table.

The younger woman starts chopping the vegetables and salts the meat. She boils the beetroot, and the potato, making a soup. Then heats a griddle iron while she sets the table for four. Then there's a sound of a key in the door. When he sees the big white shape on the threshold, a wave of nausea washes over him.

'Paul,' Mr Morton says, 'nice to see you.'

'Pleasure's all mine,' Paul manages to say.

'Are you feeling peaky? You're green in the face.'

'No, I'm fine.'

'Will you join us for dinner? Please. You must.'

'Thank you, but I was hoping to get going. Have a couple of things, deliveries actually, I'd like to get through tonight.'

'You will join us for dinner. Besides, I know you don't have any other engagements. I've made sure of it.'

The old woman sets steaming hot food on the table. Mr Morton invites everyone to sit. Then he commands them to close their eyes and bow their heads over interlaced fingers. He prays a long, convoluted and flowery prayer to Saint Christopher. When he's finished, he looks up at them. 'That's it. Your souls are now saved.'

The woman serves Mr Morton the steak along with a potato gratin, and on a side plate she cuts up the apple and the cheese for him. Then she pours him a large glass of foamy beer, and he commences to eat.

For herself, the old woman and Paul, she fills a bowl with watery soup called *borscht*.

Between mouthfuls Mr Morton tells Paul why he's here. The Russian maître d' has turned up, and he swears that the note with Ilya's fateful numbers were different from how they usually look. This both incriminates him, as he shouldn't know what the notes usually look like, and is probably the truth, as it was the second to last sentence in his life. Mr Morton tells Paul all this, in the same tone as if he was talking about the price of wheat or how to burn a brick. Non-committal, aloof.

The two women either don't understand English. Or at least they pretend they don't. All Paul can see of their reaction to Mr Morton being there, apart from fear and servitude, is the way they eye his sirloin steak.

'Now, Paul,' says Mr Morton, 'I'm not convinced about

this, but it doesn't really matter. The last sentence this man said out loud was an accusation. A pretty serious one at that. I can't know for sure he's right, as the note itself has been destroyed, but I know from experience that I run a tight ship and that incidents like these are always down to the human element. And never to me.'

Mr Morton chews with his mouth open wide, then continues, 'I've decided that even though you might not be entirely guilty, you are not entirely innocent. So, what I want you to do, which I think is quite reasonable, is to go halves with me on the money that Ilya lost me. That you lost me.'

'I don't know anything about this. And either way I have no money, none at all,' Paul blurts out.

'I know. So I'm going to lend you some, which you will then bet on yourself in a race, with rigged odds of course, and once you win, you can repay the little debt first, and then see the rest as a first payment towards the larger sum.'

'Can I think about this? You see I'm not a betting man. Not since my father lost us our home several times over.'

'You're a funny man. Of course you can't think about this. It's been decided, this is just me being courteous enough to inform you ahead of time. I'm killing two birds with one stone.'

'How? Is there more to come?'

'Not for you. But you see the younger woman? She is Ilya's second widow. I now own her and I'm taking her with me to have her installed in a place over in Ireland. She's going to be very popular with the customers I think. Look at her bone structure.'

'Please don't.'

'Do you know her?' Mr Morton asks, looking straight at Paul, as if for clues.

'Never seen her before.'

'Then shut up.'

Mr Morton pushes his plate away from him, dries his chin on the tablecloth and stands up.

'Paul I'm also a bit upset with you for other reasons.'

'I didn't do anything. The man must have made this whole thing up.'

'Don't worry your head about that. I've decided how it's going to play out and I never go back on a plan.' Mr Morton's gaze sweeps the room. He looks satisfied in the knowledge he's had the last word. 'Now, I've got a niggling feeling you're maybe getting to know one of my employees too well.'

'Who? I just pick up messages and deliver them.'

'Think hard before you speak again.' Mr Morton looks straight at Paul.

'You mean Silas?' Paul says, beads of sweat running down his back. 'I spent New Year's Eve with him, quite drunk, if that's what you mean?'

'Don't make me more upset with you than I already am.'

'I honestly...'

'I'm leaving now and I'm taking the woman with me, but I'm going to deal with you and this other situation once I get back from Dublin. Think hard about which race you want to win, and how much you need to bet to meet the targets.'

'How much is it?'

'Just win as much as you can, then I'll let you know how far off you are. Either way I have to speak to Silas first, he's your handler after all. I'm going to let the widow pack while I eat cheese and apple, might even get a cup of tea, then we're off. Now run along, Paul.'

Chapter 35

Mr Morton tells me I need to make the boy more profitable. That he has transferred some of the Russian's debt to Paul. That there will be a race in the near future I will have to place a special bet on. While I try to get my head around what this means he starts talking about medicine.

Then he mentions that he knows a doctor who's come up with some miraculous new mixtures. A doctor who's not afraid to experiment. I nod and say yes. I think about the strongbox in his office above the pub. I know it hasn't been emptied between last week and now, and the Carousel has been very busy with drinkers.

He talks about side effects and necessary sacrifices. About injections and slowly upping the dosage. I nod. Say yes. Think about the coarse twine string holding up the crucifix in his white office upstairs. Fantasize about choking Mr Morton with it.

This can't possibly continue. It has to stop. For my sake. For Paul's sake. Mr Morton talks about opiates and some of the things he has heard that they did in the war to make soldiers more alert.

I wasn't meant to notice it I'm sure, but between the cross, on the twine, next to the dull gleam of the nail driven into the wall, was another brighter speck of metal. A key.

Mr Morton tells me he might arrange for an associate of Doctor Heinrich Dreser to come over to England and run some tests on Paul in the near future.

I make myself reach over and shake his hand, tell him it's about time we took the boy to the next level. This earns me a cigar and another hour in his company.

When I finally get away from the Carousel, I sit in another

pub, where I'm unlikely to bump into anyone I know. I think about things. I think about the future. I try to make a plan and try to work out the odds of me succeeding. It doesn't look good. But then again, things can't stay the same. I have to go for broke. I celebrate with a bourbon, something I never do, but it's time to embrace the spirit of the Americas.

I decide to tell Paul about my idea for the upcoming race, the day after tomorrow. I know where he'll be racing after all, always do.

I travel back to my house and have a bath. Think things over. Then I walk over to Portobello. Mr Morton's revelations weighing heavily on me. I need to ignore it to deal with it. I know where I will end up and it's a good destination. I'm angry and hungry enough to eat an honest portion of food.

I usually make a point of letting one of the little grubby boys that hang around either outside my own house, the Carousel or the house on Copenhagen Street, know where I'm going. Not that it's their business, but Mr Morton likes to be able to get hold of me. Sometimes it's been good to be able to say to people less than eager to give up their possessions that Mr Morton knows exactly where I am. That if I don't report back by a pre-arranged time, things will get even more complicated.

This time though, I've snuck out the back. Suppose I could have told the boy a lie, but despite everything I don't particularly enjoy a straight lie. Missing someone, being away for a little while. That's just what happens in life. Lying about my destination and my intents to Mr Morton would quickly render me unable to walk.

I'm taking my time, enjoying my relative freedom. Allowing myself to think back, to dream ahead. I know the food will bring memories, it's more than half the reason I go there. Some days I emerge back out into the drab Englishness a jubilant and proud strong Greek. All of antiquity on my shoulders, modern society created by me and the generations who stride in my shadow.

Sometimes the smells, the language, the sound of the bouzouki – however badly played – make my eyes water. I measure myself and my life's progress against a different set of blueprints from most people. I am not them. I am not of this place. I might have mastered it – and if so therein lies my intelligence – but I am not of England. I like it here. Some days I even love it, but I am fundamentally torn between the two countries, always will be.

Ambling down Portobello Road, looking at things I don't need, or want, just enjoying being on my own. It's busy, but not dense, people are out on errands but not rushing around heedlessly. It's something I enjoy about the British, this determination and diligence. I pet a dog, look at a cloud of pigeons settling on a roof, consider a new pair of gloves in a very expensive shop and decide to buy them before I change my mind. Kidskin, I've never owned a pair before but now I understand why people like them. Putting them on, I walk past a Wine & Spirit dealer, a China Merchant, an Engraver & Printer, a Hat Manufacturer, and a Slater. All jolly good at what they do I'm sure. All jolly stuck.

I try to catalogue these shopfronts in my mind. Some of them look a bit run down, maybe I should come back here and ask them if they would be interested in a business loan: *Very reasonable rates of interest; Two percent per annum knocked off if you decide today; I'll come back in a little while; Let you mull it over.* That whole spiel. I know it like actors know their Tempest.

At a shop called *Henderson's Antiques*, I look at prams and tea sets, inspect the welding beads of a chair made from the wing of an aeroplane, playfully try a klaxon. The man running the shop comes over all haughty. He explains I've just touched one of the klaxons he was commissioned to send to America. 'The composer Gershwin if you must know,' he says. I can tell he's told the story before, and that he will tell it again until his grandchildren are tired of it.

'*An American in Paris*, his new big piece, uses four taxi horns, made here, in this very workshop. You must have heard of it,' he says. 'They just came back from touring the world.'

When I politely shake my head and go to put the instrument down on the bit of felt he keeps it on, he snatches it from my hands and swats me out of his shop like I was a horsefly. I batter my way back inside and buy the damned thing. For the asking price. In cash. Then I move on, making an extra note to myself to make sure he needs a business loan in the near future.

Intriguing, though, that America keeps coming up in conversation and in my thoughts. If I was more like my mother with her streak of clairvoyance – not the showy Cranbourn Street Hippodrome kind, but the real, useful kind – I could probably make sense of some of these premonitions. As it is I stagger along blindly. An understudy stumbling over the lines of my own life, re-enacting myself.

Outside the Greek restaurant I've been aiming for and avoiding most of the afternoon, a small, dark man in a beret sits smoking. When he sees me he gets up and walks off, I chase off after him, thrust the klaxon at him. He takes it, as surprised as I am. He is the old man I could have become but never will. I turn back and look at a group of sweaty white men puking up ale in the gutters, then kissing prostitutes on the mouth.

The passageway down to the restaurant is daubed in white, and it smells of lamb, thyme, honey, baklava and the coffee that I will have after the food – already making my head spin a little.

My veal arrives, and it smells like a cloud in heaven. I grab fork and knife, my mouth already filling with saliva, when a boy with soot on his face and hands, hat in hand, hair in clumps, runs up to the table. He tells me I'm to go to the Carousel immediately.

I almost lash out and smack the boy in the face.

Instead I put my napkin to the side of my plate, leave a huge tip, and wave for my waiter.

'I've been called away,' I say, and here I look skyward, as if someone close to me had died. The waiter notices the money tucked under the plate, and smiles a smile that tells me he'd be fine with any explanation.

When I get to the club I am told Mr Morton is too busy to see me.

Outside in the street I hail a taxi. Once seated and alone again in the blur of people going places, I hide my face in my hands and cry.

★★★

Paul is surprised when I pick him up from his race in Peckham the following evening. I just tell him we have some things to celebrate, and some things to discuss. Tell him to leave the bike and get into the taxi I've got waiting for us.

I get us a booth at the Strand. It could have been a very nice evening. If it wasn't for the things he tells me Mr Morton has told him. If it wasn't for what I have to tell him, the limb I have to get out on. If he wasn't so attractive. If I wasn't such an old, lonely owl. After lobster and champagne for me and beef and water for him, and chocolate mousse for both of us, I lean back and try to gather my thoughts. It won't work. My thoughts and heartbeats are like mice scurrying after crumbs of sponge cake. On the deck of a ship in a storm.

He's visibly shaken by Mr Morton's forced proposal. I am too. I tell him about my plan. Tell him it could be our plan. That in fact it will only work if it's our plan. What I don't tell him is that I want to take him with me wherever I go. That I desperately want him to see me for who I am. Someone more than a lowly moneylender, game fixer, bent landlord, debt collector.

Instead I order more champagne. Insist that I am the one to open it instead of the po-faced sommelier. Once the white foam has run down my hand, I pour Paul a glass. I know he doesn't drink or gamble, but I think since he's being forced to gamble maybe he will start to drink. Either way I like the symmetry of glass, glass, bottle.

I can't tell if he's scared, drunk or lying when he says it's a good idea. Possibly all three. It doesn't matter. He has agreed, and now I'm about to set something in motion. Finally I'm doing something. Finally we are doing something.

'Let's go, Paul,' I say, once we're finished. 'I know a good doctor who can fix you up.'

After a short taxi journey we get to Doctor Sanderson, an old friend of mine. I apologise for waking him up, and explain our predicament in vague terms. The doctor just nods and heads inside to start mixing up what he needs.

Once he comes back he places Paul on his back on the floor, with his legs up on a chair. For the blood to leave his lower body and to enter his abdomen and brain.

Doctor Sanderson and I start. I use a pair of scissors to cut off his right trouser leg. Then we plaster his left ankle and shin, almost all the way up to his knee. We're making it look like he's been in a horrible accident. Once we're done I smile to the doctor and thank him. He goes to get a pair of crutches and I sit on the floor and look at Paul's legs. Only the doctor and myself know what the two little lumps in the otherwise very smooth plasterwork are. A cyanide pill each for Paul and me. Just in case.

I take Paul to my flat. He enjoys the crutches Sanderson dug out for him, doing little tricks all the way up the stairs. I tell him to come up with a good story and to look more sorry. I tuck him in, breaking my promise to myself never to take him to my flat again. It seems like it's been a night for breaking promises.

★★★

In the morning I ply him with coffee and he laughs as we come up with a plausible accident for him to have been in. If we treat it like a game, it's actually quite funny. I ask him what he needs, tells him he's more than welcome to stay on in my apartment.

'I don't want to see you,' he says and I'm taken aback, surprised.

'That's not very nice,' I blurt out. 'Why not?'

'Firstly, because I don't want people to think we have anything more in common than being manager and cyclist. Secondly, because I was doing well before. I hate the house where I live. No disrespect, the new room is miles better than the old one, but I sleep badly. I'm cold, and angry at my circumstances. This fuels my desire to change things, to win. It keeps me in shape. I don't eat too much, relax or gain weight.'

'I see.'

'I mean, your apartment is too nice. Too comfortable.'

All I can do is laugh at him. The gall of turning down hot meals and hot baths. Thick duvets and monogrammed slippers.

'I'd love to one day get used to luxury like this,' he continues.

'And if you stayed here you wouldn't be able to see a certain someone?'

He looks up at me, alarmed. His fear frightens me. If I'm right he's dead. Parts of him will be strewn into the Thames.

I say, 'A celebrated sportsman, like yourself, must be seeing someone.' I hope he will tell me about some girl from a shop, or a governess.

'That's something to consider too,' he laughs, uneasy.

I pour him more coffee. After a while he leaves, leaning heavily on the crutches. He tells me he'd better go and see Harry. And make sure he's being seen injured around races. It falls on me to arrange the bet, drive the odds up to high heaven and chink glasses with shallow boys and men, the financiers of our stab in the dark.

It also falls on me to go and deliver the sad news to Mr Morton that his special bicycle boy can't do his job for two weeks. This will not go down well, but I'm sure Mr Morton will get over it when I offer for Paul to work for free for a month once he's back on his feet. The way to a man's heart is through his wallet.

Chapter 36

Paul sits next to Harry at the Peckham velodrome, where he should have raced. Harry talks about everything but Paul's leg. They both look like scarred war veterans, their legs straight out in front of them. Harry's leg is stiff, and his knee cap is full of fluid. It's almost a smooth ball, like a grapefruit. Next to it, Paul's white plaster and flapping, short, trouser leg. Paul makes sure to stand up and wave to the cyclists he knows, Emrys and Harry's brothers among them, and makes sure to be spotted by the ones he doesn't know. Since he's had a good season he knows that people know who he is, and that word of his injury will travel fast.

As they're sitting right next to the finishing line, Harry talks about all the close races he's been in.

Harry offers Paul a drink, but Paul's stomach turns at the mere thought of alcohol. So instead Harry muses, 'You know the drill by now. A bell. Ding, Ding, Ding. Last lap. Then a gun: *Blam*. Just the one blast, same as how the race began. Your ordeal is over.'

Paul nods, recognising the scenario. Harry continues, 'Now the pace drops. You've won you think, but looking to either side of you, you can't be sure. There are three or four racers very close by. All with their heads down. All with their chests heaving. You look up to the stands for a sign. Your head is so clogged up with sweat and counting laps, and the powders and pills, that you can't think straight.'

Paul nods to a Dutch man he has raced with – against – before.

'Then one of the other racers, one of the fast ones you've spent a hundred years trying to kill, rides up alongside you. Pats you on your shoulder, says 'Well done.' You ask if you won, and he laughs and tells you 'Yes, yes you won you mad man.' So, it seems you won.. But you're too spent to feel happy. Now off the bike. Now change shoes. Now a drink of a sugary kind. A seat, closed eyes. Wait for the shakes to subside.'

Paul smiles and nods, looks at the dignitaries about to start the race. Realises he's never really watched a race before. Just raced himself.

Harry says, 'Then an official comes walking over. A strange smile on his face. He tells you it's been a great day for racing. Then tells you they have been looking at the photo finish record and there seems to have been some confusion. There was someone else over the line before you. By a quarter of a wheel. Your mashed up head can't take that in either. You had trouble with the first idea, now that a second has come clambering for attention you give up. Breathe in, breathe out. That's the extent of it. Drink-eat-sleep, that's the only thing you can think, one long thought. You don't care, not right now anyway, about positions, remuneration, fame, glory. About anything. About anything but air.'

Paul feels himself breathing faster in recognition of the post-race feeling, as he looks at the racers lining up, taking their last normal breaths for many hours.

Harry shouts a ragged 'Good luck!' to his brothers, then turns back to Paul, 'A little later. A bit of cash, a short, curt bow from the top of a chair, this one not as high as the highest one, but higher than the lowest one. The winner bends down to you. Offering his hand as an apology. Almost. But as you know by now, a win is a win.'

Paul nods.

'You think that hopefully tomorrow you can strike gold. Twice the money. A higher tier. A line higher than before in the statistics. You smile and shake the man's hand. Why not? Today you're tired, tomorrow you'll be at each other's throats like maddened ferrets. Your Saturday and Sunday pass this way, your midweek races pass this way. But now that's not the case is it Paul? You won't be racing for a while by the looks of it.'

Before Paul can make up his mind about what to say the sound of the starter gun splits the evening air in two and the racers are off. It's a lot more exciting to watch than to race, Paul thinks, at least initially. But if this was the way he was going to spend the next six months, he wouldn't last long. He, too, would resort to drinking, he thinks.

★★★

Two and a half weeks later he's dressed in his cycling gear, ready to go. He does one last check of his medical bag, his spares and his extra layers for the ride there, and the ride home after, then he stands up. On the floor, discarded, is the cast he's been in for weeks. Now he's ready to rid himself of the yoke Mr Morton has hitched him to.

Silas has told him the odds of him placing in the top three are ridiculously high and that those of him winning are astronomical, as everyone knows that he's been on crutches for ages, and should have about two months to go to full recovery.

Then he sets off for the velodrome by Crystal Palace. It's a cold Saturday morning, and he knows Silas won't be there. They have agreed it will look better if Silas is not on the stands celebrating.

He makes sure to come as late as possible. Rolls off the street and straight into the line of racers. All of them raising their eyebrows. All of them looking down on his leg. Which is great as this means he gets the start.

The race is quite short, and Paul has decided to go all out from the beginning to build up a buffer where there's less of a chance of someone crashing and pulling him down with them. As long as he leads, he is winning. As long as he is winning, he's on his way to paying Mr Morton back the money he believes Paul owes.

All is going well, and Paul is extending his lead. Then he hears a noise. A click, not more than the closing of a door, the pick of a muted guitar string.

Then a spoke snaps behind him and his back wheel starts to wobble. As it starts to warp, two more spokes snap, and the rear wheel is now wobbling quite a bit. After half a lap the whole bike is shuddering so much it's difficult to see. More and more spokes creak and snap. He needs to change a wheel, but can't. He needs to stop, but he can't. He can't. All he can do is pray and pedal on. One lap remaining. The pack quickly catching up.

If his bike breaks it's all been a waste of time. He counts the number of yards remaining. It's not many. It might work. He gets out of the saddle. Leans forward as much as he can, to ease the weight on the rear wheel. It helps.

Time has slowed down to an almost standstill. The rim is ready to throw him off as if it was a bronco. The wheel is ready to kill. Soon touches the frame on either side of the wheel. First lightly, just a butterfly's kiss. The Jim Dunlop Pneumatic tyres he's paid so much for start whispering sweet nothings to the chain stays. Soon the tyres are stripped of most of their outer layers.

The frame starts to lose paint in big flakes. The coating comes off like the Devil's dandruff, followed by delicate canary yellow metal leafs. A disastrous confetti strewn behind him.

Paul's afraid. The wheel is beyond repair and the frame is starting to warp. Soon it's too late to straighten the frame with some planks, and a couple of Cardellini clamps. This is a welding job now, best left to professionals. If the frame is salvageable.

'Jack is going to cry when he sees this,' Paul thinks.

He can't stop. He can't go on. He knows he won't win. All he wants to do is roll over the line. Top three is all it takes.

Another spoke snaps behind him and as it catches on the frame Paul is thrown off course by the involuntary skid. He forces the bike back down on the track, turning a sudden sharp left down towards the innermost line. The pack close now. But so is the line. Just when he thinks he can regain control of the bike someone flies into him. It's a big fellow from Portsmouth. Paul can't even blame him for the crash. Paul is the one who made a sudden illogical break in his line. Paul comes off the bike and hits the track. At first the pain is white light. It's a scalpel. Then it gets worse. The pain is a rusty, serrated knife slowly separating his arm from his body. Then the pain is so intense he stops feeling anything at all. More and more bikes, and racers pile on top of him. As seconds tick by, the length of hours, his body is mangled. Pressed into the now bloody boards.

Slipping under, entering darkness is a relief. Soon his arm hangs limp at the side of his body. His yellow bike is bent and cracked beyond repair. The sticker, *Vélodrome d'Anvers Zuremborg,* flaps in the wind. Paul's torso is a battlefield of welts, blood pooling under his skin. His head rings and his legs are full of gashes and cuts. The last sound he hears before passing out are his ribs crunching like gravel.

Chapter 37

I'm in my café on Moscow road. I consult my pocket watch. About now Paul is probably setting off for the big race at Crystal Palace. We decided I should stay away, which in this weather suits me fine. I'll find out whether he won or placed lower down as soon as the race is over. I'm a bit apprehensive about the result, but I can't do more at the track than I can do from the comfort of my café.

My American papers are spread in front of me on the table. I'm reading about what they call a budding *bull market* on the New York exchange. There was a sudden fall, a sudden panic resulting in a small crash recently. A little hole in the great dam of money straining behind the walls of the exchange. Quickly plastered over with more money from some very wealthy men. There are signs that there might be a bigger quake on its way.

I don't know what to make of it. Some people say this boom will last forever, that the end of the war marked the beginning of better times. The rate of production we achieved then, and the prosperity it brought us, will rise forever. It sounds too good to be true if you ask me but I'm no economist, I am a pessimist. I'm happy for it to continue. Champagne tastes better than water after all.

In a matter of minutes Paul will line up to race. The odds are good, I've made sure they are, but that's as much as I can do. I can't make him win. Paul has borrowed, or been forcefully lent, a large sum of money by Mr Morton, to bet on himself. To try to make a dent in the Russian debt. I'll finish my breakfast, go home. Take a drink, then dress warmly and head out. But I won't stray far away from the café, as I've instructed one of the little boys to leave a message with the results of the race.

I'm about to light a cigar and order a second coffee. Last night was heavy and I need as much of the black gold as I can fit in.

The door opens and Miriam, white as a sheet, stumbles in. It looks like she's been crying. Before I can recover from the shock of her finding me, and the fact that she wants to speak to me directly, a thing that's never happened before, she tells me Paul has had a fall.

'I know. I know,' I say trying to placate her. Wishing she'd use a quieter voice, as my head is about to crack open.

'How can you know?' she asks, angry.

'I made him wear that cast to drive up the odds.' I quickly decide it's best to be honest with her. I don't really know where her sympathies lie, but if she's siding with Mr Morton he won't really mind my tactics, as long as we get the money back to him. But – and her being here, with mascara trailing her cheeks, just about confirms what I've suspected – if her loyalty leans another way, to Paul, then I might as well tell her the truth.

She grabs me by the collar and heaves me up from the seat, hisses angrily, 'I know about that. The fake plaster. This is different. This is a real accident. You'd better come with me.'

She bundles me into a taxi outside, and between rasping breaths she explains that Paul's been in a terrible accident, and is coming in and out of consciousness. She couldn't stay with him for fear of being seen.

'I thought you went to his races, and especially this one,' she says, not without an edge, 'I thought you cared about Paul.'

I start to explain, but she's clearly upset, too upset to listen to my, and his, logic.

She tells me it was only when she gathered all the little boys, right after the accident, and started doling out money, that one of them gave up the information about my favourite café.

I've never seen Miriam upset before. She's quite a sight. Eyes flashing, hands like little nervous birds. This is more than enough to confirm my suspicions. The ground disappears under my feet, but I have to go on.

★★★

On our arrival at Peckham, I immediately send one of the boys to Doctor Sanderson's house, telling him to meet me at Copenhagen Street. Then I go and have a look at Paul. He's lying on a camp bed in the officials' office. He's black and blue. Wrapped up in a blanket but still shivering.

I try to talk to him but he's not answering. I put a hand on his forehead, try to wake him from his slumber but he can't be contacted. I ask Miriam to find a car, then throw a roll of bills on the floor.

'I'm buying the bed and your help for five minutes,' I tell whoever is in the room.

Four officials, all in formal but frayed black, carry him out on the makeshift bier, Miriam and me walking behind like mourners. The rain which was just threatening in the morning is now coming down. Slow, heavy, unrelenting – English. Makes me pine for Zakynthos.

Miriam has found a covered lorry. The race officials, rain pouring off their top hats, help me load Paul onto the back of the lorry.

Miriam, with water running down her cheeks, plastering her hair to the sides of her head, jumps into the dry comfort of the driver's cab. I take a seat on an empty crate in the back and knock on the partition wall three times to let the driver know we're ready to go. As we drive through the streets, I realise Miriam must know where Paul lives. But to give her the benefit of the doubt, I also have to admit that she found me in an hour, in a small café across town, hidden behind a newspaper.

As we rock into motion I take Paul's hand. I expect cold and clammy, but I get warm and papery. His face is bruised and bloody, and one eye is closed up. I rest my head on the back panel and hold onto him.

***

The house on Copenhagen Street is dirty, neglected, and a great source of income. Looking at Paul as he is examined by Doctor Sanderson I am ashamed of myself. Of what I have become. I send Rupert out to buy hot toddy for the doctor, Miriam, myself, and as an afterthought I tell Rupert to get some for himself too. Miriam and I still haven't spoken, but I can see she's worried. I hope she's not worried about more than the investment Mr Morton has made into the body lying prostrate on the bed. It'd be better if she was viewing Paul as a piece of machinery.

Doctor Sanderson stands back and puts away his stethoscope, straightens his back and takes off his glasses. Rubs the bridge of his nose with a thumb and an index finger. He tells us that Paul needs to rest. Apart from concussion and bruised bones and a few cracked ribs, the damage is largely muscular. The sheer amount of bruising and blood lost will slow him down for a few days. I am to make sure he's contactable on the hour and the half hour all through the night, for breathing purposes, as the main problem is not his body but the head trauma suffered. We should be thankful and worried at the same time, is the doctor's conclusion. I try to give him some money, but he waves my hand away.

'Get me tickets for his next race instead. If you look after him he will be able to race again, maybe even within six months, but it won't happen automatically.'

'He can't stay here,' Miriam says once the doctor has left.

'I can't have him at my house,' I say. 'Not officially. Maybe for a night or two.'

'I can maybe house him somewhere. A hotel or something,' she says. By the way she looks at him, at me, at the door, I can tell she wants to be alone with Paul, but I can't give her that satisfaction. I don't know why. And besides he's not responsive. If he couldn't feel Doctor Sanderson's hard pokes into shattered ribs, he won't be able to feel a woman's light touch.

Eventually she says goodbye, and I stand in the room on my own, feeling the draught from the window. Listening to rodents and neighbours. I should maybe have asked her about the nature of their relationship, I'm happy I didn't. What I don't know I can't lie about if asked. I kiss Paul gently on the forehead and go over to Madame Dubois' rooms. I remind her about how she owes me a favour for letting her pay rent late, and that I want to borrow one of her girls, not for anything sordid, for something noble and at the girl's normal rate of pay. She nods and promises to see to it.

Leaving a prostitute – a young girl called Olivia – to watch over Paul's breathing, I go to my house. I soak in a bath. Then I dress as smartly as I can and head over to the Strand. Not to celebrate, that's the last thing on my mind, especially as I'm now sober, but to bump into people. I've got a few names on my list. One of them the shipping magnate's son, or indeed the man himself, but I've also read that Clarence Hatry is back from his Ivy League trip, so I set out to find him and his money. But anyone's money will do. Mr Morton is away in Belfast or Dublin again – I can't remember which – but he will hear about this within the hour.

I have to buy Paul time, and I realise I don't care if that's done by loan, theft, blackmail or worse. Maybe I can mix a dangerous cocktail of all these elements and serve them to Clarence Hatry? Putting on my twenty-four carat cufflinks, my heart soars at how low I've sunk, and how little I care.

Chapter 38

Paul hears voices and feels himself being carried, but can't do anything. Can't say anything.

***

When he wakes up something feels wrong. At first he can't work out where he is then he recognises the dining room at the Baths.

He stirs and looks around for something to drink. Then the pain whacks him over the head. Both a pounding headache and then a different kind of pain. Less sharp, but heavy; pulsating through him. Pushing in on him, like he was drowning in mud. He looks down under the covers. Sees a bruised torso under gauze. Runs a hand over his ribs and winces. He tries to sit up, but can't. Tries to speak, smell, move his fingers, but can't.

Then he hears the door open and sees Miriam's legs come towards him. That's the last thing he remembers before he has to shut his eyes again.

***

Over the next few days, Paul has only fragmentary glimpses of life. Of being fed soup. Of being washed, of his dressings being cut away from his body as caked blood and pus starts acting like glue. Of Miriam holding his head in her hands, of her trying to hold his gaze.

He tries to speak, to look back at her for as long as possible. It's all he wants but he can't. His body only allows him to be awake for a minute here and a minute there.

In the back of his mind he questions the reasons for him being nursed in Miriam's hideout flat, the risk involved, the money he now owes Mr Morton, and the futility of trying to get better, trying to stay alive. Paul thinks about Silas and wonders where he is, and if Silas knows that he is being coerced back to life in a warm, red flat across town from Copenhagen Street. These thoughts, like martins in spring, dart in and out of him. Too quick to act on, or to voice.

Silas visits and tells him that he's told Mr Morton that Paul has vanished.

'I told the old goat that you had another accident, a proper one this time, but that you escaped from the hospital.'

'It's partly true.'

'And that's the only way I got away with the lie. He's good at spotting one, but what I told him is at least fifty-one percent true.'

'Thanks Silas,' Paul says. He sighs deeply. 'We're in trouble now, aren't we?'

'That's just the half of it. Wait till I tell you the rest. I told him that the most likely place to find you would be Scotland, but that I wasn't sure where you came from, *Maybe Glasgow*, is all I said.'

'That's just a little over a half-truth,' Paul says, smiling despite the situation.

'It gets worse,' Silas says. 'At first he was just sitting there, expressionless. Then he suddenly got up and started hissing "No one makes a fool of me Silas! No one!"'

'What happened next?'

'It was absurd. Mr Morton got more and more worked up, pacing the office. Punching the walls, and then, with a shriek he tore down the grizzly bear head from the wall. Destroyed it with kick after kick, until the floor was covered with splinters of wood, hair, glass eyes. Bear canines and incisors like a pick-a-stick. I've never seen him like that.'

'He didn't do anything to you did he?'

'Not physically.'

'What then?'

'He transferred the debt to me,' Silas says, his voice flat. 'Then explained that in the light of many years of good service I have a month to pay it off. I'm now being followed around the clock.'

'I'm sorry.'

'Getting rid of the people following me isn't hard,' Silas tells Paul, 'but it is tedious.'

Paul sips water from a glass.

'You will understand that I do like my freedom,' Silas says. 'Now that's being tampered with. As for the debt, it makes no difference. I'm already dead, it doesn't matter to me. I've been dead for years.'

'Are you in danger?'

'Let's just say I'm keeping my razor sharp. Besides, he wants the money more than my life. The razor's not for him. It's for me.'

'Please don't, we'll find a way out of this.'

'Maybe,' Silas says and stands up to leave. 'Just remember to not leave the house Paul. You're under siege and if you're spotted Miriam would be in even more danger.'

'When will I get out?'

'I don't know.'

★★★

When Paul can think clearly, he fears he'll never ride a bike again. He already misses the twice-weekly race rush. The steep walls. The sea of spectators flying by. Their shouts of encouragement, their jibes, their bellows of fear of him losing them money. The sounds that ring in his hears, ring in time with his racing pulse. The faint sickness he always feels before a race, and the way it eases off as soon as he's underway. The loneliness in his individual sprint inside the orb of pain, the long hours spent in the saddle. Not glamorous or exciting, but something he's gotten used to, something he has become good at.

One morning he's aware of Miriam sitting next to him as he wakes up. She holds up a mirror and he sees his face for the first time in almost a week. He looks like a panda. His broken nose has made his eye sockets go dark.

He tries to get up on one elbow but she gently pushes him back down. He tries to speak, ask all the questions he has buzzing around, but she puts a cool, pine-scented hand on his cheek and an index finger on his lips. She leaves, and he tries to call her back, but can't. She comes back with three big sofa cushions. She props him up and gets a copper bowl and razor out. Slowly shaves him and puts a soft lotion on his cheeks. The alcohol in his normal aftershave would have stung too much, she tells him. Once she's happy with his face, she reaches for a book on the table. It's a thin volume, not more than a pamphlet with a spine really.

'I tidied up my handwriting and had my book bound,' she says. 'It cost a fortune, but I wanted to put a full stop to the thing.' She smiles and says, 'I've been staying in this week. Working hard. Looking after you. It dawned on me that I should probably clean up my family tree. Prune it a little. I did, and now I've printed four of these,' here she holds the book up in the air and sort of shakes it, as if to dry the ink, 'just for myself really. And if you wanted one.'

Paul nods. Tries to smile even though it hurts.

'There's even a verse or two about you now.'

'And you?' he says, his voice breaking and hoarse from lack of use.

'Not yet. I'm still struggling with the one about my mother.'

He looks around him and she puts down the book. Lifts a glass of water from the floor. Puts a straw gently between his lips, and a hand on his forehead.

'Will you read for me?' he asks once he's had as much water

as he can stomach, which isn't much.

'No, no not today. I would have, but no.' She looks embarrassed. Paul nods.

'Some other day Paul. You need to rest now. I'll leave the book here. You can read it yourself, maybe.'

He nods and smiles. Then the dark blanket of exhaustion falls on him again and he allows himself to drift off.

★★★

Six days later he sits in the little courtyard with Silas.

'No one saw the last accident you had, the made-up one,' Silas says. 'This one on the other hand had thousands of witnesses. And the officials would be talking about it as well, as they were the casket bearers of your lifeless shape. You can't pull off the same trick twice, but the next time isn't the same, it won't be a trick.'

Paul nods and tries to thank Silas for everything he's done.

'I didn't put you up here,' Silas nods to the walls of the Baths. 'That was her making. I thought you had died to be honest. On the night of the accident I was out trying to find money, drumming up support. Miriam moved you here.'

'How are things at the Carousel?'

'Has Miriam not told you? Mr Morton is haemorrhaging money, not just on you, and he's furious about it as you can imagine.'

'So he wants me to pay back Ilya's debt and my own? As soon as I'm better I'll race again. I'll win again.'

'It's more complicated than that.'

Paul looks at the plumes of the peacock prancing in the courtyard. The tail of the male quivering in the morning cold.

'Besides he won't wait for you to get better.'

'The doctor said I would be...'

'Never mind the doctor. If Mr Morton finds out where you are you'll need a coroner.'

'I thought you said you found some money.'

'I did, but this is mostly about his pride. And there's something else too. For the first time in years, he is low on cash. Mr Morton is holding an auction, selling off some of his assets. Turns out he took a hit on the stock market earlier this month.'

'Is the Carousel for sale?' Paul asks, almost hopeful. If Mr Morton goes bankrupt maybe there's a chance his – their – debt disappears.

'No, he'll keep that forever. And if he has to let it go, he'd set it on fire and claim insurance money. No it's an auction for some of his personal estate, you know, furniture, bonds. Maybe that place out on Nine Elms Lane, a bit of the wine cellar.' Silas looks up at Paul. Sits in silence for a minute. Then says, 'This includes Miriam.'

Paul stares at Silas. Quiet. Then Silas says, 'Seems like the trips to that brothel in Dublin have made him think.'

Paul stares into thin air. Then he sniffles. Silas pats Paul on the knee and stands up. The peacock rustles its plumes and shuffles off. 'I'll be back tomorrow,' Silas says, 'We can talk more then. I want us to think about the Good Friday race, it's really the only one that generates enough interest and money for us to have a go at. It's too close in time I realise, just six weeks away.'

'I can't Silas.'

'I know. In the meantime I won't tell anyone where you are. Just get better Paul, and let's take it from there.'

Silas doesn't turn up the next day, or the one after that. Miriam, who hasn't said anything about Mr Morton's plans, comes home late, looking deathly tired. She tells Paul that Silas is being kept under close surveillance, but that he's a slippery snake.

She's got food and clean new clothes for him, and Silas has given her some of Paul's things from Copenhagen Street, as the room is now being rented out, the story being that Paul has escaped.

Once she has unpacked, and changed into her normal clothes she comes and sits next to him on a cushion on the floor. 'Paul. I know there's a price for me,' she says. 'I know that people over in Dublin are bidding for me, and I know that you know.'

'I'm sorry, I should have said something.'

'I knew before you did, and either way, I don't want to talk about it.'

'Neither do I. I'm still hoping I will wake up from this nightmare.'

'You won't,' she says and puts a hand on his hand.

'What can we do?'

'You should get better. And then we might consider actually escaping. Either way, if they try to take me from you and send me over there they wouldn't catch me alive. There's a pearl-handled solution.'

'Miriam, don't say things like that,' Paul says taking her face in both hands and trying, and not completely succeeding, to catch her eyes.

'You don't know him like I do,' she says, voice steely.

'I don't, and that might be the only thing keeping me alive,' he says.

***

In his boredom and frustration at not being able to do anything about the situation, Paul composes a long letter to Jack Lauterwasse. It's mostly numbers and angles. Manufacturer's names and gratitude in a strange mix. After the crash Paul's bike was nothing more than scrap metal. He knows the measurements of it. He knows which saddle, which bars, which wheels and tyres he prefers, so this he puts down on paper. Gearing, type of lugs, length of stem. Like a boy's list of Christmas wishes he writes down everything he would like in a bike. Including colour and number of spokes.

Miriam is so happy to see him up and about, even if he's just limping down the stairs to the courtyard to sit all wrapped up in the weak rays of the spring sunshine, and sip tea. Miriam has even promised to buy him a bike. He's ashamed of having to borrow even more money but as he writes the letter to Jack he realises how much he misses having a bike.

Three days after the letter was delivered Miriam comes home and urges Paul to come downstairs. There's a bike, not new, not pretty, not the canary-yellow he wished for, but the numbers are almost right. Jack must have asked around in lots of shops. The only thing different from his old bike is the seat tube. It is split in two, letting the rear wheel peek through, now visible straight under the saddle. This means the wheelbase is shorter, but that can only be for the better, Paul thinks, as it makes for a bike that takes up less space and can squeeze through smaller gaps.

He asks Miriam to help him up on the bike. Then he just sits there, leaning against a wall, with one hand on her shoulder. She looks anxious at first, but when she sees how wide his smile is she can't stop herself, and breaks out in a giggle. This in turn makes him laugh, and soon they are laughing and kissing and crying. The emotions pent up from before the crash, followed by him hiding and slowly recovering, and Miriam's situation getting worse and worse by the day, come out and he climbs off the bike to hold her.

The sun comes out and bathes them both for a moment. Then he asks her to help him upstairs and asks if she wants to join him in the bath. She can't speak just yet, just nods.

★★★

Over the next two days he fiddles with the bike whenever he's not sleeping. Makes tiny adjustments, cycles slowly round the courtyard, and then makes even more adjustments. It takes his mind off things, momentarily at least.

He starts riding around the courtyard at night, first just once. The next day, twice, then in circles wider and wider. It's not big, but within a few days he manages to cycle fast enough to get his heart pumping. He quickly gets used to the shorter bike, and everything else is just as he asked for. Now he knows all he has to do is eat lots, sleep lots, cycle as much as his body will let him. He asks Miriam to see if she can find the blocks that were built for his and Emrys' Roman races. She brings a pair of them home and he installs it in the courtyard, and cycles at night, a belt around the rim of the rear wheel, a belt he tightens daily to increase the friction. Then he receives a message from Silas. It's a skull and crossbones crudely sketched with coal on brown wrapping paper, underneath it: *1 April*.

The next day there's a delivery of two large crates for Miriam. They're both empty, but inside the second one is an envelope with a train ticket for Sheerness and the address of a B&B.

The note is from Silas,

P, you must be climbing the walls. Need to train. Need air. Man to pick up you and bike, concealed in containers, tomorrow at 4am. One week to get in shape.

★★★

In Sheerness, he trains harder than ever. He wishes for the wind to be against him. To be in his face, so that he can really push himself. He goes scouting for hills. He cycles up and walks down, to strengthen his knees. He carries a backpack full of bricks. He fixes a parcel holder to the back and one to the front of the bike and attaches two seats. He's the local free taxi, the boy who happily cycles people's groceries home to them from the shop. He measures out a three-mile loop and times himself. Rages if the twelfth lap is slower than the eleventh, or the first.

He runs in boggy fields, in water, in heavy boots. All to get as much resistance as possible. He sleeps deeply, eats well and tries not to think about the reprieve he's been given. Or why a ruthless woman who could just skip out, as she's facing being sold, stays. On her own she could possibly slip through the closing net.

Instead, when he's been ill, she has laid gentle hands on his aching thighs in the evenings. Despite the overshadowing threat, the time they have spent had an air of domestic bliss. Paradoxically it's been the happiest and the most settled he's been since moving to London. Or ever.

One afternoon when he comes back from training, his landlady gives him a letter from Miriam. Harry Wylde has been taken to Saint James's hospital.

Paul immediately packs a bag and sets out on the bike. It's a fifty-five-mile journey. He knows Miriam would stop him from coming to London. And that she'd be right to. Nevertheless it's good training and it's good to see something other than the routes he's gotten used to around the little town on the Kentish coast.

Despite everything it's a lovely ride. He feels fine, maybe not as explosive as before the accident, but fine. He's warm and convinced that the saddle needs to come up one inch, and backwards half an inch.

Once at the hospital, a nurse tells him it's something with Harry's liver, 'But don't ask him about it, he flies into a rage if you tell him he's ill,' she continues. She shows Paul into a room full of beds. Harry looks old and worn out, birdlike on the pillow. After the usual small talk, and Harry asking four times if Paul has any booze with him, or if he would go and get some, they get onto the subject of Paul's bruised face.

Paul tells him about the fake injury, the bet and the fall. About the real injury, and hints at the real trouble. Paul gets the feeling that Harry isn't listening. But it doesn't matter.

After a coughing attack, Harry says, 'She's one hell of a girl. I've seen the way she looks at you. Mind, she's only been to one or two races, but I still remember her.'

Paul's too shocked to say anything.

'I know who she is. I know who her boss is, and Silas' boss,' Harry says smiling.

'You do?'

'I might be a drunk, but I'm not thick. I just hope you've got a way out of this,' Harry says. 'I can't be the only one who's noticed.'

Paul tells Harry he's got a big race coming up. One that will make or break him. It's the Good Friday meet that Harry's raced many times. Paul tells him he's more nervous than he's ever been before. Harry gets something distant in his eye, and says, 'Paul you know the track doesn't go anywhere. And you know that's one of the advantages. You don't have to stare yourself blind on the vanishing point. There's no disappearing horizon to aim for. There's no just around the next bend, it's all a bend, one long curve. There's no over the next hill, the only hill is a meandering hill of death to your right.'

Paul smiles, despite the bear trap he's in. He needs the fear to fuel him. And he needs to look beyond it to be able to race. From almost flat on the straits to the steeper turns, the long and shallow bowl at Herne Hill fills him with dread and happy delirium. Harry gestures for water and Paul passes him a glass from a sideboard, then he continues, 'A finishing line, a place in the group, a rung on the scoreboard, that's your goal. On a round track you never get there. The oval has becomes your life's perimeter Paul.'

Paul laughs, then asks, 'When are you getting out of here?'

'Who says I want out? Three square meals and a horde of pretty nurses. If I had a couple of beers, I'd be in heaven.' Then Harry turns serious and asks, 'Are you really doing this race Paul?'

Paul nods.

'If you want me to be there, I'll be there,' Harry says. 'Even if it kills me. I'd rather die at the track than in this hellhole full of carnations and disinfectant. To be honest, most of the nurses have moustaches and are not very pretty at all.'

They both laugh. Harry falls back against the pillows. In a husky voice he asks Paul something. It's hard to hear what he says, but eventually, when he understands what Harry says, Paul runs for a nurse. He promises to come and see Harry over the next few days but he's not sure Harry can hear him. He's not even sure he's awake.

Cycling back across town he thinks of the birdlike creature on the bed. He thinks about his own father who must have died all alone. Someone found him, put him in a coffin and buried him. It wasn't Paul. Despite everything, despite the money, the hardship, the love that was lost a long time ago, Paul can't stop himself feeling sorry. Not sorry that he left the farm, but sorry that he never knew his mother. Sorry his father is now dead and that Paul will never be able to forgive him.

He winds his way to the home he's been allowed to share with Miriam. Back through Camden and Kentish Town, back to the green expanses and dark ponds. When he turns the last corner, he almost falls off the bike. There's a big white Packard idling outside the front door of the Baths.

Chapter 39

I've had a horrible day of hanging around Mr Morton. Pleasing him. Agreeing with him. Being watched by him and his despicable henchman, Drago. I suspect they follow me after I leave the Carousel, but I can't be sure. Either way I don't want them to see me in my house, and I can't betray Paul and Miriam by going to Hampstead. So I remain in my dusty office at Copenhagen Street.

I've tried to explain the situation to Rupert. He's not the sharpest tool in the box, but he's trustworthy. I've arranged for him to run a couple of errands, some important, some more emotional than important. I came here to see how much cash there was on the premises and there was more than I thought there would be. A rare occurrence that all tenants have paid on time.

I'm just about to leave when I hear the familiar purr of a chain and wheels outside the office door. I jump up and stick my head out.

'Paul? What are you doing here?'

The boy looks shattered. A hull of a man. The promise I made my mother about feeding him properly still stands, I remind myself.

'Come inside the office,' I say, looking up and down the street.

Paul looks over his shoulder furtively, then awkwardly rolls the bike into the small office space.

'What's this?'

'I thought I'd come and stay here.'

'You can't. It's too obvious, and besides I've got tenants in your old room.'

'I just came back and Mr Morton was outside the Baths.

I didn't know where to go.'

I need to think about this, so I tell him to sit. Then I notice the bike. Despite everything, I'm quite pleased that I appear to have soaked up something about cycling. 'This is not the one I got you,' I say, to cheer him up, to make him think about something else.

This is as much for me as it is for him.

'That one was bent beyond repair in the crash, looked like a dried-up daddy longlegs,' Paul says. 'Miriam got me this one.'

I try to laugh at this image, but I can't. I let out a strained, horselike guffaw.

'Sit down Paul. We need to talk. We're in grave danger, you and I.'

'I know. And I'm sorry.'

'You can't be here. I thought you were in Sheerness.'

'I was, then I got a message saying Harry was in a bad way, dying.'

'So you came to see him.'

'I just couldn't let down a friend on his deathbed.'

'It might be you the next time.'

Now he starts to cry. It's an awful sound and an awful sight.

'Not to worry, we'll fix this,' I say with false confidence. A lot of it.

'How?'

'You've been injured. You were seen falling badly. That's good for us. But you're recovering quickly and you've been training by the looks of it. How are you feeling?'

'I'm fine. I've been in better shape, but I'm getting there.'

'We've only got about a week. I trust you got my note?'

Paul nods.

'That's when she's being sent out to Dublin, and when the bear claws will close on us.' I look at his legs. His shins look like a map of a mountain range. A thousand different shades.

Painful foothills and sharp crevasses. His hair, roan.

'Are you hungry?' I ask as he dries his eyes with the back of his hands.

Again he nods. Again I look at his legs. We are both dead men. I might as well enjoy my last week alive. I go upstairs and ask Madame Dubois if she can send out a couple of the girls to cause a bit of a racket outside, and see if they can flush any men watching the entrance. I watch out of the window and after a couple of minutes of the girls shouting there have not been any men watching them with professional interest. Plenty other interest though.

'Should we talk about this over something to eat?' I say and gesture for Paul to go outside.

'Sure. Fine.'

'Eel?'

'For old time's sake?'

He runs upstairs to get something he's left behind in his room. I hear him talk briefly to the new tenants, an Irish family of five, and then he comes bounding down the stairs like the Great Dane he is.

We're back where we started. In the smoke and noise of Belinda's. We ask to sit in the back room. Keep our hats on. As we wait for the food to arrive, I look at him. The youth I tried to capitalise on, and did for a while. The boy who backfired on me.

'Shame it never worked out between you and Belinda,' I joke.

'Look at her left hand,' he says quietly.

'There's no ring, I know that.'

'But there's a faint trace of white. As if she wore a ring when she wasn't here.'

'Are you serious?'

'She's a happily married woman,' is his throwaway comment.

Before I have time to laugh, Belinda arrives with two hot

plates full of mash, eel and parsley sauce, as well as my second beer and his second sarsaparilla, and I see that he's right.

'So, there's a brain on top of those legs?' I say once Belinda has retreated. He just nods, his mouth full. 'Maybe it just needed a good shake to come alive.'

'Eat your food Silas,' he says, and smiles.

★★★

Two hours and three beers later I find myself in the bowels of the Carousel. Paul's gone to a small hotel, and he's asked me to send a message to Miriam, which I've sent through Rupert, he's the only one I can trust now. The three of us are not to meet until Good Friday. Not until after the race. And probably not even then. It's best if he doesn't know where I'm staying, and it's best if I don't know what he does. As long as he trains properly. I also told him it's best if he forgets all about Miriam and he nodded as if he was listening.

The inside of the entertainment palace is dark but not deserted. Cleaners, dancing girls and bartenders loiter, either about to begin work or just finished.

I nod to everyone I see, as if I don't have anything to hide. If I lost my momentum now, I would never find it again. I would be fish food before the night was over.

I make my way upstairs and knock on the door. If Mr Morton answers I'll tell him something dull about the odds for an upcoming derby. If not, I'll try my luck.

With hands shaking so much it looks, and feels, like I'm having a seizure I get my skeleton keys out of my pocket. It's a worn set, a present from my father. I've had them in my pocket long enough that they are warm between my bloodless fingers. In my other pocket a little box that used to hold cough drops. Now there's only one capsule, resting on a bed of cotton wool. It is not a cough drop. It is the cyanide pill from Paul's plaster. The other, I keep on my bedside table, next to a gold snuffbox and a tortoiseshell comb. Memories of my mother and father.

There's no one in London who would think of breaking into Mr Morton's little temple. And even if they did there would be nothing apart from a chair and a little table to steal, apart from the crucifix.

I knock but there is no reply so I get to work. The lock is easy to pick, and gives way with a click. I push the door. It swings open with a creak and I rush over the threshold to end the sound. Once inside my heart stops. The chair is turned away from the door; its high back shielding the occupant. I see a pair of white wing-tipped shoes peeking out on the left hand of the chair, and on the table is an ashtray with a cigar. Its tip is still faintly red and there's a tendril of smoke rising from it. I say my line about the odds for the derby to the room, in case Mr Morton's not heard the click of the door. I reach into my pocket and fish out the metal box. I take a step forward, into his line of sight.

I almost vomit with relief when I realise the chair is empty. Knowing how sore his feet always get and how he often walks around in just his socks, the shoes standing to one side make sense. But he won't be far away. I run over to the cross, unhook it from the wall and thread the key off the coarse bit of string. I was right, but now I am a dead man. I place the key next to the pill on the cotton wool. My hands are now shaking so much I have trouble hanging the cross back up.

Then I hear steps approaching, and I realise I've left the door ajar. Not much, just an inch, but still visible. The slow, shuffling thread of what sounds like a heavy man comes closer and closer. I look around the room for somewhere to hide but there's nowhere. The steps are coming nearer and nearer, and the person walking towards me is whistling. The melody is atonal, seems to go wherever it wants to. Sounds old and religious in its minor nature. Maybe a catholic hymn, something for Lent.

The footsteps stop by the door. The whistling ends, and

the door moves. I jump into the chair and pull my legs up. I hunker down so that the back of the chair shields me from the view of the door and grab the cigar. It's a beautiful Princeps, and I give myself to the smell of it, and to my fate.

The hinges creak, a bow pulled over a slack cello string. Then I hear the voice which always sends shivers down my spine, 'You want this closed?'

I don't say anything.

'You want this closed Mr Morton?' Drago repeats.

I pull hard on the cigar and blow out a big cloud of smoke. I grunt, trying to sound as much as I can like the albino elephant. At first nothing happens. Then I hear the hinges again. I can't tell whether Drago is coming in or out. I take another puff, but my heart is beating too fast for the smoke to go anywhere.

I hear the click of the door and his steps retreating. Light-headed, both from the smoke and from the relief I stagger up out of the chair and over to the door. I put my ear to it, and silently count to sixty. I open the door and quickly step out into the corridor. Close the door and raise my hand, so that it looks like I was just about to knock in case someone spots me. No one does and I start for the stairs.

Water flushes in pipes and someone lets out a loud burp. The lock of the bathroom at the end of the corridor starts to rattle. I look down at my hand and realise I'm still holding the cigar, so I open the door and throw it in the direction of the chair. I quietly run down the stairs, and manage to duck into the floor below just as I catch a glimpse of white trouser legs and argyle patterned socks. I stand still with him right above me, trying not to breathe. Then he opens the door of his white office and walks inside. I tiptoe slowly towards the next set of stairs, and then I hear the shriek. His voice as high as a girl's, 'Help! Fire!'

He comes out onto the landing again, screaming hysterically. *The cigar hit the chair*, I think as I rush downstairs. Doors are opening and people are running. The braver ones upstairs to save the building, save Mr Morton and make a name for themselves. The smarter ones, doing what I am doing, dodging downstairs and outside.

After the maze of stairs and landings, I come to the room with the octagon and the red lines on the floorboards. I walk over to the wall and slide in behind a curtain. I pull out the box and look at the key. Listen to the shouts from upstairs about organising a chain of buckets. About axes and wet handkerchiefs over peoples' mouths. There's no way of telling whether the fire is spreading or if it is being stopped.

The key is gleaming dully like a fish in a strong current. I peek out from behind the curtain. It's suddenly gone quiet. The ones upstairs are upstairs, the ones outside are outside. I'm the only one who has stuck myself firmly in this limbo.

I take out the key and put the box in my pocket, then I make a mad dash for it. Just ten minutes ago someone running would have looked out of place. Now, not so much. I run out to the bigger room, sprint up the stairs and into the second office above the stairs.

The safe is a squat cube in the corner of the room behind Mr Morton's desk. I try the key. It doesn't work. I try it again. Still not. Now I'm really panicking, and I'm angry with myself for being such an idiot, for taking such a risk. For all I know this key is for Mr Morton's diary, or a shed where he keeps doves or tackle.

I notice that the lock of the box has been forced and gutted. Not recently. There's a coat of paint over where there should have been scratch marks. In place of the cylinder is just a dark slit, and as I put my eye to the hole I see a bill. I realise the safe is so full that bills are pushing up against the lid.

I look at the back of the box. There's a new padlock. I try my key and the shackle slides out of the body. It's the most beautiful, and most terrifying, sound in the world. I open the lid and look at the sheer amount of paper bills. I realise I have nothing to carry the money in. I walk over to a sofa and take all three cushions off. I peel off the covers and stuff bills inside. The filling from the cushions I put in the bottom of the strongbox, then I scatter notes in an inch-thick layer on top, so that if anyone looks through the hole where there used to be a cylinder, the safe looks as full as before.

With the cushions tucked under my coat, I run down the stairs and out into the street. Fortunately it's raining and there's a big crowd of people, both staff and onlookers, I weave my way through, hat pulled low, as people are looking at the Carousel, partly blinded by the floodlights that illuminate it. Some hoping, some fearing the place will catch fire.

Although there's always a line of taxis waiting outside the club I avoid them, can't be sure the drivers don't keep a tally on comings, goings and addresses. Instead I hurry across the street and jump on a bus. It's been a long time since I did that. I take a seat and watch the rain turn to sleet as Elephant and Castle disappears behind me. Halfway across Southwark Bridge the conductor comes around and asks to see my ticket. I laugh out loud, quickly realising the man must think I'm drunk. I tell him I have no money, which is true. I don't have any coins on me. I made sure to empty my pockets before I walked into the Carousel, didn't want any jangling change to give me away. So despite having enough money to buy a townhouse in Chelsea in my armpits and on my lap, encased in silk cushion covers, I can't pay the bus fare.

The man takes a look at me, peers out through the window at the weather, then he puts a hand on my shoulder and says, 'You're alright.'

I almost cry. I don't know why. It's the conductor's kind words, it's the sensation of being alive.

The bus makes a stop not far from Liverpool Street station. I disembark, thanking the conductor, even shaking his hand. I'm not travelling anywhere, I just want to make sure that I've not been picked up and followed since I came out of the

Carousel. I enter the busy station. I walk to a track with a waiting train and get on, then I run through the carriage and come out of the door further to the front, looking for people either following or keeping an eye on me. I do this three times with different trains. On the last one, which isn't leaving for another twenty minutes I duck into a toilet and opening a pillow I get a couple of notes out and cram them in my pockets.

Satisfied I'm not being followed I buy a suitcase from one of the many stalls on the station concourse. It's nothing fancy, just a blue cardboard frame with reinforced metal corners. I fling the cushions into the suitcase and walk outside for a taxi.

I ask the man to take me to a mid-budget hotel in Bayswater. The choice is his. I'm trying to make myself invisible, and one way to do that is to not go to the kind of hotels in the parts of town I would choose, or indeed anywhere diametrically opposed. So I'll settle for something bland and boring. It's only for a couple of nights anyway. The first or last few nights of my life.

Tomorrow I'll try to go to Chinatown to have the razor sharpened. Other than that I will be in the hotel room. The money is not enough for freedom – but enough for a good bet. I fall asleep quickly, for the first time in three weeks. Silk cushions under my head.

Chapter 40

It's Good Friday 1929 and a record crowd has paid to see the cyclists. Down on the oval I watch Paul focus on his hands. Hands that used to handle white-eyed horses, deliver lambs, right fence posts blown over in Campsie gales and put his drunk father to bed. Hands that have killed by proxy, thrown bodies down a shaft to decompose. Hands that have caressed a body belonging to Mr Morton. Hands that have shaped my future like an amateur potter. I've not seen Mr Morton yet, but I'm sure he'll come. Once he finds out that Paul is racing he'll come. I've still got a few days to repay my debt, and so far I've been free to come and go as I please, but that won't last. He knows I know better than to try and escape.

One of Miriam's friends, a hunkering great girl called Brenda, told me that Mr Morton had been visiting the Baths on the same day that Paul decided to come back and visit his sick friend. Brenda told me Miriam was shaken, but that she had showed Mr Morton her rooms and as Paul had taken all his things with him she had nothing to hide.

Poking around the courtyard Drago found the block Paul had put his bike wheel into, but she managed to say she had taken it for firewood, and it seemed like they believed her. The next day Mr Morton sent a big load of wood to the Baths. Not sure if it was a sort of apology, if he actually believed she needed the fuel, or if he was being ironic. It's very tiring interpreting the actions of a despicable man.

These thoughts whirl in my head as I pretend to drink tea and watch the racers prance around. All of them apart from Paul who has straddled his bike and is standing as still as a rock.

Then *Crack!* With a jostle of elbows and straining thighs they're off.

The first hour is torture. Paul drops down a little in the field. Not much, but steadily losing places. He's not too far down in the field, and neither is he out front for too long, tiring himself. I drink too much, too quickly and soon I'm forced to go to the toilet, looking over my shoulder the whole way there. When I come back the bunch of cyclists have changed. Now Paul isn't among the first three, or even the first ten.

Now, time passes differently. It's because of the gin, and it's because of the implications. My fingertips tingle; the crowd sense that something is about to happen. The mauled mongrel from Scotland has put up a good show but now he's flagging. People love to see a plucky underdog die. Still he hangs on.

I spot Mr Morton. He looks smug, turning a ring on one of his fingers. He's wearing a white fur coat and he is looking straight at me.

I wave to the elephantine monster. Make a sign of downing a glass, as if I'm off to get another drink. Soon I'm vomiting in the gutter outside the velodrome and while doing so I drop the key to the strongbox into a drain. My sickness the perfect cover in case I'm watched. Then one of my grimy boys come up to me.

I run. Not away from the velodrome as my brain tells me to, but towards it, following the detrimental instinct of my heart. The sharp taste of gastric acid burns in my throat. My lungs shallow. Turns out there's been a big crash. A whole throng of racers have been injured. For Paul's sake I hope he's in a coma. Or mortally wounded, a chain wound around his neck, his heart spiked by a broken spoke. Then the grimy boy still at my side tells me Paul was so far behind that the crash was nowhere near him. That Paul, exhausted, could easily ride around it far up on the banking, wobbling all the way to the line.

I can't believe it, my heart is trying to escape out of my throat. He's won! We've won! 'Take that!' I shout, to the world, but mostly to Mr Morton, who I am sure is still somewhere in the stands.

The plan was always to return the borrowed money plus the money we owed to Mr Morton, to settle our debt. But riding on that wave of emotion I decide then and there not to return any money to him. What an awful day it's been. What a fantastic day it's been. I want to run down onto the track and kiss Paul, but I want to be away from Mr Morton more than anything else.

As we had agreed in case of a win, I go straight to the bookmaker on Compayne Gardens, via a shop where I buy two of the biggest suitcases available. In the taxi on the way over I can't think straight, it's too much of a shock, but a plan starts to form in my head. One taking things one step further than we had originally planned. One involving Sebastian.

I go to the bookmakers to collect the bet I placed with all of the money from Mr Morton's safe. He looks pale and tries to protest that he hasn't enough to keep his business going, but he knows who I am, and he knows I could not care less. I allow myself a chuckle at the thought that it's Mr Morton's reputation that's helping me to escape from Mr Morton himself. With so much of his money. I consult my watch and calculate that Paul should have been able to get to my office, our post-race meeting point, by now.

I sit in the back of the taxi. The two suitcases, one empty, one full, bounce against my leg, and I almost cry. I'm not cutting Paul into bits with cheese wire, we're taking a train to Southampton. Half the money in my suitcase, the other half in his. With hats pulled low and scarves pulled high we're sailing off on the first available ship. Then as we cross the equator we'll toss our disguises in the ocean. I can see this in vivid colours. Too vivid.

Once at the house I open the door of the *Ofiss* just an inch, and my heart stops. The first thing I see is a white suit jacket flung over a chair. I should have snuck back outside, bought a car and driven to Calais, but something holds me there. Then I hear Paul's voice.

'I'm sorry Silas.' He's on his back on my desk, one arm handcuffed to the steel bars over the window. He is pale, and his eyes are closed.

He tells me that he was in such a state after the race that he requested an ambulance. Partly for his own safety. The ambulance was sent away and instead he was driven back to Copenhagen Street in Mr Morton's car. But not before Mr Morton picked up a rumour that someone had gotten very rich from the race.

'Where is he?' I ask.

'He's coming back. He's got men at the Baths too. Leave while you can. I can't. I'm stuck.' He shakes his arm and the rattle from cuffs against bars is awful. 'He is just getting Drago, and he said together they would get the whole story out of me.'

There's a knock on the window – like the sound of a bird colliding with the pane – but I can't see anything. Then there's another, and I look outside. It's a streetgirl, throwing pebbles. I look again, and realise it's not a prostitute. It's a woman in disguise. Miriam. She looks left up the street. Then right. Then she waves to me. Frantic. Urgent. Shivering. I raise one palm.

'When did he leave?' I ask.

'I don't know. I don't know anything. I'm in so much pain it's unbearable.'

'Take some of your pills. Now is not the time to break down. Pull yourself together Paul,' I hiss.

'I've had so many. If I have any more I'll be a vegetable.'

'Take a couple and stay still.' I hiss. I dig out the skeleton key and start to work on the handcuffs. They're well made, good quality ones, and the minutes tick by as I work. My heart almost stops at every little sound out in the street, and there are drops of sweat, and drops from my runny nose dripping on my hands. Then there's a click and the clasp opens.

I give him one of the suitcases. The empty one. Not the one carrying a fortune. I ease the front door open. All quiet, so I edge out, nodding to Miriam the mock prostitute across the street. I carry the big suitcase full of cash and my heart leaps at the possibility of us getting away. If we can just make it away from the building there's a chance. If we are quick we can disappear in the city, until we can leave the country. Then, like a glimpse of the sun over the horizon at dawn, but horrible, I see the bonnet of a big white car turn a corner. It's now or never so I take a deep breath and push Paul out in front of me. I stumble after, both of us slowed down by our bags. I pull him into a service alley, hoping Miriam will follow. Then I hear the roar of the engine echoing between the houses of Copenhagen Street. I should've been quicker, but there's a chance he didn't see us.

Chapter 41

Paul hears the engine come closer. He knows it well. Twelve cylinders of relentless power, so different from the horsepower his legs produce. The revs of the engine are awful but what comes after is worse still. The screeching tyres, pushing loose gravel into two straight lines, maybe ten, fifteen yards long. Then the silent engine. Around the corner, in the alley, Paul inches even closer to Silas. Two doors open and they hear the heavy puff of a fat man and the deadly tread of Drago. Mr Morton tells the driver to stay where he is, to keep an eye, then they both enter the building. Paul lets out a breath, nods to Silas and then they both run.

Before they get far there is a shrill, castrato shout behind them. Wordless anger. Drago comes running into the alley, a filleting knife, held flush against Rupert's throat. Drago pushes Rupert away from him, slashing him vertically down the arms. Ripping Rupert's coat, leaving long, bleeding lines.

Paul, exhausted from the race, and Silas, in slippery shoes, a man who's not been forced to run for many years, sprint down the alley. Drago is quickly catching up and Paul gestures for Silas to give him the other suitcase. At first Silas won't do it, but when he sees how close Drago is getting, Silas hands over all the money he's ever made to the ginger giant.

Carnegie Street, busy as always, is just in sight at the end of the alley. Caledonian Road, with its crowds and mass of vehicles, beyond that, and further still the river. Drowning seems like a good way out at the moment.

Drago is now so close that they can hear his steps, and the end of the alley, where there will at least be potential witnesses, is just beyond them. They enter Carnegie street with the man in black just behind. Hear a screech and a dull thud. Turning back, they see Drago on the ground, bleeding from the head, and Miriam holding a brick.

'Belinda can hide us,' Paul says.

'I don't know,' Silas answers, struggling to breathe, hands on his knees.

'I've been down in the basement, for sarsaparilla, it's huge.'

'I don't want to involve her.'

'Mr Morton won't look for us there.'

'He will. He might already have.'

'Why?'

Silas straightens up, pulls a hand through his damp hair. 'She's my wife.'

Paul looks at him, wide-eyed. 'I didn't know you were married,' he says.

'Mr Morton doesn't trust unmarried men. I saved Belinda from a man. She saved me from women. Apart from a trip to Eastbourne we have never stayed under the same roof.'

'Let's go,' Miriam says, her voice high and broken. 'But not to Belinda's.'

By running through houses, through peoples' homes, by going into pubs with two doors, entering one, exiting through the other, by moving for almost an hour, in taxis, on buses, on trams, running, always running, they leave Mr Morton behind. Their combined knowledge of the streets, in different social strata as well as false cul-de-sacs and shortcuts through parks and greens now comes in very useful.

They come to a standstill in a street neither of them know. Wet and shivering, despite the mad dash. This is the first time they have allowed themselves to stop. Paul's pupils are pinholes and he has a buffoon's smile plastered across his face. The last time he was lost was in the rain in Marylebone. He's not used to it. Silas stands shivering on the pavement, eyes half-shut. Paul tries to backtrack, talks out loud, but can't remember much.

Miriam has turned her back to the street and is leaning

against a wall, her forehead resting on a film poster of *Spangles*. The celluloid beauty of Fern Andra's melancholy face level with Miriam's. Paul gently turns her away from the wall, picks up her hat from the pavement. Her golden feather is missing. Silently he makes her move. To move is to stay warm, is to not be found.

Silas urges them along the street, but they are walking, not running. Both because they are too tired to run, and because walking people attract less attention. Paul's in a daze and keeps tripping on invisible things. He asks Silas, 'Where will we go?'

'You or you two?'

Miriam takes Paul's hand and says, 'Us two.'

'And you, too, Silas. You can't stay here,' Paul says.

'I'm not emigrating again. It broke my heart the first time.'

Paul opens his mouth and starts saying something, but Silas cuts him off.

'America, that's where you two are going. It's got to be somewhere where he can't reach you.'

'I don't know anyone in America,' Paul says.

'You're a big boy now. And besides, cycling is big business over there too. Much bigger than here in fact.'

'I don't know.'

'What's the alternative? Stay and pretend nothing's happened? Don't worry. You'll quickly find your feet, just make sure you change your name.'

'But I left my bike at the velodrome. Only got to use it once.'

'You can get a new one once you're there. A better one.'

'How will we even get there?'

'By boat, you lunatic.'

'I don't have that kind of money. I can't just go up to the ticket office and get a ticket,' Paul says. Miriam looks at her shoes, ruined.

'You do. You do, Paul. It's not the money that's the problem. It's your name, your looks, and the fact that you have neither a passport nor a visa. And that Mr Morton will have people at train stations and port offices,' Silas says.

'So what should we do?' Paul asks.

'I know a boy. His father owns ocean liners. And he still owes me a portrait,' Silas laughs.

They come to a run-down café. It looks closed but through the grimy windows they can see a woman shuffling along behind a counter. Silas hands Miriam some money from his pocket as Paul still looks too groggy to be trusted. Silas tells them to wait, to be careful, and sends them inside.

Two hours later Silas comes back, tells them a reservation of sorts has been made for them on a ship, at no insignificant sum. Then he sits down across from them. His hands are shaking almost uncontrollably. Miriam gets up and brings him a cup of tea, and he nods at her thankfully.

Once he's had his cup of tea and a piece of stale pineapple cake, Silas tells them he has secured passage between Southampton and Ellis Island. He can't tell them much more than to ask for a stevedore named Raul once they get there. Apparently someone else is going to get caught in customs tomorrow, and Paul and Miriam will take their cabin.

'Beyond that you're on your own.'

Silas waves to the woman to get another cup of tea, but she can't see him, so Miriam gets up and comes back with a teapot. Silas looks Paul straight in the eye, and puts an urgent hand on his arm. 'Make sure you wear your racing top when you're boarding the ship.

'The one I'm wearing now?' Paul says and unbuttons his jacket a little. 'The one you gave me for Christmas?'

'Well, the one Jack gave you first...'

'Will you say goodbye to him from me by the way? And Emrys?'

'No I won't. You send them a letter. Just no return address please. You need to use your head a little in the coming months.'

'Why should I wear the racing top? Don't I want to look nice and respectable for the trip?'

'For luck.'

'But it's sweaty.'

'Paul, when you're properly out at sea, once you can't see land any more, and as soon as you're convinced no one has recognized you or followed you, go to your cabin. Lock the door, then, and only then, take a pair of scissors to your top.'

'Why? It's my lucky top.'

'You see, there's a lump, a little bag with five lumps, under the *three*.'

'Lumps?'

'Each about a carat.

'Rings?'

'Diamonds.'

'Yours?'

'No, no. Mr Morton's.'

'Won't he miss them?'

'Yes, immensely.'

'And I've been cycling around with that since Christmas?'

Silas nods and finishes his tea. His hands now a little steadier.

Paul says, 'Thank you Silas. You've always been too good to me.'

'If you play your cards right, it could set you up quite nicely. Just don't sell them too cheaply.'

'I won't. I wasn't born in a barn you know.'

'I know you were, so just be quiet.'

Paul laughs, and when he falls silent they look out into the street. Then they shrug into their coats and walk out into the street. Silas looks at his hands and then at Miriam.

'Miriam, this is goodbye. I know you understand the magnitude of what's happening. I appeal to you.' Silas opens his arms as wide as he can, and she comes to him for a hug. He whispers loud enough for Paul to hear, 'Take care of him.

Promise me you will.'

Her eyes well up, start to glitter, and she swallows several times before giving up on speaking. Just nods.

'We've had a strange few years, Miriam,' Silas says. 'We've both hated working for Mr Morton I think, but we both, up until now, failed to find the courage to do anything about it. Until Paul turned up. But not even then did we combine our forces properly, but pussyfooted around our common enemy for too long. Now we have acted. Maybe because we had something in common? Loving him.'

'Oh Silas, come with us,' she says. Silas just shakes his head.

'What are you going to do?' Paul asks.

'I don't know. Stay here maybe?'

'That would be insane. You can't.'

'Buy a boat and sail to Greece,' Miriam says.

'Be serious. I'd drown before I was out of the harbour,' Silas says. 'For the first time in many years I don't know what to do.'

'You'll figure it out,' Miriam says, putting her hand on his shoulder.

'He knows about all my other places, the flat on Ossington Street. The cubby hole at the Peacock club,' says Silas wistfully.

Suddenly Paul's face lights up, and he says, 'I'm going to give you the farm.'

'What are you talking about?'

'You once said you had had enough of the city. That you wanted a simpler life, something more real, less flashy.'

'Maybe I did.'

'And now you need to go and hide somewhere remote where he won't look.'

'I can't take your farm.'

'I don't want it. I can never return.'

'I don't know anything about farming.'

'You've got a bit of money. You've got common sense and you're savvy, more so than anyone I've ever met. You'll work it out. Hire people, ask people, get to know them. They're a friendly bunch. They will be once they realise you're there to stay. Once they realise you're a friend of mine and not my father's.'

'I can't.'

'You provided me with a roof over my head when I came to London.'

'That was different.'

'You trusted me, took a chance on me, a stranger.'

'It wasn't quite like that.'

'Now I'm repaying the favour. Just you're not a stranger, you're a friend.'

'About that time, the time at King's Cross when I first met you, I need to tell you something.'

'Whatever it is, it can wait. We have to go. Thanks for everything Silas. I'll write. To the farm.'

'You insolent pup,' Silas says, 'I wish you were wrong, but there's some sense in what you're saying. I can't stay. I can't go to any of my known haunts. Not till this has died down at least. If it ever will.'

Paul runs back into the café and borrows a pen and some paper. He writes a quick note to his uncle. Not much more than his name and that he's giving the farm to Mr Silas Halkias. He folds up the paper and writes his uncle's address in terrible copperplate on the back, then rushes out and hands the paper to Silas. Presents his family farm to Silas.

'Paul, Paul,' Silas shakes his head, then takes Paul's hand solemnly. The Greek's eyes shining. Then Silas looks at Miriam who nods and then he says, 'Fine. There's nothing else for it. I need to disappear from the face of the earth and what better place than Lewistown?'

'Lennoxtown.'

'What?'

'Lennoxtown, that's where I come from. That's where you're going. Well first to Edinburgh, to see my uncle.'

'Wait here you two, I need to use the bathroom,' Silas says.

He motions for Paul to hand him the suitcases. Silas walks off back into the café and navigates past the counter and into the kitchen, suitcases held high. A minute later he comes back and hands Paul one of the suitcases. They are now equally heavy. Paul opens it an inch and peers inside, and Miriam who's standing next to him sees the stacks of notes too, and gasps, putting a hand to her mouth.

Silas says, 'So what are you two waiting for? Scram.'

'Scotland will do you good Silas,' Paul says, holding the handle of the suitcase extra tight. 'I know where you are. I know exactly where you are. Take care of the old house.'

Silas stands on his tiptoes and kisses Paul on his stubbled cheek. 'It's been a pleasure Miriam,' Silas says and kisses her on both cheeks. 'I've always loved the way you smell of pine, lemon, geranium,' he says. She smiles.

'Come on Little Crow,' Paul says to Miriam and Silas cries openly as the couple walk off. They are soon swallowed by a curtain of rain.

Chapter 42

Paul and Miriam get on the last train of the day to Southampton. No luggage apart from the suitcase and Miriam's handbag. Paul is still in shorts and his racing top, a quilted jacket on top. Miriam is wearing a dress with tiny specks of Drago's blood on it. She's too breathless, too scared to talk. She imagines spies and grimy boys reporting back everywhere. Thanks to the drugs, Paul is much calmer. 'We must have passed thousands of people giving us away on the way to the station, a whole army, a nation of snitches just waiting for their reward,' she whispers to Paul.

She pulls the curtain of the compartment they're in and leans back in her seat peeking out through the inch-wide gap. Her chest is rising and falling quickly. Her cheeks flushed. Her eyes are big and her hair is dishevelled. She's nothing like her usual self.

Then they hear the first creak of the carriages. The whistle and the goodbyes shouted out through compartment windows. For the first time since getting on the train she looks over to Paul. He's sleeping, childlike. An arm draped across his forehead. The blue panda marks on either side of his boxer's nose now fainter.

She keeps an eye on the door to their compartment and her hand on the ivory gun inside her bag. It's not until they have been on their way for almost two hours that she relaxes.

She prods Paul awake. Knows that he needs to drink and move for the drugs to leave his body. He doesn't want to open his eyes, but she won't let him sleep. She opens the windows, forces him to stand up, which he does with eyes closed. Forces him to move his limbs. Once he's awake she tells him she'll read for him. 'For a change,' she says.

'That's nice,' he says and sits down again. Comes close to her.

'I wrote this one in Coventry. When you were in the bath. Remember we had just had that fight,' she says.

'I do,' Paul mumbles.

'I was so afraid of losing you, but I didn't know how to tell you.' Miriam now puts her handbag on the floor, covers her gun with a scarf. 'I did some thinking in that hotel room, and I decided I don't want to be like my mother. She had a terrible life, but she let her circumstances shape her. I won't let that happen to me. This is her one.'

Paul closes his eyes.

No. 50
I watched her become more thorn than rose
Cut off from all that blossoms and grows
I saw how her scars made her wither and die
Unable to love, unable to fly
The greatest promise I can make
Is this, I won't make the same mistake

'She had a man for a few years, Frank. He was nice to her. Nice to me and my brother, but she didn't treat him right. Not because she didn't want to, but because she couldn't do it. She wasn't very good with people after everything that happened to her.'

Paul opens his eyes.

'I'm not leaving you Paul. I'm not like the people who came before me.'

He sits up straight and kisses her. She cries a little. Then he sits back and says, 'It's so nice to hear you read. It's a shame we've not done it before.'

'There'll be plenty of time on the boat.'

'The boat,' Paul says. 'America.' Then he tells her about the time she brought him up on the roof of the Baths. Makes sure she remembers the towel she dropped and the dogs that ripped it apart. She laughs. He can tell she also remembers what happened once they went downstairs.

He brings out the box he meant to give her then. He has kept it behind a loose brick at Copenhagen Street and only remembered to pick it up before his last supper with Silas. The pendant, shaped like an eight, made from a link of bicycle chain, hangs beautifully around her neck.

As the train picks up speed thousands and thousands of chimneys, millions of lives, billions of coincidences pass by outside their carriage window.

Chapter 43

It's easy to stand here and philosophize about how great things are, seeing the rear lights of their train recede into the tunnel to what I sincerely hope is the safety of the sea and the anonymity of a new continent. It's easy to forget about my own peril, but when it comes back to me it lands on me like an anvil dropped from the fourth floor. The relative relief of seeing the two of them disappear matched with the sudden insight of my impending death, unless I somehow convince myself I can cut it as a Scottish gentleman farmer, buckles my knees.

I suddenly feel sick. My inner ear off-kilter. The schism between hope and reality widening. I can't leave London. I can't stay in London. I can't be anyone else. I can't be me.

My father would have gone straight to the lion's lair and fought. My mother, always the wiser, wouldn't have mixed up courage and stupidity. She would have known when to keep quiet and run away. Survival is the highest proof of intelligence, not bravery or bloodshed.

At King's Cross I board the first northbound train that comes in. It's only for Liverpool, but at this stage I don't mind. Anywhere is better than home. Anywhere is better than what, and possibly who, I've been.

I'm now as rich as I would ever need to be, but I'm a fox listening out for trumpets and dogs. If I run fast, if I run far, those will fade away behind me.

Once underway I ask a conductor, to take me to a first-class carriage. I tell him there's a little something for him if he can find me an empty compartment, which he does. I sit down, facing the direction of travel. Facing the new. Lennoxtown at the end of the ball of string in front of me. London, that cesspool of rats and bets, soon nothing but a story. I smile a little. I relax a little. Open the window four inches, a horse hand — Paul would have known. I watch the smokestacks and coachworks of London town recede. Watch the world I know fade into a memory.

I'm away. I'm scot-free. I smile sadly at my joke.

I had a good run with the boy, I had a good time with him. It's not for me to find someone to share everything with. It's not for me, this domestic happiness seen in others.

I close my eyes and think of the race and the lucky pile-up, of meeting him at King's Cross, of him starving himself half to death in that disgusting house. The tenants will come to grief, probably Rupert too, as a result of me jumping ship. It can't be helped. If you want to make an omelette you have to break some eggs. I think of the humiliation Mr Morton put him through. The poor Russian secretary, evicting the Sorensens with no explanation, the evenings I spent following Paul, at a respectful but watchful distance, to Hampstead Heath.

I look at the way the trees line the railway line. Real trees, ones that grow where they want to. Not where they were planted, not in a park. I realise I've not properly been outside the city for years. Not since Eastbourne.

Even when I did go, it was always to civilised places, to bars, cafés, hotels, parks. Other towns and cities, little islands of the burgeoning bourgeois looking at, and laughing at races. Men or horses. I forgot to look beyond. Never to nature, never to the unspoilt. The exact qualities I enjoyed in Paul.

The sky is a beautiful purple. The whole carriage at the back of the train, far from the noisy engine, seems shushed and the sound of the wheels on the tracks, the sleepers and seams in the metal offer a steady rhythm to the journey.

I wake up with a start. The first thing I do is to pat the air between my legs for the suitcase. It's still there and my heart comes back into its casings in my chest. I touch my throat and the speed of my pulse scares me.

A man sits across from me. From what I can see of him from

behind the broadsheet he's unfolded between himself and me, he's dressed entirely in black. Like an undertaker. A shadow.

I look up and smile, only the masthead smiling back. I look at his shoes, often an easy way to judge character. Black brogues, neither here nor there. Old but well kept.

I keep the smile on, remind myself that I'm good with people. I don't want the company, but if this man is travelling somewhere and has decided to come and sit facing me, even though there seems to be a lot of space in the first-class carriage, I'll make it a pleasant, if unremarkable, journey for him. I won't be too quiet or too talkative. I won't say, or do, anything out of turn. I won't offer too much information nor hide any if he asks. Lies, obviously: Edward S Penderton, shipping merchant, the company has been in the family for generation, going to a funeral up in Liverpool, an old aunt, not seen her for years, the wife would have come but has been feeling under the weather the last couple of days, think the damp has gotten into her lungs a bit, nothing serious, prefer doing the trip on my own anyway.

Then a few questions, maybe a clarification or two about my own circumstances, barring the unfortunate event of the man also being a shipping merchant, in which case I will backpedal a little, tell him I'm very detached from the running of it, hint at old money. Then a little chat about cricket, which I know nothing about, rugby which I know a little about, and horses, which I know a tremendous amount about, but would pretend to be only marginally interested in, intentionally getting facts muddled up.

I look at the man's hat jutting up over his paper. He is either sleeping, or engrossed in an article because he hasn't turned the page since I woke up.

I settle in the seat, glance out over the pastures and towards darker clouds on the horizon. It's a bank which looks like it could bring lightning and thunder, both things quite nice when you're in a cosy compartment flying north. I'm just about to take off my coat, when the man across from me folds down his paper, clears his throat and looks straight at me.

'Silas. Silas.' He sounds disappointed. I know him. It's Drago, the bastard.

For the second time in a short space of time my heart flies up into my throat. A sensation I've not felt for many years. One I've made sure never to have to come to experience, and when I've been forced to feel it, I've trained myself not to gasp, or get confused. Not to feel anything, show anything. But this, this I can't fence off.

'We are not happy about this Silas,' he continues. 'Mr Morton saw great potential in you. And in your boy. But now...' here he opens his arms in a gesture of a stingy embrace, then clasps his hands in the manner of a preacher praying.

He looks out the window, and my gaze follows his. It's now dark. All I see is the reflection, like a pear cut in half, our faces staring back at us.

The grip and hammer of a well-oiled gun sticks up out of his armpit in a tight holster, in his belt a pair of handcuffs. How proud he is to show them to me, as if by accident. What kind of a man does this? A dog on a leash hoping for a sausage, that's who. A coward who can't be bribed. Not because he has any moral standards. But because of his fear. Because of his unquestioning respect for his master. I have seen this class of men before. Subservient and vain. I have made use of them myself, I'm not proud to say, and from experience they have been very efficient.

My dreams of freedom, of Lennoxtown and – this I hadn't even admitted to myself until this black bishop appeared – of one day crossing the Atlantic. Pulling into New York, finding Paul somewhere. His name in letters as tall as double-decker buses on a sign outside Madison Square Garden, inside he's mid-race. After we would go for eel or whatever the equivalent is over there, and talk about the past, laugh about this whole mess.

'Silas, what do you propose we do about the situation?' Drago's question pulls me out of my self-pitying reverie. He continues, 'I know you took the money, I know you gave some to the boy and that whore. I know you sent him somewhere, it's just a matter of time before they are found. And dealt with.'

'I'm not afraid you know,' I say. 'This is something I can explain to Mr Morton. He knows me. I've known him a lot longer than you have.'

'I don't think you can. He sent me. He wants you. Dead or alive, he doesn't care. And he knows he can trust me to do the job properly,' he says and begins to study his fingernails.

'You've got quite the reputation,' I say. At this he merely bows his head. Self-important prick, proud that his fame has preceded him. Which is fine with me. A bit of pride might be a loose rock in his wall of Eastern European stoicism, one I can prod.

'I've got nothing to hide. I'm a man on a train. Going to Liverpool to visit a friend. That's all,' I continue.

He looks up and says, 'I don't have a preference. I don't mind what happens to you, I am just a courier. But you and I are returning to London. You are telling me where your prized horse and his whore are right now and I will cable the Carousel. Once we are back you can tell Mr Morton in person.'

'I don't know.'

'My medical training and scalpels,' here he pats the pocket of his suit jacket, 'says you do.'

I look out of the window. He is sitting with his back to the direction of the train, but I have a full view of the track. Up ahead there's a slow right, going into a series of tunnels. I pull on my left kidskin glove, put my right hand in the pocket of my coat, look him in the eye and say, 'I'm going to close the window, seems chilly all of a sudden.'

'I always took you for a weakling Silas.'

I ignore this. Continue, 'Then let's get this over and done with. I'll come with you if that's what you want.'

I put the right glove on, as if I need a better grip on the mechanism. I look at him, smile and continue, 'Actually I'm very impressed you found me.' This puts him at ease. The little rock possibly looser.

I focus on my hands. Hands that used to handle white-eyed horses on race tracks, then white-eyed men. Hands that delivered money first to my father, then to Mr Morton. Hands that have broken open hundreds of lobsters at the Strand, hands that have put hundreds of drunk men to bed. Hands I once hoped would make me enough money to not worry about money. Hands that over the years and through the things I have seen have always been steady. Only once or twice have my palms been wet from nervous sweat. Last time it was at the race. Now I can't afford that. Now I wear gloves.

'Drago, you must be very good at what you do,' I say.

My hands are calm enough. Instead it's my legs that shake as I stand up and reach for the clasp of the window. I pretend to struggle, notice Drago's snigger. I buy time until the last second before the train rushes into the tunnel.

The compartment is plunged into darkness. Now I pull the straight razor out of my pocket. I unfold it, secure it and plunge it into Drago's throat. While he's still surprised, I hack, saw, push. Lean into him, almost breaking the blade. In a rage I've never felt before I go and go and go until the hilt is stuck and his eyes show white. Until he stops gurgling, until his rasping, wet breaths are spaced out, stop altogether. His hands, at first clasped around my sawing arm, slowly lose their grip. Then his arms flop onto the seat with a meaty thunk.

I shudder. Look at my ruined gloves. Dry the blade on his right lapel. First one side, then the other, with a care that surprises me.

Instead of closing the window I gulp air, though we are still in the tunnel. I pluck the gloves off, soaked finger by soaked finger. Drop them out of the window. I take down my hat and my mohair scarf from the coat rack. His head lolls in time with

314

the train. Severed tendons, a lump I realise is his Adam's apple cut in half. Red blood, a torrent. White bone and cartilage remaining ivory white in the dusk of the compartment. I gingerly wrap my scarf around his throat, concealing the wound.

The river of blood has soaked his clothes and his shameful goatee, but as they are both black it's not too obvious at a casual glance. I put my hat on him, pull it low as if he was sleeping, cover him in my coat. I close the window and place my ticket on the little table between us. The conductor should leave the man alone all the way till Liverpool.

I peer out into the corridor. I thank a God I don't believe in and Drago's inflated confidence. It seems this bishop came alone. Now he's dead, lying across the board he thought he knew how to play. He met his match. He met his Queen.

This will not go unnoticed and I will never be safe, especially once the great white authority finds out I've slaughtered his favourite pet. I have delayed the wire being sent. I have hopefully held up matters long enough for Paul and Miriam to find a way onto a ship.

I pick up the suitcase, and move to sit in third class. Smoke cheap cigarette after cigarette, bought from a man smelling of chicken feed. I get off at the first station we come to, almost before the train has stopped, but not in too much of a hurry. I walk out of the station, make sure the train sets off before I return. Once back I buy a cup of coffee. If nothing else it stills and warms my hands.

I stand on the platform, thinking about the implications of what I've just done. I weigh Past and Future and find one side of the scale heavier, and more important. I realise my troubles will never end unless I put an end to the matter. He will find me, he will send more men, more trained pets with sharpened teeth, wherever I go. I had just warmed to the idea of rural Scotland, of the quiet and calm of a backwater.

Eventually he will find Paul and he will find Miriam too,

whether they are together or not. I know only too well how he treats people who cross him. I've been an instrument of destruction myself. My only regret is that I should have done this years ago.

I get a ticket back, again first-class. None of the fantastic omens I saw on the way north show themselves on the way south.

Once in London I take a taxi to my flat where I wash the razor blade, and dress in my best suit, a beautiful cobalt number from Henry Poole. It was made for a special occasion, not for a day like today, but it can't be helped. Then I spend an hour putting my papers in order, downing tumblers of the most expensive spirits in the house.

Once I am done I hail a taxi, patting my right pocket. Dressed for a wedding or a coronation I set out for the Carousel. To lie. To buy more time. To die. Or kill.

Acknowledgements

Thank you to my family: Lucy, Elias, Alma, Mika, Mormor, Mamma, Pappa, Ann-Cathrin, Klas, Gabrielle, Jakob, Jennifer, Rebecca, Phil, Flo, Ewan, Myra, Vicki, Susie, Jeff, Ethan, Rachel, Jack, Emily, Georgia, Abigail, Bethany.

Thanks also to Johannes, Oskar and the whole Karlsson clan, Emma and Ivan Naismith-Zetterström, the Stockholm Book Club, Mary Dolmar, Helena Ydén, Zoë Strachan and everyone in the 2014 Glasgow Uni reading/writing group and beyond, the Hackney Hotchpotch, the Clouston Community, the Garrioch Gang, Richy Carey, Libby Walker, Helen Sedgwick, Sarah Macintyre at Scottish Cycling, Gail McConnell, Peggy Hughes and everyone at Literary Dundee, Russel McLean, Ed Wilson, Adrian Searle and everyone at Freight Books.

A whole host of folk have contributed, knowingly or not, with practical and emotional support over the years. Thank you.

PRINCE ALBERT PUBLIC LIBRARY
33292900181540
Devil take the hindmost